SANCTUARY

SANCTUARY

A Legacy of Memories

T. M. BROWN

Palmetto Publishing Group
Charleston, SC

Sanctuary: A Legacy of Memories
Copyright © 2017 by T. M. Brown
All rights reserved

Second Edition

Printed in the United States

ISBN-13: 978-1-64111-073-0
ISBN-10: 1-64111-073-2

"Have them make a sanctuary for me, and I will dwell among them."
— Exodus 25:8, NIV

CHAPTER ONE

Until three years ago, the Adams County Courthouse proudly stood since the Civil War as the landmark in Shiloh. After the powers-to-be transferred the county seat to Alexandria during the Depression, the majestic edifice underwent renovation to appease the folks in Shiloh and became the town's city hall. The elegant lady wore her nostalgic brick and stone exterior well, but the makeover had been superficial.

Questions have lingered since city officials reported the fire as accidental, cause unknown.

———

A PROLONGED INDIAN SUMMER GRIPPED GEORGIA. Though already the first Sunday of November, hot and humid weather more suitable for early September caused sweat to trickle unabated down my neck dampening the collar of the fresh cotton polo I had just yanked over my head. The moving truck had pulled away while Liddy patiently watched from her passenger window. I walked up the sidewalk one last time and locked the front door of the colonial brick suburban house we had called home for the past seven years.

I jumped into the driver's seat, buckled up, squeezed the hand of my wife of forty years, and then reached for the gear shift. "Any regrets?"

Liddy raised her window and turned her gaze straight ahead as a silly smirk appeared. "Nope, Let's roll! We've got a moving truck to meet in Shiloh tomorrow."

My foot slid from the brake to the accelerator and our Expedition jolted forward with the packed trailer in tow. Liddy stared straight ahead for the first few minutes. She caressed the manila envelope stuffed with photos, brochures, and paperwork about the house we contracted to purchase for our retirement, but soon dozed off after we turned south onto US Highway 19. I settled in for the long afternoon drive to our destination an hour below Albany.

The all-too-familiar gated communities and shopping centers under Atlanta's ever-present shadow faded in my rearview mirror. I snapped a farewell salute as we passed Cornerstone Publishing where I served as chief publishing editor until one week ago. The historic highway narrowed as the scenic panorama of autumn colors revealed more and more farms, fields and forests along the landmark route.

Liddy stirred just long enough to adjust her position and place a small pillow between her head and the window. Glancing at her as she fell back to sleep jogged my memory of the first day my eyes fell upon her on the Athens campus forty years ago. My smile over the memory faded when I glanced at the stranger in the rearview mirror. Gray had infiltrated my dirty blonde hair, and crow's feet pointed to sagging eyelids. After an extended sigh, I reminded myself that I no longer was that spirited undergrad Liddy first met, but a second glance at Liddy returned a grin to my wrinkled face.

When Liddy first suggested I consider early retirement, I turned a deaf ear. Undeterred, she persisted. "Theo Phillips, it's high time you realized that you can afford to do what you've always wanted. Walk away from that job you've grown to resent and invest the time to write your own stories as you've always envisioned?"

Once my hard head embraced the idea, Liddy wasted little time. She arranged the sale of our home, scoured a mountain of listings, made countless phone calls, and endured long day trips, while I fulfilled my promise to my boss and worked until the end of October. Liddy strutted about the day our home landed an eager buyer, and the following evening methodically spread a collection of photos on the kitchen table of a picturesque, historic home located in a South Georgia town aptly named Shiloh. Not far from our childhood hometowns, the pictures brought back fond memories for both of us. We both felt God had answered our prayers when a day later we received acceptance of our cash offer.

On the outskirts of Albany, Liddy stirred and wiped her eyes as the late afternoon sunlight glistened between the treetops. She cleared her throat and lowered her sunglasses from the top of her head. Surveying the passing scenery, she asked with a drawn-out sigh. "Where are we?"

I pointed to a well-timed road sign. "Albany's 30 more miles. Reckon we'll arrive in Shiloh a little before six." The news earned a smile as she stared back out the window.

Liddy soon turned with a curious grin. "What were you thinking about while I was asleep?"

Without losing my focus on the road, I said, "How lucky I was to have stolen the heart of the prettiest girl that ever graced the Athens campus."

Liddy giggled. "I feel the same about you."

We soon turned onto the Flint River Highway, the homestretch leg of our journey. The amber glow grew darker as the sun disappeared below the distant treetops.

Liddy bit her lower lip and clenched my hand. "Do you think we did right? I mean… buying this house and leaving Peachtree?"

A chuckle erupted first. "Hun, I've no doubt that the vetting process you orchestrated selecting this house removed any reservations I might have clung onto about my retirement or our decision to pack up and move to Shiloh."

Her cheeks glowed. "Me neither, but I wanted to be certain you weren't just trying to appease me. I'm truly looking forward to sinking deep roots and making a slew of friends."

My wink brought a smile to Liddy's relieved lower lip. "You're right," she said. "But how well do you think we'll fit in?"

"Trust me. A town like Shiloh won't allow us to remain anonymous long."

Liddy laughed and agreed that Shiloh would be like the small towns we remembered growing up, where even strangers passing through town were addressed as "friend" or "neighbor," and names were exchanged during a hearty handshake or hug.

Liddy eyed a distant weathered barn donning a rusted tin roof. "We must be getting close."

She begged me to stop when we passed an abandoned mansion with discolored columns and rickety shutters no longer protecting shattered windows. With critters and termites likely the only tenants, I convinced her we should save a close-up inspection for another day. Plantation oaks with dangling moss lined the rest of the way into Shiloh. The Expedition's automatic headlamps attacked the growing dark shadows and distant lights welcomed us into town.

On Main Street, Liddy urged me to slow well below the speed limit as we drove into the center of town. She pointed out the quaint drugstore, barbershop, and the other storefronts surrounding the town square. We reminisced about fifty-cent Saturday matinees as we rolled past the movie theater with its illuminated marquee. In fact, Shiloh revealed family-owned shops and businesses, a fading memory in most small towns throughout the South.

The Chamber of Commerce brochure depicted a majestic, antebellum, red-brick courthouse anchoring the center of Shiloh. Instead, we discovered a newly constructed brick and granite city hall with a grand portico and well-lit main entrance. Decorative red-brick walkways cut through manicured lawn and meticulous gardens. As we crept along, Liddy pointed to an illuminated, life-like bronze statue of a young man at one corner of the town square.

"I wonder who he was?" Liddy asked. "He looks so young. There's nothing in the literature about it."

I managed a shrug as I searched for the street that led to our house. The word SOLD stood out on the Arians Real Estate sign in the front yard of our corner property. Liddy left little doubt about her eagerness to show me more of the house, but darkness, the growl of our stomachs and fatigue begged otherwise. A couple of blocks further into the quiet neighborhood, Liddy exchanged smiles with two red-haired girls playing out front of one of the elegant mansions among other comparable homes at that end of Calvary Street.

Shiloh's unified school complex at the southern end of town brought back memories of our school days. The buildings and grounds appeared recently renovated. The football stadium and athletic fields behind the school appeared larger than one would expect for a town of Shiloh's size.

Once I turned back onto Main Street, flickering yellow and blue neon lights identified our destination for the night, the Shiloh Motel. "Thank goodness! I'm so ready to crawl out from under this steering wheel. Not to mention, I'm famished."

Liddy lowered her window. "Hey, look next door, Bubba's BBQ. Sure smells good too."

Inside the motel office, a silver-haired woman dressed in a blue and white flowered frock eyed us as she slurped down the last of her drink, managing a warm smile at the same time. She yanked off her makeshift paper towel bib, dabbed her cheeks, moments before she wriggled out of her armchair. A sauce-stained, white porcelain platter next to her chair held remnants of her dinner, a couple of ketchup ladened fries alongside a neat stack of sucked-clean rib bones. With a flick of her remote, she muted Aunt Bea from *Andy of Mayberry.* She adjusted her dress as she approached with contagious smile that made us respond likewise, but her shrill greeting we'd never forget.

"Welcome, folks to Shiloh. Y'all mus' be Mista an' Missus Phillips. We've been expectin' y'all."

Liddy froze but managed an abbreviated nod. I continued up to the counter, choking off an escalating chuckle. Instead, I feigned a cough before greeting the jovial hostess with a suitable grin.

"I'm Barb, Barb Patterson. Me and my husband Bubba are the proud owners of the best motel and barbecue restaurant in Shiloh." Her cheeks flushed as her fingers sought to stifle her cackle. "Oh, me. Oh, my. The truth is, we own the only motel and barbecue restaurant in town." A burst of self-indulgent belly laughter followed.

"Well, Barb, thanks for such a pleasant greeting," I managed to say after snickering briefly. "We're glad to be here after our long drive." I nudged Liddy. "I'm Theo, Theo Phillips, and this is Liddy, my wife. I believe the two of you spoke this morning."

"Y'all mus' be plum tuckered out." Her fingers flitted in the direction of my hand reaching for my wallet. "Just keep your wallet in your pants pocket for now." She slid a registration form and pen in front of me. "Just sign right here. We've got our best room reserved for you. We'll deal with the formalities in the morning."

I pointed to our name and new address already filled in as I slid the signed form back to her. "Thanks, but how'd you know?"

Barb muffled another high-pitched cackle. "Honey, Mista Nick is not just the realtor in town but also a dear friend and regular customer. He stopped by for lunch and told us all about you and that y'all are buying Miss Betty Priestly's old home." She stared at Liddy's raised brow. "Hun, everyone in Shiloh knows the Priestly house. Y'all sure are getting a mighty special home." She pulled the form off the counter. "Will you need one or two keys."

I showed her one finger and promptly received a brass key with the number 10 stamped on it.

Liddy's composure returned. She reached out to thank our capricious but jovial hostess. Barb received Liddy's hand. "Hun, if you need anything, just dial the desk. It's a genuine pleasure to be the first to welcome y'all to Shiloh."

"Thank you, Miss Barb. We're glad to be here too." After Barb released Liddy's hand, Liddy asked, "How late is the restaurant open?"

"Just hold one second." Barb lifted the receiver of her yellow rotary phone, dialed and momentarily tapped her cherry red fingernails on the counter. "Cecil? The Phillips just checked in, and they's mighty hungry. Will you take special care of 'em? Maybe seat 'em at one of the winda' tables? ...Thanks, Ceec. You're a doll." Barb hung up and looked at Liddy. "Miss Liddy, y'all are all set. Hope y'all are hungry. Bubba's ribs are 'specially good tonight."

Liddy smiled and glanced at Barb's empty platter. "Thank you, Barb. I think we'll give those ribs a try. We haven't eaten since we left Peachtree."

A tall, silver-haired African-American gentleman approached us with a broad, toothy grin as soon as we walked into Bubba's BBQ. His white bib apron wrapped comfortably around his slim frame allowing him to tie it in the front. A damp towel draped over his shoulder and provided clear evidence of his busy day.

"Y'all mus' be the Phillips. Welcome to Bubba's. My name's Cecil, and that's Bubba over there."

Cecil then turned his head and yelled. "Bob, say hello to the newest folks in town, the couple Mista' Nick spoke about this afta'noon."

Bubba, a rotund man with graying dark hair, raised his free hand and shared a sweaty smile but returned to tending the carousel of meat rotating over the smoke pit.

The table Cecil offered us provided a clear view of Main Street. Liddy and I handed the menus right back without opening them.

"Barb recommended Bubba's ribs. How about two platters with sweet tea?"

Cecil affirmed our choice with an appreciative nod before he headed towards the kitchen and yelled, "Two more ribs."

Liddy and I soon were ready to bust and shoved our near empty plates aside. When Cecil inquired about dessert, Liddy raised her hands and shook her head.

After we paid for the meal and expressed our appreciation to Cecil and Bubba, we decided to stretch our legs and walked into the center of town. Liddy found a bench next to the brick walkway and admired the unique architecture of Shiloh Baptist Church across the street. My interest fell upon the illuminated bronze statue we saw earlier.

Spotlights highlighted the young man's chiseled face. His collared polo shirt had an "SHS" monogram above a fleur-de-lis over his heart, and a coach's whistle hung from his neck. A Bible rested in one hand while the other pointed upward. The life-like detail monopolized my attention until my eyes drifted to the plaque at the base.

JESSIE MASTERSON, BELOVED COACH AND TEACHER, SACRIFICED HIS LIFE SAVING THE LIVES OF TWO OTHERS THE NIGHT OUR HISTORIC COURTHOUSE BURNED TO

THE GROUND, DECEMBER 8, 2010.

I stood arms crossed allowing my thoughts to conjure the possible bigger story that earned this young hero such recognition. Liddy walked up and clutched my elbow, disrupting my thoughts. Her weary eyes told me it was time to head back to the motel. Before we left, I peered over my shoulder at Jessie Masterson and then said, "I was thinking... what a tragic tale that memorial represents. My instincts tell me I should try to learn more about that young man. What do you think?"

Liddy squeezed my hand and winked.

CHAPTER TWO

DANGLING SAFETY CHAINS AND THE RATTLE of trailers awoke me our first morning in Shiloh. I squinted at the illuminated 4:35 on the bedside clock before lowering my head back onto the pillow but struggled to block out the pre-dawn sounds of rural South Georgia. Gradually the long-forgotten sounds dissipated as visions of family, autumn foliage, and pumpkins ready for harvest captivated my mind's eye.

South Carolina led Georgia by six points when the whistle blew to mark the end of the first half. Tommy, our youngest, and Ted, Junior to the family, occupied the front seats of my Expedition with the doors swung open as the game blared on the radio. I sat on a nearby ice chest and enjoyed Tommy and Junior's expert commentary about why our beloved Dawgs trailed the Gamecocks.

I laughed along with my sons as we discussed their slanted opinions until Liddy shouted, "Lunch is ready! Guys, go round up the kids."

Kari and Stacey, our daughters-in-law, offered support for their husbands' pressing missions.

"You heard your mom," Kari yelled.

Stacey added, "And for heaven's sake, don't you and the kids forget to wash up."

Liddy stood under the pavilion with hands on her hips and a proud smile as her family scurried about on their assigned missions.

I maintained a safe distance. "Don't you girls fret none, I'll make sure they all get cleaned up for supper." Liddy smirked as I added, "By the way Hun, good timing. Halftime just started, but I'm sorry to report our Dawgs went into the locker room dragging their tails between their legs."

"Theo Phillips, Coach Richt will take care of our Dawgs. You mark my words. Now, skedaddle and help the boys round up the kids."

Tommy flushed his kids from the nearby woods bordering the lake. Buzz, a three-year-old with reckless abandon busted out first, stopped, cupped his hands over his mouth and yelled, "I won! I won!"

Teddy, Buzz's ten-year-old brother and future professor exited the woods next and stared back over his shoulder and huffed, "Come on slow poke."

Sissy, our eight-year-old granddaughter, Poppy's princess, sulked as she cleared the woods. She stomped and fussed as she wiped her cheeks and red eyes, and then ran headlong into my waiting arms and tattled on her brothers. I lifted her into my arms, grabbed my handkerchief and dabbed her damp cheeks. She clung to my neck while orchestrating a barrage of sniffles and whimpers.

"You didn't lose," I told her. "Look, your daddy's last."

She raised her head off my shoulder and pulled her hair from her face as she exchanged sobs for giggles while she pointed to her father brushing himself off at the foot of the trail.

Laughter announced the arrival of Junior with three-year-old Conrad on his shoulders as they chased Eddie, our other ten-year-old grandson, affectionately nick-named Bubba. Sissy tee-heed as Bubba ribbed his dad and little brother about their feeble attempts to corral him. Junior lowered Conrad from his shoulders and tried to catch his breath.

Bubba ran up. "You okay dad?"

Slumped over with his hands on his knees, Junior managed a thumbs-up between gasps. "I'm fine… just can't keep up with you while carrying Conrad anymore."

I chuckled and said to Junior, "Sounds like old age to me, son."

Junior rolled his eyes before we both broke out laughing and chased the kids toward the pavilion. Liddy surveyed each of us before she gave her approval and we all found our places around the end-to-end picnic tables.

Liddy's fried chicken never disappointed, and the boys and I risked her wrath grabbing a taste before passing the other side dishes.

We were about to pray when Buzz and Conrad clamored with hands raised high. "Can we say the blessin'? Pleez, pleez, pleez!"

I walked to their end of the table, grabbed their hands, and the three of us said our special family prayer. "God's great, God's good, and now we thank him for our food. By his hands we are fed, thank you, Lord, for daily bread. Ah-man!"

At the end of dinner, Liddy tapped the side of her glass, which caused even

Buzz and Conrad to stop and stare. Liddy then pointed to the head of the table and announced, "Poppy's got something to share."

I swallowed one more gulp of tea and then forced a cough in a feeble attempt to dissolve the growing lump in my throat. "It's no big secret that Grammy and Poppy have been searching for a place in the country to retire." Clearing my throat once again, I glanced at my two sons. "Well, we've found our retirement home, and we'll be moving next month."

Teddy, the oldest grandson, raised his hand. I grinned at his welcomed interruption.

Teddy blurted, "Poppy, excuse me, but where exactly is your new house?" Stacey placed her hands over her mouth at Teddy's question, but I raised my hand as I prepared to answer his question.

I looked upward for divine intervention as all eyes focused on me. "Good question, Teddy." I pointed to the far end of the lake, and said, "Just follow the water." Teddy scrunched his face. "Do you see where the creek begins at the far end of the lake?" Everyone turned their heads while Sissy and the three-year-olds stood up on their seats.

"I see it!" Sissy shouted.

"It flows into the Flint River just south from here and then flows through Albany, right by the small town of Shiloh."

Teddy's eyes lit up. "That means we can take our boat to your new house?"

Liddy jumped in. "Of course, a boat trip would be fun, but it'd be much easier and faster if your mom and dad drove you there."

"And... Grammy and I expect all of you to still share Christmas with us, except in Shiloh this year."

Tommy nodded as Junior said, "We'll see you and mom just like always. A few miles won't change our family's tradition."

Squealing brakes and the growing rumble of trucks woke me again. This time the clock read 5:30. Liddy remained fast asleep. I pulled on my pants and shirt and then stepped out of our motel room.

———

The smell of fresh coffee lured me toward the motel lobby where I met a full-figured, affable African-American woman with an inviting smile. Her name tag introduced her as Cora. She wore a light gray uniform with a broad lace lapel and a starched white apron. Her short, black hair tucked beneath a hair net accented the fullness of her cheeks and bright red lips that framed her wide white smile.

"Good morn' sir. I 'magin you'd be Mista' Phillips."

I generated a pre-coffee grin before a stifled yawn brought a more somber look. "Good morning... at least I expect it to be shortly." I poured some coffee and then enjoyed the warmth of the cup between my hands.

Cora continued to wipe off the table where Barb Patterson enjoyed her dinner a few hours earlier, and then paused, looked out the window, and said, "That morning sky tells me it's goin' to be a mighty fine day Mista' Phillips." Her ever-widening smile put an exclamation on her confident prediction.

After a quick sip, I nodded before I asked, "By the way, how'd you know my name?"

"Well sir, my husband told me about you and your wife. Besides, we didn' have too many folks last night..." Cora blushed, and her smile disappeared. "Mercy sakes, pleaz' forgive me Mista' Phillips if I've said anything wrong."

"Oh, no Cora. You're fine. I was just curious." I took another short sip and then asked, "So, would Cecil be your husband?"

Her smile returned. "Why, yes sir."

"My wife and I enjoyed meeting him. He took real good care of us."

"If you and the missus are hungry later, Cecil's famous around these parts for his breakfast fixins. Ever had ol' fashioned red-eyed gravy with your grits and biscuits?"

"Sounds tempting. It's been quite a long time since I can say I had-"

"Well, you won't be disappointed, Mista' Phillips," Cora blurted and then reached for a framed photo on Barb's desk. She grabbed her dust rag, wiped it, then showed it to me. "This here's Cecil and Bubba when they cut the ribbon to open the restaurant. They's been partners and best friends since their Navy days."

"Sounds fascinating." My eyes darted toward the door. "If you'll excuse me I've some reading to do, but thanks for the coffee and pleasant conversation, Miss Cora."

Cora smiled and then returned to her cleaning. As I closed the door behind me, I heard her humming. "Oh, When the Saints Come Marchin' In."

Back at the room, Liddy remained curled up under the blankets. I dug in my bag for my devotional journal and closed the door behind me. I settled into one of the chairs in front of our room, read a bit, and wrote about my dream and the sights and sounds of my first sunrise in Shiloh.

"Tap, tap, tap." I craned my neck to see Liddy's cheery face looking out the window. I smiled back and held up one finger before she disappeared behind the drawn drapes.

A few minutes later Liddy stood all dressed, fussing to herself in the mirror while I slipped on my socks and shoes. Liddy boasted how peaceful she slept as she drew open the drapes and looked out the window. "Theo, Shiloh sure shines in the morning light." Then she squealed. "Hurry up. You gotta see this. There's a parade of pickup trucks on Main Street."

I arrived by her side with an irresistible smirk. Liddy and I joked back and forth with each passing sight and sound. We both agreed that Shiloh reminded us of our childhood hometowns.

Old and new, small and large trucks, many with trailers in tow, rolled past weighed down with all kinds of farm equipment and supplies.

Liddy grabbed my arm and pointed. "Theo, check out that shiny black pickup truck — the one with all the chrome. It doesn't look like it's seen a lick of work."

Without much effort, I spotted the gaudiest four-door dually I'd ever seen. It's chrome accented metallic black exterior sparkled in the morning sunlight, while the chrome brush guard on the front bumper gave the truck a pretentious smile.

I said flippantly, "I wonder if the owner of that truck lives around here. If he does, he sure ain't a farmer."

"Yep, I agree. But did you catch the license plate?"

"Yeah, sure did. SHILOH 1."

Liddy laughed nearly hard enough to disguise her sarcastic barb. "Be nice. I think it's kinda cute. Be honest now. Wouldn't you like that fancy rig in our driveway?"

"Sorry ol' girl. I'm not looking for that kind of attention. Besides, I like our paid-for, bug-riddled, dusty, reliable SUV." I stared proudly at our Expedition with the rental trailer hitched behind it.

"If you want breakfast, let's go buster. We've got a 9:30 walk-through at the house."

"Yes, boss." I grimaced lugging our bags through the doorway. "Go on ahead. I'll meet you outside the office."

Barb Patterson remained seated in her chair when we entered the lobby. "You caught me again," she confessed as she laid aside her half-eaten glazed doughnut, grabbed the napkin from her lap, wiped her face and her hands as she stood. "Aah, that's better. Good Morning. Did y'all enjoy the room?"

"Everything was awesome. We both enjoyed a good night's sleep." I handed Barb my credit card and room key. "By the way, would there be any problems if we decided that we needed a room for one more night?"

Barb paused and smiled. "Knowing Nick, everything will go jus' fine today. But if y'all need a room tonight, we'll have one for you."

Cora greeted us in the restaurant and poured hot coffee just before she pointed to the blackboard menu that revealed the breakfast choices. Liddy inspected her choices as Cora said, "Mista' Phillips I reckon this is your wife."

Liddy looked up at Cora and then over to me. "I'm sorry," I said. "Honey, this is Cora, Cecil's wife. We met this morning when I went looking for a cup of coffee."

Liddy turned and extended her hand. "Nice to meet you, Miss Cora."

Cora placed the coffee pot down on the table, wiped her hand on her apron and shook Liddy's hand. "Pleasure's mine, Missus Phillips."

Liddy smiled. "Please, call me Liddy."

"Yes ma'am, that's a pretty name. Thank you. Do you know what you'd like this morn' Missus Liddy?"

I spoke up while Liddy's eyes returned to the blackboard. "Well, I know what I want."

"Okay Mista' Phillips, what's it gonna be for you this morn'?"

"I'll try Cecil's country breakfast special. Can I have my eggs sunny-side up?"

"Umm, umm, Mista' Phillips, one country breakfast it is. Any juice?"

"No ma'am, just coffee will suit me just fine."

Liddy hesitated as she turned and looked at Cora. "I guess... Oh, heavens-to-Betsy. I'll try the cheese grits with two plain biscuits, and can I have some honey with that? And oh yes, a glass of orange juice too."

Cora never wrote anything down. She just grinned and nodded and then walked away as she cried out to Cecil. "One red-eye sunny-up and a cheezy with biscuits."

Cecil smiled and waved his spatula. "Good mornin', folks."

A few minutes passed before Cora returned. "How's about some mo' coffee. Y'all's orders will be up shortly."

Before Liddy and I engaged in more conversation, Cora reappeared with our breakfast.

"If y'all need anything else, just ask."

Cora topped off our coffee mugs before handing Liddy a glass jar of honey.

Shortly after I crumpled my napkin and tucked it beside my empty plate, Cora scooped up our dishes and slid our ticket face down in front of me. I flipped it over and gave Cora a puzzled look as I showed Liddy the smiley face.

Cora chuckled. "Y'all just promise to come back as soon as y'all get settled... Welcome to Shiloh."

CHAPTER THREE

N$_{}$ICK A$_{}$RIANS SUGGESTED HIS BROTHER, Joe Arians, handle the closing after disclosing that Joe also happened to be the trustee of the Betty Priestly estate. We expected a smooth transaction with only a few legal documents needing our signature before we exchanged our cashier's check for the keys to our new home. But first, we arranged to meet Nick's assistant, Miss Jeannie Simmons, at the house for the final walk-through and approval of the renovations we requested.

Liddy dialed Jeannie's cell phone as we pulled away from the Shiloh Motel. Her ear-to-ear smile drew a raised eyebrow from me as she ended the call. "Step on it. Jeannie's at the house, waiting for us."

Our drive covered only a handful of blocks, but the anticipation made that trip across town feel farther than the couple of minutes it took. Liddy's eyes widened when we turned off Main Street at the north end of Town Square onto Broad Street.

Just beyond the shadows of the stores and office buildings surrounding Town Square, our new neighborhood displayed a patchwork of quaint homes with manicured lawns. Most of the houses appeared reasonably modest in size and offered little doubt that more than one generation raised their families in them. Mature magnolias, moss-ladened stately oaks, as well as picturesque pecan trees, watched over the homes. The patched sidewalks and curbs reflected decades of children on bikes, mothers pushing baby carriages and couples taking a stroll. Inconspicuous narrow alleys ran behind each row of homes. Wrought iron or painted picket fencing with appealing stone or brick walkways welcomed guests to the front porches.

Liddy said as we slowly drove past Battery toward Calvary, "This is so beautiful. I can't wait to see all these azaleas and crape myrtles in full bloom."

As I turned onto Calvary Street, Liddy unbuckled her seatbelt before I pulled into our driveway. A yellow VW Beetle sat along the front curb, and an attractive younger woman with long dark hair stood by the front porch rail. Her wave and welcoming smile prompted Liddy to exit our vehicle before I shifted into park and turned off the engine.

"Mister and Missus Phillips, good morning. I imagine y'all are a bit excited?" Jeannie cradled a black leather portfolio against her chest.

Liddy said, "Of course we're excited. Glad to see you again Jeannie. This is my husband, Theo."

Liddy led the way as I walked a bit faster to keep up. She pointed to a new sign displayed in the front yard - Welcome to Shiloh Theo & Liddy Phillips.

At the top of the porch steps, Liddy said to Jeannie, "We want you to know that both of us are already falling in love with this town and I'm anxious to check out our new house, especially the upstairs renovations."

Jeannie grinned as she stepped aside to reveal a wicker basket beside the front door. Liddy knelt down to inspect the contents. I peeked over Liddy's shoulder and watched her behave like a little kid on her birthday.

"Look Theo, flour, sugar, salt, coffee, and even a sack of your favorite yellow grits."

Jeannie giggled. "Bet y'all have never received a welcome gift like this before."

Liddy looked up at Jeannie. "It's certainly unique."

Jeannie bent down beside Liddy and said, "It's a 'pounding gift' from the Shiloh Cooperative Church Fellowship."

"A what-gift?" I said, examining the items in the basket.

Jeannie responded, "The churches in town work together stocking a central pantry that helps families in need, and fulfill the long-held tradition of providing a 'pounding gift' to new homeowners in Shiloh."

She chuckled as she pointed to each sack. "You know… a pound of this and that, but since we don't get too many new residents in Shiloh, they kinda go overboard."

Liddy giggled as she poked through the basket and pulled out gift certificates from local merchants, two free movie passes and a laminated map and directory of city and county services. She stood and handed the basket to me as Jeannie smiled and tugged on the handle of the glass storm door. I held it open as she pulled a ring of keys from her pocket.

"Would you like to do the honors?" Jeannie then handed over the keys, and Liddy led us across the threshold of our new home.

Liddy had painted a vivid portrayal of the charm of the house, but we both anticipated layers of dust requiring hours of cleaning before we could move in. However, to our surprise, the walk-through revealed glistening wood floors, clean countertops, and dust free window sills and wood trim. We stood with our mouths open as Jeannie stood off to the side with a sheepish grin.

I asked, "Who did all of this?"

Jeannie's dimpled cheeks reddened. "My family thought it was the least we could do."

"Your family did this? Why would y'all do this for us?" Liddy inquired.

"Well, to make a long story short, after my dad and brothers finished all the work upstairs, there was so much dust and dirt. Well, the whole family decided to pitch in and make sure you'd be pleased with your new home."

I looked towards the stairs and asked, "Can we go check it out?"

"Of course." Jeannie chuckled.

Liddy brushed me aside and bounded up the stairs with Jeannie in tow. Liddy inspected each room and then smiled at Jeannie. "Your father and brothers did all this? Please share that we'd like to thank them personally. This is better than we dreamed."

Further inspection downstairs revealed a welcome card on the kitchen counter with a handwritten inscription. Liddy read it, "Please stop by today or tomorrow before five o'clock. We'd like to welcome you to Shiloh and answer any questions you may have. Hal Archer, Shiloh Utilities Office."

Jeannie said, "I'm glad y'all are pleased. Unless you've got any other questions, I guess we can head on over to the office."

———

We followed Jeannie back to Town Square and parked across the street from the Arians Building. Jeannie pointed toward the stairwell entrance next to the Arians Real Estate and Property Management office.

"Joe and Nick are waitin' for y'all upstairs."

At the top of the stairs, we walked down a short hallway and opened the frosted glass door with painted letters, "Joseph P. Arians, Attorney at Law."

"Good morning. You must be Mister and Missus Phillips. Please come in and have a seat." The pleasant woman behind the desk pointed across the office toward a waiting area that rivaled any elegant living-room with its plush brown leather sofa, antique coffee table, matching end tables, and two high back lounge chairs arranged upon an expensive Persian rug. A narrow serving table against the far wall held a coffeemaker and a small refrigerator.

"Mister Arians will be ready for you in just a moment. Would you like a cup of coffee?"

Liddy shook her head, but I smiled and accepted the offer of hospitality. Mr. Arians' assistant got up from her desk and walked toward the coffee pot.

"By the way, my name's Susanna Simmons. I believe y'all met my daughter already."

Liddy looked at Susanna with a curious grin. "Jeannie's your daughter?"

Susanna looked at Liddy and offered a mother's smile.

"Then, according to Jeannie, I guess you lent a hand cleaning the house?"

Susanna handed me my cup and said to Liddy, "Yes. My whole family pitched in."

"Well for goodness sakes, I want to thank you and your whole family. The house looks magnificent. How can we ever thank you enough?"

Susanna revealed the same reddened dimples as her daughter. "It was our pleasure. We just wanted to do our part to help you feel welcome here in Shiloh." She returned to her desk and stacked some folders into a neat pile.

Just then, a man wearing a gray three-piece suit appeared in the doorway to the private office beyond the waiting area. He said, "Hey folks, sorry to keep you waiting. I'm Joe Arians." He escorted us to the conference table in his private office. "I believe you already know my younger brother, Nick."

Nick rose from his seat to greet us. "Missus Phillips, it's a pleasure to meet you again." He then reached toward me and smiled as he said, "Mister Phillips, glad to finally meet you."

As we found our seats, Susanna entered with a folder and sat next to Joe. "Y'all ready to get this done?" Joe said as he opened the file Susanna handed him.

The closing took no longer than the time needed to sign a half-dozen prepared legal documents. During the process, Joe and Susanna focused on the business at hand with nothing but warm smiles between directives. I sensed an air of solemnity and meticulous care I had never experienced before at a closing.

With all the necessary papers signed, Liddy exchanged our check for a ring of keys along with an envelope containing our copy of the documents. With formalities completed, Joe and Nick relaxed their professional demeanor. We stood, shook hands, and both men accepted hugs offered by Liddy.

After echoed offers of assistance to help us settle into our new home, Nick asked, "I know y'all just arrived, but do you have plans to join a church once you settle in?"

Although the question caught me off guard, I welcomed his genuine interest. "Absolutely. We're looking forward to finding a church home for sure."

"I'd like to invite you and Liddy to be our guests at Shiloh Baptist Church. It's that big, red brick church on the corner." Nick pointed out the window diagonally across the street to the largest of the three churches in the center of town.

I eyed all three and smiled. "Well, since we're not Presbyterian or Methodist, sounds good to us. What time are services?"

Nick said, "Services begin at eleven o'clock sharp. Doctor Wright is pretty punctual at the beginning of each service and most of time ends on-time also." We exchanged a chuckle over the pastor's perceived punctuality.

Joe said, "And, no pressure, but if you're free, stop by Wednesday night at seven o'clock. It'll be a good opportunity to meet the pastor and get introduced to a few others in our church."

Liddy stopped at Susanna's desk on our way out and shook her hand before following me down the stairs. We walked across the street to our vehicle, looked back up at Joe's office and saw Joe and Nick talking. They waved as if we were already good friends.

———

I started to unpack the trailer while Liddy went inside to call the moving company driver. As I walked through the front door balancing two boxes Liddy looked in my direction with two raised fingers and pointed to her watch while she continued to give the driver final directions.

With the trailer emptied in short order and the moving truck still a couple of hours away, Liddy suggested we visit the city utility office before we get some lunch. During our walk into town, we cheerfully returned greetings from a few of the neighbors but resisted stopping and chatting since there would be plenty of future opportunities to get acquainted.

CHAPTER FOUR

THE SMELL OF FRESH PAINT and absence of scuff marks on the walls or polished granite floors revealed the newness of Shiloh's City Hall. With each step, the soles of our shoes squeaked as we walked down the hallway to the Utilities Office.

"Good morning, can I help you?" the clerk behind the counter asked.

"My name's Theo Phillips, and this is my wife, Liddy. We're the new owners at 10 Calvary Street..."

Before I could finish, she said, "Oh, we've been expectin' y'all." She pushed her chair back and disappeared into a corner office.

A moment later, a pleasant young man with almost shoulder length brown hair and dark brown eyes returned.

"Mister and Missus Phillips, I'm Hal Archer, Shiloh's Utilities Department Director. I wanted to personally welcome you and offer any assistance to make your move to Shiloh a pleasant experience."

"Thank you, Mister Archer."

"Please call me Hal. Mister Archer's my father, and happens to be the mayor." Hal's eyes and voice dropped as if searching for his next thought. He then fumbled with a pre-filled green account form, grabbed the pen clipped between the two top buttons of his blue knit shirt, and pointed to where I needed to sign.

"If you'll put your John Hancock right here, that'll be all we need."

"That's easy enough," I said, offering the pen back to Hal.

Liddy asked, "When should we expect the bill each month?"

"Bills go out the fifth of each month. You can either mail or drop off your payment. If you ever have any questions, please feel free to call me." He reached out to shake my hand while fumbling in his pocket for a business card he offered to Liddy.

———

Lunch became the next order of business. We decided to try the cozy restaurant next door to Nick's office, across the street from City Hall.

After we crossed Main Street, we realized the line of customers had grown to the doorway. Liddy pointed to the sign overhead, "The Butcher Shoppe," and peeked inside.

Hardly a vacant seat remained inside, leaving little doubt this was a favorite lunch spot in Shiloh.

Liddy squeezed my hand as she stood on her tiptoes and whispered. "Hun, this reminds me of that sandwich shop in Athens. Do you remember the name of that place?"

I closed my eyes tight and then whispered back, "Of course, Dawg Bonz." My nostalgic senses surveyed the uncanny similarities to our old campus hangout. A sign over the set of French doors to our immediate right read, "Fresh Meats and Cheese."

I nudged Liddy and pointed. "They also have a deli and butcher shop."

Liddy smiled and said, "We'll have to check it out after we eat."

My attention shifted to the handwritten menu on the blackboard above the counter. As the line inched forward, I felt a tap on my shoulder.

"Do you mind if we join you?" Joe said with a smile standing with his brother Nick.

I nudged Liddy. "Mind if Joe and Nick join us for lunch?"

Liddy peeked over her shoulder. Her face lit up. "Hey, what a wonderful surprise. Maybe one of you can help us pick something out for lunch."

While Nick offered a couple of suggestions, Joe stepped aside and shouted, "Hey everyone. Can I have your attention? I'd like to introduce

Theo and Liddy Phillips. They're Shiloh's newest residents."

Curious, smiling faces enjoyed our stunned expressions. To make matters worse, the gentleman busy taking orders at the counter called out, "Hey Joe. Please, bring Mistor and Missis Phillips up here."

The customers about to order stepped back and made room for us. The man behind the counter clapped his hands and said, "Bravo, bravo. Thank you very much. These are guests today."

Liddy dug her fingernails into my bicep as we stood at the counter embarrassed.

When the brief round of applause ended, our dark-haired host raised a generous smile beneath his bushy mustache, reached over the counter and grabbed my hand. His strong accent required my full concentration. "My name is Silas Thrope. Welcome, Mistor Theo to my restaurant. Please, whatever you and your wife want today is on the house."

"Thank you, Mister Thrope. That is most gracious. Since this is our first time here, what would you suggest?"

"Don't you worry. I fix something special for both of you." Silas released his firm grip on my hand and turned toward the other end of the counter. "Bernie. Alex. Please come here. I wanna you meet Theo and Liddy Phillips."

A young man sharing Silas' Mediterranean features sans the mustache appeared. A red apron protected his long-sleeved flannel shirt and blue jeans.

Silas puffed out his chest. "Please, Miss Liddy, this is my son, Alex. He'll take good care of you. He's a good boy."

Alex's polite but wrinkled smile appeared to share our awkward embarrassment. Liddy smiled as she said, "Nice to meet you, Alex."

"Yes ma'am, thank you."

Silas' wife wiped her hands and then greeted us. Her dark hair, olive complexion, and deep brown eyes matched her husband's appearance. "Missis Phillips, my name is Bernie. Kaloos Oreesa-tay."

Liddy glanced at me, but I returned a likewise puzzled look.

"Kaloos Oreesa-tay means welcome in Greek," Bernie said with a broad white grin.

Liddy's eyes lit up. "Oh. Thank you."

I turned to Silas. "How'd you and your family land in Shiloh, Georgia?"

Silas laughed as he paused to count on his fingers. "Umm, just about twenty years ago, I told a business friend I wanted to find a place of my own and move out of Atlanta. He told me about this butcher shop. So, here we are."

Bernie barked at Silas. "Enough, our customers are hungry." Her hands-on-hips bluster made Liddy smile. Bernie waggled her finger. "Back to work old man."

Moments later, Alex carried Liddy's tray and led the four of us to a table near the front window. We savored the first bites of our gyro, stuffed with seasoned lamb, feta cheese, and grilled onions, and a side of fries. As the pace of our eating slowed, and our small talk grew, Liddy asked Joe and Nick about their families.

Nick said, "Momma and I share our family's original home not far from your house. Thankfully, she spends most of her time at our family's Saint Simon Island summer home. Dad passed away eight years ago, and not long afterward, my wife died in an auto accident. Momma and I have sorta been taking care of one another ever since."

Liddy responded. "I'm truly sorry about your wife. Do you have any children?"

"No, but I've got precocious twin nieces." Nick peered toward Joe's crooked smile.

"What about you Joe?" I asked.

Joe smirked at Nick. "Well, let's see here. I cut the umbilical cord from Momma twelve years ago after I married Melissa." Nick returned a humorous wrinkled look as Joe continued. "My wife Melissa, Missy to most folks around here, and I have two daughters, Lizzie and Lucy, spirited, red-headed eight-year-olds. Our home is across from Nick and Momma. I hope you can meet Missy and the girls soon, and of course, Momma when she gets back in town."

Nick then asked about our family. Liddy talked about our two sons and their families, and how they planned to visit for Christmas, while I looked across the street at the bronze statue.

After a few more minutes of small talk, I blurted, "Excuse me, but what can either of you tell me about that statue across the street?"

Our small talk abruptly halted. Nick and Joe glanced at each other, as their playful smiles disappeared. Nick spoke up first.

"You mean Jessie Masterson. He was a dear friend, and it's safe to say about everyone who knew him loved him. Though he's gone, he'll always remain a hero in the hearts of just about everyone in Shiloh."

Liddy asked, "What happened?"

Nick looked out the window toward City Hall. "Well, until three years ago, you'd be staring at the original Adams County Courthouse. The night it burned down, Jessie and a group of students met in the basement as usual. Based on the various accounts of that night, after the building caught on fire, Jessie mustered the students to safety before he ran back into the burning building to save two others trapped upstairs."

Nick paused and sighed before his sad eyes connected with mine.

"The fire department reported it as an accident, cause unknown, but —" Nick looked at Jessie's lifelike statue.

"But what?" I asked.

"First, no one has shared what happened on the inside just before the ceiling collapsed? The fire had been so intense that night that only Jessie's gold necklace miraculously survived beneath some smoldering rubble near the front entrance."

"There's gotta be more to the story," I urged as I examined Nick's and Joe's sullen expressions.

"Only the two Jessie saved know more of the story about that night," Joe answered. "You see, he saved Hank and Hal Archer, the mayor's sons, which leads to a second unresolved mystery. No one has gotten a straight answer out of either one of them since that evening."

My eyes lit up. "Wait a moment. We just met Hal a short while ago at the City Utilities Office." That inquisitive itch I first felt after visiting Jessie's memorial the previous night returned.

Nick nodded. "From the testimonies we read and heard, Hal and

Hank scrambled out the front entrance, flames licking their heels, seconds before the main floor ceiling collapsed." Nick paused. "To this day, it's hard to swallow that Jessie couldn't have made it out, but Hank and Hal have added nothing."

Joe interrupted. "But Jessie's a hero in the eyes of all those grateful students and their parents. Even the mayor praised Jessie as a hero because of what he did for his two sons. I won't hesitate to tell you though, in our minds, it's the untold story behind Jessie's death that's the real tragedy."

Liddy squeezed my hand. "We didn't mean to stir up such sad memories."

"Liddy's right. Please forgive me."

Joe placed his hand over Liddy's and mine. "Hey, you didn't do anything wrong."

Nick added, "It's just that we were close friends, but-"

"Look here, today's supposed to be a happy day. There'll be plenty of time to talk more about Shiloh's history." Joe smiled as he steered the conversation to cheerier, more pressing matters.

Before we left, we thanked Joe and Nick and reiterated our intentions to take up their offer and visit Shiloh Baptist Church.

———

As soon as the empty moving truck pulled away, I surprised Liddy when I said, "I've got dinner covered." She followed me into the kitchen. "While you were busy with the movers, I spent most of the afternoon meeting some of our neighbors." An array of casseroles and baked treats filled the kitchen counter.

Liddy's tired smile reflected how overwhelmed she felt with all the unopened boxes stacked throughout the house. By the time we ate and put the food away, we located the box containing our familiar sheets and pillows.

Liddy fell right off to sleep, but my mind wrestled with the unrevealed aspects of the horrific story Nick and Joe shared.

CHAPTER FIVE

THE HUSTLE AND BUSTLE OF unpacking lasted two arduous days, but Liddy orchestrated all our belongings into their new proper place.

Our white wooden rockers and matching tables fit well on the front porch. But something seemed amiss as I reexamined the porch scratching my chin.

Liddy yelled from the other side of the kitchen window, "What's the matter? You look puzzled."

"Honey, our chairs, and tables look great out here, but somethin's missing."

Liddy opened the front door, a dish towel draped over her shoulder, and her hair pulled into a neat ponytail. Her faded jeans and gray cotton shirt showed little evidence of how much the two of us had completed since breakfast. She dabbed her cheeks with an end of the dish towel while puffing at a couple of stray locks tickling her face. A twinkle in her eyes accompanied a cute smirk. "Everything looks just fine, but I thought you decided to hang your hammock out here?" She winked and then retreated to the kitchen.

An hour later, my hammock swung from new hooks installed in the porch's ceiling beams. I flopped into the cotton netting for a quick test and then hollered, "Oh Liddy. Got a second?"

Liddy giggled as she climbed next to me. After a few snuggles, I said, "Now, this makes our new front porch complete."

Liddy kissed my cheek. "The kitchen's almost done. I'll be back." She scooted out of the hammock, looked down and added, "Why don't you just relax out here a while longer? You earned it." She then handed me a copy of yesterday's local paper.

A soothing Gulf breeze soon arrested any intention I held to read the paper. My eyes grew heavy, and the newspaper wound up tucked by my side. I felt myself gradually drift off until the sounds of car doors and shuffling feet warranted a curious squint.

"Mister Phillips, good afternoon. I hope we didn't disturb you."

I lifted one hand and mustered a grin to dismiss any pretense of an interrupted nap. I firmly planted both feet on the floor and took stock of our approaching guests. His starched white dress shirt, Windsor green and yellow silk tie, and pleated gabardine slacks matched his neatly groomed short, graying brown hair combed to disguise a receding hairline. She wore a navy skirt with a gray sweater top that with her stylish, short gray-streaked dark hair complimented her thin features.

"I'm Larry Scribner, and this is my wife, Martha. We own the Shiloh Sentinel, the town newspaper."

I arose from the edge of the hammock and politely extended my hand.

"What do you think of our little town, Mister Phillips?" he asked before I got any words out.

"Please, call me Theo…" Larry returned my smile as I replied to his question. "Shiloh's been a pleasant surprise, unveiling itself so far to be everything we hoped it'd be." We broke our handshake, and I looked at Martha. "Would you like to come inside?"

Liddy stepped onto the porch adjusting her ponytail. I said, "Honey, I was about to invite Larry and Martha to come inside to meet you."

Larry waved his hand. "No, no. Please. We only wanted to stop by to introduce ourselves." Martha smiled as her eyes connected with Liddy's.

Liddy pointed to the rockers. "Well, would you at least have a seat for a few minutes?"

Martha glanced at Larry and said, "Maybe for a few minutes. We feel bad enough disturbing Theo's nap."

After we all found our seats, Larry said, "We just stopped by on behalf of Shiloh Baptist Church. I ran into Nick Arians, who mentioned that you might visit our church this Sunday and...well... maybe tonight as well?" Larry's eyes floated between Liddy and me.

Liddy peeked over at me and she asked, "What time does the service begin?"

Martha grinned. "At seven o'clock, but if you get there early, you'll discover that we're pretty friendly at Shiloh Baptist. Besides, I'd like to introduce you to Pastor Wright and his wife, Judy."

I looked at Liddy and shrugged with a conciliatory look.

Liddy said, "That settles it. We'll be there a little after six-thirty."

Larry turned to me. "By the way, I understand you just retired from Cornerstone Publishers as Chief Editor and have some newspaper experience too."

I hesitated, not knowing where Larry learned about my background. "Well, I reckon that's pretty accurate. Why?"

"Nick mentioned it because he figured I might be interested. It's not often someone with your background moves into town." His curious stare indicated he had unasked questions.

"Sure, I guess that makes sense," I stammered.

Larry stood and extended a hand to Martha. "Look, we won't take up any more of your time, but I'd like to talk to you some more in a day or so. Would that be okay?"

I tried to disguise my curiosity and said in a matter-of-fact tone, "Sure, that'd be fine."

Shortly after six, Liddy grabbed her sweater and handed me my red Georgia Bulldog windbreaker. After a short walk, we crossed Main Street and stood at the bottom of the steps leading up to the main entrance of Shiloh Baptist Church. Plenty of people milled along the sidewalk, while a few, none in any real hurry, made their way up the stairs and entered the large red doors.

Once inside the church, the Scribners whisked us toward a tall, distinguished gentleman wearing a light blue open-collar dress shirt beneath a maroon v-neck sweater and gray dress slacks.

"Pastor Wright, I'd like to introduce to you, Theo and Liddy Phillips. They're the new couple I spoke to you about," Larry said.

"Welcome to Shiloh Baptist Church. Please, feel free to call me Arnie. Everyone else does." He then glanced briefly at Larry as his smile broadened after a light chuckle as we shook hands.

"Thank you, Arnie." I felt a little awkward addressing any pastor so informally, but it indicated that this church might be a good fit for us.

Arnie checked his watch. "Oops, I'm sorry. If you'll excuse me, I have a lot to do before we start tonight. However, would you mind if my wife and I stopped over for a brief visit after the service tonight?"

"Uh, sure." I glanced at Liddy's it's-up-to-you-look. "No, not at all. Do you know where we live?"

Arnie replied, "Absolutely. I promise we won't dilly-dally. We'll be at your house no later than, let's say eight-thirty." He eyed Liddy for her approval.

Liddy beamed as she chimed in, "That'll be fine Pastor Wright… I mean Arnie. Do you and your wife prefer regular or decaf coffee?"

"Decaf will be fine," Arnie said before heading into the sanctuary.

Larry and Martha gave us a quick tour of the church before we entered the sanctuary, which offered comfortably padded wooden pews and a broad center aisle. A large open Bible sat atop an ornate, carved table in front of the pulpit. Two high back chairs sat to one side just below where the organist waited with her hands in her lap, eyes glued on the ebony concert piano's unoccupied bench on the other side of the raised platform.

Arnie entered from a side door and stood at the head of the aisle on the main floor. He greeted everyone with a pastoral smile and spoke briefly on various church matters, but meant little to us.

Martha pointed to a young woman with long blonde hair seated on the front row and whispered, "That's Mary, our daughter. She leads the music program." A moment later, Mary took her place at the piano and nodded at the organist. The congregation stood and sang three familiar praise songs.

After prayer and praise requests, Arnie shared a brief message about how our faith determines our relationship with God. He referenced Abraham's story of faith as the inspiration for his mid-week sermon. Arnie shared how Abraham left behind his familiar home and community to journey to an unknown destination that God promised him.

While listening to Arnie, I surveyed the room full of strange faces. After the closing prayer, one of the few familiar faces, Nick Arians, hustled between two rows of pews and caught up with us in the aisle.

"Glad you could make it."

Liddy asked, "Where's your brother and his wife?"

"He's stuck at the office working on some legal mumbo-jumbo. Missy scooted straight out to fetch the twins."

"Well, please let them know we asked about them."

"Absolutely. I'm sure Missy will feel bad that she missed you, but they should be here Sunday."

I extended my hand and said, "Thanks again Nick."

"For what?"

"For helping us to feel so welcome."

"Hey, that's what friends are for, right?" Nick slapped my shoulder and shot Liddy a boyish grin.

———

Waiting on the porch for our guests to arrive, I heard the hiss of the coffeemaker as Liddy gathered coffee mugs and put a dish of her homemade ginger snaps onto a tray. The Wrights pulled up promptly at 8:30 and walked hand-in-hand up the walkway. Judy's fit figure complemented Arnie's athletic appearance. Her shoulder-length, silvery blonde hair bounced as she walked. Her designer jeans and fashionable long-sleeved maroon and navy sweater coordinated with Arnie's gray slacks and his solid maroon sweater.

Arnie said, "Thanks for having us. Getting settled into a new house is a lot of work. Besides, I know I kinda invited myself, but Judy wanted to meet both of you as well."

Before I could respond, Liddy rushed out the front door and greeted Judy and her husband as though they were already dear friends. "Welcome, I've made fresh decaf coffee, or if you prefer, I can offer you some tea."

Judy, still clinging to Arnie's hand, said, "Thank you, Missus Phillips. Coffee will suit both of us just fine. Can I help in any way?"

Without blinking, Liddy said, "Please call me Liddy." She then grabbed Judy's hand and pointed with her other hand toward the rocking chairs. "Preacher, you and Theo make yourselves comfortable? Judy and I'll be right back."

I overheard Judy giggle and ask as soon as they stepped into the living room, "Would you mind giving me a quick tour of the house? It's been ages since I stepped into this house. I'm just dying to see what you and Theo have already done inside."

"Aah. This is nice," Arnie sighed as he slowly rocked.

"Yes, this is what I've missed all those years living near Atlanta. All these stars remind me how truly awesome God is."

"I agree, Theo. In the twenty-five years that Judy and I've lived in Shiloh, I've never lost the awe of clear nights like this." We continued to rock in silence and stared into the night sky until Arnie asked, "So Theo, I understand you're retired?"

"Yes, but I'm still adjusting to the idea and trying to figure out what that means for me."

"What do you mean?"

"It's been less than a month since I left my position as the chief editor at Cornerstone Publishing."

Arnie chuckled. "You worked at Cornerstone? I have several books in my library that Cornerstone published."

"Cornerstone's a good company, but it was just the right time for me to call it quits. Truth be told, I grew weary evaluating other writers. I'm ready to dabble doing some writing again."

"Maybe you can find some inspiration around here. Shiloh's a sleepy little town, but with a little digging, you'll likely stumble across some stories worth writing. Heck, I bet old Larry Scribner at the local paper would love to take advantage of your background."

"Funny you mentioned that; Larry and his wife stopped by earlier today."

A sly grin grew on Arnie's face. "Yeah I heard, and Nick Arians told me that you and Liddy might consider joining our church?"

"I've nothing against other churches, but Liddy and I just feel much more comfortable in a Baptist Church."

"I understand. As far as I know, God welcomes all his children into heaven, but I hope you'll find Shiloh Baptist a good fit for you." Arnie stared blankly at the porch floor.

Arnie's casual conversation felt natural, not forced as with pastors I had met in the past.

Arnie lifted his eyes and asked, "What do you think about our little town and those you've met so far?"

"To be honest, at this point, I'm a bit skeptical."

"What do you mean skeptical?" Arnie's brow wrinkled.

"Well, truthfully, so far Shiloh's everything we hoped it'd be, and unbelievably friendly."

Arnie rocked back in his chair. "So what's not right?"

"That's the problem. It's too good. You know, scary nice…" I paused before adding, "Umm, makes me wonder if Liddy and I'll fit in."

Arnie reached over and slapped my knee. "Theo, trust me. Shiloh ain't nowhere near perfect, my friend. Don't get me wrong, though. It's certainly friendly enough, but it has its share of moments that'll make you scratch your head. Just give it time… you'll see what I mean."

I offered a tight-lipped grin and nodded.

"Theo, I think you need some convincing. I'm making a trip tomorrow to visit a wonderful lady who lives just outside of town. Her name is Marie Masterson, Jessie Masterson's mother."

I interrupted, "The same Jessie Masterson memorialized across the street from the church?"

"Yes, the one and the same."

"Nick and Joe shared a little about what happened to him during our lunch the other day."

"Well, there you go. There's a story that you might find interesting to write. So how about it? You wanna tag along for a visit? It'll give us more time to talk."

"Well, sure. I'd love to."

"How about I call you in the morning?" Arnie sat back in his rocker. "By the way, has anyone told you that you're living in Jessie Masterson's great aunt's house?"

My eyes widened. "Seriously?"

"Betty Priestly was Marie's aunt. Betty and her husband, Zack, were the reason Jessie and Marie moved to Shiloh years ago."

Then Arnie lowered his voice. "But in the meantime, let's not talk about Jessie anymore tonight. Judy still gets pretty emotional whenever the topic is brought up."

I nodded and said nothing further, but my curiosity stirred all the more.

The glass storm door opened as Liddy and Judy chatted back and forth as they brought out the coffee and cookies.

When Judy and Arnie stood to leave, Liddy glanced at me and said, "By the way sweetie, you'll have to occupy yourself tomorrow afternoon. Judy's invited me to a women's luncheon."

Arnie said, "Well, I guess that'll mean Theo can spend some time with me. I've got a visitation planned that Theo may enjoy accompanying me on while you ladies do your thing." Arnie winked as he and Judy got up to leave. "Theo, I'll call you in the morning."

We left the window slightly ajar in our bedroom that night, so Liddy pulled the comforter over her shoulder and cuddled as she whispered, "That was a pleasant visit tonight. Judy seemed nice and knew a lot about this old house too."

I turned so I could see her face and kissed her on the forehead. "Arnie shared something about the house too."

"What'd he tell you?"

"Betty Priestly was Jessie Masterson's great aunt."

"Really? No wonder everyone we've met comments about the house."

"Well, then you'll find this of interest. Arnie invited me to tag along when he visits Jessie's mother."

Liddy's weary eyes perked up. "Jessie's mother? Sounds like this Jessie fella' and his story is growing on you."

CHAPTER SIX

A FAINT GLIMMER OF DAWN disturbed the darkness by the time I found my familiar recliner. The soft light of my Tiffany reading lamp welcomed me back into my quiet time regimen.

I peered out the living room window and surveyed the colorless blanket of leaves covering our almost dormant lawn. I dismissed any further notions about the leaves, preferring to stare at Liddy's favorite patchwork quilt draped across her ottoman in front of her plush armchair. Each scrap that Liddy meticulously sewed together to make her cherished quilt, she cut from old clothes our family had worn over the years. Each patchwork held a special memory.

I reached down beside my chair and found my Bible and daily devotional journal. Both shared dog-eared pages, a rainbow's worth of highlighted passages, and years of scribbled notes. After reading about Abraham's journey of faith in Genesis, I wrote in my journal for Thursday, November fourteenth, "Father God, sorry it's been so long since we sat down together, but whatever reservations I privately had about our move to Shiloh, I now set aside. Whatever you have in store in the days ahead, I accept by faith. Thanks, Lord."

After returning my Bible and journal beneath the end table. I savored my first cup of coffee. Treetops and rooftops blocked my view of Town Square, except for City Hall's copper-clad cupola and three crosses atop the churches in town.

The unmistakable grinding sound of a bike chain and evenly-spaced thumps brought me to my feet. I cinched my flannel robe and ventured onto my porch to investigate. A young lad, maybe ten or eleven, pedaled his way down the street, launching his arsenal of folded newspapers onto walkways on both sides. He wore a gold ball cap bearing a green S, a Shiloh Saints athletic sweatshirt, and blue jeans rolled high on his calves.

He came to a skidding halt by the curb, and a swift swing of his foot dropped his kickstand. Bearing the reddened freckled cheeks one would expect on a brisk autumn morning, he marched up to my porch. "Good morning, sir. I thought I'd stop later this morning but saw you on your porch. My name is Tim."

I greeted Tim at the bottom of the steps. His professional demeanor and confident handshake surprised me. "Well, good morning to you. My name is Theo Phillips."

"Would you like me to deliver your paper to you?" Tim asked, all businesslike. "I promise your paper will be right here at the foot of the steps every morning, bright and early."

"Well, Tim, it looks as though you deliver pretty early, which suits me just fine." I crossed my arms and sized up his confident pose.

"I promise your paper will be here every morning before six-thirty," Tim smirked. "That makes certain that I'm also never late for school which I promised my mom and dad." He pulled a copy of this morning's edition from under his arm. "Here, can we say I made my first delivery to you starting today?"

"Deal," I said tucking the paper under my arm.

He reached into his pocket, pulled out a small notebook, and then scribbled down my name and address. "What's your phone number?"

"Hmm, good question...I have to think a moment." My grin twisted. "Sorry Tim, guess I'm getting old and its too new for me to remember it."

"Oh, that's okay. Just write it on your payment envelope next week." Tim reached back into his pants pocket and pulled out a Shiloh Sentinel business card. "If you've any questions, just call."

"Hey Tim, thanks for stopping."

"Have a great day Mister Phillips, and welcome to Shiloh." He hopped on his bike, swept the kickstand back, and disappeared around the corner.

As soon as I closed the door, Liddy's sleepy voice came from the kitchen. "Who was that?"

"Tim, our paperboy."

Liddy raised her eyes just above the rim of her coffee cup. "When was the last time we had a paperboy?"

"I was just trying to remember, but it's certainly been a long time. Of course, I remember delivering papers on my bike for my Dad's newspaper."

—

Following breakfast, I hung one framed picture or painting after another under Liddy's watchful eye, until a knock at the door interrupted us. I left Liddy contemplating the placement of the last few family photos in the hallway.

Larry Scribner's polished grin greeted me when I opened the door. Although he owned a small-town newspaper, he embraced a big-city image with his blue-striped dress shirt and blue and red silk tie tucked beneath a khaki three-button vest and matching dress slacks. Fortunately, Larry's friendliness separated him from the stuffed shirts I remembered from my publishing days.

"Howdy Theo. By the looks of things, Liddy's keeping you pretty busy."

A relaxed grin emerged as I welcomed him into our living room. "Glad you stopped. We enjoyed our visit to the church last night."

Larry sat across from me in Liddy's armchair. "Well, we sincerely hope you and Liddy like it. I'll admit right off, it isn't perfect by any stretch, but it's got far more upsides than downsides."

I nodded with a hopeful grin. "I can honestly say, so far we've seen mostly upsides."

Larry's demeanor turned more businesslike. "That's good to hear. Look, I don't want to hold you up, so I'll get right to the point. Martha and I would like to do a down-to-earth feature article on you and

Liddy. We'd like to take a couple of snapshots of the two of you and create a nice piece telling the town a little about you."

I gave Larry a long, blank look. "I'm not sure what to say. I've never been on this side of a news article." I turned in the direction of Liddy pretending to be preoccupied. "Liddy, would you join Larry and me for a moment?" The sound of the hammer being tossed into the toolbox followed.

After I reiterated Larry's offer, Liddy attempted to muffle her giddiness as she asked, "Why would you want do a feature on us?"

Larry looked baffled. "Well Liddy, this town doesn't get a lot of new faces, and you and Theo have an interesting background to share. Besides, there're a bunch of folks already wanting to know more about the new owners of Betty Priestly's home."

Liddy looked at me with a curious stare.

Larry added, "Look, Liddy, I'll respect your privacy. It'll be a great opportunity to be introduced to your new town. How about it?"

Liddy's tight-lipped grin met Larry's persistent hopeful look. "Sure, on one condition." Liddy raised her index finger.

Larry stood up. "Name it."

"We get to review the final copy before it goes to print."

Larry stuck his hand out. "I personally guarantee it."

Before I shut the front door after Larry left, the phone rang. Arnie asked if I still wanted to go with him to meet Marie Masterson, and then mentioned she insisted on feeding us lunch.

An hour later, we pulled into the church parking lot. Not sure of the length of my and Arnie's visit with Marie, I tossed the keys to Liddy before she headed off with Judy to their luncheon.

———

A few minutes later Arnie drove his Tahoe onto Main Street while I filled him in on Larry's visit.

Arnie chuckled. "Larry means well. Besides, the article sounds like a good idea. Just don't be surprised if Larry's got another motive behind it."

"What do you mean?" I asked with some reservation.

Arnie glanced at me and said, "I could be wrong, but don't be surprised if he uses the friendly gesture as a stepping stone."

I nodded with a puzzled stare and then said, "Arnie, tell me a little more about the connection between Marie Masterson and Betty Priestly."

"What do you want to know?" Arnie glanced at me again before returning his eyes on the road.

"Until you said something last night, Betty Priestly was just a name on the paperwork at the closing of the house."

Arnie cleared his throat and said, "Until Betty Priestly passed away about three years ago, as far as I know, a Priestly family member had always lived in that house. However, Miss Betty only lived in the home after her husband, Zack, died eleven or twelve years ago. Before that, their son John lived in the house while Zack and Betty remained full time on their farm until Zack passed away. In fact, it's where Marie now lives."

"What happened to the son, John?"

Arnie's demeanor saddened. "John Priestly was a respected teacher and coach in this town. He earned admiration from of all his students who passed through his classroom, as well as all those he coached at the high school. That changed though when he faced felony charges for the theft of school funds."

"Huh? What happened?"

"Because it involved school money, the district attorney pushed hard for a felony embezzlement conviction, though the evidence appeared circumstantial at best. However, when I visited John after his arraignment and bond hearing, he told me, 'Preacher, I know you and a lot of folks will be confused about this, but I'm going to do what's right and trust the truth will prevail.' A week later John accepted a plea bargain and pled guilty. He's still serving out a five to seven-year sentence."

"You make it sound like a fishy deal went down. Do you believe

John was innocent?"

"Yes, I do. And ever since John asked me to trust God and pray, that's what I've done almost daily. It's sad to think it's been over three years since they took him away." Arnie sighed as he continued. "The hardest part of John's story involved Miss Betty. She suffered a stroke and died a few weeks after he landed in prison. They allowed him to attend the funeral, but two sheriff deputies escorted him." Arnie's sadness filled the car.

"I'm sorry to hear that. Shiloh just doesn't seem like a place where that kind of thing would happen."

Arnie gripped the steering wheel tighter and gave me a serious stare. "Look, Theo, don't get me wrong. Shiloh's a great place to live and raise a family, but we all live on the wrong side of heaven to claim any place to be perfect. Like I told you last night if you want to write about Shiloh, there're plenty of interesting stories beneath the surface you might find worthy of your time and talents."

"I guess that explains why the house remained empty all that time before we moved in. How did Marie end up on the farm?"

Arnie's grin reemerged. "Now that's a more pleasant story. Fifteen years ago, Marie and her son Jessie arrived in town. At first, they lived with John in the house, but they also spent a lot of time out on the farm. Betty already struggled with health issues, so Zack and Betty willed the farm to Marie and Jessie. After Zack died, Betty moved back into town with John while Marie & Jessie moved onto the farm."

"How old was Jessie when they arrived?"

"Let me see. He'd just graduated from Georgia Christian University when John helped him land his teaching and coaching position at Shiloh. So I guess he was probably twenty-two or three when they first moved here."

"How's Marie handled all the responsibilities of a farm since Jessie died?"

"She keeps pretty much to herself nowadays, except for when she needs something in town."

"But what about the chores around the farm? Does she handle

them all alone?"

Arnie chuckled, "Heavens no! She's got plenty of help on the farm."

"What do you mean?"

"You'll see."

CHAPTER SEVEN

EXCITEMENT CRISSCROSSED MY ANXIOUSNESS OVER the prospect of meeting Jessie's mother as Arnie drove toward Marie's farm. I tried to calm myself by absorbing the countryside scenery along the way, all the while reconciling in my mind that, at worst, Marie Masterson will turn out to be an old recluse struggling with the loss of her son.

Arnie snapped his fingers and called out, "Theo. Theo. You okay?"

"Sorry, Arnie. Guess I zoned out on you, deep in thought about what to expect when we get to Marie's place."

Arnie smirked as he peeked out the corner of his eye. "I guarantee you'll enjoy meeting Marie, and you can thank me later for inviting you."

Five miles from town, Arnie turned off Old Mill Road onto a gravel road surrounded by woods. Dust billowed in our wake as the road narrowed. Arnie slowed as we approached a one-lane bridge with rusting steel girders and rails long overdue for paint. The Tahoe crept across the bridge as he pointed to the lazy water flowing below. "That's Shiloh Creek," he said.

A minute later we drove beyond the woods, and saw Marie's farmhouse and adjacent barn. An open gate welcomed us onto her property, as wood-fenced pastures filled with harvested bales of hay and distant cattle and horses grazing on remnants of green grass led the way. A crude wooden bridge spanned the winding brook running through the property. The thumping loose boards announced our arrival as we crossed.

A tall, rugged young man with a friendly smile appeared from the barn and greeted Arnie. I remained seated but overheard the young man's deep voice. "Preach', what brought y'all out here today?"

After a brief chat, Arnie walked to the house, and the red-haired young fella walked around the front of the Tahoe to greet me. I got out and extended my hand. His calloused grip swallowed mine as he said, "Mista' Phillips, I'm Pete. Preacher says you're new in town?"

I felt small next to Pete and pushed a smile through my discomfort. "Glad to meet you, Pete. And, yes, my wife and I just moved to Shiloh. Do you work for Miss Masterson?"

Pete's easy laughter delayed his response. "Well, not exactly, Mista' Phillips. Gosh, unless ya' count the great fixins Miss Marie provides when I'm here, helping Miss Marie with some chores just ain't work in my way of thinkin'."

"Hmm... that sounds nice of you. How long have you been helping out here?"

"Well Mista' Phillips, she's a wida', and her only son passed away three years ago. Me, my brother, and a couple of my cousins just decided it was the right thing to do."

"There're others?"

"Yes sir, but don't think for a doggone moment Miss Marie don't do her share out here." Pete's smile dissolved into a tight-lipped grin. "Mista' Phillips, why exactly are you here with the preacher anyway?"

I felt uncomfortable sharing too much with my new ruddy acquaintance until I got to meet Marie. I crossed my arms to match his stalwart, guardian pose. "Preacher invited me to tag along, so I'd get the chance to meet some more folks."

Pete scratched his red curly head and then massaged his unshaven burly face. "Umm, you seem like a nice enough fella. Heck, anybody preach' vouches for is okay in my book." Pete's jaw relaxed as his smile returned. "If'n' ya need help with anythin', you just let me know. Me and my brother Andy will stop by and say hey sometime."

"Do you know where we live?"

After a hardy chuckle, Pete said, "Of course. Me, dad and Andy worked on y'all's house. Shucks, I handled the plumbing."

"Really? Susanna's your mom, and Jeannie's your sister?"

"Yes, sir. That ol' house sure carries lots of memories for me and my family."

"Seems a lot of other folks feel much the same about that old house. You and Andy stop by anytime. I'd love to hear about some of those fond memories."

Arnie's voice interrupted. "Theo. Come on in."

Pete smiled. "Go on. You don't wanna keep Miss Marie waitin' on ya. But do me a favor?"

"Sure, what's that?"

"You and Preach gotta promise to save me some of them cookies she baked."

I winked back at Pete as I headed to the kitchen door.

Arnie said, "Come on in Theo." A petite woman in work jeans and a denim shirt tucked in offered a pleasant smile accented by her well-tanned face.

Marie stepped to greet me as the screen door snapped shut behind me. "Welcome, Mister Phillips." She pointed to the table by the window in her cozy kitchen. "Come, join us for some lunch."

Baked ham and a wedge of yellow cheese sat next to a loaf of fresh-made bread on a cutting board.

Marie asked, "Sweet tea okay? I just made it this morning."

I nodded with a smile as the aroma of still warm bread and cookies caught my nose. I sat across from Marie. Arnie faced the window. We each made a sandwich while Arnie shared a little about Marie's farm.

After we finished our sandwiches, Marie pulled a porcelain pitcher from her refrigerator and slid a plateful of chocolate chip cookies onto the table. With a sly grin she asked, "Mister Phillips, you ever tasted fresh cow's milk before?"

"Golly, I haven't had gen-u-ine cow's milk in forty years, but I'm game. Thank you."

Marie and Arnie giggled at the delight I showed in my first bite. I swallowed and then confessed, "These cookies are sinfully good." I grabbed a napkin and wiped the crumbs from my lips.

I noticed Marie had leaned back in her chair and looked intensely at me. Her countenance changed, but her curious stare lingered even as she sipped on her milk. In an almost inaudible whisper, she muttered, "Theo Phillips, I just know we've met before."

I washed down the last morsel with a gulp of milk. "We have? When? Where?" My widened eyes darted between Marie and Arnie.

"I knew you looked familiar when you first walked in, and now it's coming back to me. You've got, or at least had, a really sweet wife named, uummm... let me think a moment...Linda? No, it wasn't Linda."

With hesitation, I said, "No not Linda, but-"

Marie placed her hand on my arm and placed a forefinger near my lips. "Sshh! Give me a second." She stared at the untouched cookies on her plate and then her head popped up. "Lydia. That's it."

Arnie and I stared at each other as I slowly nodded.

Marie continued. "What's it been? Maybe thirty-five years? But some people you never forget. It was in Richmond Hill?"

Dumbfounded and puzzled, my mind raced back to my first job after college. Liddy and I had moved from married campus housing to our first house in Richmond Hill in 1976.

"As a matter of fact, Lydia, or Liddy, is having lunch right now with Arnie's wife. But I'm still trying to recollect when and how we met." I stared harder at Marie's suntanned face and tried to picture her as a much younger woman.

"See if this helps. The first time we met, you and Liddy stood behind me in the checkout line at the A&P in Richmond Hill. I struggled with my then infant son fussing in my arms when I realized I didn't have enough money to purchase his formula."

"Oh my God. I remember." I looked at Arnie who sat back and simply observed with amazement. Images from that day flooded my memory. "Your baby squirmed and hollered. Liddy handed me a twenty dollar bill when she saw your tears, which I gave to a surprised young cashier, who then tried to hand me the change, but I told him to give it to you."

Marie's eyes teared up. "Yeah, but I also remember how I left the store so upset and embarrassed, toting the formula in a brown paper bag in one hand, my pocketbook slung over one shoulder, and Jessie cradled in the other arm."

I glanced at Arnie and said, "But Arnie, catch this… Liddy and I paid for our groceries and loaded them into the back of our Bronco just as dark clouds overhead dumped rain on us. We pulled away from the store, but before I pulled out into traffic Liddy begged me to stop. She pointed at Marie drenched, her baby tucked under her jacket, struggling to keep a firm grip on a wet grocery bag. We pulled beside Marie and offered to drive her and her baby home."

Arnie finally entered the conversation. "And here you are thirty-five years later meeting this same young mother you helped."

The three of us sat frozen in silence. This meeting exceeded sheer coincidence. Self-conscious of my own emotions, I noticed Marie's flush cheeks and a slight grin. Arnie simply stared upward.

I looked at Marie and said, "As I remember, we parked outside your apartment and spoke until the rain let up, but never talked to you again after that. For the longest time, Liddy and I prayed for you whenever we saw you with your son around town. We certainly never expected our paths to cross four decades later."

Marie's misty eyes confirmed the significance of our connection. Her voice cracked as she spoke. "I can't explain it, but never before that day or since have I felt comfortable accepting generosity, especially from total strangers, but you and Lydia served as my guardian angels that day. You gave me much more than money and a bag of groceries. Your compassion is why I've held onto the memory for so long."

I turned to Arnie. "I don't know what you're thinking right about now, but I've just acquired a far stronger sense of God's providence in the affairs of man than we're comfortable admitting most of the time."

Arnie shook his head. "Amen brother, I agree."

A single teardrop left a moist trail down Marie's cheek. "Theo, that young child was the only child God blessed me with, and his name was Jessie." Marie's tears increased, and she stopped to dab them with her napkin. "Please forgive me. A terrible accident took Jessie from me."

I placed my hand on her forearm. "I have to admit, the loss of Jessie was the reason I wanted to visit you today. Ever since Liddy and I arrived in Shiloh, I've felt drawn to his memorial in the center of town. I've asked several people all sorts of questions trying to know more about him." I tried to make eye contact with her watery eyes. "Do you believe in divine appointments?"

A sniffle brought a small grin as she looked into my eyes. "I do now."

"Look, I've spent the last four decades in the publishing business and not once has such a burning desire struck me like the one growing within me these last few days. I believe Jessie's story deserves to be written." Our eyes reconnected. "Would you allow me the opportunity to write Jessie's story?"

Marie grabbed her napkin again and wiped her tears. She paused and slowly nodded. "You'd do that?"

Arnie leaned forward and said, "Marie, I believe this is something that not only Jessie deserves but you as well. Sharing his story with someone like Theo and then seeing Jessie's legacy preserved will bring a special blessing to you and a bunch of other folks too."

Marie stared at Arnie and then back at me. Her sad blue eyes pierced my heart as she took my hands into her calloused palms and squeezed tight for a moment before letting go. "Tell me what you need from me."

Holding back the enthusiasm I felt beneath a rising grin, I said, "Just time to talk about the last thirty plus years, but ... we shouldn't start until you and Liddy get together. She'll never believe me when I tell her about our conversation today."

Marie allowed a stifled laugh as her head swayed back and forth. "I can only imagine, Theo. I definitely would like to meet her again."

"How about if you come visit us at our house?"

Marie's eyes lit up. "You bought Aunt Betty's ol' home didn't ya?" I nodded as she added, "Just give me a call early next week."

Although anxious to learn more about Marie and Jessie, I also sensed we needed a couple of days for the significance of our divine appointment to sink in. I reassured her we'd call to arrange a time to meet.

On the return to town, Arnie shared more about Marie and her relationship with her volunteer farm hands, Pete, Andy, Jay, and Jim. I learned that Jay and Jim were the sons of Zeb Adams, owner of Adams Feed and Hardware in town. Arnie said the four of them grew up together, and Jessie became more like a big brother to them after he came to town."

When Arnie pulled into my driveway, I said, "You know, Liddy's never going to believe this! Thanks."

Arnie laughed. "Didn't I tell you that you'd thank me later?"

CHAPTER EIGHT

LIDDY HAD WHIPPED UP A BATCH of my favorite pancakes and freshly squeezed orange juice by the time I got out of bed. While she filled my coffee cup, she blurted, "I still can't stop thinking about Marie Masterson, after all these years." Liddy stared at the calendar beside the refrigerator. "Let's see… I've been thinking about us hosting a cookout. We can invite the Wrights, Scribners and maybe the Simmons family to thank them."

"When are you thinking?"

Liddy slid her finger over the calendar. "How about next Saturday? That'll give us plenty of time to pull it off."

"Sounds like a good idea. Let's ask Larry and Martha when they stop by this afternoon."

Do you think Marie would come too?"

"I'm not sure but it won't hurt to ask her."

One more unseasonably warm day found its way into mid-November. Two piles of leaves stared at me in defiance as I paused to wipe the sweat off my face with my sleeve when Larry arrived with Martha and their daughter Mary in their white Buick sedan.

"Theo, the yard looks great. Hope you and Liddy aren't too busy."

"Nah. Y'all have a seat," I said as I reached for the door. "Let me see what Liddy's up to. I'll be right back."

Liddy straightened her ponytail as she stared into the mirror in the hallway. "Is Martha with Larry?"

"Yes, Mary too..." I said as I headed toward the bedroom. "And she brought a camera."

Liddy snarled as she followed me into the bedroom. "Oh, fiddlesticks. Theo, please hurry up. I need you to buy me another five minutes."

"You look fine." I washed my hands and face and pulled on a fresh shirt and pair of jeans and combed my hair as I headed to the porch.

A couple of southern minutes later, Liddy apologized as she joined us on the porch.

Martha looked up and smiled. "No need to apologize. Theo's been keeping us company."

Larry handled the interview and asked a few mundane questions about our ordinary past, while Martha took copious notes in shorthand and Mary took candid photographs. Then he asked, "What led you to choose Shiloh and this house?"

Liddy placed her hand on my knee and then said, "Truthfully, looking back, we didn't exactly choose Shiloh, Shiloh chose us."

Martha laid her pen down and looked up for the first time since the interview began. Larry paused, stared at Liddy and asked, "Can you elaborate a little on that?"

"Larry, it's hard to explain in a few words. After thinking about the people we've met and the stories we've heard in the short time that we've been here, Theo and I feel we just can't take credit for choosing Shiloh."

Larry massaged his chin. "What exactly are you saying? Give me an example, if I can ask."

I squeezed Liddy's hand and said, "Larry, the quaintness and friendliness of the town has certainly exceeded our expectations, but what I think Liddy is trying to say..." Liddy and I shared a quick reaffirming grin. "Ever since we arrived, I've felt drawn to find out more about Jessie Masterson and what happened to him. Thanks to Arnie, I visited Jessie's mom yesterday. You'll never guess what role providence played during that visit." I paused to consider my words carefully.

Larry leaned closer. "Are you going to tell me?"

"This may seem hard to believe, but it turns out that Liddy and I met Marie and young Jessie thirty-five years ago. That brief encounter stirred Marie to recognize me during our visit."

Martha picked up her pen and began scribbling again. I leaned over and gently put my hand on Martha's pad. "Please, let's consider this off the record for the time being." I then looked at Larry. "Do you understand now why we believe that Shiloh chose us?"

Larry gently pulled the pen out of Martha's hand and slid it into his shirt pocket. "We'll work around that part of the story for the time being."

At that point, Liddy invited Martha and Mary to take a tour of our house. After the women disappeared, Larry asked, "Theo, on another note, would you consider doing some writing for the paper? I'll be glad to work around your schedule and interests. Fact is, you may be a godsend for me too. Theo, our paper sure could use your kind of experience and fresh perspective."

I wasn't quite sure what my gut tried to tell me as I absorbed the offer. "Let me give it some thought. Can I stop by your office in a day or so?"

Liddy stood in the open doorway with one of her curious looks and asked, "You'll give what some thought?"

Larry explained his offer, and when he finished, Liddy stepped beside me, grabbed the back of my arm, and said with a playful grin, "If you can use him and take him off my hands a few hours each week, you've got my blessing."

I laughed. "I promise, we'll talk in a day or two."

Larry appeared pleased. "That's fine, and I promise the article about you two won't go to print until we get y'all's approval in *my* office next week."

I nodded as Liddy turned to Martha. "We've got a question for the three of you before you leave. What're you doing next Saturday?"

Martha thought a moment. "Nothing I guess. What do you have in mind?"

"Theo and I want to host a cookout, and we'd like you to come. We're also inviting Arnie and Judy, maybe the Simmons and Marie."

"Sounds like a great idea."

Larry smiled as Mary said, "We'd all love to."

After our guests drove away, Liddy whispered, "I think you should really think about Larry's offer."

———

The next morning, I got out of bed early and mulled over Larry's proposition. The thought of working for the paper sounded more and more practical to me. There was little doubt that the paper would provide access to invaluable resources about Jessie Masterson as I gathered facts to write what I hoped to be a worthy story. The next logical step, I concluded, involved getting Larry to consider making Jessie Masterson's story my first special interest assignment.

The sound of Tim's bike spurred me from the comfort of my recliner. A minute later, I dropped the paper on the kitchen table and sat down after pouring a hot cup of coffee.

Not long afterward, Liddy appeared and rested her hands on my shoulders. In a quiet, raspy voice she inquired, "What's the news in Shiloh today?"

I looked up at her smiling yawn. "Not much to report. The highlight seems to be an article on how last night's Shiloh's football season mercifully ended after another disappointing season. According to Larry's column, the third coach in as many years announced his resignation right after the game. Otherwise, it appears the advertisements and classifieds are more newsworthy than the rest of the news. Maybe that's why Larry made his plea."

Liddy poured some juice and reached for the paper. "Maybe so." After a quick sip, a smirk appeared. "But before Clark Kent's head gets too big, I hope he takes care of his yard. Perry White's offer at the Sentinel can wait a couple more hours."

"Geez. As soon as I remember where I left my phone booth, your

Superman will save us from the merciless onslaught of those nasty leaves." I received a well-deserved slap on my wrist and spent most of the day outside as I promised.

Shortly before three, I latched the door of my shed and walked into the kitchen. Liddy yelled from the rear bedroom we converted into her craft room, "Hurry up and get a shower. The game's about to start." By kickoff, we lounged on our sofa sharing a bowl of popcorn, ready to rally our Dawgs to victory.

———

Sunday marked our first week in Shiloh. We both overslept and tag-teamed between the bathroom and grabbing a bagel and cup of coffee before heading to our first Sunday service at Shiloh Baptist Church.

By 10:30, the crisp fall breeze lost its nip to the morning sunshine. A crowd milled in front of the church as smiling faces greeted one another while others worked their way through the maze of people entering the large foyer just beyond the main doors. Greeters handed us a bulletin with a guest packet and a friendly handshake.

I attempted to inspect the bulletin, but Liddy grabbed my arm and said, "There's Martha and Larry."

Larry and I discussed the football game while the girls talked about the different activities the church offered. Out of the corner of my eye, I noticed Nick Arians with Joe and his family heading our way. Nick said as he approached, "Glad to see both of you this mornin'. Every-thin' going okay at the house? Y'all gettin' settled in?"

"Yes, we are. The house feels like home already," I said.

Nick pulled Joe and his family away from greeting a nearby cou-ple. "Theo, Liddy, you remember Joe, but this is Missy and their two daughters, Lizzie and Lucy."

Missy greeted Liddy with a lady-like handshake. The twins, dressed in matching red dresses and black patent shoes, huddled close to their mom.

"Missy, they're so adorable," Liddy said, as he leaned closer and eyed the black bows that decorated their curly red hair. "They remind me so much of Sissy, our eight-year-old granddaughter." Lizzie and Lucy giggled at Liddy's fussing but still clung shyly to their mother's side.

Nick looked at his watch. "We're late. We need to run."

Joe looked at me apologetically. "Thanks, Theo. Hey, we're late for choir rehearsal. We can chat later."

After Joe and Nick disappeared through a door at the end of the foyer, Missy sighed. "And I need to check the girls into the children's area before service begins. Let's plan to get together soon."

Liddy spotted Judy Wright and darted off while I stayed with Larry and Martha. Liddy beamed upon her return a moment later. "I just invited Judy and Arnie to the cookout next Saturday, and she's pretty sure they'll be free to come."

We sat with the Scribners during the service. Their usual pew in the back of the sanctuary suited me fine as I watched all the people take their seats. Sitting directly in front of us, I recognized the curly red hair of Pete Simmons but not the three young men next to him talking back and forth. A few seats away from Pete and his friends, I recognized Susanna and Jeannie Simmons.

I nudged Liddy. "There's Jeannie and her mom, and over there's Pete, the fella I met at Marie's."

Liddy caught Jeannie's attention and exchanged friendly smiles. Then Liddy said to me, "I presume next to Susanna is her husband, Sam."

Promptly at eleven, the buzz in the sanctuary hushed as Arnie stepped onto the platform and sat in one of the high-back chairs behind the pulpit. Mary Scribner and the organist played as the choir members in crimson choir robes entered and took their seats. Liddy poked my side and nodded when she recognized Nick and Joe in the top row of men.

After a few songs, Arnie began his message by asking, "Who is your neighbor?" The question connected as I looked over the sanctuary brimming with folks we did not know. I held Liddy's hand while we listened intently to Arnie's timely message.

After the service, we followed Larry and Martha into the center aisle and filed back into the crowded main foyer where no one seemed in a hurry to leave, and chatter filled the air. Arnie and Judy shared pleasantries and smiles as folks trickled by them and went outside.

Liddy leaned close. "Can we say hello to our new neighbors, the Simmons family?"

I surveyed the foyer and had little difficulty spotting Pete's red hair, and then recognized Susanna, Jeannie, and Sam nearby. I tugged on Liddy's hand, and we excused ourselves.

Pete waved as we approached. "Mista' Phillips, good to see you, and this mus' be Missus Phillips. It's a pleasure to meet ya. Mom and Jeannie told me about ya."

Susanna and Jeannie stepped aside and gave us room to join their family circle. Sam stood stoically poised. Susanna's eyes lit up. "Liddy, how'd you and Theo like the services?"

"Arnie speaks from his heart. I like both him and Judy."

While Liddy engaged in conversation with Susanna and Jeannie, I reached out and grabbed Pete's paw. "Glad to see you again, Pete. Miss Marie doing okay?"

"Yes, sir. She's fine. Probably busy feeding her animals." Pete put his hand on his dad's shoulder. "Dad, this is Mista' Phillips."

Sam loosened up as he spoke. "Glad to meet ya', Mister and Missus Phillips." He glanced at Susanna and Jeannie. "I've heard plenty about the two of you." Sam looked at Liddy. "Ma'am, sorry I haven't been by sooner. Susanna and Jeannie did tell me you wanted to meet me. I hope you're pleased with all our work."

Liddy said, "You and your boys did a marvelous job. And the way y'all cleaned up the house… Oh, my! Thank you so much."

"Ma'am, the credit should go to Pete and my other son, Andy, who handled most of the work. I mostly helped them and did a little painting."

I said to Pete, "I'm truly impressed, but I feel bad that I didn't make more of a fuss when you told me that the other day. I didn't realize the connection when we spoke at Marie's, but I'm very impressed and thankful to you, your brother, and your dad."

Pete's ruddy complexion deepened. "Mista' Phillips, by the time I realized who you were, we didn't have much time to say more."

Liddy looked at Pete and then said to Susanna, "How about you and your family join us at our home next Saturday? We have a cookout planned. The Scribners, Wrights and hopefully Marie will be there. It'll be our way to say thanks for all your family has done for us."

Susanna eyed Sam and then Pete. "If food is being served, I know Sam and the boys are up to it. What can Jeannie and I bring with us?"

CHAPTER NINE

MONDAY MORNING ARRIVED TESTIFYING TO South Georgia's unpredictable autumn weather. The temperate Gulf breezes wrestled with a cold air front sweeping down like Sherman's Army from Atlanta.

My reading lamp provided temporal comfort against the grayness looming beyond the living room window. My morning devotion offered commentary on the nature of man which proved timely. The metaphor, the light had come into the world, but people loved the darkness rather than the light, left an uneasy feeling in my stomach. I removed my glasses and closed my eyes.

A few minutes passed when a whisper stirred me from deep thought. "Honey, would you like some more coffee?" Liddy then reached across me to collect my coffee cup.

"Yeah, thanks." I watched her walk away before I got up and followed her into the kitchen. While she poured coffee, I leaned on the counter next to her and shared my intentions to accept Larry's offer and then stop by Nick Arians' office.

A little before nine, I pulled on my red Georgia windbreaker, slipped the keys into my pocket, and kissed Liddy. I chuckled to myself as I got behind the wheel of my Expedition. I'd likely consume more gas cranking the engine than it'd take to drive over to the newspaper office. However, this particular damp morning nixed any rational reason to save fuel walking into town.

At the Sentinel office, Martha greeted me with a barely audible, "Good morning." Uncertain if I should interrupt her or wait, she finally looked up and said, "I'm sorry, Larry's in the back." The familiar sound and smell of printing presses stirred memories.

I stood in the doorway until Larry acknowledged me with a cheesy grin. "Hey, look who the cat drug in. Come on in and have a seat. We didn't get much of a chance to talk at church yesterday. What's up?" Larry wrinkled his forehead as he sat across from me in front of his desk. "Well?"

"I've thought it over and would like to accept your gracious offer."

Larry leaned back looking pleased. "I'm certainly glad to hear you say that."

I raised my hands to stop him before he celebrated. "But first... it's important we come to an understanding concerning a particular story that's on my mind. Although, I think you'll be interested."

"Okay, I'm listening."

"This Jessie Masterson has intrigued me since I arrived. The more I learn about him, the greater this nagging itch gnaws at me. You know what I mean?"

Larry scooted to the edge of his chair. "Yep, guess I do. Keep going."

"I know there's a bunch more that I need to dig into about Jessie, but I sense there's a broader and likely deeper story here than meets the eye. The more I ask about Jessie Masterson, the more John Priestly's name pops up. My gut tells me their back-to-back tragic circumstances are linked beyond the fact they were cousins and worked together. I'm just not sure how yet."

Silence dominated until Larry leaned closer and waggled his finger as if trying to kickstart his words. "Listen carefully, my new friend. You just might be the perfect person to investigate what happened to Jessie. Lord knows, who'd fault your naïve inquiries about Jessie Masterson that might shed some light on what happened to John Priestly as well." Larry scratched his jaw while his furrowed brow stare met mine. "But, be forewarned. You'll find snooping into what happened to John Priestly to be far more challenging than you might imagine."

"Why'd you say that?"

Larry stood poised ready to answer but paused momentarily. "Tell you what. Let's get some coffee."

We walked into the break room and returned to Larry's office without saying a word.

Larry sat and asked, "So, what'd Arnie tell you? About Jessie and John, I mean."

The significance of a possible link between Jessie's and John's story weighed heavily upon me. Had I bitten off more than I bargained? I measured every word to control my swirling thoughts.

"Arnie talked mainly about when Jessie and his mom arrived in Shiloh years ago and how John helped Jessie land his coaching and teaching position with the school."

"What about Marie? Did she say anything more?"

"No, not really, but I can tell you that she's certainly a sweet but tough lady." I guarded against saying any more about Liddy's and my prior connection with her. "Would it suffice Marie gave me permission to write the story about Jessie and offered to help me as she can to write it?"

"She agreed?"

I leaned forward with my coffee cup cradled in my hands. "So, what do ya' think? You interested? I believe you and the paper can get some profitable ink out of this. Of course, if by chance I stumble across a promising angle related to John Priestly, that'll be a bonus for you, me and the paper."

Larry stared into his cup as if his decision rested there. "Theo, tell you what I'm going to do. I'm going to roll the dice on this. I've long wondered if we'd ever know the whole truth about John and Jessie, but I've been reluctant to stick my nose out too far. You just might be able to open some doors I felt best remained closed." Larry stood and paced in front of my chair.

"Yep, it's high time any lingering doubts get removed, and the truth dragged from behind those blasted closed doors. Marie deserves it, the whole town deserves it, and hell's bells, those two young men deserve it most of all."

I arose and looked into Larry's face with my hand extended.

Larry feigned spitting into his palm and grasped my hand. "Theo

Phillips, maybe God brought you and Liddy here for more than just a laid-back retirement." Larry's expression matched his solemn voice as his left hand covered our intertwined hands. "But when you're digging around, be extra careful whenever it involves any of the Archer family. Harold Archer's been the mayor for three decades, and he's also the richest and most politically connected man in these parts. Mark my word, they'll make their presence known to you soon enough."

I gave Larry a sideward glance. "I've met Hal Archer already. He seems friendly enough."

Larry released our lingering handshake and waved his finger back and forth below my chin. "Just remember what I said. Be careful. Even Shiloh has its skeletons, and some people might take it personally when you start prying."

"Got it. Thanks, Larry."

———

I pulled along the curb in front of Nick's office, Larry's words still echoing in my mind, but I wanted to ask Nick more about Jessie and John.

As I entered Arians Real Estate and Property Management, Jeannie looked up from her desk. "Good mornin', Mister Phillips. Everything all right at the house?"

"Everything's fine, thanks. Liddy's hanging more family pictures and decorating for Thanksgiving. Is Nick in?"

Jeannie disappeared down the hall. She tried to hide a grin when she returned to her desk.

Nick's bravado laugh preceded him into the front office. "Theo, it's good to see you."

"If you've got a few minutes to kill, I'd like to share some thoughts with you."

"I'm always available for my friends. Come on back." Nick pointed to a black leather armchair in the corner as he rolled his executive desk chair from behind his desk. "So, what do you have?"

My initial words revealed my awkwardness. "Thanks for seeing me. But, I'm here in a kind of official capacity."

Nick sat back, fingers interlocked. "What do you mean, 'kinda' official capacity?"

"Well, as of this morning, I'm working with Larry Scribner for the *Sentinel*."

Nick grinned, pulled one leg over the other knee. "That so? What's that old geezer got ya doin'?"

"I've decided to tackle special assignment writing for him. Liddy figured it'd keep me out of her hair a few hours each week."

Nick chuckled, "I'm sure the *Sentinel* and its readers will benefit from your experience."

"Thanks for the vote of confidence, Nick. Thought you'd like to know, the first story I'm working on is Jessie's, and I'd be interested in his relationship with John Priestly."

Nick clasped his hands behind his head and rocked slightly. "Um... How can I help?"

I sat back in my chair attempting not to appear overly anxious. "Remember our lunch conversation last week?"

Nick nodded with an affirming grin.

"It was pretty clear that Jessie's tragedy touched a nerve with you and your brother. Would you mind talking a little more about Jessie?"

Nick got up and closed the door to his office, and scooted his chair closer, but held onto a reserved grin that kept me at ease as he sat down. "Theo, when you first asked about Jessie, we weren't sure what we should say. Yes, Jessie and John were good friends to Joe and me. Heck, it wasn't hard to like either of them."

"I've heard that more than once the past few days."

"As far as what happened to John, Joe is John's attorney. Joe sees him pretty regular since arranging John's relocation to a safer state prison farm not far from here. Plain and simple, Joe's your best contact regarding John Priestly. But, if it means anything, we both believe John's charges were trumped up. Heck! The State's evidence was circumstantial at best. Furthermore, you should know, no one but John knows his reasons for not fighting the charges. Beyond that, Joe's your best bet."

"So I guess you and I can talk more about Jessie then?"

"I'm not sure what more I can tell you. I'm not aware of anything more I can tell you about what happened. No matter how the fire started, Jessie lost his life just being Jessie. Sure, we've heard the rumors. Joe and I have gone round and round about the curious coincidences involving the Archer family with what happened to both John and Jessie, but I don't want to speculate or contribute to any of the rumors."

"I appreciate your frankness."

"I think what you're doin' is long overdue and hope Joe and I can help you more."

"By the way, Arnie Wright took me to visit Jessie's mom."

"You met Marie Masterson? Isn't she a peach? It's sad she doesn't come around much since Jessie died. I've visited a couple of times, but she likes her privacy. Jeannie keeps me informed, though, thanks to Pete and Andy."

"She's got a pretty place, and she sure seems pleasant enough."

"Sounds to me like she warmed up to you. If it turns out Marie trusts you, she'll be a bigger help than most folks around here regarding any questions about Jessie and John."

"Fair enough. One final question. What's the history between the Mayor and his family and John or Jessie?" I knew that was a loaded question but figured it warranted hearing Nick's response.

Nick shot me a curious stare. "Why'd you ask about Harold and his sons?"

"Uh, well, Larry mentioned that I should be aware they'd come up when looking into what happened to Jessie and John, that's all."

Nick's eyes glazed as he answered in a somber voice, "It's Harold Archer and his son Hank who turned on John during the investigation. Also, if you remember, Joe told you that Hank and Hal were the two fellas Jessie saved the night of the fire when he died."

"I remember that, but I didn't know about their role in what happened to John."

Nick ran his hand through his hair. "I'm not sure if this had anything to do with anything, but you might want to look into the ruckus between John and the Archers over accusations that Archer Construction Company attempted to shortcut a lucrative contract involving renovations at the school facilities. Larry Scribner wrote the article about what followed which resulted in a very costly, public apology by Harold and Hank Archer. It shouldn't be hard to find the article." Nick smirked as he added, "It even made the front page of the *Atlanta Constitution*."

I leaned back, arms crossed. "So you think there may have been some sour grapes over the incident between the Archers and John Priestly?"

Nick stared out his office window. "You could say with certainty friction remained between them after that happened."

I thanked Nick as we stepped toward his office door, but when Nick gripped the doorknob, he said, "Look Theo. Take extra care sharing much of this until you've got the facts to back up anything else you find out." As he opened the door, he added, "One more thing. I know you already have a good relationship with Arnie, but please don't share too much with him. Harold Archer's on the church's leadership board. Please keep what you learn close to your vest for now."

"Sounds like solid advice. Let's have lunch again soon."

"It's a date, and I'll speak with Joe for you," Nick said as I waved at Jeannie on the way out.

———

I shared with Liddy about my visits while we enjoyed a nice lunch waiting when I came home.

"I knew you and Larry would hit it off." She slid her honey-do list onto the table for me to see.

"Is this all?" I muttered with a playful grin and a roll of my eyes. "And I suppose you'd like this list done this afternoon?"

"No real hurry. You just need to finish before Marie visits Wednesday."

"Wait! What? You spoke to Marie?"

"Sure did. We talked for at least thirty minutes, and I found out she'll be in town Wednesday, so I invited her to have dinner with us."

CHAPTER TEN

LIDDY'S HONEY-DO LIST SEEMED ENDLESS. As fast as I completed and crossed off tasks, new ones mysteriously appeared. Wednesday morning before Marie's visit, Liddy commandeered my services. She had me buff the hardwood floors, although, to my eyes, the house already shined like a showcase home.

After lunch, Liddy came up from behind and nudged my shoulders back into my chair before I got up from the table. "You did such a magnificent job this morning and hardly complained. I'll finish up in here." My shoulders relaxed as she stroked my hair and straightened my part. "But before I release you for the rest of the afternoon, would you please wipe down the rails and sweep the porch?"

The prospect of fresh air suited me as did the notion no more than thirty minutes of cleaning kept me from my hammock. "You sure?" Before Liddy could respond, I added. "I'll even sweep the walkway too."

Just as I swept the last remnants of debris from the porch steps, a silver pickup pulled up. A young man exited the driver's side, while Sam Simmons stepped out from the passenger side holding a manila envelope. Both wore similar plaid flannel shirts and khaki work pants.

"Theo, glad to catch ya' home. This here's my son, Andy," Sam said as he slapped Andy's shoulder.

Unlike his brother Pete, Andy had short auburn hair and a clean shaven chiseled face. Though nearly as tall with square shoulders, his slim waist contrasted Pete's heartier stature.

"It's a pleasure to meet you finally. We've heard much about ya' and admired your handiwork upstairs."

"Thank you, sir." Andy's firm grip matched his muscular appearance, but his dark, hazel eyes looked everywhere but at me.

"Andy's my quiet son. He makes up for Pete's..." Sam glanced at Andy's smirk. "Let's call it, friendly exuberance."

I chuckled understanding well how two sons could be uniquely different. My hand rested on Andy's shoulder. "Heck, I respect a man whose deeds and attitude speak louder than his words. Now, come on inside. Liddy'll be glad you stopped by."

Liddy appeared from the kitchen. "Sam, is this Andy?"

Sam slapped his son on the back. "Yep, this is Andy."

Andy's dimples deepened in depth and color as Liddy said with a widening grin. "Well Sam, he's too good lookin' to be this bashful."

Andy turned his head attempting to wipe away his reserved, partial grin. "Yes'm. It's nice to finally meet y'all too."

"Liddy, why don't ya' show Sam and Andy how the upstairs turned out?"

Liddy beamed. "Land's sake! Of course." She rambled as Sam and Andy followed up the stairs.

Sam and Liddy ventured into the bedroom on the right, while Andy drifted to the other. I noticed Andy's satisfied grin as he ran his hands along the wood trim before he opened the attic access door and peered inside. I wondered what he thought about as he stared at the bare attic on the other side of the wall.

At the top of the stairwell, Sam said, "Thanks, Liddy," as he looked at the envelope he brought with him. "Oh yeah, almost forgot. We stumbled upon these while we worked on the house." He pulled out several yellowed documents. "Andy found these wedged behind some of the lath boards along the back wall." He pointed to the bedroom that Andy just left.

Liddy examined the stained Sears Modern Homes brochure and then thumbed through the discolored drawings and invoice. Her queried glance spurred me to inspect the invoice. Beneath its Sears Modern Homes masthead, it identified Ezra Priestly, Shiloh, GA as the customer, dated June 6, 1922. "Who was Ezra Priestly?"

Sam shrugged and said, "I think he was Zack Priestly's grandfather or one of his great uncles. We aren't certain, but he must've been the one who built this house." Sam pointed. "And paid $2,794.00 to boot."

Andy opened the drawings and pointed out the modifications to the home since its original assembly. "I researched on the internet and discovered this particular factory-built home was quite popular about that time. Everything got crated and shipped, except the foundation and the labor."

Sam added, "By no means is this house the oldest in town, but it's one of the earliest twentieth-century so-called modern homes ever built here."

Liddy gave a warm hug to Sam and Andy, then stepped back and looked at Andy. "Almost forgot. Are you coming Saturday?"

"Yes, ma'am. In fact, Pete and I were thinkin', would y'all mind if Jay and Jim Adams came with us? They're good friends, and you'll enjoy meeting them. We'll all be at Miss Marie's Saturday anyway and figured we'd come with her if that'll be okay with y'all?"

Liddy responded without hesitation. "Absolutely. We'd love to have Jay and Jim too."

———

Later that afternoon, a faded dark green pickup pulled into our driveway, stirring me from my nap. When I recognized Marie behind the steering wheel, I climbed out of my hammock. Before I could call out, Liddy stepped off the kitchen stoop with her hair freed from her ponytail, combed neatly off her shoulders.

Marie scanned the property as she stepped from the truck. I caught up to Liddy at the corner of the driveway where we waited patiently.

"Theo, the place looks as good as it ever has," Marie said before she and Liddy embraced like long-lost sisters.

"Liddy, this is amazing. You look just as I remember," Liddy confessed as she stepped back.

"That's so sweet. In that case, I think we've both aged pretty well."

Inside, Marie stood in the living room and stared at the walls and floors. "Mercy, it looks as if you've lived here for years, but the wonderful memories I have from this old place are still here."

"Let me show you the rest of the house. Just wait until you see the upstairs." Liddy glanced at me. "Coming hun?"

"Y'all go on ahead, I'm right behind you."

Marie reminisced as Liddy walked her through every room. Upstairs, Marie shared what her first days in Shiloh were like when they slept in what had been the drafty old attic.

"Wait until Liddy shows you what Andy and his dad found," I said with a wink that brought a widened stare from Marie.

Marie sat on the couch in the living room while Liddy and I sat in our respective chairs. Tears emerged as she admired the nostalgic papers and shared memories of the house and how well Betty, John, and Zack treated her and Jessie.

Apparently moved by the connection between Marie and the Priestly's, Liddy asked, "Marie, it sounds like God blessed you and Jessie with these memories of your Uncle and Aunt, but I can't help but wonder how you're doing since Jessie passed. Our hearts ache over what happened."

Marie readjusted herself on the sofa, then looked at us. "Liddy, I wish both of you could have gotten to know Jessie. He and his cousin John loved making a difference in this town, especially with the youngsters."

"It's pretty clear to me, that memorial in the center of town testifies of Jessie's love for this town and the town's love for him," I said.

Marie gazed out the window in the direction of the statue. "Who would've guessed how well that fussy infant you remember would turn out? He led a full life, and I cling to my belief that he and his father are sharing good times in Heaven together."

In response to the sullen looks on our faces, Marie scooted to the edge of the couch, and her eyes bounced between Liddy and me. "Hey, Jessie's right here." She touched her heart. "It's okay to talk about him.

God's taking good care of my boy."

Liddy grabbed a tissue and through tears asked, "Marie would you like some sweet tea?"

After Liddy returned, Marie kicked off her shoes and folded her socked feet under her. "Theo, how about I share what very few in town know anything about, my life before Shiloh. I've never bothered to share those rougher days for Jessie and me, but I think you deserve to hear what happened to us before we moved here."

"Do you mind if I grab a pad and pen? I'd love to include a little bit about Jessie's upbringing before y'all arrived in Shiloh in the story I want to write."

"Of course…," she thought for a moment. "Well, let me see. I just can't remember everything we shared all those years ago, so I'll start when Joe and I met in the spring of 1975. The American troops had long been home from Viet Nam, and Joe had just been discharged from the Army."

Liddy said, "I remember when all the soldiers arrived home back then. It wasn't like the movie, Forrest Gump. We know how hard it was for so many friends we knew during that time, but I'm sure you experienced that too."

I asked, "So what happened when Joe got back? When did you meet?"

Marie's face lit up. "Oh Liddy, you'd have wanted to meet Joe in his uniform. Wait! I've got a picture of him." She set down her glass and pulled her billfold from her pocketbook and handed me a faded Polaroid of Joe in his Army uniform.

When I passed it to Liddy, she blushed and said, "Marie, I can see why you fell for Joe."

Marie's face beamed when she took the photo back from Liddy. "Let me see. We met in Savannah and only dated for three months before he proposed. We both wanted to raise a family together, but only frustration and disappointment came. A specialist, our doctor recommended, examined both of us and concluded that Joe's combat wound made it impossible for him to father a child. We considered adoption, but six months later God answered our prayers. I discovered I was pregnant. We celebrated and told our parents the great news over that Memorial Day weekend, and Jessie arrived on Christmas Eve."

"That certainly made for a special Christmas." Liddy's exuberance brought her to the edge of her chair.

Marie paused as if to dwell on the memory a moment longer. "Yes Liddy, it was the best Christmas ever. Joe cried when he saw Jessie for the first time in the hospital. He pulled cigar after cigar from his stuffed shirt and coat pockets. He hugged and thanked the nurses and doctors for two days."

"I remember acting pretty stupid myself when we had our first son," I confessed.

Marie's apparent glee disappeared as she focused on the next part of the story. "I'll never understand why God blessed us with so much joy but then allowed the miracle to be followed so soon by a tragedy that I thought I'd never get over."

"What happened Marie?" Liddy became concerned over Marie's sudden change of mood.

"Joe worked for an Army contractor. He sacrificed to help the family and accepted the fact his work required occasional trips away. His last trip took him to Huntsville. He was gone only a couple of days and called nightly as usual. Just before he boarded his flight home, he even called from a pay phone at the airport and told me how much he looked forward to a quiet dinner together after he landed."

Marie's eyes watered but waved off our anxious looks. "The plane crashed as it tried to land in the middle of a sudden storm at Savannah's airport. Sixty-six onboard died. By God's mercy, twenty survived. Joe was initially one of the survivors but sustained severe injuries. I raced with Jessie to the hospital. By the time I arrived, he was out of surgery and in the ICU." Marie paused, and Liddy handed her a box of tissues. Marie wiped her eyes and took a couple of sips of tea before she continued.

"I remember like it was yesterday. Reporters were everywhere. How they knew who I was I don't know, but they circled me with their questions and cameras. They mostly drowned each other out, but I did hear one reporter ask, 'Did you know your husband was a hero? He assisted passengers who couldn't get out on their own. Ma'am, at least half of the survivors owe their lives to him.' I remember feeling numb. All I wanted was to talk to Joe. I carried Jessie in with me to Joe's ICU room. Joe kept repeating, 'I'm sorry.' I stroked his forehead as he told me he had peace in the knowledge he'd live on through Jessie. He made me promise to be strong and raise our son to be proud of his dad and never forget how much he loved him. Joe told me to tell Jessie when he was old enough to understand that his dad would never leave his side, and whenever he found himself in a difficult situation, never fail to do the right thing because his dad would be there with him. I promised Joe just before he passed away that evening that Jessie would never know any father but Joseph Masterson." Marie exhaled and sank back into her seat.

My heart ached over Marie's courage. Our providential encounter with her and Jessie shortly after Joe's death now seemed surreal as I realized how much Marie faced standing alone in the rain with her infant son all those years ago.

Marie blew her nose and cleared her throat. "The weeks and months after Joe's death were tough as I struggled to make ends meet. There wasn't a lot of insurance money, but God faithfully provided people like you at just the right times. I survived by clinging to my faith in God, my promise to Joe, and our love for Jessie." A long exhale followed as she gathered her emotions.

Liddy asked, "Where were you before you moved to Shiloh?"

I had intended to ask that very question and smiled at Liddy's intuition. I wondered how Marie raised Jessie since his legacy reveals such a secure foundation.

Marie folded her hands and rested them on her lap. She stared for a moment at her fingers as they lightly stroked a tissue. Finally, she cleared her throat and continued.

"My days in Richmond Hills were hard. Initially, I refused help from my family, but Joe's parents insisted and became an invaluable lifeline connection to Joe. We found a sanctuary in their home and had good memories in Whitesville, North Carolina. I returned to church, and God brought peace to my heart about Joe's death. Joe's mother passed away right after Jessie turned ten, and Joe's father fell victim to a stroke shortly after that. Jessie and I inherited the home but felt isolated, so we sold it and moved to Beaufort near my parents. Jessie finished high school there. My family had a small farm on the edge of town, and that's when I renewed my love for farming."

Marie paused, snickered, and put a hand over her mouth in embarrassment. "I'm sorry. I had a brief flashback. When I finished high school, I told my dad how much I hated the farm and wanted to find my own life to live."

"I can remember telling my dad I wanted nothing to do with the newspaper business or becoming a journalist," I blurted at the tail end of a chuckle.

Marie's face brightened, and her eyes became clear again. "Yeah, as funny as it seemed, Jessie became attached to the farm and my father. Jessie not only discovered how smart he was but also how much he enjoyed playing sports, and turned out to be naturally good at 'em all. Football, basketball, and baseball kept him busy, but he never neglected his family time and chores on the farm. However, a heart attack took my father away just after Jessie turned sixteen. Jessie took his grandfather's sudden death hard and tried to fill my father's shoes on the farm, but it was just too much. A year later, Jessie finished high school and offers from colleges poured in. Eventually, he decided to attend Georgia Christian University in Waycross after my mother encouraged him and sold the farm. That's when Aunt Betty reached out. My mother moved into an assisted living center in Alexandria. I lived upstairs in this house in the beginning, and Jessie visited on and off since school was just two hours away. During that time, John became the new head football coach at Shiloh High School, and their relationship blossomed until, well, you know the rest." Marie again stared into the distance.

Liddy got up and sat beside Marie. I watched Liddy and Marie connect while Jessie's story seemed to inscribe itself on my heart. I knew I had more to learn in the days ahead, but for now, my mind felt at ease.

In addition to Liddy's scrumptious dinner, laughter filled us as Marie shared fun memories of Jessie's glory days at GCU. We also shared some of our funnier stories about Junior and Tommy during their college years.

After Marie's truck tail lights dimmed into the distance later that night, Liddy and I sat on the porch and talked about Marie's inspirational faith and courage. We shared how it appeared that so many people in this town knew and loved her, but hardly anyone knew the story she shared with us that day.

CHAPTER ELEVEN

As I WALKED TO THE rear parking lot of the church, Arnie exited the church office with a brown leather satchel over his shoulder. With his cell phone to one ear, he stepped toward his Tahoe, but concluded his call right after he noticed me approaching.

"Good morning Theo. What can I do for you? I'm headed out. Seems there's always someone to visit in the hospital."

"I imagine that can grow tiresome."

"Sometimes, but it comes with the job." Arnie pointed upward with a smile. "Besides, today's a busier day than most. I've got a meeting at City Hall right after lunch. We're finalizing plans for this year's annual Christmas in Shiloh schedule of events. It's a big thing around here. Folks come from all parts of the county each evening. You and Liddy will enjoy what's in store for your first Christmas in Shiloh."

"Sounds great to me. Our whole family should be in town."

"They'll love it, especially your grandkids." Arnie slid his satchel off his shoulder and fiddled with his key fob. "So how can I help you?"

"Thought you ought to know, Marie stopped by the house yesterday. The three of us caught up on the past thirty-five years."

Arnie grinned and said, "I'm pleased to hear you and Liddy hit it off with Marie. I think she's ready to move on with her life. Maybe you two came along just in time to help her to do that."

"For Marie's sake, I hope that'll prove to be true. Oh yeah, two quick things before you run off. First, I accepted Larry's offer and I'll be writing some special interest pieces for the paper. In fact, the first series of articles will be about Jessie Masterson."

Arnie smirked. "You and Larry will make a great team. Your background and unique perspective should offer a fresh voice for the paper's readers. You might also want to know that his memorial will be dedicated the first evening of Christmas in Shiloh." Arnie winked with a grin as he unlatched the Tahoe's door locks. "I'm sorry. I gotta run." Arnie pulled his vehicle door open and lifted his satchel onto the passenger seat.

"I almost forgot. Are you and Judy good for our cookout this Saturday?"

He paused with a curious look, and then pulled his black appointment book out of the side pocket of his satchel. "Let me see here…" He mumbled as he flipped open the book and slid his finger across the week of scribbled notes. "What's this?" He turned the book toward me and pointed to the neon pink highlighted note written in black ink across Saturday's space. "Liddy's Cookout!!!" Arnie laughed. "Well, it certainly looks like the boss' writing. I reckon, unless God has other plans, we'll be there."

"I'll let Liddy know. See you Saturday at one-thirty."

"By the way, Judy already told me she's bringing her favorite chocolate cake." Arnie let out another chuckle. "See you then."

After Arnie drove off, I walked across the street to visit the Shiloh City Library.

The library maintained plenty of articles and photos portraying Shiloh's long history. I learned more about the original antebellum courthouse and how Shiloh had been the original county seat until the powers-to-be in Adams County precipitated the transfer of the county seat to Alexandria during the Depression. One article attributed the decision to Shiloh's reluctant growth and modernization, but another cited the controversial rerouting of the new State highway in favor of Alexandria.

Renovations in the 1950s transformed the old courthouse into a more suitable city hall. I made copies of photos that showed what Shiloh looked like shortly after our house had been built. Only the recently built city hall and expanded football stadium offered notable exceptions to Shiloh's reputation for resisting change through the decades. By the time I left the library a little before noon, I better understood the construction and layout of the original courthouse. Little doubt remained in my mind that the two-story brick and granite exterior served as a chimney when the original sesquicentennial milled wood rafters, joists and timbers became the kindling in a careless fire.

———

Friday morning, shortly after Timmy delivered another edition of the *Sentinel*, Liddy joined me at the breakfast table. We discussed the remaining preparations needed for our cookout. This time, I drafted my own "to-do" list.

After lunch, I drove the two short blocks to the Butcher Shoppe and parked across the street. Silas and Bernie waved when I entered. Only a couple of late-lunch customers occupied their attention. I smiled and pointed through the doorway to the cut-to-order meats, cold cuts, and cheeses in their deli.

Bernie yelled into the back kitchen, "Alex, Mistor Phillips needs help in the deli."

I waited in front of the sparkling porcelain and stainless steel counters while Alex wiped his hands dry.

"Good afternoon, Mister Phillips. How can I help you today?"

"Let me see… I need some ribs and chicken for a cookout."

"How many people are you expecting?"

I calculated with the aid of my fingers. "I reckon fifteen, but I don't want to run out. We've got some hearty appetites coming."

"Who's coming? Family?"

"No family. Just some of the folks we've met since we moved here. The Simmons, Scribners, Pastor Wright and his wife, Miss Masterson, and we believe, Jay and Jim Adams are coming as well."

Alex's eyes lit up. "I know Jay and Jim. They're certainly big eaters. Are Pete and Andy coming too?"

"Yep, Pete, Andy, and Jeannie too." I chuckled.

"If I may suggest, you should buy enough for at least twenty guests. Pete's my friend, and I know how he loves to eat." Alex stood behind the counter with his arms crossed and a patient smile.

"That's a fine suggestion. How about five fryers quartered and twenty pounds of ribs? By the way, how do you know Pete?"

Alex started to carve five chickens he pulled from the display. He worked with his back to me but continued our conversation over his shoulder.

"Oh, Pete and Andy helped coach at the school during my high school years. They tried to get me to play football, but momma wouldn't agree to it." Alex twisted around and laughed at his lean frame. "But I liked to run and joined the cross country and track teams."

"You look like a runner."

Alex pointed with his knife towards the corner desk. A framed picture of him in his cross country uniform hung on the wall. A gold medal dangled by its blue ribbon over the corner of the frame. More trophies lined the shelf above the desk.

"How'd you win that gold medal draped on your picture?"

Alex shrugged his shoulders and acted embarrassed. "Momma hung it there. I placed first at the state cross country meet my senior year."

"Now I understand why Pete and Andy wanted you to play football."

"I tried out for the basketball team, but Coach Masterson asked me if I wanted to be the team manager after he watched me dribble and shoot during tryouts."

"Ouch! So basketball wasn't for you either."

Alex turned his head with a playful grimace. "Coach Masterson tried his best, but if the sport needed more than my feet, I just wasn't very good."

"What'd you think about Coach Masterson?"

"Oh, Coach Masterson was very good to me. He invited me to his weekly Sanctuary meetings, which helped me to fit in and make friends."

"Was it hard for you to make friends?"

Alex paused a moment. "There aren't any Greek Orthodox churches anywhere near here. The only time my family goes to church is when we visit family in Atlanta, but Coach Masterson welcomed everyone to Sanctuary. He said God didn't care about such distinctions, so we shouldn't either."

"Do you miss Coach Masterson?"

"Yes, sir. After he died, my senior year, Sanctuary stopped meeting too."

"Alex," I said with a serious tone. "Thanks for sharing. I'm writing about Coach Masterson for the *Sentinel*. Would you mind if I used what you shared in the story?"

"I guess not. If what you write honors Coach, how can I say no?" Alex turned toward me toting a corrugated box filled with neatly packed ribs and chicken.

I tried to hide my grimace as I paid the bill but knew the investment already reaped a worthwhile return. With both hands needed to carry the box, I backed my way out the door of the Butcher Shoppe.

I began to step beyond the curb to walk across the street where I had parked when an ominous black and chrome pickup rumbled slowly around the corner. Its over-sized tires and flashy chrome rims advertised how badly the owner relished the attention his vehicle drew. Around Atlanta, such outlandish trucks earned the reputation as being redneck limousines because their overpriced, showy accessories served no purpose other than for show.

Tinted glass prevented me from identifying the driver, but as the truck came to a stop, the window lowered. Country music blared, but mercifully the volume got adjusted in time for me to hear a deep, raspy voice say, "Mister Phillips. My name's Hank, Hank Archer, and this here's my brother Hal." Expensive aviator sunglasses hid his eyes, but he had slicked down black hair and a hardened, tanned face covered with dark day-and-a-half old stubbles. "We noticed your vehicle parked across the street. Hoped we'd catch you. Thought it only right to stop and welcome you to Shiloh. How y'all like our little town so far?"

I stared at myself in the reflection of his glasses as I recalled Larry's warning about the Archer family. I lowered the box to the sidewalk and stepped closer to the driver's window. Hank reduced the volume more and tilted his head as he lifted his glasses onto the top of his head.

"My wife and I are settling in quite nicely, thanks for asking." I maneuvered to also look at Hal in the passenger seat. He wore a faded baseball cap tilted to cover his forehead. He slouched in his seat with one of his fancy leather boots propped against the dashboard. He raised the bill of his cap and looked back with sleepy eyes and gestured, lifting his left hand.

Partly to preserve my recently-purchased, unrefrigerated meat but mostly to keep this encounter brief because of its blatant pretentiousness, I stepped back and picked up the box. "Hank, I appreciate you going out of your way to introduce yourself, but I've got to get this meat home right away. Anytime you're runnin' around town and have a few minutes, you and Hal please drop in at the house."

Hal gave a slight nod and raised a thumb. Hank stared down and examined the boxful of wrapped meat and said in a thick drawl, "We'll do that Mista' Phillips. Thanks for the invite. It looks like you're fixin' to have a big shindig."

"As a matter of fact, we're havin' a cookout tomorrow, which is why I better get this meat into my refrigerator before my wife fusses."

Hank acknowledged with a casual hand salute a moment before the tinted window brought an abrupt end to our meeting. Their music blared again as Hank pulled from the curb and rumbled away. I slowly exhaled as I walked across the street to my vehicle.

81

CHAPTER TWELVE

SHORTLY AFTER ONE O'CLOCK THE next day, a sputtering rust-bucket pickup pulled up in front of our home. Over the clatter of its idling motor, the dented passenger door let out a crack and a squeal as it swung open and then shut. Marie yelled back toward the driver. "I expect to see you and the others shortly. Finish what y'all are doing and get back here straight away. Thanks for the lift."

When I greeted Marie at the curb, Pete leaned toward the open passenger window and hollered. "Hey Mista' Phillips! I brought Miss Marie, but I've got to wrangle the others up. What time you plan'n on eating?"

"About three," I said, but Pete grimaced and shook his head.

I tapped my watch and raised three fingers as I shouted, "Be back by three!"

Pete signaled that he understood and then grabbed his gear shift, let out the clutch and roared off.

Marie shook her head. "What Pete sees in that ol' beater is a mystery to me, but he fiddles and fusses enough to keep that ol' rattle trap runn'n."

South Georgia offered a picture perfect blue sky for our afternoon cookout. I kept busy setting out additional chairs on and around the deck, while Liddy and Marie hung out in the kitchen.

The Scribners and Wrights arrived simultaneously. Before I could greet any of them, Martha asked if Marie was inside. Judy carrying a large Tupperware container asked, "Where do you want this chocolate cake?"

I nodded at Martha, and then said to Judy, "I imagine Liddy wants that in the kitchen."

The crescendo of Marie's and Liddy's laughter through the open kitchen door drew a smile from the ladies as they stepped onto the stoop.

I said to Larry and Arnie now standing with me, "That's all I've heard pouring out from the house since Marie arrived."

Arnie said, "Marie and Liddy sure seem to be having a good time in there."

Larry and Arnie followed me to the safety of the deck out back.

A little before three, Sam and Susanna arrived in his silver pickup. Jeannie followed in her Yellow VW. Susanna and Jeannie joined the other ladies in the kitchen while Sam looked relieved when he saw us out back.

Sam plopped into a deck chair. "What time are them ribs goin' to be done?" As he rubbed his stomach, I realized Pete's voracious appetite likely came from his dad.

A few minutes later, Liddy brought out a bowl of her kettle cooked sweet potato chips along with her secret dipping sauce. Judy followed with a pitcher of tea and glasses.

Liddy said, "Hope this'll keep y'all happy 'til Pete and the boys get here."

We did not have to wait long. Pete maneuvered his clunker around the other cars parked in the driveway.

"Okay, the party can begin now," Pete bellowed as he got out.

Sam's glare worked no better to muffle Pete's loud voice than the muffler did to quiet his old red truck. I yelled in the direction of the kitchen. "Liddy, I believe the last of our guests are here."

Pete and Andy waited beside the truck. "Mista' Phillips, I've been tellin' Jim and Jay so much about you and Missus Phillips, and they've been hankerin' to meet you ever since." The suspension of Pete's truck rose a couple of inches once Jay and Jim hopped out of the truck's bed. "Come on guys. He don't bite."

When the two brothers turned, I took a double take. They not only shared six foot four muscular builds but also had similar length, dark brown hair, blue eyes and pearl-white grins.

"Mister Phillips, I'm Jay, and this is my brother Jim. Glad to finally meet ya'." Jay offered his hand. "Pete and Andy said y'all just moved here a couple of weeks ago." Jay's voice struck me as confident and polite. His sturdy but friendly, calloused grip enveloped my hand.

Andy asked, "Mister Phillips, where's Missus Phillips?" I gestured for him to turn around. Liddy waved from the concrete stoop by the kitchen door.

Andy said, "Come on guys. Let's say hey to Miss Liddy."

I followed, but my stride stretched trying to match their casual gait. "Honey, these are Pete and Andy's friends, and I believe cousins as well, Jay and Jim Adams."

"Missus Phillips, I'm Jay, and this is Jim."

Liddy grinned and attempted to distinguish between the brothers. "I don't mean to stare, but I've never been around identically attractive brothers like you."

"Missus Phillips-" Jay began before Liddy interrupted.

"Please, I'm Liddy."

"Yes ma'am, Miss Liddy. We're more different than you might think at first glance."

Jim boasted through a widening grin, "Yes, ma'am Miss Liddy. Jay's right. I'm easy to pick out...I'm the better looking one."

Jay smacked his brother on the back of his head and then said, "If it'll help, my hair's parted on the left, and I'm right-handed. Jim's one of those goofy southpaws and parts his hair on the right. Our momma used to say God had a sense of humor when he made us mirror images."

Liddy peered around Jay and smiled at Jim. "Don't you mind about that goofy southpaw business, our older son's left-handed too." Jim grinned and poked Jay in his side as Liddy asked, "Are you young men ready to eat?"

Although Liddy stood on the stoop, Pete looked nearly eye to eye with her after he pushed his way by the others. "Miss Liddy, we're ready. Mm, mm. It all smells good."

Susanna's voice rang out from inside the kitchen. "All four of you march inside and get cleaned up first. There's a bathroom around the corner." Marie smiled as the boys filed past.

In almost no time, the trash barrel by the edge of the deck soon overflowed with paper plates, meatless bones, and crumpled napkins. Susanna and Martha carted the almost-empty bowls of Liddy's potato salad and three-bean salad back into the kitchen just before we all sat on the deck. Each of the families shared their stories about when they first met Marie and Jessie at this very house. The boys added humorous tales involving the farm, including a couple of encounters with an old mule Marie inherited from her Uncle Zack.

Sam recollected as he pointed to the side yard. "Jessie and John wrestled with the boys right out here on many occasions." He described how the boys looked up to Jessie and John long before they became their coaches and teachers at Shiloh High School.

After Pete scarfed down a huge piece of Judy's chocolate cake, he retrieved a football from his truck and tossed it towards Andy as he swallowed his last bite. Jay and Jim trashed their empty plates and joined in. Before long, Larry, Arnie, Sam and I found ourselves egged into a game of touch football, and each of us pretended we could compete against the four younger athletes. As the sun began to set, we stood with our hands on our knees gasping for breath, thankful our gridiron exploits had finally ended.

After everyone pulled away, Liddy rested her head on my arm as we swayed in the hammock soaking up the starlit sky. Liddy's head soon relaxed as she dozed off.

When sunlight broke the following morning, two realities quickly became evident. First, Liddy was already up. Hissing and clanking followed by the smell of bacon, eggs, and coffee woke all my senses. Then the second reality became painfully clear. My back, shoulders, and thighs testified to the tragedy that befalls old men who dare to play as if they were still young men. Only the thought of a long, hot shower enticed me from under the comfort of my comforter. I did my best to mute my groans and grunts as the hot water soothed my afflicted joints.

Liddy popped her head into the bathroom and dropped off my first cup of coffee, and couldn't resist her extended giggle. "Breakfast will be on the table in ten minutes, champ."

My stride mercifully loosened somewhere between home and church. When we arrived at the church, Liddy pointed across the street. Mary and Martha exited their Buick and patiently waited as Larry struggled out of the driver's seat. Mary ran up to us, struggling to restrain her laughter. "Mister P, what did you do to my daddy?"

I shot back, "Me? I didn't hold a gun to his head. I even tried to warn him, but he chose to give it all he had against those younger guys."

Martha walked just ahead of Larry as he shuffled over to say good morning. Both Larry and I shared a grimace at the bottom of the steps as we looked up toward the church entrance. We arrived three steps behind the women, too busy in their conversation to notice our struggles.

We followed each other into our pew, and I spotted the back of Sam's head next to Susanna in their usual seat. Pete sat beside Andy and Jeannie, and he pointed to his dad with a silly grin.

Larry leaned toward me and nodded at Arnie. "I wonder how Arnie feels this morning?" Our dignified and respected pastor then rocked his body and relied on the arms of the chair to push himself up when the time came to greet the congregation.

A voice from one of the front pews inquired, "Long day yesterday preacher?" Laughter and snickers followed.

Arnie showed little signs of his discomfort as he proceeded with the morning worship service, but his hands anchored him to the pulpit. His sermon message, "Living the Strong and Courageous Life," from Joshua's exchange with God served as a welcome distraction.

At the conclusion of the service, Liddy and Martha pointed out the Simmons family's quick exit out the back of the church. Larry laughed and looked back to me as we found our way into the aisle. "I bet Susanna drove this morning and intentionally parked in the back parking lot to avoid Sam negotiating any stairs. Wish I'd have thought of that."

Arnie stood next to Judy at the main door as folks filed out. Larry and I exchanged handshakes with him before we broke into contagious laughter, joking about our heroic achievements the day before. After a few minutes, a deep and authoritative voice interrupted our levity.

"Well done, Pastor Wright."

A gentleman in a distinguished three-piece pinstripe suit stepped between Larry and me. "Hello, Larry and Martha." He turned toward Liddy and me. "And these must be the new folks in town, the Phillips." Liddy wrapped her hand around my arm while I accepted his clammy handshake.

Arnie noticed the puzzled look on Liddy's face. "Harold, I'm pleased you're here. I'd like to introduce you to Theo and Liddy Phillips." Arnie looked at Liddy and me. "Liddy, Theo, this is our mayor and one of our longstanding leaders here at Shiloh Baptist Church, the honorable Harold Archer."

Without apology, Harold wedged further into the gap between Larry and me, imposing his corpulent stature and high-spirited persona into the center of our conversation. He wore his thinning salt and pepper hair slicked back. His dark gray eyes scrutinized each of us through gold rim spectacles. His bellowing voice dominated our otherwise normal conversation, but his jovial demeanor appeared genuine. Although, Liddy's tightened grip indicated her rarely mistaken sixth sense regarding something amiss with Harold Archer.

Harold's thumbs rested in his vest pockets, and he said intending others to hear, "Mister Phillips, my sons, Hank and Hal behind me, told me about bumping into you a couple of days ago."

I peered over my shoulder and noticed Hank and Hal talking with each other, disinterested in their dad's conversation. Harold motioned to them, but they ignored the invite. Hank appeared aloof and continued his chat with Hal, while Hal seemed far more interested in the laces of his shoes with his hands deep in his pants pockets.

Harold grunted, shrugged his shoulders and said louder, "Anyway!..." He then looked at his third son standing separated from his two older brothers. "This is my youngest son, Phillip." We stepped back and enlarged the circle to make room for Phillip.

A couple of acne blemishes dotted his youthful face, but he looked smart in his maroon blazer, charcoal slacks and plaid rooster tie that dangled from his open shirt collar. Harold rumpled Phillip's short, neat hair. Phillip winced before he ran a hand through his hair.

He shook my hand while I said, "Glad to meet you, Phillip." I gently nudged Liddy. "This is my wife, Liddy. We look forward to getting better acquainted with you and your whole family." I peered over my shoulder. Harold clung to his affable yet plastic grin. Hal removed one hand from his pocket and offered an abbreviated mock salute, and Hank even managed a poker-faced nod.

Hal caught Harold's attention. "Oh yeah dad, I meant to tell you. When I met the Phillips at the utility office, Mister Phillips extended an invitation to stop by anytime, but I figured they'd be too busy getting settled and plumb forgot to say anything to ya." A short shrug and wrinkled grin followed.

Harold groaned and turned his reddened focus to Liddy and me. "Had I known sooner, I'd have certainly made it my business to stop over by now."

"Mister Archer, please accept our invitation for you and your sons to stop by whenever it best suits your busy schedule," Liddy said.

As we shook hands again, Harold laid his left hand over our clasped hands. "Theo, I appreciate the invitation. As Mayor, I feel remiss in my duties. For heaven's sake, you never know, I may need your vote someday..." Harold's belly laughed before he said. "Come to think of it, I'll be out and about town this afternoon. Would you mind if I stopped by for a short visit?"

Liddy looked for my reaction before she responded. "Please, that'd suit us fine."

Hal and Hank disappeared long before Harold completed his final wave and left with Phillip by his side.

CHAPTER THIRTEEN

AFTER OUR SUNDAY DINNER OF leftovers, I attempted to make sense of the last two weeks while I cleaned up the remaining evidence of our cookout. Then Arnie's morning message calmed my thoughts. "Wherever God calls us to go; we never go alone. God always prepares the way and never forsakes or leaves us on our own." His closing remarks affirmed in my heart what I knew I had to do. "Courage is not intended to remove but overcome our fear of the giants we'll certainly encounter as we follow God's lead."

I sat on the edge of the picnic table and prayed. My silent "Amen" ended abruptly at the sound of truck doors. My eyes opened, and I muttered an impromptu postscript. "Okay Lord, I think one of those giants just arrived."

Harold and Phillip talked back and forth as they walked toward the front porch, failing to notice me quick-stepping from around back.

"Harold. Phillip. Welcome. We've been waiting for you." I led the way up the steps and grabbed the door. "Please, come on in." Harold stepped inside with Phillip a step behind.

Harold surveyed the front rooms of the house. "It's been a long time since I put a foot inside this house. Miss Betty, God rest her soul, was a charming woman, as is this house." A fond chuckle followed. "Now Uncle Zack, that cantankerous ol' codger, I gotta confess, I miss him too. He sure kept me on my toes, especially whenever we butted heads over what we both thought was best for Shiloh."

Liddy took their jackets and asked, "Would you like something to drink?" After we all requested tea, she hung their coats and disappeared into the kitchen.

Harold and I exchanged idle quips about the Georgia versus Georgia Tech annual rivalry next Saturday. A couple of minutes later, Liddy shouted "Go Dawgs" as she brought our drinks.

Harold roared, "Bravo. Missus Phillips. Them Dawgs are sure to dismantle the Ramblin' Wreck this year."

"Amen Harold," I said. "And as fellow Georgia fans, please call us Theo and Liddy. And that goes for you too Phillip."

Harold leaned toward me. "I understand, you and Larry Scribner have gotten pretty close, and you've agreed to write for the *Sentinel*."

"Yeah, Larry and Martha have been most helpful and friendly since we moved in. As far as my writing for the paper..." I leaned back and confessed. "I imagine I'll be focused on special interest stories to help me get introduced to the folks in town better."

Liddy returned, and Harold sat more relaxed on the sofa. As Liddy topped his glass off, he looked at me. "Your father used to publish the newspaper over in Douglaston, didn't he? How is it then that you retired as chief editor for a corporate publishing house in Atlanta?"

Taken back but equally impressed by Harold's well-informed inquiry, I rendered merely a tight-lip grin.

Harold returned a self-conscious grin, and said, "Sorry, but today's internet can provide information on just about anyone. Please accept my apologies. I merely wondered why a nice couple from Atlanta would choose to buy a home in little old Shiloh as their retirement preference. It surely wasn't to pursue our magnificent golf and bridge clubs."

I managed a crooked smile while I tried to conjure a better response than a shocked nod.

Liddy's ordinarily cordial persona hardened. "Harold, please excuse me, but now I'm a little confused. Why not Shiloh?" Harold's eyes widened beneath his arched brow. "I don't mean to be rude, but what's wrong with us choosing to retire in such a beautiful, quaint house in a quintessential South Georgia town like Shiloh? Is there any reason we should wonder about our choice of this house or Shiloh?"

Harold hesitated and squirmed, his lips moved, but no words

came out. Instead, a defensive chuckle surfaced before he stammered, "Please, Miss Liddy. I didn't mean to imply anything by my silly questions. Y'all certainly appear to be nice folks. I truly pray a host of others like you and Theo will make the same choice."

Liddy's gracious spirit responded. "Oh Harold, we hope so too, but not too many, mind you. We like Shiloh just as we have discovered it. In this crazy world, bigger isn't always better. Shiloh's an oasis for folks like Theo and me."

Harold looked at me. "I like your wife, Theo. She's got a genuine fondness for the simple life we want to keep here in Shiloh. Do you agree?"

"Yes, I agree. We both grew up not far from here and miss simpler days. Shiloh appears to offer a rare haven for those desiring a slower heartbeat far removed from the bustling Atlanta shadow. But I've a question."

"I reckon we're all on the same page when it comes to Shiloh. What's your question?"

"Not to change the subject, but I've taken an interest in that bronze memorial in the center of town. What's the story behind it?" Phillip's eyes darted towards his dad.

"Theo, what've you heard so far? Is it safe to assume I'm not the first you've asked?" Harold sent a quick glare toward Phillip before looking back.

"From what little research I did at the library, it seems that Jessie Masterson died in an accidental fire three years ago saving your two older sons."

Harold's head drooped with his eyes closed as he gripped his hands, white-knuckle tight. Phillip's eyes darted between his dad and me.

"Harold, I'm sorry. It's clear the memory of that night still bothers you. It's just that I committed to writing about Jessie Masterson and my intuition tells me there's much more to his story beyond the tragedy."

Harold sighed. "Nothing to forgive. I'm eternally thankful for what Jessie did for my boys. Writing about Jessie Masterson actually might serve a fortuitous purpose. Who else have you spoken to about your interest in his story?"

"Larry Scribner thinks it'd be good for the town and agreed to publish it as a series of articles and Marie Masterson has already given her approval. So, do I have your support too?"

Harold paused, then slapped his thigh. "Sure. Sounds like a mighty fine undertaking. Besides, the city plans to dedicate Jessie's memorial and the new city hall building during the opening night of our annual Christmas in Shiloh celebration. Think your story will be ready before that? It oughta generate additional interest in the dedication ceremony." He paused and then his eyes widened as he added, "I know. Maybe you can include something about the recent construction projects being like Shiloh's phoenix rising from the ashes of our past?"

I glanced at Liddy and Phillip who shared curious looks. Then I said with some reservation, "Sure...ah, I guess I could work that in somehow. Sounds like an interesting image to consider."

Harold's previous dark mood brightened. "You know...we can't let the past keep us from bringing our community into a better future. Whatever you need from me, my door's always open."

Liddy raised an eyebrow as I said to Harold, "All right, I'll take that as your official approval. Maybe when you've more time, we can talk in-depth about your recollection of what happened and how Shiloh has moved on since then."

"Be glad to Theo. I'm indebted to Jessie for what he did for all my sons." Harold glanced at Phillip. "In fact, did you know that Phillip helped Jessie escort the kids to safety after the fire broke out that night?" Harold reached across the sofa and ruffled Phillip's hair. "Yea, Phillip's a hero too."

Phillip stared at the floor as his head swayed ever so noticeably as he straightened his hair.

"My apologies, young man. I didn't know. You must've been pretty darn close to Jessie. I hope I didn't make you feel uncomfortable. Maybe we can talk sometime? I'm sure your dad wouldn't mind..." My eyes rolled toward Harold. "In fact, I'm certain your dad will agree that talking about these kinds of matters helps."

Phillip checked Harold's reaction. "Mister Phillips, I mean Theo, I'm not sure what benefit I'd be to your story. Coach Masterson was the hero, not me. I just miss him and the whole gang who used to attend Sanctuary."

I recalled Alex Thrope's mention of the group. "Can you tell me more about this Sanctuary?"

"Coach Masterson and Coach Priestly started it. Each week during the school year Sanctuary provided the opportunity to talk about real-life concerns and hear some devotional insight on subjects that mattered to us. The group began meeting at the school, but right after I joined, we relocated to the basement of the old courthouse."

"Why? Did it get that big?"

"Yeah. Coach Masterson insisted no one should be turned away from the group."

"Interesting you said that. Alex Thrope mentioned that to me too."

"Oh yeah, Alex enjoyed our meetings."

Liddy smiled and asked, "Phillip, how many students came to your meetings?"

"Hard to say exactly, Miss Liddy. The group grew well beyond just jocks and cheerleaders. It got big enough that even the churches in town eagerly volunteered their facilities when we began looking for a new place to meet, but Jessie wanted to avoid any specific church affiliation."

Liddy asked, "What did he say about the value of attending church?"

"Oh, he and Coach Priestly made it clear that Sanctuary was never intended to be a replacement for church. They told us that the group served only as an oasis for fellowship, just as the Bible emphasized."

Liddy leaned closer to Phillip. "So I imagine we're talking more than a dozen or so students by the time it met in the courthouse?"

"Yes, ma'am. It varied, but I reckon at least a couple dozen middle schoolers and nearly twice that many high school students attended each week."

"So how did the group end up in the old courthouse?"

"Well, actually, my dad worked it out." Phillip grinned at his dad.

"After Coach Priestly left, Coach Masterson struggled with the group's size, but a couple of recent graduates like me helped out each week."

"So Sanctuary moved into the courthouse after Coach Priestly was gone?"

"Yeah, not long after, I guess. My dad and Coach Masterson felt it'd be a more suitable location." Harold listened with a smug stare.

I asked Phillip, "How was the group funded?"

Phillip looked puzzled. "I just figured Coach Masterson and Coach Priestly-"

Harold interrupted. "Theo, I know for a fact there were some in town who wondered about the group's funding as well, but I never had any reason not to believe that Jessie Masterson and John Priestly funded the group's activities from their own pockets."

Harold tapped Phillip on the knee. "Come on big guy." They both rose to their feet. "We've taken up enough of their Sunday afternoon. There'll be plenty of time for us to talk more. Besides, Maddie'll be wondering where we are." Harold stood and looked at Liddy's puzzled look. "Oh, excuse me. Maddie's our live-in housekeeper. She's lived with us so long she's family."

"We enjoyed your company," Liddy said. "You and your wife should stop back sometime."

Harold cleared his throat. "Liddy, thanks for the kind offer, but I've been divorced since Phillip ran around in diapers."

Not knowing how to respond, we smiled and thanked them for stopping. Harold stopped and turned when he stepped onto the porch. "By the way, what are y'all doing for Thanksgiving? Do you have family plans?"

"Things have been so busy around here we hadn't thought about it. Our family won't be here until Christmas," I said peeking at Liddy.

"I reckon you both have a lot to be thankful for and might enjoy a quiet day. Of course, Christmas with the family sounds nice too. They'll be here before you know it."

As Harold drove off, Liddy snickered. "Look. We now know who belongs to that SHILOH1 license plate."

CHAPTER FOURTEEN

THE FRONT PAGE OF THE following morning's *Sentinel* immediately caught my attention. The caption beneath our smiling faces under the centerfold read, "Theo and Lydia (Liddy) Phillips, Proud New Residents of Shiloh."

Without reading anymore, I dropped the paper into my lap. "Liddy, got a second?"

She leaned closer and placed a hand over her mouth. "I wish I'd have known our photo would be on the front page. Oh, look at my hair!" She took a second glance and mumbled through her fingers. "Theo, did you approve this before it went to print?"

"Of course. You look great in that picture."

The sounds of Liddy fixing breakfast mixed with her continued murmuring. Over and over she said aloud, "Wait until I catch up with that rascal, Larry Scribner." Each outburst then ended with the sound of self-indulgent snicker which brought a smile to my face.

In the meantime, my morning devotion came from Proverbs. *"A young man is known for his actions and behavior, especially when they are pure and upright."* It directed my attention to the testimonies of so many people, especially young Phillip only yesterday, regarding Jessie Masterson.

Liddy called out from the kitchen. "Theo Phillips, if you and God are done, do you want your breakfast out there or in here with me?"

I closed my devotional journal and said, "Coming dear. Smells delicious."

After breakfast, Liddy announced as she cleared the table, "I'm sure you won't mind if I run off to get some shopping done today?"

"No, of course not. I planned to walk over to Larry's anyway. I'll be sure to tell him how upset you were about the photo."

Liddy protested. "You'll do no such thing." She brushed her fingers through her hair and smiled. "You can tell Larry how flattered I felt to make the front page of his paper."

"Okay, I'll tell him," I said with a huge grin. "I plan to delve into the *Sentinel*'s archives today, so I may be there past lunch if you need to find me."

———

A crystal blue sky provided a pleasant walk through town. I stopped across from City Hall and tried to visualize the old courthouse in its place and wondered what the *Sentinel*'s archives might reveal beyond the copies of pictures and articles I collected from the library. Surely I'd find more photos and articles about the fire.

"Hey, Theo!" I turned in the direction of my name being called. Joe Arians held a plastic cup in one hand with a briefcase hung over the other shoulder. He stood beside the street level entrance to his office.

"Hey, Joe. Good mornin'."

Joe adjusted his shoulder bag and managed a quick handshake. "Nick told me you're serious about writing Jessie Masterson's story and possibly include his relationship with John Priestly. Is that true?"

I smiled at the question. "Absolutely."

"I've some pressing court matters today, but if you're free tomorrow, let's say about noon, I think I've an intriguing proposition to discuss with you over lunch."

"Sure, that suits me."

"Look, I gotta run. Susanna's goin' to shoot me if I'm late. But, I'm glad I caught you this mornin'."

———

"How did Liddy enjoy the paper this morning?" Martha said with a cheerful smile when I entered the Sentinel.

"Liddy joked about her hair but told me to tell you how flattered she felt with the front page notoriety. As for me, heck, people will re-member Liddy's face anyway, not mine."

Mary let out a snicker from her desk nearby. "Mister P, somethin' tells me you'll be more recognizable in town than you may realize."

Martha added with a smile. "You do realize there's more coming about you and Liddy, right? Larry's working on the article. He wants the town to know more than what you look like."

"I didn't forget. Maybe y'all can tuck it inconspicuously on the society page." Martha nor Mary failed to appreciate my humor. "Just joking. I'm sure it'll be just fine. Where's Larry hiding anyway? Is he feeling any better?" Mary chuckled and pointed to his office.

I knocked and stepped into Larry's office. "How are ya feeling this mornin'? Those legs loosen up any?"

Larry looked up from his desk. "Yes, no thanks to you guys." He massaged his thighs as he stood. Beyond a couple of subtle moans, he appeared a far sight better than yesterday. "What's up with you today?"

"I'd like to scrounge around in your archives, so I can see what you've got on Jessie Masterson and John Priestly for my story. Would that be okay?"

"That's fine. Look, I've got to prepare for a meeting later, but hold on a sec." Larry called Mary and asked her to set me up in the back storage room.

Mary unlocked the room, flicked on the lights and said as she pointed, "File cabinet drawers are typically labeled chronologically, although the alphabetical ones contain notes and photos for significant newsworthy topics." Mary pointed to the dusty overhead storage box-es. "Those contain our oldest files if you think you need to go back that far." She then pointed to a rickety step ladder tucked in the corner.

"I hope I can find what I need in these filing cabinets. Thanks."

"Mister P, if you need anything, just ask. I'd like to help any way I can. My dad believes you're the fresh eyes and ears we've needed to write Coach Masterson's story."

"Thanks, Mary, I'll do my best. You can count on me calling you if I need any help." Mary turned to leave. "Oh, if you don't mind, where can I find an empty box?"

Mary disappeared and returned a moment later toting an empty storage box. "If you need more they're in the supply cabinet."

"Thanks. And, I do have one more request. Can you and I sit at lunch, if you don't mind? I'd like to ask you some questions about Coach Masterson and Coach Priestly."

She smiled and nodded as she turned to leave again.

I shouted, "Oh yeah, I know you call Liddy by her name, so please, Theo will be fine for me too."

"I'll try to remember. Thanks, Theo." The click-clack of her heels then faded down the hallway.

The musty archive took me back to my distant past when I worked for my father at the *Douglaston Dispatch*. The familiar dank odor of forgotten, yellowing newsprint, aging photographs and reams of legal notepads stuffed into manila folders offered a tantalizing reminder that the *Sentinel* remained removed from the 21st-Century digital era that most modern newspapers capitalized upon.

With a sigh of relief, I realized everything I needed could be found without scavenging through the dusty storage boxes overhead. First on my list, the courthouse fire. This topic provided a trove of before-and-after photos, scribbled notes, and news clippings about that fateful night and Jessie Masterson's funeral. I paused over a dated five-by-seven color yearbook picture of Jessie the *Sentinel* used in its feature article about the funeral.

While I set aside what I felt I needed to review later, Mary appeared in the doorway. "Theo, would you like a cup of coffee or maybe a Coke? I need a refill anyway."

"Thanks, Mary. Actually…a cold Coke would be nice."

A moment later Mary returned. "Here you go. Finding everything okay?"

"Yep. I'm finding plenty of photos, notes, and articles to go through after I get home and have time to sort through them more thoroughly. Got a few more things on my checklist, though. I'll holler if I need you."

After I found what I felt I needed on the courthouse and Sanctuary, the last item on my checklist, John Priestly's arrest and his subsequent court appearances, sat in three stuffed file folders. John's resigned, distant stare in his arrest photo and the candid courtroom shots provided a stark contrast to his confident grin found among the myriad of school and Sanctuary photos. As I stuffed the folders into my box, it seemed even the *Sentinel's* archives raised more questions than answers as to what happened to John Priestly.

After two hours of scouring through file cabinet drawers, my stomach growled. I flicked off the lights and closed the door as I carried the full box into the press room and scrubbed the newsprint and dust off my hands.

"Is Larry out? His light's off."

Martha turned with the phone cradled to her ear. "Yeah, I'm talking with him now."

"Tell him I'll catch him tomorrow. I've got plenty of homework to go over."

I looked over at Mary behind her oversized computer screen. "Still up for a quick lunch? I'm buying if that's okay with your mom?"

Martha smiled and motioned for Mary to wait for a second. She put Larry on hold. "Mary if you wouldn't mind, it looks like I'm stuck here. Can you bring me a sandwich back?"

"Look, how about if I run over to the Butcher Shoppe and get each of us a sandwich?" I said.

Mary suggested, "How about I drive you? If we hurry, we can beat the lunch hour rush."

Thirty minutes later, Mary sat across from me in the press room. She had just shared with me about her Journalism degree from the University of Georgia and asked questions about Atlanta and the prospects of her landing a job there someday. "Don't get me wrong, I love Shiloh, and my parents are great, but those last two years on the Athens campus opened my mind to all the possibilities outside of Shiloh."

"Atlanta's a big city full of opportunities for any smart and talented young person, but I suggest you consider what you have here. Heck, you could end up running the Sentinel before too long."

Our conversation then drifted to her days at Shiloh High. She had been an honor student and a cheerleader, which provided plenty of opportunities to be around John Priestly and Jessie Masterson.

"What was it like for you at Shiloh High?" I asked.

Mary laughed and said, "For years, all of Shiloh's athletic teams struggled. Everyone wanted Shiloh's football team as their homecoming opponent. Heck, the old stadium held more band members than spectators on most Friday nights. But everything changed after Coach Priestly arrived. By the time I graduated from middle school, the Shiloh Saints had enjoyed winning seasons. That's when I decided being a cheerleader would be fun."

Why do you think Coach Priestly made such a difference?"

Mary thought a moment as she propped her chin with one hand. "Good question. I'm no expert, but he sure invested the time and effort like no one before him. He also knew the value of surrounding himself with good people too. Folks from all over town gravitated to Coach Priestly and offered their help and support, and after Coach Masterson arrived, winning became a habit in Shiloh."

"What do you mean?"

"Coach Priestly had earned the respect and support of the town, but when Coach Masterson arrived, the people looked up to him as a real live sports legend. Coach Masterson's contagious, smiling wit always seemed to come up with the right words for any given situation. He proudly wore his GCU National Championship ring and conspicuous gold cross around his neck to inspire the players on the field and his students in the classroom."

"How so?"

"He said the real value of his ring and cross rested upon what they symbolized. He said their real values were established by the example of the person wearing them not the retail price in a jewelry store."

"I can understand why so many loved Coach Masterson." I then asked, "So how would you describe Coach Priestly?"

"Umm, Coach Priestly worked tirelessly but also made time for everyone, and preferred leading from behind, redirecting any credit that came his way toward others. At the start of each game, Coach Masterson lead the team onto the field while Coach Priestly, although the head coach, jogged in behind the players. Does that make sense?"

"Yeah, I think I see what you mean. Look, but how'd the town handle what happened to Coach Priestly and then Coach Masterson?"

She looked away and contemplated her response. "I remember that year. I still commuted to the University's campus in Alexandria." She stared at her fingers before she continued. "I guess you could say the wheels fell off the bandwagon pretty fast. Before people could even speculate on Coach Priestly's guilt or innocence, he went off to prison. It all happened so fast, but the town rallied around Coach Masterson. That fall, the football team continued to win every game, at least until the regional playoff game right after he died. His death knocked the wind out of Shiloh's sails. The team suffered the worse defeat in memory that night."

"Mary, thanks. You've helped me see a perspective I hadn't heard yet. I still need a lot more time to wrap my head around how this town dealt with such a tumultuous year."

Mary got up. "Somehow I think you will. I just hope I've been a little help."

"You certainly have, young lady, but you need to get back to work before your mother glances at me again."

"Anytime, Mister P, I mean Theo. If I can help more, just let me know."

Larry returned just as I headed to the front door and held the door open. "Did you find everything you needed?"

"Sure did."

Larry looked at his car keys still in his hand and the box on my shoulder. "How about a lift?"

On the drive to my house, I thanked Larry and shared how helpful Mary had been. I also mentioned my lunch plans with Joe Arians. I reached behind me and tapped the box in the backseat. "I hope all this will help me not only with Jessie Masterson's story but also to get a clearer picture of John Priestly before I meet with Joe tomorrow."

The kitchen light highlighted Liddy's silhouette through the window as we drove into the driveway. I waved as Larry pulled away and then toted my late-night homework assignment on my shoulder into the house.

CHAPTER FIFTEEN

THE EVENING CONTINUED WELL INTO the morning hours, long after Liddy surrendered to her drowsiness. I nodded off at some point after raking through and sorting the myriad of articles, notes, and photos from the *Sentinel*'s archives.

Liddy nudged my shoulder as she called my name.

My glasses miraculously remained perched on my nose until Liddy stirred me, and then fell harmlessly to the floor, along with my scribbled notes and red Sharpie. Liddy gazed at the former contents of the box now organized into neat piles around my chair. The morning sunlight forced me to squint while I tried to wipe away the fuzziness.

As the cobwebs dissipated, the plausible threads between what happened to Jessie Masterson and John Priestly and how they pointed to the Archer family returned. Though my candlelight vigil presented nothing concrete, a list of questions now served as a roadmap forward.

After breakfast, Liddy watched in her chair with a curious stare as each pile disappeared into labeled folders and I meticulously deposited them in the corrugated storage box.

"Are you going to at least tell me what you're so enthralled and energized about this morning?"

I paused from packing my box. "I'm just about certain the circumstances behind Jessie Masterson's death has a connection with what happened to John Priestly. I'm not sure how exactly, but maybe today's visit with Joe Arians will shed some light."

Liddy scooted to the edge of her seat. "How so?"

"Questions about John Priestly's arrest and conviction kept me up late last night." I raised an index finger. "Why would John Priestly risk his career and reputation for something so asinine as stealing $5,000 from the school's football program?" I raised a second. "More perplexing, why didn't John defend himself in court? Why accept a plea bargain? Either John's guilty, implicated somehow, or covering for someone."

Liddy wrinkled her forehead. "Do you think Joe knows anything?"

"I don't know, but he did offer to have lunch today." I loaded the last labeled file and slipped my pad of notes into my leather attaché.

Liddy nibbled on her thumbnail. "Yea, but Joe's John's attorney. I'm not sure there's much he can tell you."

"That's true, but maybe he can tell me how the Archers fit into what happened to John Priestly since Hank and Hal Archer were the last to see Jessie alive not long after that. Was it coincidental? I just don't know."

Liddy attempted a reassuring smile as she handed me the keys and my attaché.

"Sweetie, I'm sorry I'm investing so much time on this, and looking into what happened to John Priestly will require even more time."

"Theo Phillips, I know you're doin' all this for the right reasons. You've also got Marie Masterson to consider. Just let me know what I can do to help you."

———

"Damn good question!" Larry blurted with a puzzled look when I asked why no one dug any deeper into the Archers' possible connections with what happened to John Priestly and Jessie Masterson. Larry shoved his mahogany leather chair out from under his desk. "Darn good question, I mean."

"Yeah, I agree it's a darn good question."

Larry stepped to his office window that offered a view of the idle printing presses in his print shop. He remained frozen in silence.

I asked, "You okay?"

Without turning, he said, "Theo, over the last four or five years there's more that has happened around here that reinforces the validity of your question."

I spoke to Larry's reflection in the window. "Like what?"

"Well, it's a fact this whole town has wrestled with John's conviction and then Jessie's death." Larry stepped away from the window. "But, why others, including yours truly, have ignored any connections is a good question."

"There may be a lot of unintentional reasons-"

Larry cut me off. "Unintended reasons or not, I'm certainly not goin' to ignore it any longer even if I've known Harold as long as I have. I just pray that pompous ol' windbag's hands are clean with what happened to John or Jessie. We've had our differences, but I'd be shocked if he knowingly did anything that would hurt this town or one of its citizens." Larry walked over and rested his hand on my shoulder. "But I'm a newspaperman, and the truth is what we're after. What do you suggest we do next?"

Larry's attitude confirmed my instincts about him. I rose from my chair and looked him square in the eyes.

"I'm meeting Joe Arians at noon, and John Priestly will be our topic of conversation. Then, I would like to talk to Marie. She might be able to provide some additional details related to what happened to both John and Jessie."

"What can I do to help you?"

"You mentioned other events over the last four or five years. What else should we consider looking into?"

Larry thought a moment and then said, "Five years ago, Harold Archer turned over Archer Construction to his war hero son, Hank. But Hank's return came after several weeks in a rehab facility. Harold wasted no time though and put Hank right to work. Less than a year later, amidst a major contract the company won to renovate and expand facilities at the school complex, John Priestly went public about costly mismanagement concerns. Harold got involved, and the contract got completed, but I think he and Hank harbored hard feelings over the embarrassing publicity John stirred up."

"Certainly sounds like that might be worth investigating further. Can you put something together for me?" As we shook hands, I added, "If anyone asks, I'm just working on my story about Jessie Masterson."

"I understand, and I've got your back. If we're wrong, and it gets out that we're looking into any connections between the Archers and what happened to John and Jessie…"

"Don't worry Larry. I understand your paper's investment in this."

"Theo, let's not be wrong, or else I'll have to hitch my wagon to yours as we both leave Shiloh. Now get going!"

———

"Theo, it's not noon yet is it?" Susanna glanced at the clock on the wall. "Joe's on the phone, but he's expecting you. Can I offer you some coffee?"

"No thanks. I know I'm a bit early. I'll just grab a seat." Having missed my morning devotion time, I thumbed through the Bible on the coffee table hoping God would tell me where to stop and read.

Joe opened his office door. "Come on in, Theo." We sat in two leather armchairs near his desk. "So Theo, has Liddy got you two settled yet into your new home?"

"Thanks for asking. We're both enjoying the house, and Susanna, Martha, and Judy have been more than helpful. They've recently pointed her to Alexandria so she can shop for those things you can't find in Shiloh."

"Lord, don't let Missy hear about Liddy shopping in Alexandria. That'll become another reason for her to harp on the fact Shiloh doesn't encourage fancy, big-name retail stores within the city limits. But enough of that. I also heard through the church grapevine that you and the fellas played some backyard football this weekend."

"Instinctively, I rubbed a phantom muscle twitch in my thighs. "Yeah, just glad the younger ones went easy on us old geezers."

"Theo, before we head to lunch, I hoped we could talk a bit without a crowd around us."

"That suits me."

"I know you're working with Larry and he'll certainly help you get a lot more of the answers you inquired about when we first talked. I wanted to talk to you privately because I'm sure you know by now that John and Jessie were like brothers. John's conviction and incarceration deeply impacted Jessie, and when the news of Jessie's death reached John, it nearly crushed him."

"I've been told how close they were."

"That's why I told John about you and Liddy, and that you're writing Jessie's story."

"What'd he say?"

"He's willing to meet you, but you need to understand that John's been lock-lipped for the past three years."

"Look, Joe, I get it. Tell me what I need to do."

"John and I've talked about your background. He seemed to accept the idea that you're not some opportunistic journalist but still requested this meeting be off the record. Until John says otherwise, anything you talk about is confidential. Agreed?"

I nodded. "Do you think John will at least talk about his relationship with Jessie before his arrest and allow me to share some of his fonder memories about him and Jessie?"

Joe paused and stared at the sunlight shining through his window blinds. "Ask him when we meet. I believe he'll agree if it honors Jessie."

"While we are here in your office, I've got a couple of questions to ask you about John's arrest and conviction."

"Such as?"

"To begin with, the charges and severity of the sentence, especially after a plea bargain, don't add up. Why do you believe John pled guilty? Did he accept the plea deal to cover up for someone else?"

Joe responded without hesitation. "I'm not sure. And if I knew the answer to the first, I might be able to answer your second question. If it helps, I'm not sure if John will ever say more either, but it'd be a fair question to ask him. Maybe you'll have better luck than I've had."

"What can you tell me, off-the-record of course?"

Joe chose his words carefully. "I reckon there's no harm in sharing; I'm confident John is serving time for a crime he didn't commit." Joe leaned forward with a broad smug smile. "Fair enough? How about lunch?"

On our way out the door, Joe stopped by Susanna's desk. "Would you notify the prison that Theo Phillips will accompany me this Friday?"

"Consider it done. And will you remember to leave the beach house early enough Friday morning to be here by noon? You did tell Missy and your mother about having to visit John Friday?"

Joe chuckled. "You get Theo approved for the visit. I'll take care of Missy and Momma." Joe looked at me. "You're free Friday, right?"

I peered at Susanna and then Joe. "Friday's fine. What time?"

"Noon, and I'll arrange for a lunch to eat on the road."

"What'd you mean, you'll arrange?" She gave a got-ya smirk.

Joe laughed and raised both his hands. "Guilty as charged. Susanna will make sure we have lunch Friday. Now, let's get downstairs. Maybe the lunch line won't be too long." Joe looked at Susanna. "We'll be back within the hour. Do you mind waiting until I get back before you cut out for lunch?"

Susanna pointed to the fridge in the corner by the coffee pot. "I'm good. Now, y'all skedaddle so I can get some work done and enjoy my holiday weekend."

———

While we waited to place our order at the Butcher Shoppe, I asked, "Where's Nick today?"

"Nick's checking out some property near Alexandria, then heading to our family's house at Saint Simon's Island. Momma's already there."

Then I heard Silas's thick accent. "Theo, Joe, my friends, what can I get you today?"

We ordered and found a table that Alex cleared as we arrived.

After we discussed the upcoming Georgia game Saturday, I asked, "Joe, I gotta ask one quick question about John. How was Harold involved in what happened to John?"

"Theo, I'm not sure why you asked that, but..." Joe looked for prying ears. "All I know is the DA's office moved quickly and aggressively. I felt like someone applied pressure for an expedited process. I don't know if Harold was behind that, but I do know that he urged the school board to push for John's resignation within forty-eight hours after his arrest. The judge mandated at the arraignment that the case would proceed without further delay to trial. My attempts to sway the judge's decision were repeatedly denied. I figured with Harold's political strings, he most likely made some phone calls to high places."

"What motive do you believe Harold might have had?"

"Theo, you're asking the same questions I've asked myself for the past three years."

I fell back in my seat and wiped my face with a napkin. "All right. I'm sorry. We can talk more Friday."

Joe grinned and nodded as his cheeks bulged from a bite of his hamburger.

"I know I'm writing Jessie's story, but John's could be the bigger one."

———

Liddy applauded the good news, but I needed time to process the significance of my meeting with Joe Arians. I grabbed a rake and wheelbarrow from out back and pruned and cleaned the gardens while lingering questions wrestled and tugged at me.

Haunted by the fact that I needed to protect myself from relying too much on the opinions of my new friends when it came to investigating about what happened to Jessie or John, I realized all the more the need to maintain objectivity in order to find the truth. My father's voice echoed in my mind. "Any important, worthwhile story will be fraught with many shades of gray where latent truth resides. Don't be fooled. Follow the facts and not opinions to the truth. Love your friends and family, but love the truth more when writing a story that others will read and believe."

I looked up and whispered, "Thanks, Pop."

CHAPTER SIXTEEN

THE STREETLIGHTS HAD FLICKERED ON by the time the sound of a truck pulling up followed by the shutting of its doors caught my attention. Jim, Andy, and Pete waited by the curb as Jay lifted a box over the tailgate.

"Evening Mister and Missus P. Hope y'all don't mind we stopped by without calling, but Miss Marie asked us to drop this off for her," Pete yelled spotting Liddy and me at the foot of the porch steps.

Jay lowered the box off his shoulder, and she raised a corner of the burlap cover, and her hand shot to her mouth. "She shouldn't have," Liddy mumbled as she turned to me.

"Marie butchered one of her hogs this weekend and thought you'd like a butt and a shank cut, which makes a tasty picnic ham."

Marie's gift required both hands as Jay handed me the box. Liddy then latched onto Jay and Jim's arms and eyed Pete and Andy. "Come on inside. I think there's some banana pudding in the refrigerator."

A few minutes later, Jay spoke up with a bowl of pudding in his lap. "We're sure glad Miss Marie asked us to stop by tonight. We got to talking on the way over, and, well, we felt bad we didn't get to talk much with y'all Saturday." He turned to me and added, "Besides, Mister P, you asked us to stop back when it suited us, so here we are."

I lowered a spoonful of pudding back into my bowl. "I sure did. So, if you guys don't mind, I'd love to hear some of your stories about being raised here in Shiloh."

Over the next hour, these native-born sons of Shiloh tag-teamed, sharing about growing up together. Even though each went away to

college, they offered no regrets deciding to return to Shiloh. Pete left
to go to school ten years ago, while the others graduated together and
went their separate ways the following year. Pete and Andy returned
and have grown their father's plumbing business into a more diverse
home construction enterprise. Jay and Jim helped their father modern-
ize and expand Adam's Feed and Hardware, a landmark in town.

Liddy pointed to the scraped clean bowl on the kitchen table.
"Y'all still look hungry. Would you be ready for some dinner in about
an hour? I assume you boys would like to stay a while longer and eat
with us?"

Awkward stares went back and forth. Each seemed hesitant to say
yes until Liddy's playful pout broke into a smile as she said, "Theo
would love hearing more about y'all's glory days in Shiloh."

Pete opened his mouth to speak, but Jay responded first. "Yes,
ma'am. That'd be great. What do you say, guys?" Each nodded their
acceptance.

Liddy peeked at me, smiled and then disappeared into the kitchen.
"Y'all go on with your stories. I'll listen while I start dinner."

"Guys, I've heard you played when Shiloh won two state championships in football, and that success spilled over on the basketball and
baseball teams too. What I'd like to know, do you guys have any interesting stories about Coach Priestly and Coach Masterson?"

With the ice officially broken, they launched into another round
robin of ball field and court-side stories, probably embellished, but
they laughed as they shared locker-room anecdotes that presented
their unique, inside perspective of both Jessie and John. Their stories
offered plenty of color and details after I suggested that I'd consider
using their stories in one of my articles about Coach Masterson.

Their laughter and back and forth banter filled the room, rib-
bing each other about the accuracy of their memories. All the while,
I flipped page after page in my yellow legal pad recording as much of
their colorful details and quotes as I could manage.

After Liddy called us to the table, more stories continued, but the
tone of their voices became more respectful and reverent when I asked

for their opinions about Coach Masterson and Coach Priestly.

The guys helped Liddy clear the dinner plates before we settled back into the cozy confines of the living room. As I stoked the fireplace, I felt our relationship with the boys warmed as well.

Liddy and I heard tales of how their relationships with Coach Masterson differed from the reverence they held for Coach Priestly, which intrigued me because it closely mirrored Mary Scribner's testimony about John and Jessie.

Andy said, "A couple of years after Coach Masterson joined the staff, Coach Priestly asked him to take over our varsity basketball program. It was the best thing that happened as far as I am concerned."

I asked, "How so?"

"Coach Masterson played both football and basketball at Georgia Christian. He not only showed us exactly what he wanted from us, but he taught me what it would take to play both football and basketball at the college level. I owe him a lot for helping me chase the dreams I had."

Jay blustered in jest from his seat on the ottoman. "Andy, each of us wishes we had been as gifted as you were."

Andy glared at Jay.

Jay chuckled. "Andy, I was just joking. You know we all feel fortunate for the blessings we received."

Pete gave Andy a nudge, and they both busted out in manly snickers.

Jay smiled and said, "Hey, Andy do you remember the night we celebrated in the locker room after our basketball season ended during our junior year? As usual, we horsed around while Coach Masterson had his feet propped up in his office. The cheerleaders waited for us in the gym with their high pitched giggles and constant chatter reminding us of our promise to stop by Bubba's."

Jim laughed. "I remember. We clowned around with Pete about his contribution to the scoreboard." Jim's big grin turned to Liddy. "You see, Miss Liddy, Pete played basketball like he played middle linebacker and fouled out of most games."

Pete's face reddened as he grinned at Liddy and me. "I wasn't that bad. You never minded my picks so you could make all uncontested layups. And Jim, you appreciated the rebounds I grabbed following your errant rim shots."

Andy stood up from his seat on the sofa and pointed to Pete. "Touché brother." Then he said with a smothered smile, "Come on guys, Pete deserves a lot of credit for making the most of his unique basketball talents by the time he graduated. I'm sure, Pete'll give all the credit to Coach Masterson." Andy sat back down grinning at Pete while the twins tried to control their laughter.

Liddy smiled at Pete. "I'm sure your valiant effort made them all look good out there."

"You've spoken mostly about Coach Masterson. What about Coach Priestly?" I asked as our laughter subsided.

Jim said, "I think all of us agree. Coach Priestly could be summed up in three words: firm, fair and frank."

Andy said with a thought-filled grin. "However, Lord, don't be the brunt of one of Coach's righteous tirades." Andy's eyes drifted to the floor.

"You ought to know little brother." Pete chuckled. "But truthfully, Coach Priestly deeply cared about not only every athlete but also every student in the school. He never pushed his faith upon anyone, but when asked, you'd quickly learn how God directed his life. Coach Masterson might have become the spokesman for Sanctuary, but God gave Coach Priestly the vision to start it."

Liddy shared a warm grin and asked, "Why do you think he never married?"

They all laughed as they jokingly confessed, a wife would've played second fiddle to the school and the program. None of them remembered seeing John on a date, and outside of school, they said, he spent his time caring for his mom.

I looked at my watch. "Guys, it's late, but one last question. Do you believe Coach Priestly was guilty?"

The four stared at each other and none said a word before Pete broke the silence. "Mista' P, Coach could no more have done what they said than me outrun Andy. Anyways, he didn't need money. Since his dad passed, he devoted himself to caring for his mother. Nope. Ain't no way. But I'll tell you what he told me and Andy before they took him away. 'I'm doing what I am doing because I have to. When the right time comes, you'll understand better than all the others why all this happened.'"

I examined their stalwart faces and asked, "I imagine you all agree with Pete?"

"Yes, sir," they whispered in unison.

Liddy offered her calm assurance. "Please listen to me. Sometimes wrongs happen to good people and can't be explained. Sometimes they're made right and sometimes not, but I'm glad to hear y'all believe in Coach Priestly."

After the young men walked off the porch, Pete yelled from the darkness, "Thanks for the spaghetti and banana pudding."

I flicked off the porch lights. Liddy stood behind me and snuggled her arms around my waist. "Did our unexpected dinner guests help paint a good picture of Jessie and John for you?"

I rotated in her loose embrace and looked into her hazel eyes. "These young men made me wish our boys had experienced John and Jessie as their mentors and coaches."

CHAPTER SEVENTEEN

"Theo... oh, Theo... Are you waking up? Breakfast is ready." Liddy's voice stirred me from the comfort of my pillow.

"I'm up," I said with a touch of reluctance, sitting on the edge of the bed. My hand instinctively found my glasses on the nightstand and then fumbled for the pen next to the scratch pad. I jotted a reminder to talk to Arnie, and then slid my feet into my flip-flops, grabbed my robe and headed down the hall.

Liddy set the morning edition of the *Sentinel* next to my plate. The lead article on the front page referred to the Mayor's press release announcing the city's schedule of events for this year's Christmas in Shiloh celebration. Larry's article highlighted the city's decision to purchase new holiday decorations and light displays to illuminate Town Square. The week-long celebration would kick off on the Wednesday before Christmas with the lighting of the town's tallest Christmas tree ever right after the dedication of the new City Hall and Jessie's Memorial.

Liddy hovered over my shoulder as I pointed to the article and said, "Hey, I bet the grandkids will get a kick out of seeing the tree lighting ceremony. What do you think?"

Liddy huffed, reached over my shoulder, flipped the paper open to the centerfold, and pointed to Larry's promised follow-up story beside the same photo from last week's article. The caption now read, "Theo and Liddy Phillips are evidence of Shiloh's draw for new residents looking for a special place to call home."

In the article, Larry highlighted our recent years in Atlanta, our

University of Georgia alumni status, thankfully without revealing our graduation year, and the fact we chose Shiloh because of our southern Georgia roots. Larry ended the article quoting Liddy. "We look forward to our two sons and their families arriving for Christmas, so that we can show off our wonderful new town."

I looked up. Liddy held her hand over her mouth. Teary-eyed, she gasped. "Theo, oh my gosh! I've got so much yet to do. Gifts to buy." Her eyes darted back and forth as a cute smirk emerged. "The move put us way behind. We still need to buy gifts for all the grandkids." She then squeezed my hand, and uttered through a coy look the dreaded words, "Why don't you come with me? We can visit the shopping mall in Alexandria."

My mind raced seeking the right response when, as fortune would have it, the phone rang. Liddy answered it but handed it to me with a puzzled look. "It's the Mayor's office."

A polite, perky voice on the other end said, "Mister Phillips, the mayor will be right with you. Please hold for just a sec."

Harold's unmistakable laugh followed. "Theo, sorry to call this early."

"No problem. What's up?"

"Nothing official. I thought about our conversation Sunday evening. How'd you and Liddy like to share Thanksgiving with me? My sons announced they'd rather spend the day hunting turkeys rather than eating the big one Maddie's preparing. So, unless your plans have changed, it looks like both of us will be without family for Thanksgiving. How about it? Maddie's fixin' a huge tom turkey."

I posed the question to Liddy's equally inquisitive stare. She glanced at the oven, sink, and cupboards, then grinned as she whispered, "Sure. Why not?"

"Harold, that'll be great. Liddy's smiling at your kind invitation."

"Fine. I'll have directions and my home phone number delivered to you later this morning. You'll be home won't you?"

My face lit up. "Yes, I'll be here."

Harold asked, "Would two o'clock tomorrow be good for you?"

"That'll be just fine. We look forward to it."

After I hung up the phone, I looked at Liddy acting disappointed. "Gee willikers. Looks like I've got to stick around this morning. Harold's dropping off directions to his home later this morning."

Liddy sighed and then giggled. "Phew, thought for a moment you might want to spend the day shopping with me."

"Maybe next time," I said with a shrug, and eagerly volunteered to clean up the kitchen.

About the time I finished wiping off the counter, the jingling of car keys caught my attention. Liddy stood at the door and announced. "Hun, I'm leaving."

I kissed her after a grateful hug. "See you later this evening I imagine."

I called Arnie right after she left. He promised to stop by after making his appointed rounds this morning. Not long after I hung up, I heard a gentle knock at the door. When I opened the front door, a young woman with a friendly smile and white envelope greeted me.

"Mister Phillips, I'm Megan from the Mayor's office." She handed me the envelope. "These are the directions Harold promised, and the home phone number is at the bottom of the map, but y'all should have no problem finding the address."

I concluded by the handwriting that Megan prepared it rather than Harold. "Thank you, Megan."

"You're most welcome," she politely responded and then walked back to her sporty red Mustang convertible parked out front, though its black cloth top remained latched this morning.

With Harold's directions in hand and likely more than a couple of hours before Arnie's arrival, I grabbed my windbreaker and headed across town for a brief visit with Larry.

———

I entered the Sentinel's office and immediately said out loud, "Larry, you cost me a bunch of money this morning." I looked over at Martha's startled face and put my finger over my mouth. "Shh!"

"Hey, what's all the fuss out here?" Larry stomped out of his office and looked for the source of the ruckus. His search abruptly halted as he put his hands on his hips. "Oh, it's only you."

"Whoa, there, big fella'. You're in big trouble." I strode toward Larry as Martha hunched over grinning.

"What are you squawking about?"

"Because of your article, Liddy made me walk across town to express her feelings about it."

Larry appeared puzzled and stammered, "I...I...I thought she'd like what I wrote."

"You can relax Larry. She loved your article. That quote at the end of the family visiting for Christmas tugged on her emotions and my checkbook." I slapped him on his shoulder and laughed at Larry's perplexed, scrunched face. "Yep, your article is costing me a small fortune today."

Larry's tongue appeared stuck between laughing and utter confusion.

"Liddy's headed to Alexandria to catch up on her Christmas shopping. I'll be a pauper by nightfall."

We both broke out into laughter and entered his office.

"Of course, I thought you'd also like to hear that Joe Arians is taking me to visit John Priestly on Friday."

Larry's face lit up. "That's great news. Does John know you're coming?"

"Yes. Joe vouched for me and told him how Marie had approved of my writing about Jessie."

"You'll handle your meeting with John fine, especially with Joe breaking the ice for you."

"Oh, and Pete, Andy and the Adams twins stopped by last night too."

Larry leaned back in his chair and smiled. "So how'd your visit with the famous Four Horsemen of Shiloh go?"

"Liddy fed them while they recanted their glory days and shared some notable memories of Jessie and John."

"Theo, you'll hear similar tales about Jessie and John from a lot of folks in town."

"Guess that's why I'm turning my attention more to John Priestly. I've concluded that no matter how well I write Jessie's story, I can't change what happened to him, but it just might unearth the truth about John. What do ya' think?"

"Glad you brought that up. Want to know what I dug up about Archer Construction?"

"Absolutely."

Larry reached for a file on the top of his desk and flipped open to his notes inside. "Archer Construction won both of the largest construction contracts this town has known for decades, the school's renovation and expansion project and the building of the new City Hall." Larry flipped to photocopies of the contracts. "But, catch this. In both instances, Archer Construction won the contracts without being the lowest bidder."

"How was that even possible?" I asked with a puzzled look as I checked over the contract copies.

Larry leaned back in his chair. "Each contract included a provision extending a ten percent advantage to any local owned contractor over other bidders. It's right there." Larry pointed to the highlighted portion of the bid paperwork.

"Is that legal?"

"Yeah, it's called a preferred bidder clause. In other words, the county or municipality feels a particular contract would best serve the interest of their citizens if a local business wins the bid process since it employs local workers and has a vested interest in the local economy, not to mention the tax revenue benefit. The clause doesn't guarantee a local contractor always wins against larger companies, but offers an edge."

"I'd say it would."

"Now, here's the most interesting part. After Archer Construction started both projects, they received contract addenda worth thousands of dollars."

"Sounds like hometown cooking to me."

"Well, to be honest, everyone around here rooted for Archer Construction to win the bids. Local businesses and a bunch of folks benefitted from the work. Legal? Technically, yes. Hometown cooking? No doubt."

"But Harold Archer's mayor? Wasn't that a conflict?"

"Archer Construction may be legally owned by the Archer family, but Harold relinquished control of the company to Hank after Hank returned from the Army. The city council awarded the contracts to Archer Construction, not Harold's company – at least officially." Larry smirked.

"Can you give me some of those numbers and details for my records? And one final question before I get outta your hair. Do you believe Harold Archer would ever break the law for his personal or family's benefit?"

Larry scratched his scalp a moment. "Whoa. He's far too cagey and wily to do anything illegal. Of course, if you'd have asked me if he'd do anything underhanded, he's the consummate politician. He knows how to manipulate every angle to gain an advantage politically or personally. Harold may be a hard-headed pain in the butt, but there's no law against that. If there were, I'd have to plead guilty. But why do you ask?"

I hesitated. "Just thinking aloud about John and the Archers."

CHAPTER EIGHTEEN

I WALKED HOME FROM LARRY'S OFFICE and fixed sandwiches for Arnie's impending visit before deep thoughts about what Larry revealed accompanied me onto my hammock. I drifted off until I felt Arnie nudging my shoulder and squinted at his shadow hovering over me.

"Hey, Theo. Sorry, I'm later than planned. You can blame Harold. I tried to scurry out right after our meeting at city hall, but he stopped me before I could get away."

I sat up on the edge of the hammock and checked my watch. "No problem Arnie. I was…uh, just resting my eyes waiting for you. Lunch is ready."

Arnie stared at the two now iceless glasses of tea sitting in puddles on the kitchen table. "Are we going to eat in here?"

"Yep, grab a chair." I opened the fridge, pulled out two Dagwood sandwiches and condiments, and then grabbed a bag of chips on top, and sat across from Arnie.

After a few minutes of small talk about the boys' visit, I directed the conversation to what I had intended.

"Arnie, I want to thank you and Judy. Liddy and I genuinely appreciate how you both reached out to us. We consider you both friends."

"Thanks, Theo. We feel the same about you and Liddy." Arnie stared at his glass. "Am I here as a friend or your pastor?"

"I guess mostly as a friend, but because you're also my pastor, I promise I'll be brief so you'll have plenty of time to get ready for tonight's service."

"That's fine Theo, what's on your mind?"

"Promise me if our conversation makes you uncomfortable, you'll let me know."

Arnie smiled and nodded.

I slouched over and inspected my half-empty glass. "Thanks. I need some man-to-man advice."

"Like what? Everything okay with you and Liddy?"

"Gosh yes. I'm talking about what I'm working on so I can write Jessie's story. I'm afraid it's grown much bigger and more significant than I anticipated."

Arnie crossed his arms. "How so?"

"Every new question I ask seems to drag me further away from that simple commemorative story I first envisioned. It seems there are some dark, hidden truths about what happened to Jessie that keep pointing back to John Priestly. Does that make any sense to you?"

"Theo, before I answer, have you considered the likelihood that God directed you to Shiloh for more than just a peaceful retirement?"

I responded with a cockeyed stare.

"Look, you and Liddy brought fresh eyes and ears as well as good hearts with you. The Shiloh that attracted you to invest your lives here has struggled in recent years. I guess you can say Shiloh's still suffering from a mild case of PTSD... you know, post-traumatic stress disorder."

Arnie sipped his tea before he continued. "In fact, you've already met some good folks who have suffered one way or another from what happened to Jessie and John, and nobody expected anything like what happened to either of them to take place in Shiloh either."

"Wow. I hadn't thought about it that way."

"I'm not sure what I can say or what you're even looking for me to say, but I sense this tribute to Jessie has mushroomed well beyond a simple story about one tragic night three years ago."

My head slowly bobbed while I stared at my empty glass.

"Theo, what happened to John and Jessie crushed a lot of hearts and dashed plenty of hopes for this town's future. I mean, consider what happened to Betty Priestly. I believe she succumbed to a broken heart after John landed in prison. Her poor health couldn't handle it.

For that, I feel like I didn't do enough."

The painful reminder of Betty's passing tugged at my heart. "Look, Arnie, I'm sure you did what you could. We understand." I spread my hands and looked around. "Let's face it, Liddy and I are dealing with the fact we purchased her house. We also sense how much Jessie's loss impacted Marie. Without a doubt, I'm now more acutely aware how these two tragedies have left their mark across the whole town, and how the grieving silently lingers for so many."

Arnie's somber stare spoke louder than his words. "Too many, including yours truly, have forgotten the good we enjoyed. We let our grief cloud our vision, but that's why I believe with all my heart that God brought you and Liddy here to provide a fresh perspective for all of us to see. You've already uncovered much we quite frankly have kept hidden in the shadows of the past."

"Funny you put it that way, that's what Larry pointed out too, but it doesn't make the task any easier."

"Theo, God doesn't always send us on easy, comfortable tasks. However, if it'll make you feel any better, I believe that God selected you and Liddy for this time and purpose."

My clenched fist bounced off the table. "But that's why I wanted to talk with you, Arnie… Why me? Why did God pick me? I'm not some hard-nosed investigative reporter like my father. My journalistic talents kept me anchored safely behind a desk all these years. I just wanted to write a simple tribute regarding a young man who died to help others… but, we've long left simple."

"I'm not God. However, I can tell you this… Shiloh's existed for decades isolated from the harsh effects of scandals like what fell upon John and the tragic loss of Jessie. When that last dump truck left with the final load of rubble and the bulldozers arrived to prepare the foundation for the new city hall, a huge piece of Shiloh's past got buried too. Shiloh's no more equipped to cope with these tragedies than you are to write about them. Like you put it, most folks would rather continue to keep the past under the rug rather than face the dark truths and answer the question, 'Why did this happen?' Thankfully, people like Larry, Joe, and Nick, as well as a few others have not given up. They want closure, so the town they love can move on."

"But outwardly at least, Shiloh's moved forward. What about the new City Hall and Town Square? They've given the town a facelift."

His sad eyes met mine. "Theo, my friend, bricks and mortar can never replace human lives. A bronze statue can't walk and talk or touch the people like the person it honors. Shiloh's linked by family ties and bonds of friendship forged and passed on, one generation to the next. For the last quarter of a century, Judy and I've been a part of this community and we've witnessed firsthand that in Shiloh, change arrives late, is received reluctantly, and meets significant resistance. To my knowledge, only a few in Shiloh have the authority or influence to instigate or advocate change. And of those few, only the boldest agent of change would see the recent events as an opportune time to introduce more change as a cure-all for the doldrums."

"Who would be the boldest agent for change?"

Arnie gulped the last of his tea and allowed it to make its way down his throat before he spoke. "I guess it'd be no surprise that Harold Archer and his sons would be the likely bold agents of change. Look, Harold genuinely believes what he does is for the good of the town, but I believe his intentions come from his aspirations." Arnie's head swayed, eyes closed. "I'm truly sorry Theo. I've never shared this with anyone else, and maybe I shouldn't have said it to you, but I know this to be true about Harold."

I raised my hand. "Wait! Harold sits on the church's leadership board."

"Theo, thanks for being concerned about me. I can handle Harold, but you best be careful with him and his sons. Harold's shrewd, powerful and well-connected, all the way to Atlanta. I've had to work with and often around him on church matters for more years than I care to count. I still don't fully trust him because I don't believe he trusts anyone but himself."

"The Archer family is linked to what happened to both Jessie and John. Maybe it's just a small town coincidence, but it's something I've got to look into."

"Theo, just be careful what you say and to whom you say it to about the Archers."

"I will Arnie, thanks…So why have you tolerated him for so long?"

"Well, for one, he's hard to miss or dismiss." We shared small smiles in agreement. "Secondly, when I get his support, things get done. Lord forgive me, but I've learned how to handle a crooked stick when it's useful for the right purposes." Arnie prayerfully looked up with a twisted grin.

I paced the kitchen floor as my mind tried to grasp what Arnie just shared and what I believed I knew about Harold. The same man Liddy and I had in our home and agreed to share Thanksgiving dinner with.

Arnie sat quietly and patiently as I paced.

My thoughts grew audible. "Since I met Harold that first day in church, I've felt uneasy about his sincerity. Even when trying to be friendly, his pompous attitude serves as a shield and makes him hard to get to know."

Arnie spread both his hands in my direction and grinned. "You seem to have Harold Archer pegged pretty good. And yes, he's a hard man to understand and to measure, so err on the side of caution around him. He's like a billow of smoke, hard to ignore but not easily grasped." Arnie grabbed for the imaginary smoke then revealed his empty hands.

I leaned against the kitchen counter with a puzzled stare. "Doesn't that make you a little uncomfortable to cooperate with someone like Harold?"

Arnie paused before he carefully chose his words. "Theo, I've been pastor at Shiloh Baptist for a long time now. As much as I'd like to say it's not been an issue, there've been times and situations where I've wrestled with 'playing politics' inside the church. That may not sound very spiritual, but pragmatic solutions often allow spiritual matters to move forward. As Jesus said, 'Give unto Caesar what is Caesar's, and to God what is God's.'" Arnie shrugged and smiled, looking for my approval.

"Trust me, I understand, but Harold's a tough representative of Caesar."

"Just because he's good at politicking, does that earn him any favoritism from me? Trust me. There're plenty of times I've prayed for real change to occur in Harold's spirit, but I reckon Harold's even testing God's forbearance. But God won't give up, so neither will I." Arnie offered a half smile then looked skyward again and whispered almost inaudibly, "God, please forgive me for saying that so bluntly."

"If it means anything, I forgive you." It wasn't my intention to make Arnie, my new pastor, and friend, uncomfortable or feel embarrassed. I came to him for encouragement and now felt obligated to comfort him.

"I'm truly sorry... I hadn't considered what you've dealt with for so long. If it helps, you've helped me realize that God has a bigger story for me to tell. It doesn't make me feel any more capable. Quite the contrary. Now I'm afraid God wants a story of redemption that will manifest itself though Jessie and John's stories."

Arnie raised his eyebrows. "Look, between you, me and God, you may have something there. You're in the unique position of doing far greater than just pay tribute to Marie Masterson regarding Jessie. Remember, God's in the redemption business."

"If I amen that, will I feel better?"

"Probably not, but it's a good start. Just believe God won't ask you to do anything you can't handle, and I've got no doubt he's picked the right person."

"Well gee, thanks, Arnie. I'll try to remember that when I have Thanksgiving dinner with Harold tomorrow."

"Oh yeah, Harold mentioned that when I was at his office this morning." Arnie stood, pointed to me and added, "That reminds me, I can't tell you everything, but heed my advice. Don't get Hank riled, and never meet with him alone. Just trust me on this. Since he returned from serving in Afghanistan a few years ago, let's just say he can become extremely abrasive and often combative if the mood strikes him."

"Thanks for the warning. He's been okay so far. What about Hal?"

"For the most part, outside of City Hall, Hal serves as Hank's handler, for Hank's sake I think. Hal's pretty much the quiet one, and you already realize that Phillip's a decent good kid. How Harold raised those three after his wife left him is beyond me. One thing I can say good about Harold is he's tried to be a good father to all three."

"I've met them all, and so far I've seen nothing that bothers me except I can tell Hank and Harold seem a little at odds with each other."

"Theo, just remember what I said." Arnie looked at his watch. "I've gotta run. Hope our chat helped, but feel free to call me anytime."

CHAPTER NINETEEN

LIDDY HANDED ME THE BAGS she carried only to turn and wrestle even more out of the back of the Expedition.

"I found some great deals and checked off most of the gifts on our list."

"Most?" I uttered maneuvering through the doorway.

She removed her jacket, and then eyed the half-empty glasses and scrunched napkins still on the table. "How'd your lunch go with Arnie?"

A guilty-as-charged look accompanied my reply. "Arnie left about an hour ago." I grabbed the glasses and laid them in the sink. "You'd be surprised to know how down to earth he is."

"I guess you didn't miss me too badly."

With my best sheepish smile, I said, "Uh... of course, I missed you. Arnie and I had a good chat over lunch, but he's hardly a worthy replacement for your company."

"Aren't you sweet." The flutter of her eyelids and coy look lasted until she pointed to the living room. "Now, go sit down. I'll show you what I got for all the kids."

———

Other than the Arians, the familiar faces of our new friends congregated in the main foyer by the time we arrived. Jay and Jim stood talking to whom, by his similar features, appeared to be their dad.

As we approached, I said, "Hey guys. Good to see you again. Is this your father?"

"Mister Phillips. Good to see you too." Jay responded and then looked beyond me. "Missus Phillips. We were just bragging on your cooking to my dad."

Jim looked at his father. "Dad, this is Mister Theo Phillips and his wife, Liddy. They're the ones who bought Aunt Betty's old home."

Mister Adams's bearded face beamed as he extended his hand. With a friendly, hearty voice, he said, "Glad to meet y'all. The boys sure have bragged about both of you. They're mighty partial to football and food, and it sounds like you two scored on both points."

Liddy accepted his hand. "Why thank you, Mister Adams. They're both mighty fine young gentlemen, and we think highly of them already. I'm sure you're proud."

"Please call me Zeb."

"Thank you, Zeb. Please call me Liddy and my husband, Theo."

"Sorry, I haven't met you sooner. It ain't my usual nature to miss church meetings, but it's busy this time of the year." Zeb pointed in the general direction of Adams Feed & Hardware. "With the growth of our farm equipment and warehouse business, I've been more sidetracked with this year's longer-than-usual harvest season, which overlapped with the time we usually begin our store's holiday preparations."

"Theo and I've driven by your store several times. It seems hardly ever empty of customers."

"I hope it stays that way, to be honest. My family established the original general store before the Civil War, although it's grown a bit over the years." Zeb chuckled with his chest puffed out and rocked on his heels. "You should stop by and visit. We've preserved the original building and it's attached to the main feed and hardware store."

I said, "Zeb, I'm impressed. I imagine your sons are a big help to you."

"Yes they are. I'm glad to have 'em around too. Both have been a huge help in expanding our business. They've introduced all sorts of new-fangled ideas and computer stuff that our business needed. I'm just glad they understand it all because I'm too old to fuss with it."

I laughed. "Trust me, I can relate to that. My sons refer to me as a digital Neanderthal."

"I couldn't manage the business anymore without them." Zeb slapped his sons across the back of their shoulders.

Liddy offered a proud mother's grin at Jay and Jim. "Mister Adams, I mean Zeb, we'd love to have you stop by the house anytime to visit, and bring your wife along too."

Zeb reached out and gently touched her upper arm. "Liddy, I appreciate the invite, and I'd love to enjoy some of that mighty fine cooking I've heard about, but I reckon the boys didn't tell you their momma went to be with the Lord a long time ago."

Liddy's eyes dropped. "I'm so, so sorry."

Zeb grabbed the shoulders of his two sons. "Miss Liddy, no need to feel sorry. The good Lord's taking good care of their momma." Zeb widened his warm smile. "I know. How about you and Theo stop by the store? It's all decorated and stocked for the holidays, and a load of fresh Christmas trees just arrived."

Zeb dug into the top pocket of his shirt and handed me his business card. Zeb's head then turned toward the sanctuary. "Oops, sounds like we better find our seats."

Zeb offered his arm to Liddy while I headed in with Zeb's sons.

Jay pulled me aside before we got inside the sanctuary. With a serious look, he whispered, "Mister P, listen. I need to warn you 'bout somethin'."

"Warn me? About what?"

In a hush-hush tone, he said. "We've heard around town that Hank and Hal Archer are asking questions about you and what you're doing."

"How should that bother Hank or Hal?" I responded, puzzled.

"Look Mister P, Shiloh's a small town. Nearly everyone knows you're now writing about Jessie Masterson for the paper, but the word's spreading that you're also asking about what happened to John Priestly."

"That's all true, but why should I worry? I'd like to talk to Hank and Hal anyway."

Jim stared at me and emphasized, "Look, you don't understand. Hank can stir up plenty of trouble. And don't be fooled by Hal's laid-back manner, his first allegiance is to his family."

Jay added, "All we're sayin' is be careful. We don't think they'd do anything stupid, but we've had a couple of, let's say, heated run-ins with Hank since that hotheaded rat accused Coach Priestly of stealing." Jay's face reddened, and his stare hardened.

Outwardly I grinned, but inwardly my gut wrenched. "Look, guys, thanks. I'll be careful. Besides, I believe I know four pretty capable sentinels who'll keep an eye out for me." My half-hearted chuckle got a similar response from both of them.

Jim and Jay slipped past Liddy and found room next to their dad while I stood next to Liddy with a sheepish grin. She grabbed my arm and stopped singing long enough to whisper, "What took you so long?"

"Sorry, they just wanted to tell me something about Hank and Hal. Nothing to worry about." I turned my head and started singing along to "How Great Thou Art." Liddy kept peering at me as we sang but said nothing more.

Before sitting back down, Liddy pointed to Harold and Phillip. During the greeting time, we made our way to where Harold greeted others around him. When he recognized us, his jovial voice escalated. "Miss Liddy. Theo. Good to see you this evening. I trust you'll have no problem with Megan's instructions tomorrow."

"Thank you. They appear crystal clear. Where's Hank and Hal?"

"They're not as enthusiastic about attending church as I wish they'd be. They decided cleaning guns had priority." Harold tried to smile but grumbled under his breath. Phillip winced and offered a slight shrug as he glanced at Liddy and me.

Liddy offered a lighthearted response. "Oh Harold, I'm sure we'll enjoy the afternoon together. The boys just might straggle back before our visit's over."

"Possibly. Anyhow, I'm looking forward to sharing tomorrow with y'all."

Arnie opened his message reciting from Psalms. "O, God... I have seen you in the sanctuary, and there I saw your power and glory because your love is better than life."

Arnie continued his message, but I turned a deaf ear when an "aha" revelation struck me. The young people of Shiloh deserved their Sanctuary resurrected. What a sad testimony if Jessie's and John's efforts remained sealed in the past. I scribbled "Sanctuary" on my bulletin, circled the word, and tucked it into my Bible.

I surveyed the sanctuary and noticed the lack of young people actually in the service. It reminded me of what I had heard; how Jessie and John made it their message to the youth that attending Sanctuary did not replace church, but the students in Shiloh lost the encouragement and example of Jessie or John, and no one picked up the mantle.

Before Arnie closed in prayer, he asked, "Mindful that our heart is our sanctuary, how long has it been since the Lord made his presence known to you in your sanctuary?"

During the prayer, my heart, soul, and mind struggled with my thoughts about Shiloh's Sanctuary, but then I heard Liddy's prayerful whisper, "Thank you, Lord."

Harold and Phillip walked by as we exited into the foyer. "Harold, see you tomorrow." To Phillip, I added, "Good luck tomorrow. Hope you bag a turkey."

Phillip returned an awkward smile as Harold put his arm on his shoulder. "Yeah sport, you'll bag a big ol' bird. Thankfully for us, Maddie's already bagged our bird, stuffed it and it's headed for the oven." They both waved and disappeared out the front of the church.

At the bottom of the steps, Liddy clutched my arm, and we paused to admire Jessie's bronze statue across the street before we started to walk home.

I asked, "Did anyone ask you about your little shopping excursion into Alexandria?"

Liddy giggled. "We're already discussing a ladies day out to do some more shopping next week." Her stride lengthened, and I felt a slight tug on my hand. "When do you want to visit Zeb's store? We should think about getting a tree anyway."

Liddy then wrapped her arm around my waist and said, "I'm not sure why I need to say this, but I'm glad to be sharing Thanksgiving with Harold. Somehow I think he needs us there too."

CHAPTER TWENTY

TIME CREPT. MINUTES BECAME HOURS. Every attempt to capture any semblance of actual sleep proved futile. Capitulation arrived shortly after four when I poured a cup of coffee and sat down in the living room.

The bulletin from last evening's service bookmarked the passage Arnie referenced in his message, but my Bible soon rested open on my lap. I massaged my eyes and petitioned, "Okay Lord, what're you trying to share with me?"

When I read one more time, "I have seen you in your sanctuary..." my thoughts went into overdrive. I lowered my Bible again, laid my glasses on top, and stared at the colorless shadows beyond the window.

Stumped, I placed my glasses back on my nose and shut my Bible. As the pages flopped together, the bulletin floated onto my lap. I slipped it inside the front cover just as the sound of a stifled yawn drew my attention.

Rubbing her eyes, Liddy mumbled, "How long have you been up?"

I got up from my recliner and pointed to the kitchen table. "Sit down, and I'll pour you some coffee. Did I wake you?"

Liddy propped her chin on the palms of her hands. "Nooo... I rolled over to cuddle but found only your pillow. Anything wrong?"

I placed a cup of coffee in front of her, topped off my own and then sat across from her.

"No, nothing's wrong. I couldn't get rid of a dream that haunted me through the night, so I got up and read a bit. I hoped I might at least understand why I couldn't dismiss it and fall back to sleep."

Still groggy, she wrinkled her nose. "Hun, you're just getting too stressed over this Jessie Masterson and John Priestly project of yours."

"Just hold one sec. Let me show you something." I fetched my Bible, opened it and pulled out the bulletin again to bookmark the passage, but my circled reminder, "Sanctuary," caught my eye.

Liddy raised her head off her palm. "What's the matter?"

"Hmm… you're probably right. It's just my imagination working overtime, I reckon."

My lopsided grin lingered as I recalled why I wrote the reminder. "How would you feel 'bout you and I looking into helping to restart Sanctuary?"

She pulled the bulletin from my grasp and carefully inspected it, and then inquired, "Do ya think Pete and the others would be interested? I mean, we literally couldn't restart it on our own."

"Of course not. I didn't mean we'd lead it but offer support from behind the scenes. I bet Mary, Jeannie, and likely Phillip would be interested in the idea."

Liddy fiddled with her cup in one hand, holding the bulletin in the other. "It actually could be a great idea. It'd serve as a remarkable legacy to Jessie. Not to mention, we could do it together." Liddy grabbed my hands, kissed them, and looked back up with a confident smile. "Want some breakfast?"

"Yeah, but only toast for me. We've got Thanksgiving dinner at Harold's to look forward to today."

———

We left for Harold's around one thirty. As we passed Adams Feed and Hardware, Liddy said, "Let's not forget, we need to stop there. How about Saturday?"

"Absolutely. We're going to need a bunch of new Christmas decorations this year anyway."

Liddy craned her neck as we passed. "Hey! There's the fresh load of Christmas trees still on the trailer too. Saturday… It's a date."

We followed Megan's easy-to-read directions and turned onto River Road as we left town. A few minutes later we pulled in front of an impressive gated entrance.

"Well, I guess we're here."

I lowered my window and pushed the red call button on the speaker. A polite voice promptly responded, "One moment please."

The black wrought iron gates crept open seconds later.

The oak-lined drive wound back and around to Harold's two-story estate home complete with an oversized detached three-car garage. Harold's secretary waited on the front steps as we exited our vehicle. She waved and greeted us with a warm smile.

Liddy and I walked hand-in-hand to the grand front entrance. "Megan… what a surprise," I said with a slightly puzzled look.

Megan smiled and said, "Mister Phillips, good to see you again. This must be Missus Phillips."

I glanced at Liddy's surprised expression. "Liddy, this is Megan from Harold's office. She's the young lady who dropped off the directions that guided us here so precisely."

Liddy offered her hand. "Pleasure to meet you, Megan. Your directions were most helpful. Thank you. Are you joining us today?"

Megan giggled beneath her hand, masking a coy smile. "Why yes ma'am. I live here." She received Liddy's hand and then declared matter-of-factly, "Harold's my father-in-law."

"Which Archer are you married to, if I may ask," I said.

"Hank's my husband. I believe you've met him."

"Why yes. In fact, we've met all of Harold's sons and can tell he's quite proud of them all."

We removed our coats in the foyer and admired the double stairwell leading upstairs from opposite sides of the expansive front entry. A wide hallway led into a massive great room with seating on each side of a floor to ceiling, stone open-hearth fireplace. Two sets of patio doors on either side provided access to the veranda. Panoramic window panes offered an unobstructed, breathtaking view of the manicured fenced yard, rolling hills, and distant meadows.

Megan broke the silence. "Beautiful, isn't it? I just can't get enough of it either."

Liddy recovered from her open-mouth stare. "Is all this part of your family's property? It's absolutely breathtaking and beautiful, as is this house as well."

Megan smiled with a rehearsed nod and pointed to two imposing tan suede leather sofas. "Please join me. Harold's upstairs and will join us shortly. He asked me to keep you company."

Liddy, a pro at small talk, put on her most polite, inquisitive smile. "Megan, excuse me, but I was just wondering if you and Hank have any children."

Megan's smile tensed. "No, ma'am. Not yet, but Hank and I expect to surprise Harold soon. We just celebrated our fourth anniversary, and hope to be in our own house that'll include a nursery by the time we celebrate our next anniversary."

I said, "I bet Harold will make a proud grandpa. There's nothing like it."

Megan wrung her folded hands, though her posture and tone appeared relaxed.

Liddy rescued Megan and asked about the new house.

Megan's tentativeness eased as she spoke. "Hank and I plan to build on the property Harold set aside as our wedding gift." She pointed out the picture window behind her. "You can't see it well from here, but it's just beyond those trees. It's a beautiful piece of property with a view of Shiloh Creek, ideally suited to raise a family."

I smiled and nodded.

"Mister Phillips, how many children do you have?"

"Please, Theo and Liddy."

"Why thank you, Theo." She turned to Liddy. "And, Liddy is such a pretty name. Is it short for Lydia?"

Liddy blushed as she nodded. "Yes, it is."

Megan said, "Lydia's one of my favorite names. In the Bible, Lydia was a strong and confident business women who helped launch a church."

Liddy's reddened cheeks grew as she smiled and sat an inch taller in her seat. She knew the story of Lydia from Philippi well and enjoyed the image of her namesake.

Liddy held up two fingers and said, "We have two wonderful grown sons, and they'll be visiting Shiloh with their families for Christmas."

"That's wonderful. Bet you're anxious and counting the days." Megan sighed. "As for me, I was born and raised right here in good ol' Shiloh. My mom and dad still live just outside of town. And since I don't have any brothers or sisters, mom regularly harps about any news regarding the prospect of their first grandchild."

Uncomfortable, awkward silence followed before I changed the subject. "I'm not sure if Harold said anything, but did you know I'm working on a story about Jessie Masterson? Since you were raised here, I'd love to talk about your experiences and memories related to Coach Masterson. I imagine he was at Shiloh High when you went there."

Megan beamed with the mention of Jessie, but an exuberant laugh interrupted our conversation.

Harold looked down from the balcony rail. "Theo! Liddy! I see you're enjoying the company of my charming and talented daughter-in-law."

Liddy and I both rose to our feet as he approached. He shook my hand and gave Liddy a generous smile.

CHAPTER TWENTY-ONE

"Mista' Harold, you and your guests, 'bout ready?" said Harold's matronly gray-haired African-American housekeeper. She stood patiently at the doorway leading onto the veranda wearing a traditional white broad collared maid's uniform with a starched apron.

"Maddie, if you're about ready out there, I reckon we're ready."

With a little huff, Maddie said, "Come on then. I've been waitin' on you folks, Master Harold, and I'm sure these nice folks has been waitin' on you." She opened the door and pointed to a table all set for us.

Harold sat at the head of the table, and we sat across from Megan. A plump, partially-carved roasted turkey accompanied by butter beans, green beans, collards, mashed potatoes, a sweet potato casserole, dressing and both pumpkin and pecan pies covered the other end of the table.

Harold pulled a bottle of Chenin Blanc off the side cart behind him and popped the cork. He rotated the label for us to see.

I smiled. "Yes, looks like a nice wine choice, thank you, Harold," and then he filled four crystal glasses and passed them to each of us.

I took a sip pretending to know a little about savoring wines. I offered a modest grin of approval. Liddy took a smaller sip and smiled politely towards our host before she placed the wine glass down and nonchalantly reached for her glass of tea.

"I'm glad y'all approve. Thought it'd be an appropriate complement to Maddie's honey-basted turkey." Harold extended his arms wide, drawing attention to Maddie as she prepared a plate for each of us.

As I waited for my plate to arrive, I said, "Harold, this is a nice treat, and the Lord certainly gave us a beautiful day to eat outside like this." I then pointed to his immaculate lawn and gardens. "How do you find time to take care of all this? I'm jealous."

Harold's laughter filled the veranda. "I'm far too busy. We've got a regular crew that maintains the grounds around here for us. But Theo, it's me who's jealous. You've done wonders with the old Priestly home. It's obvious, y'all don't mind getting your hands dirty."

Maddie laid a full plate in front of me, careful not to disturb the pan gravy that floated atop the cornbread dressing and mashed potatoes. "I hope you ladies and gentlemens are hungree." She pointed at the far end of the table. "There's plenty more but leave room for some pie, and I'll be right back if ya needs me."

Harold applauded. "Maddie, mm, mm…you've outdone yourself, once again. Thank you."

Liddy said, "Yes. Thank you, Miss Maddie." Maddie's round cheeks blushed as she stepped away.

Throughout the meal, Harold directed the conversation and offered an endless history of the house and the property that had been passed down to him. He boasted about his family's long history in Shiloh that began not long after the Civil War ended.

He looked at Megan with a twinkle in his eye. "And it looks like Hank and Megan will be the first of my sons to build their own home. I've little doubt that Megan's ready to move into her own house after putting up with four men coming and going all the time."

Megan's cheeks turned pink, but she continued to focus on the food in front of her.

After we finished eating, Maddie reappeared over each of our shoulders and set a white coffee carafe on the table. "Missus Phillips, would you like pum'kin or pee-kan or maybe a little of each with your coffee?"

Maddie served each of us with the same soft voice question. She wasted no time or motion as she efficiently tended to each of us. She then loaded each of our dirty plates along with the leftovers onto her wooden serving cart and rolled it away.

Between nibbles, Megan shared stories about serving as Harold's administrative assistant. She left little doubt that she enjoyed the status of the position, and Harold glowed as Megan told stories about him.

At a point during the playful and respectful roasting from Megan, Harold pushed his chair out from the end of the table, grabbed his empty dessert plate in one hand and leaned toward me. "Theo, now you'll see why I struggle with my weight." A jolly laugh followed him to the other end of the table.

Megan's stories continued as her eyes appeared to scold Harold.

"Ah come on Megan, it's Thanksgiving. You know Maddie always serves me just a tiny piece anyway," Harold said before he gobbled down a loaded forkful of pecan pie and tapped his belly. "Um, good. Don't you agree, Theo?"

I looked at Liddy, leaned back in my chair and tapped my stomach. "As for me, if I ate another bite, I'd bust, not to mention Liddy will make me walk home."

After our dessert plates disappeared, Harold stood. "Megan, why don't you offer Liddy a tour of the house and the grounds while Theo and me take a drive around the property."

Liddy smiled at Megan and nodded, then I looked at Harold and said, "Sounds great to me."

Before Harold and I walked away, he said to Megan, "We'll probably be a couple of hours. I've got my phone if you need to reach me." Then he looked at me. "We'll go in my truck if that's okay with you?"

"Sure," I said as I looked over my shoulder and saw Liddy and Megan disappear into the house. "Harold, you've got a great daughter-in-law."

A slight grin appeared on Harold's face. "If only you knew how exceptional she truly is. That boy of mine doesn't deserve her. There're times I wonder why she puts up with him. I hope they'll settle down soon because I just couldn't do what I do without her."

Harold pushed his truck's key fob as we approached the garage, and his black dually's diesel engine roared to life. "Door's unlocked.

Hop in. You can just toss my satchel in the back somewhere." Country music already filled the cab but thankfully more appealing to my ears than Hank's taste.

I adjusted my seat and buckled up. "Harold, this is nice. I'm impressed." I ran my hand over the personalized logo burnt into the chaparral leather that covered the center console.

"I put a lot of time in my truck. Being mayor and all the other stuff I'm involved with around town; I figured long ago that I might as well enjoy my ride, don't you agree?" He maneuvered the huge dually onto the gravel road and drove us to what he referred to as the Pine Groves. When we arrived, we stretched our legs along the path that wound through the property.

Harold boasted about the work involved in the maintenance of a profitable harvest of timber. I admired the patience and persistence required to cultivate and harvest pine trees.

"Harold, clearly your family's been a big part of this community, and you've well-established deep roots on this property and in town."

"That's true. The family still owns 500 acres, but going way back, we once owned two thousand of the most fertile acres that ever produced cotton and peanuts in these parts. There's been an Archer on this land since General Sherman served as military governor of Georgia. Sadly, though, my great, great grandfather sold much of the property during some tough times that ravaged the plantation owners around here about 100 years ago. Although he did hold onto the most fertile acreage."

"How did your family end up in Shiloh? It's been my impression that your family's always been here."

Harold hesitated before continuing in a loud whisper. "Shh... we've Yankee roots. My family migrated from Pennsylvania. The story goes, not long after the war ended, my great, great, great grandfather heard about the abundance of fertile plantation land being auctioned off for taxes, so he sold his farm near Gettysburg, packed up and came here."

The word "carpetbagger" crept into my mind, but I kept that thought to myself. "I imagine he bought the land for pennies on the dollar. Although much of the original land got sold off, I'm sure you're still proud to one day pass your family's land and heritage on to your sons."

Harold smiled and nodded.

"By the way, how long have you been the mayor of Shiloh?"

Harold stopped, inhaled deeply and then slowly exhaled. "Lemme think a minute… twenty-five, no, twenty-six years. Umm, seems like a lifetime, but I've enjoyed the satisfaction I've gotten from being the mayor." He started walking again.

"Twenty-six years is certainly a long time. Have you considered a future in politics outside of Shiloh?" My hands entered my pockets as our pace slowed.

"Do you mean like at the state level?" The wrinkles on his forehead arched as he pondered the inquiry. "Actually, I'm mulling over running for the State Senate, but I'm not sure what to do yet. I still have until after the first of the year to declare my candidacy, but I'd appreciate it if you'd keep that quiet for the time being."

"No problem Harold, but you sound like you have some reservations?" I mirrored his tone of voice and stride.

Harold stopped and hesitated again as if wanting to validate my sincerity. I believed he wanted to confide in me but erred on the side of caution.

"Theo, you should well know how rough the media can be on politicians."

"Yeah," I muttered almost inaudibly but nodded as well.

"But what you may not know is that the picture they depict is far tamer than what lurks behind closed doors."

"I've never been behind the closed doors of political life, but I imagine it can be rough."

His smile vanished, and his jaw tightened. "Theo, even right here in little ol' Shiloh, politics has its challenges. All the appropriations and grants Shiloh depends upon don't grow on trees. In the political arena, everything's earned quid pro quo. Between you and me, when you climb the political ladder, you're either a prostitute or a pimp exchanging and earning favors so you can stay in office."

I looked up with a naïve stare. "That certainly paints a nasty picture. So what you're saying is that successful, powerful politicians know how to be a prostitute, a pimp or become merely a puppet?"

"Yep. You've got a clear picture." After a careful look, he continued. "I had the chance to run for the State Senate three years ago, but it didn't work out."

We both stood kicking dirt while our hands remained tucked in our pockets.

"What happened?" I said. "Was it the timing? Did the publicity surrounding the Courthouse fire affect your decision?"

Harold's hard persona softened and became more transparent.

"Without a doubt, the fire brought a lot of publicity to the town, but it arrived in the form of favorable sympathy and support. What hurts the most was the publicity surrounding John Priestly's arrest and conviction. It put my electability in doubt with my political buddies in Atlanta. They suggested I hold off running for the Senate until things settled down in Shiloh."

My stare went through Harold as I wrestled with how John Priestly's case could have affected Harold's opportunity to run for State Senate. I decided to continue with great caution.

"I'm sorry. What could you've done differently?"

Harold again deliberated before he responded. "I have no idea, but looking back, I probably hurt myself by being so visible and outspoken against John. The media might've been less voracious when they covered the story. Having my name and picture in the papers, especially the *Atlanta Constitution,* with all the controversy surrounding the case certainly hurt my electability. Let's face it, and I'm sure you know by now, John Priestly was a popular figure throughout the entire county. A lot of good folks in Shiloh were ready to string me up over what happened. Know what I mean?" Harold turned and squared up to the path facing back to the truck. "Come on. Let's head back."

"I guess if you weren't highly popular at home, getting elected to the State Senate was out of the question. How'd that make you feel?"

"Pretty disappointed, but I, fortunately, managed to eke out another term as mayor. Maybe enough water has passed under the bridge, and that's why I'm considering the State Senate again."

Harold's demeanor reverted to his light-hearted self. "Can I count on your and Liddy's votes?"

"Well, I can only guarantee my vote."

"That's a start. I'll hold you to it." We laughed as our pace picked up on our return to the truck.

On the drive back to the house, Harold bragged about how he pulled political strings in Atlanta to finance the work that took place on the school facilities. He said the rising reputation of Shiloh in sports and academics helped him leverage support in both Alexandria and Atlanta.

"I know I can get elected if I can get the town's name in front of the right people as I did before to gain their support." Harold stared ahead like someone plotting his next battle strategy.

After we parked and walked toward the house, I asked, "By the way, how long has Maddie worked for you? She seems nice enough, and she's an outstanding cook."

"Maddie? She's been a part of my family since before I got married. But I'll tell ya' something about ol' Maddie... After my wife dumped us when Hank and Hal were hellions, and Phillip still needed diapers, Maddie stepped up and mothered them boys. She's a charmer when she wants to be and sociable enough most of the time, but the boys'll tell you how she handles them whenever they sass her. Wooie! Hank and Hal still to this day know when to stop fooling around when Maddie says, 'enuf is enuf!'"

Maddie appeared at the front door and waggled her finger. "Miss Megan and Miss Liddy are on the porch waiting on y'all. They's been gigglin' and carryin' on like two school gals."

———

After I pulled onto River Road, headed back into town, I asked Liddy,

"Did you enjoy your girl talk with Megan? Maddie said y'all got along pretty well."

Liddy grinned. "She's a sweet girl, but I sense she's not happy in her marriage."

"I sensed Megan was hurting when we talked earlier. I'm glad you enjoyed the time with her."

"I invited her to visit anytime she wants. I got the impression she doesn't have anyone outside of Maddie she can talk to. She admitted she isn't very close to her parents but changed the subject when I asked why."

"I'd like to talk more to Megan if I get the chance. In the meantime, I bet Mary and maybe Jeannie know Megan from their school days together."

When I shared a little about the Archer family's history in Shiloh, Liddy voiced what I couldn't. "Harold's ancestors were nothing but low-down, dirty carpetbaggers?!" Liddy's head swayed back and forth in disbelief as we pulled back into town.

CHAPTER TWENTY-TWO

TIMMY RODE BY AND WAVED as he tossed the morning paper onto the foot of the porch steps. I acknowledged him from my living room window but let the paper lay where it landed. The relationships we had formed since our move to Shiloh had captured my attention, which I concluded, none developed happenstance.

"Good morning," Liddy said as she stepped into the kitchen. "Did you get any coffee yet?"

"No, not yet. Why don't you grab both of us a cup and come sit out here with me?"

With today's important visit on tap, I hoped Liddy could help me process what Harold shared yesterday and possibly add more from her one-on-one time with Megan.

"Here you go dear." Liddy handed me a cup and then sat across from me, feet perched on her ottoman. She clutched her cup with both hands and stared out the window.

The emerald flecks in her sunlit eyes mesmerized me until she turned and pointed. "Hey, the paper's still out front. Whatever you're mulling over this morning must be important."

"We both know that Jessie's death and the destruction of the old Courthouse certainly disturbed Shiloh's tranquility, but Shiloh's problems began well before the fire, and even John's incarceration."

She lowered her half-empty cup and held onto a wide-eyed look. "Okay, so Jessie's death led you to John Priestly's scandal, which led you to ask more about the Archer family's prior relationship with John and Jessie. And..." She stopped, mouth wide-open, waiting for me to continue.

"Well, everyone has tried to comprehend what happened rather than why, and I certainly don't know the connecting 'whys' yet, but I'm convinced that once I discover the motive behind one, I'll likely discover what instigated the other."

"What do you mean?"

"Well, I'm hoping my visit with John Priestly this afternoon will help figure that out."

She cocked her head. "I thought John's not talking about why he pled guilty."

I slowly exhaled, and then said, "I believe if John sheds some light on what happened to Jessie, it might offer a clue as to why he's so reluctant to talk about his circumstances. They're linked. I just know it."

As if she could read my thoughts, Liddy asked, "You believe Harold's implicated?"

"I don't honestly know." Liddy's question confirmed what already cluttered my thoughts.

Liddy clung to her concerned look, so I added, "What I do know, John and the Archers had a history before his arrest. John had confronted Hank about Archer Construction's shoddy work and costly overruns on the school restoration project awarded to them four years ago."

Liddy's jaw dropped. "Theo, those are serious accusations. What happened?" She pulled her knees tighter to her chest and rubbed her chin against her kneecaps.

"Honestly, I'm still confused on the extent of the accusations, but Archer Construction must've feared whatever John knew. The City Council released a statement not long after John went public. They announced all parties reached an amenable agreement for the completion of the school project. Miraculously, the City Council reported no wrongdoing. Instead, they emphasized that Archer Construction agreed to repair and resurface the stadium's parking lot at no additional cost to the city. Although they never mentioned Harold by name, the City Council announced how pleased they were by Archer Construction's good faith gestures to soothe any unresolved concerns and expected completion in time for the new school year."

"How did John take the news?"

"I'm not sure, but there's a photo that accompanied the article with Hank shaking hands with John in front of the old stadium just before they tore it down."

Liddy replied, "John might'a felt vindicated, but I wonder how that sat with the Archers. By the way, did you talk to Harold about any of this yesterday?"

"Heck no! It wasn't the right time for that discussion."

"I agree. Probably wouldn't have been good timing. He was such an amiable host yesterday wasn't he?"

"Yes, he was. Besides, what he told me about John's arrest indicated he wasn't behind the accusations brought against John. He did admit he may have overreacted after the fact, but said nothing to indicate he held a grudge against John leading up to that point."

Liddy's distant misty-eyed stare and long face caused me to pause and ask, "What's the matter?"

"It just dawned on me that John's sitting in a prison cell, while we're sitting in his former living room talking about what happened to him." She turned her head. "His mom made him meals in that kitchen, but he doesn't have her anymore either. Theo, please let me help you. We have a vested interest in making this right."

I looked intently into her teary eyes. "You've already helped more than you might realize. We'll figure this out together, okay? I promise we'll talk more tonight after I get back. In the meantime, why don't you look into visiting with Marie? Perhaps she'll share something with you that'll help. How's that sound?"

Liddy grabbed a tissue, blew her nose and nodded. "I think talking with Marie, mother-to-mother, is a good idea. Come to think of it, I bet she'll also be interested in the restarting of Sanctuary. What do you think?"

I clutched her soft hands and smiled. "Great idea. We can't bring Jessie back, but for Marie's sake his legacy certainly deserves more than a bronze statue."

Liddy swung her legs off the ottoman and jumped to her feet. "We've both got things to do. I'll fix breakfast. You get the paper."

I climbed from my recliner and headed for the front door. Liddy's countenance soon reflected an optimistic smile with silly giggles when she considered asking Marie to join her and Judy on their planned shopping trip next week.

———

Shortly after eleven, Liddy dropped me off at the Sentinel. I wanted to check with Larry for any additional information before I headed over to Joe's office. I hoped the meeting with John would help me to earn his trust. Any additional tidbits I could learn from Larry might prove helpful and I certainly didn't want to waste the extended windshield time with Joe either.

No one occupied their desks, so I tapped the bell on the counter. Larry appeared from his office. "Come on back."

"Good morning. How's my part-time boss and full-time friend?" I chuckled and offered a smart salute, which earned one in return.

"I thought you were headed to see John today?"

"I am. We leave at noon." I sat in the familiar chair in front of Larry's desk. "Thought I'd check in on you and fill you in on our visit with Harold yesterday."

"That's right. How'd that go?" Larry raised his brows in anticipation.

We laughed about how Liddy and I came to realize Megan's in-law status with Harold. Larry got an extra chuckle when I told him about how Harold sparred with Maddie a bit and otherwise turned out to be a gracious host. Then I brought up how John Priestly's incident caused Harold some political fallout and ruined his run for State Senate at that time.

Larry smirked, which led me to believe that Larry already knew something about Harold's political plans, but I promised Harold that I would not tell anyone about his renewed interest in running for the State Senate.

Larry leaned back in his chair, and admitted, "Interesting. My capital contacts tell me Harold's on the radar as a candidate again."

Straight-faced, I said, "Seems like we'll know for sure after the first of the year, don't you think?"

"I expect so." Larry leaned forward and gloated. "But wait until I tell you what I found out."

I scooted closer to the edge of his desk.

Larry gave a smug grin. "I got wind of discussions regarding a parole hearing for John Priestly. I'm curious if Joe knows anything about it."

My jaw dropped. "Larry, any reason to think Harold knows about it?"

"I can't say. It'll be interesting to see if he'll use as much influence to get John out of prison as he used to get him in. Harold's political clout could be decisive in John's parole decision, but then again he might like to drag out any parole decision until after the election if he's running next fall."

I relaxed back into my chair and took a moment to clear my thoughts. "Larry, I'm on board with you about the likelihood John was framed. I also believe he may have been a victim of a vendetta by the Archers."

Larry leaned toward me. "Welcome aboard the conspiracy theory wagon. I'm glad to know I'm not driving it solo."

My heart beat faster. "What more did you find out?"

Larry's smile widened. "Catch this… the contract awarded to Archer Construction came as a result of them being a local contractor which afforded them that ten percent advantage in the bid process."

"Yeah. We already knew that."

"Right, but now you might want to get your notepad out. Archer Construction won the bid with a two percent advantage to spare." Larry looked at my expression to see that I followed what he was telling me.

"Are you telling me they were eight percent above the lowest bidder?"

"Exactly. Here's the kicker. After the smoke cleared and the tempers of the other contractors had long dissipated, Archer Construction banked an additional $2,500,000 for approval of discretionary add-ons for the project."

I felt the wrinkles on my forehead burrow deeper. "Larry, what was the original contract value?"

Larry held a Cheshire Cat grin. "$9,750,000... $750,000 above the lowest bidder." He slouched into his executive chair and stretched out his hands as if he just gave me a big box with a bow on it.

"That's a three-quarter of a million dollar advantage by my calculations."

"I'll save you some calculating. Archer Construction received a total of $12,250,000 for the contract after the add-ons. Virtually all of the money came from federal grants earmarked for school construction projects and matching state grants, thanks, I'm sure, to Harold's political wrangling. Swallow that whole if you can." Larry looked like a prosecuting attorney who just completed a signed, sealed, and delivered closing statement before a jury.

My fingers played with the numbers, and it dawned on me that amidst the political mumbo jumbo, Archer Construction ultimately received over three million dollars more than what the lowest bidder valued the contract to be worth. This fact gave me three million additional reasons to dig deeper into what happened to John Priestly. But I wondered what John knew for sure and how that played into him being set up.

Larry and I discussed the possible implications at work in what we now knew. To start, we decided to check into the City Hall project. With the additional information about the school contract payouts, Larry and I decided getting the files on that project might prove equally revealing.

Larry's news about a possible parole hearing pending made my trip with Joe to see John more pressing. We joked briefly about our wives' upcoming shopping trip as he walked me to the door. Mid-handshake, Larry's demeanor changed.

"Does Liddy know what's going on? I'm going to fill Martha in this weekend."

"Yes. Liddy's on board, even wants to help."

"Good. Now pay attention. This could become a scandal that gains statewide attention. We need to be sure of our facts before going public. This could be the biggest story the *Sentinel*'s covered since carpet-baggers under the guise of Sherman's orders sold off a good portion of the land illegally in Adams County."

———

Nick sat in Susanna's seat when I arrived at Joe's office. "Hey, Theo. Did you have a pleasant Thanksgiving?"

After erasing my blank stare, I said matter-of-factly, "Yes, we sure did. Liddy and I ate dinner with Harold Archer and his daughter-in-law Megan. His boys were off hunting turkeys while we ate ours. Where's Joe?"

"He's back in his office on the phone," Nick said with his feet propped on top of the desk. "I drove back with Joe this morning so Missy and the girls could stay with Momma a couple of extra days. I didn't mind, though. I had enough family if you know what I mean."

"I might if I didn't miss my sons and grandkids so much."

"Well, maybe today'll help. You ready to meet John?"

"Sure am. I've heard and talked so much about him I feel like I know him personally already. Liddy and I even talked this morning about how odd it is that we live in the house where his mother cooked meals for him."

Nick picked his fingernails with a letter opener. "You do know John holds the key to his prison cell, right? He's had a case of lockjaw whenever anyone tries to talk about what happened to him."

Nick paused and focused on his manicure before he continued in frustration. "Theo, I hope you have more success than Joe or I have had in talking some sense into John. He can be one to die on a hill of righteousness rather than give any ground."

The door of Joe's office swung open, "Theo! You ready?"

CHAPTER TWENTY-THREE

WITH HIS COAT AND LEATHER SATCHEL in hand, Joe locked his office and caught up with us at Susanna's desk.

"Glad you could join us, Joe," I said. "I've got some great news. There's a parole hearing being scheduled for John." I glanced at Joe and then Nick. Both sported smug, know-it-already grins.

Joe shook his head side to side and sighed. "Larry never ceases to amaze me. I just hung up the phone with Cal Barnard, my contact on the State Board of Pardons and Parole, who just now told me that John Priestly's case received a green light Wednesday for an expedited decision. Cal also indicated he was surprised by all the strings being pulled from Atlanta to get this done before Christmas."

Nick said, "Man, I wish I could come with you guys. I'd love to see John's face when he hears this news." Nick left Susanna's chair and slapped Joe and me on our shoulders. "You two need to get a move on. You've got a long drive ahead of you."

Between bites of sandwiches, Joe shared more about what to expect in the next few days. He told me the district attorney's office had signed off on John's early release motion, and William Paraman, the assistant district attorney handling the case had called and said John was eligible for a work release provision, which would expedite his release. Judge Fitzgerald signed off on the motion Wednesday morning, and the final decision now rested with the parole board next week in Atlanta.

I tried to absorb the intricate details of the parole process and remembered from my conversation with Harold that there had been political forces at work that landed John in jail.

"I'm curious," I said. "It sure sounds like there are some external influences at work to prod the process along."

"You know, Theo, the same thoughts ran through my mind. It doesn't hurt that John's been a model prisoner, and the warden wrote a letter of recommendation that found its way onto the governor's desk."

A large green and white road sign identified the Clearwater State Prison entrance. I commented about the neatness of the grounds and read every sign aloud as we walked side-by-side toward the main administrative entrance. How much of my nervous chatter Joe listened to was unclear. He seemed focused on the concrete sidewalk in front of him until we reached the door.

"Theo, excuse me for interrupting, but I was just contemplating Harold's response when he hears about John."

Joe winked and pulled the door open. We showed our identification, and a guard escorted us along the walkway between the buildings. Razor wire topped chain link fencing separated us from inmates wearing gray D.O.C. stenciled uniforms in the exercise yard. Some milled around while others played basketball or curled barbells as guards watched.

Joe whispered, "And this is a medium security prison farm."

We entered an empty cafeteria, evidence of a lawyer's advantage over other visitors. Our escort directed us through another door into a room for lawyers and clients to talk privately. Wire reinforced glass panels across the front wall of the room provided the guards with visual monitoring of the otherwise private room.

We waited beside an institutional gray metal table with four matching chairs. Joe whispered, "Look, you'll get the chance to talk to John in a minute, but let me introduce you and give him the news about the parole board meeting first."

The buzz of a security door announced the return of the guard escorting a tall, muscular young man with long, finger-swept dark hair and a scraggly beard.

I whispered a prayer. "Lord, may all we say, think, and do be according to your will. Please stir John's heart so that the truth will come out. Amen."

Joe patted my back and stepped forward to greet John. My heart thumped against my chest while I watched Jessie's cousin enter the room.

The guard grabbed the door and said, "Mister Arians, you have ninety minutes." He pointed to the red intercom button by the door. "If you need anything, I'll be over there." He pointed to a glass-enclosed room at the end of the hallway. Joe dismissed the guard with a polite smile and a nod that reflected his familiarity with the routine.

Joe guided John to the table with one arm draped across his broad shoulders. "John, this is Mister Theo Phillips. He and his lovely wife now live in your mom's home and have become a welcomed addition to Shiloh recently."

John gradually turned his head until we stared at each other across the table.

I stretched my hand out and stammered, "John, it's a real pleasure to meet you finally. My wife and I've heard so much about you."

John's unshaven face and shaggy hair hid his chiseled features. His gray, peppered temples and beard made him look much older than the pictures I found of him.

John's first words were deliberate but soft. "I'm sorry Mister Phillips. I don't get many opportunities to greet new people in this place." His gritty stare gave way to a slight grin just before he coughed to clear his throat and continue.

"Joe's told me a little about you. Thanks for coming today." A playful smirk appeared as he glanced towards Joe. "I just feel sorry for you... I know all too well how dry and humorless Joe can sometimes be."

Joe sneered. "Hah, hah. Come on. Let's sit down."

John and I laughed at Joe's expense.

A twisted smile softened Joe's sneer. "Well, I'll try my best not to be so dry and humorless today. Why don't I start out by sharing some good news?" Joe reached across the table and rested his hand on top of John's. "The parole board's holding a hearing next week to get you released before Christmas."

John's tired eyes flew open, and his jaw dropped. "You sure? Is this for real?" He pulled his hand out from under Joe's and wiped his eyes with his gray uniform sleeve.

Joe sat back. "Yep, it's true. Even Judge Fitzgerald agreed to this as did the DA's office. Once I know exactly when you'll be released, I'll personally bring you home."

Joe and I watched as many of John's deep-set wrinkles disappeared as a wide grin pushed out the sides of his scraggly beard. He then stood, leaned across the table and ruffled Joe's meticulous hair.

John looked at me and laughed. "I guess I should take back what I said about this old buzzard being boring and dry. I love this guy! Nobody's got a better friend than I have in Joe."

Joe swept his fingers through his hair. "All right, all right. We can swap compliments after you're home, surrounded by your real friends. But first I'll arrange with old man Edwards to give you a first-rate haircut and shave."

John ran his hand through his scraggly beard and swept his long locks behind his ears. "How's Marie doing? Does she know?"

Joe laughed. "Marie's great, and I bet she'll have a welcome home shindig when you get back. Oh, and catch this, Ol' Zeb already has a job lined up for you. He didn't hesitate when he heard how that would help with the parole board's expedited work release decision while your parole paperwork gets finalized." Joe tipped his chair back on its hind legs and crossed his arms as John absorbed the news.

John's expression turned solemn as he leaned onto the table. "What about the Archers? Does Harold know?" John stared at the table and waited for Joe to answer.

"I'm not sure." Joe turned towards me. "Maybe Theo can share what he knows."

John's eyes turned and searched mine as I cleared my throat. "Well, my wife and I had Thanksgiving dinner with Harold yesterday."

John rocked his chair back onto its two rear legs, and his dark brown eyes zeroed in on mine. "Sounds like old Harold's interested in you for some reason. What have you been up to since you moved in?"

John's dark stare unsettled me. "John, I'm sure Joe told you, and it's certainly no secret now, that I'm writing about Jessie for the local paper. In snooping into Jessie's background, like any good writer, I began to realize who you were and what happened to you."

John crossed his arms and gave me a firm, cold stare. "Okay, go on."

I hesitated before I continued. "John, I got to a point, looking into what happened to Jessie, that I realized while I can't change what happened to your cousin, I might be able to help you."

"How's that Mister Phillips?"

"Like most of the folks I've talked to about you, the deeper I dig, the more I'm convinced you were either framed or made the scapegoat for the missing money. I also believe your run-in with Hank Archer and Archer Construction over the school project is likely connected."

John cocked his head. "Do the Archers know this?"

"Heavens no. Harold thinks I'm just writing about Jessie, but I suspect he's curious about why I've been asking about what happened to you as well. And before you ask, I also got wind just this weekend that Hank Archer has started asking questions about my inquiries."

John uncrossed his arms and returned all four legs to the floor. "Just be careful. The Archers don't take kindly to anyone snooping into their business. Tell me, what did ol' Harold say yesterday?"

"After dinner, we drove out to see some of his property. That's when we ended up talking about you. Harold admitted how badly he felt about the harsh sentence you received."

"Really? He said that? Were any of his sons there?"

"Only Megan joined us at dinner. His sons thought turkey hunting was preferable to eating turkey with their dad. I'm not sure how either Hank or Hal will respond, but Phillip sure will be elated about your return."

John scratched his bearded. "How's Megan?"

"Liddy and I enjoyed meeting her and she sure dotes upon her father-in-law, but we got the sense that she's lonely in that big old house."

"Glad she's okay…" He paused briefly and cleared his throat. "What do you know about what happened to me and about Jessie's death?"

I glanced at Joe, and he offered a reassuring nod. "John, let me be honest. I'm no seasoned investigative reporter, but it appears Shiloh's still unsettled over what happened to you and Jessie. That's why I'm here talking with you."

John glanced at Joe before he motioned me to continue, sat back and crossed his arms again over his uniformed chest, but with a more relaxed demeanor.

I sat back as well. "To be blunt, I believe what happened to you is also connected to whatever happened the night Jessie died, but that's where the fuzziness begins. I hoped you could help."

Joe glared at John, but John focused on me. "Like how? What do you think you know? I was here when Jessie died."

I swallowed to wet my dry throat before I continued as boldly as I could. "Please forgive me, but let's face it, you and Hank Archer didn't exactly see eye to eye during the school renovation project. Your accusations against him and his company teetered on claims of fraud and theft. That said, it's clear you knew or claimed to know enough to have caused Archer Construction and the City to renegotiate the remainder of the contract. I read about their gracious concessions that silenced the matter. Behind closed doors, though, I don't imagine the Archers were happy. Even in the short time I've lived in Shiloh, the Archers don't strike me as the type to back down easily. You must've had some significant evidence to back up your claims."

Joe leaned towards John and implored him with an intense look on his face. "John," he said. "You've kept all this wrapped up inside for a long time. I know you had your reasons not to fight the charges, but I've sat silently on the sidelines far too long. So when Theo came to me with his concerns and shared what he uncovered, I knew we needed to act. If you were framed, we could make your parole become a step closer to an exoneration. But you need to help us make it right."

John rocked back in his chair again, glanced at both of us, then stared at his prison-issued boots. He propped one leg over his knee and picked at the dry mud on his soles. He finally looked up and said, "Look, Harold Archer did what he thought was right. When the hammer of justice fell as it did, it hurt me deeply, but my decision had nothing to do with whatever motives might have been behind the charges coming against me. What I'll tell you is this: I had nothing to do with the missing money. A promise I made prevents me from saying more. Please… the truth will come out, but it just can't come from me."

Joe groaned and gritted his teeth. "John, for Pete's sake, who the hell did you promise? What did you promise? Why is this damn promise so important? John, do you want to be a convicted felon for the rest of your life? Parole will get you home, but you'll never teach or coach again. Is this person you promised worth it?"

John tightened his crossed arms and snapped back, "The person may or may not be worth it, but my word is."

I decided to take a different approach. "John, look. I get it. If you were my son, I couldn't be prouder of your stand. I've learned in the last few weeks and seen today that you firmly believe in what is right and oppose what is wrong. Since you've as much as told us that your decision is firmly rooted in this promise, can you at least answer one question? Does your promise have to do with who or why the money went missing? As Joe said, help us help you." I locked eyes with John.

"Look Joe. You've been a loyal friend, and you only want what's best for me. And Theo, I'd rather not answer that question. I've faith that my decision is the right one. I pray to God daily for peace over it. I simply can't break my promise, just as God never breaks his promises to me."

Joe kicked into lawyer mode. "John, is it at least okay with you if Theo and I keep digging? Three years in prison and now a lifetime as an ex-convict is a high price to pay. Heck, the town will embrace and defend you either way, but these same folks want the truth to help clear your name and Shiloh's past. If Theo's instincts are right, and I believe that they are, Jessie paid the ultimate price because of that almighty promise you made."

"Joe, I'll never be able to face myself if I turn on this promise. I know Jessie would've agreed, and I'll say no more about this." John looked squarely at both Joe and me and added, "However, if the truth surfaces through your investigations, I won't oppose you."

Now I understood what Joe meant about John's rock-hard stubbornness. I also realized John's unrelenting obstinance was not prideful but deeply rooted in who he was. I couldn't help but respect and admire his resolve.

For the remainder of our visit, John asked questions about the changes Liddy and I had made to his old home. I assured John our efforts maintained the original charm of the house and invited him to stop by after his release. Joe told John about this year's Christmas celebration and the tribute to Jessie during the dedication of the new City Hall. John admitted he was anxious to see the changes in town, and wanted to see Jessie's statue and visit Marie. John appeared quite ready to leave behind the dreariness and despair of prison life.

During the drive home, Joe and I again agreed there was much more remaining of John's story. We challenged each other about what we might have overlooked, and our discussion continued throughout our return to Shiloh.

CHAPTER TWENTY-FOUR

SLEEP TUGGED ON OUR EYELIDS, but the prospect of sharing the good news about John with Marie kept both of us up until well past midnight. After Liddy finally turned out the light, and her head sank into her pillow, she mumbled, "Remember, you promised to stop at Zeb's place tomorrow. We should get there early enough to pick out the best tree before his stock gets picked over. We'll visit Marie after lunch." Liddy's rhythmic breathing arrived before I could respond, and I too faded off.

Early Saturday morning, I reached across the bed but found Liddy's side empty. I listened but detected no movement in the house. A moment later, I walked into the kitchen and saw a fresh pot of coffee but no Liddy. I then heard grumbling outside. Her head bobbed up and down as she paced back and forth just beyond the porch rails.

I stepped onto the porch with a cup of coffee. "Mind if I ask what you're doin' out here on such a dreary morning?"

Liddy, looking frazzled, snarled, "What's it look like I'm doin'? I'm figurin' what additional Christmas decorations we need to buy." The hood of Liddy's gray sweatshirt failed to shelter her face and hair from the constant misty drizzle. The smudge marks on her forehead and rosy cheeks attested to her frustrated attempts to push her unruly soaked strands of hair out of her eyes.

I savored a couple more sips of coffee before I said with a muzzled grin, "Hun, I already calculated what I thought we might need. Why don't you come on inside? We can compare notes over breakfast before we head to Zeb's."

Liddy huffed as she brushed her hands against her jeans and swatted at more of her unruly hair. "I guess that works. Wish you'd have said something last night." She handed me her pen and pad as she walked by and disappeared through the door without further resistance.

———

Only a couple pickups occupied Zeb's parking lot when we pulled in.

Liddy said, "Looks like they're still unloading the trees. C'mon, let's go on inside first."

Liddy grabbed my arm as we both admired the rustic pine floors, scarred by decades of traffic entering and exiting the landmark store. Unpainted rugged timbers braced the wooden beams and joists overhead. An eclectic mixture of racks and display shelves defined the aisles of merchandise.

Liddy drifted toward the aisles, but I clutched onto her hand and guided her through the archway leading into to the "Old General Store," where Shiloh's preserved heritage greeted our senses.

We walked back in time and discovered the charm of Shiloh's 19th Century historical roots. Penny candies and chocolates in large glass jars lined the glass top counter. Antique artifacts and dated pictures displayed Shiloh's past on shelves high above the candy. Beyond the candy jars, an inventory of toys and games from an era long before electronics and computers sat ready for little hands to enjoy.

Liddy yanked on my arm. "Look, Raggedy Ann and Andy. Bet Sissy would like those, and look over there!" She dragged me toward the Tinker Toys, Lincoln Logs, and Erector sets on display above painted wood rocking horses, colorful wooden block sets, doll houses, scooters and wagons on the floor. Shelves along the back wall displayed cast iron cars, trucks, boats and trains next to trinket boxes for boys and musical jewelry boxes for little girls.

Liddy opened one of the music boxes and squealed. "Oh my, I used to have one of these when I was little."

I wandered beyond the center rack of children's classic books, coloring books, and comics. A potbelly stove with a large black coffee pot on top sat between painted columns framing an area set aside for checkers and idle chatter.

I smiled and said, "Gossip central."

Although no one occupied the rocking chairs at the moment, the trash bins and checkers lying askew revealed its intended purpose. A faded hand-painted sign hung above the chairs and checkerboards. "Sit long, talk much."

A moment after Liddy found me, we heard, "Theo. Liddy. Sure glad you stopped by this morning. Sorry, I didn't catch you when you first walked in. I was out back."

Zeb Adams wore gray bib overalls with a red and green plaid wool shirt over a crew neck flannel shirt. His shaggy, gray hair hung over his ears, and his weathered face partially hid beneath his mostly white beard.

We shook hands as I said, "Zeb, I love this old store. Sure brings back a lot of memories."

Liddy nodded and said, "All the history on display is amazing. I'm flabbergasted by all your toys and games."

Zeb drew his fingers through his disheveled beard and laughed. "You'd be surprised at how popular they still are, especially during the Christmas season."

"No, I have no doubt. In fact, you can count on us taking some off your hands." A coy grin appeared beneath Liddy's scrunched nose.

I pointed towards the checker tables. "So, is this where the ol' codgers hang out and share scuttlebutt and fish tales?"

"You mean where the real gossip starts in town? Shucks, some days more traffic mingles back here than in the main store." Zeb looked at Liddy. "So how can I help you today? Looking for anything special?"

Liddy glanced at me as her rosy dimples deepened. "Well Zeb, we need more Christmas decorations for the house and of course a tree too." She pulled her shopping list from the pocket of her purple parka.

"Yes ma'am, follow me." Zeb turned and led us back to the hardware store.

Liddy turned toward me. "Why don't you chat with Zeb while I wander around and check everything out. I'll come get you if I need you."

"Looks like we'll be here for awhile," I said to Zeb.

Zeb stuck his hands into his overall pockets and rocked on his heels. "Come on. I'll show you around."

I laughed as we walked across the colorful floorboards that surrounded where custom paint got mixed. "I bet there's a lot of history behind every drop and glob of paint spilled over the decades."

Zeb chuckled. "Yeah, it's pretty safe to say every house in Shiloh is represented on that floor. I can't even remember the last time we even tried to scrape it back to bare wood."

Zeb took us beyond a large sliding door into the warehouse where they stored bulk stock and pallets of farm goods. A couple of pigeons fluttered away as our chatter disturbed their siesta. Jay and Jim tossed salt licks and bags of feed onto a flatbed trailer.

"Hey, Pop! Do you want Jay and me to get this out to Marie's place now?" Jim shouted standing beside the trailer as Jay drove the forklift. He ran up and shouted above the noise of the forklift. "Hey Mister P! Glad you could stop by."

"When you see Miss Marie, please tell her you saw us, and that we'll be by after lunch. We've got some wonderful news."

Jay ran up the ramp. "Pop, you might want to order some more salt licks and oats. We're getting pretty low again." He wiped his brow with his sleeve, turned toward me and answered for both he and Jim. "You can count on us. We'll pass the message on to Miss Marie."

"You both ain't goin'!" Zeb barked. "Only one needs to go. The other needs to lend me a hand. We've got a lot of trees to move today."

Jim and Jay echoed, "Yes sir, got it." They jogged side by side back to the trailer. Jim got into the truck while Jay disappeared out the back door of the warehouse.

"Zeb, you've been here a long time, haven't you?" I asked as we walked back into the store.

"Sure have, all my life. What's on your mind?" Zeb's smile faded as he seemed to sense more inquiry coming his way.

"Liddy and I shared Thanksgiving with Harold Archer, and I had an interesting one-on-one chat with him after dinner. We talked a little about Jessie Masterson, but our conversation shifted to John Priestly."

"How can I help you?"

"Since you've evidently got a finger on some of the talk in town, I was wondering, how did Harold get along with John and Jessie?"

Zeb inspected the paint residue on the floor before he answered. "Theo, I'm not sure what you know, but I'll tell you this… As far as Harold Archer and Jessie Masterson go, I believe they got along fine. But then again, everyone liked Jessie. As for John Priestly, well, he was more like his dad and wore his emotions on his sleeve. Don't get me wrong, John rightfully earned his reputation as a reserved, behind-the-scenes gentleman, but he could get his dander up when a wrong needed to be made right. And Harold and his older boys provided ample opportunity for him to get his dander up."

"What do you mean?"

"To say it plainly, John liked doing things the right way, whereas the Archers liked having their way on certain matters. I witnessed a few of their heated exchanges at some of the booster club meetings when Harold wanted his say over the school's athletic program, but John fought back for what he felt served the best interest of the school and his players. Thankfully, Jessie kept the peace. He'd call a timeout and negotiate a compromise or weasel a concession out of John or Harold."

"That's interesting. I can see where John's strong personality might've been a thorn of contention for Harold's personality."

Zeb continued but in a more subdued voice. "Let me give you an example. But mind you, I can't say it's one-hundred percent true or not, but I'd say it's likely truer than not."

"I'm listening. Is this about the school contract?"

"Why yes, it is. So you've heard about this then?"

"Larry and I discussed it."

"I'll tell you what I know. During the middle of the project, John confronted Hank about shortchanging the work they were doing. Hank responded by demanding John and his staff clear their offices and the locker room. Even though work on the gymnasium and locker rooms were the last to be completed according to the project's master plan, Hank argued the change was needed to finish the project ahead of schedule. John challenged Hank about it, and tempers flared."

"I don't understand John's anger even if it meant some inconvenience. Wouldn't it have benefited John and the staff for the work to be completed early?"

"Now listen carefully. John had already openly expressed concerns regarding renovations in other areas of the school. When the schedule of work got reshuffled, John accused Hank of manipulating the master plan to get him and his staff out of the way so there'd be no looking over their shoulders while they finished the work. John vocalized what others at the school were afraid to voice out loud because they feared the Archers. But John refused to back down."

"Sounds like John and Hank weren't best of friends."

"You could say that. In one particularly bad instance, from what I understand, Harold walked in and prevented the exchanges between John and Hank from escalating. He assured John that he'd look into his concerns. But John made sure that Harold knew how Hank manipulated approvals on work not completed satisfactorily, and he could prove it. John threatened to go public if the wrongs weren't made right."

"I read about that in some press releases I found. After their rift went public, Hank publicly apologized. Archer Construction agreed to correct any valid issues and renegotiated the remaining work on the contract, but what you told me helps to clarify some of the accusations."

Zeb's chin hardened. "I believe Harold resented John's accusations, and the timing came at a crucial point for him. It was no secret that Harold had aspirations to get elected to a state seat in Atlanta, but the bad press that followed the ruckus between John and Hank caused Harold unwelcome notoriety. As a result, Hank felt Harold's wrath, but neither Harold's and Hank's relationship with John recovered after that."

"Was it possible that when charges came against John a few months later, Hank and Harold saw it as an opportunity for revenge?"

Zeb placed his hand on my shoulder and looked into my eyes. "As my pappy told me long ago, 'Where there's smoke, the source of the fire must be nearby.' As far as what happened to John, it was wrong, plain wrong."

"It appears that way to me too."

Zeb lowered his voice to almost a whisper. "Theo, I've been burdened by what happened to John. I think you're on the right track, and I appreciate what you're doing to honor Jessie Masterson too."

I recognized Liddy's excited voice from the end of the aisle. "Oh, there you two are! Theo, I need you to check out what I found."

Zeb sighed and smiled. "Go on. I'll see the two of you up front in a minute."

Several minutes later, we rolled a cart loaded with Christmas decorations to the front counter. She asked Zeb to also ring up the Nativity and Santa with sleigh yard displays.

Zeb winked with a jolly grin and pointed to the side of the building. "Miss Liddy, Jay's out there with Pete and Andy. They'll be glad to help you pick out a nice tree."

"Pete and Andy are here today?" I asked.

"Yeah, they pitch in selling trees every year. They donate their commissions to the City's Benevolence Food Pantry."

We walked out to the side of the store where several families browsed through the maze of trees in spite of the persistent chilly mist. Liddy came in her parka and gloves, so nothing could deter her quest to bring home what she felt was the perfect tree for our first Christmas in Shiloh.

Jay, now wearing rain gear, leather gloves, and a soggy, sad-looking Santa hat, found Liddy first. "Miss Liddy, please allow me to help you."

My choice of only a windbreaker over my sweater provided my excuse. "You two go ahead. I'll start loading our vehicle."

Jay and Liddy turned away without another word. Liddy stretched high on her tiptoes to mark the height she desired for the tree and spread her arms to indicate the girth. Jay intently watched before he led her toward a stack of trees.

Inside, Zeb manned the cash register as business had picked up and many new faces ventured through the aisles. Zeb wished everyone a jovial "Merry Christmas" as each customer walked up to the counter with their purchases.

I meandered into the Old General Store and looked out the window. I watched Liddy and Jay shake out one tree after another. Based on Liddy's facial expressions and gestures, I had plenty of time to enjoy some coffee before I loaded our purchases into our vehicle.

Silas' unique accent caught my ear. "My good friend Mister Theo. Good morning to you."

"Why good morning Silas, and you as well, Bubba. What brings the two of you here this time of the morning?"

Bubba slapped Silas on the back and said through a burst of shared laughter, "To tell ya the truth, we're kinda late for our weekly game of checkers. We don't have long before we must scoot back to help with the lunch crowd."

I looked puzzled and asked, "Do you come here every Saturday?"

Silas laughed, "Sure. Our wives think we're just picking up supplies, but we always squeeze in an hour of checkers before we head back. Don't you tell Bernie or Miss Barbara."

I chuckled. "Your secret is safe with me."

As I slammed the tailgate shut, Jay called out. "Come see the tree Miss Liddy picked out. What'd you think?" He bounced the tree a couple of times on the loading platform. I gave a hearty thumbs-up, and Jay secured the tree to our roof rack.

Liddy stepped outside shaking her head. "Hun, Zeb gave us a discount on everything we bought today. Isn't that sweet?"

"We'll need the savings to pay next month's electric bill."

"Oh, hush you ol' Scrooge. By the way, I talked with Jay about the boys stopping over tomorrow after church."

"What'd you tell him?"

"Just that we had something we'd like to share with them. Now let's get home, so we can eat lunch before we head to Marie's."

CHAPTER TWENTY-FIVE

As we made our way to Marie's, Liddy stared out the passenger window and said without turning. "I almost forgot how raw and exposed the fields looked after the harvest."

My tight-lipped smile offered my agreement while my eyes remained glued to the road ahead. I didn't want to miss Marie's larger-than-most faded green mailbox that marked where to turn off the highway.

Marie's warm smile greeted us as we exited our vehicle. After we exchanged quick hugs, I said, "Marie, I'm sorry we're a little later than we hoped, but we kinda' got carried away at Zeb's place this morning."

Marie grinned. "Don't fuss. I wasn't going anywhere. Besides, ol' Zeb's got a mighty unique store to browse through on your first visit."

Marie handed Liddy two cups of coffee, and then sat down opposite us and reached for an official looking envelope on the kitchen table. "Look what I got from our good Mayor."

Marie pulled out a handwritten letter on City of Shiloh stationary and handed it to me. *Dear Ms. Masterson: Please accept my personal invitation to serve as the guest of honor at this year's annual Christmas program on Wednesday, December 17th. In addition to officially dedicating the new City Hall, we will recognize Jessie's memorial statue that evening as well. My office will be in touch with you to discuss the details, but I personally hope you will accept this invitation to join us as our special guest. Sincerely, Harold Archer.*

I handed the letter to Liddy and turned to Marie. "Well, you gonna go?"

Marie raised her eyebrows and a sly grin. "I'll tell you my answer after you tell me your news. Joe said you had something good to tell me."

Liddy looked up and her eyes twinkled with excitement as Marie's eyes darted between us. I could not resist smiling as I cleared my throat and said, "We've got an early Christmas present for you."

Marie looked over at Liddy giggling. "Theo, what the Sam Hill are you talking about?"

Liddy slapped my arm. "Theo! Please tell her for goodness sakes."

"There's a parole hearing in the works for John. He should be home before Christmas."

Tears welled in the corners of her eyes as I grabbed her hand to lessen her fingernail grip on my forearm. "Marie, before we left to see John yesterday, Joe confirmed only formalities and paperwork remain."

Marie released a gush of happy tears, which only stirred Liddy to follow suit. The two women hugged and shared a joy-filled moment of weeping and laughter. Marie suddenly raised her head from Liddy's embrace, wiped her moist cheeks and asked with a puzzled, blank stare, "Where's John going to live? You own his former home."

I squeezed Marie's hand and glanced at Liddy. "Good question, but Joe already worked that out. Zeb Adams guaranteed the Parole Board that John has a job and a place to stay waiting."

Marie abruptly interrupted, "That's mighty nice of Zeb, but no one, I mean NO ONE is going to offer John a home but me!"

"Exactly what Joe said you'd say."

Marie's exuberance turned into a long sigh. "Oh my goodness. I need to fix up Jessie's old room... and decorate for Christmas... and... "

Liddy tugged on Marie's hand. "Marie, there's plenty of time. We're here to help you. And, I was gonna tell you later, but Judy and Martha invited us to go shopping with them next week. Now you've got a great reason to say yes."

"Liddy, I could sure use some help..." Marie paused as her eyes widened. "But what if he doesn't want to live here with me?"

My chair rocked back as I laughed and said, "Marie, John loved the idea but worried you'd be uncomfortable having him stay with you at the house."

"You tell him that's just plain silly. I won't take no for an answer."

Over the next hour, we walked throughout her house and discussed what needed to be done to make John feel at home. Marie said she had done little around the house since Jessie's death, and she started crying again.

"Christmas used to mean so much to me." Marie stared at a photo on the mantle of Jessie. "Christmas Eve was Jessie's birthday, but…"

Liddy embraced Marie and tried to comfort her. "I understand. You just leave it to your friends, and we'll get this ol' house ready for Christmas. And listen to me. Even though Jessie won't be here, we'll still hang his stocking next to one for you and John on the mantle. What do you think?"

Marie pulled her head back from Liddy's shoulder, sniffed and slowly whispered, "That'd be nice."

I placed my arms around both of them. "I'm glad you ladies have this worked out. How about a Christmas tree? I happen to know where to get a nice one."

Liddy looked at her watch and added, "If we're going to get that tree before they close, we need to hurry along." Liddy grabbed Marie's hand. "But before we run off, I've got a great idea. How about Theo and I pick you up tomorrow morning, and we'll go to church together? I think God deserves some credit for John's return. What do you think?"

Marie said, "Sure, but y'all don't need to come all the way out here. I'll meet you at your house. I've been avoiding church long enough. God's certainly earned my thanks for all he's done and is doing, and that includes special thanks for bringing you and Theo back into my life."

"We feel the same about you, Marie," Liddy said. "Hey, how about adding to the celebration a little get-together after church? I'll invite some of your closest friends for a decorating party. Theo and I will take care of everything. We'll all pitch in and get this house ready for John's arrival."

Marie giggled. "Well. I guess… Sure. Why not?"

Liddy handed me my jacket and said to Marie, "Alright then. Coffee will be ready by nine. We've got to run, so we can get you that tree we promised."

———

Back in town, we found an empty parking spot out front of Zeb's. Jay stood on the front platform with a puzzled look. Except for a couple of families still milling around the trees, they looked ready to close.

"We need another tree!" I faked my panicked plea.

"Another tree? What happened?"

"Not for us. Everything's fine. In fact, better than fine. We just left Marie's and promised we'd get her a tree by tomorrow morning. Can you help us?"

Jay jumped into the air and pumped his fist. "Miss Marie's going to decorate her house for Christmas. Well hallelujah!" He turned and yelled at the others by the trees. "Hey, we need to pick out a special tree. Mister and Missus P are getting Marie a tree for Christmas."

Jim stared with his jaw unhinged. "How'd you... What'd you do? Miss Marie is gonna celebrate Christmas? She hasn't celebrated Christmas since..."

I pointed upward and smiled.

Jay and Jim scurried among the trees and argued over a couple before they finally agreed and tied one onto our roof rack. Jim reached into his shirt pocket, pulled out his black marker and wrote across the tree's tag, "PAID IN FULL. Merry Christmas!"

I stared at the ticket and smiled. "Guys, thanks. Marie's goin' to be tickled to death."

Liddy stood by watching us share high-fives and then laughed. "See you guys in church, right? Marie'll be there."

Pete and Andy came out of the store and interrupted. "Excuse me... Did you say Miss Marie's goin' to church too?"

Liddy grinned and said, "Yep, she'll be there. And, there's been a small change in our plans. Instead of meeting at our house, we need your help over at Marie's after church instead. We're all goin' to pitch in and help her decorate her house."

Jay shouted, "That'll be fine with us!" The others nodded with big grins.

Liddy looked at Jay. "One more thing, will you and your brother swing by Bubba's after church? I'll call and place an order. It'll be waiting for you."

Jay looked at Jim and said, "We'll take care of it. See y'all in the morning."

———

After sunset, Liddy and I stood outside and enjoyed the festive lights we hung in front of our house. The Nativity glowed softly on one side of the front walkway, while Liddy made certain Santa and his reindeer pointed in the direction of the manger on the other side. Later on, inside, we shared stories as we hung each ornament on our tree. After forty years, we had quite a collection of memories hanging on our Christmas tree in the corner of the living room. We enjoyed each of them anew with the prospect of the new memories we were creating.

CHAPTER TWENTY-SIX

LIDDY GREETED MARIE AT OUR DOOR Sunday morning while I fumbled with my tie. I stopped fooling with it long enough to take Marie's coat as Liddy said, "Marie, you look fantastic." Marie's nervous grin accented her youthful appearance as well as hinted to her shyness.

"It's the only dress I felt comfortable wearing to church. I reckon I've shed a few pounds and grown accustomed to my jeans and boots the last couple of years." She inspected her dress for wrinkles. "But I figured it's best to wear something nice today."

Liddy looked at Marie. "My oh my, you certainly look just fine in that dress." She then reached for my dangling tie-ends. "You need help?"

I dropped my arms while Liddy fidgeted with my tie until Marie interrupted. "Liddy, I think Theo looks just fine without a tie."

"Why thank you, Marie," I said, giving Liddy a wide grin.

Liddy pulled the tie from my collar. "At least put on your maroon sweater vest."

Liddy and Marie were sipping coffee in the living room by the time I returned. "Much better," Liddy quipped as she pointed to my coffee on the table next to my chair.

After some light chatter centering around Marie's fond stories about John and Jessie, Marie suddenly lost her grin. "Please excuse me, but I've been thinking. What John has had to endure is plain wrong and simply scandalous. The more I think about it, the angrier I get. I'm not sure we'll ever know the truth. Even Jessie told me John wouldn't confide in him about what happened. The only thing Jessie confessed to me was John admitted to him that it all had something to do with not breaking someone's trust to prove his innocence."

I looked into Marie's distant stare. "What Jessie told you puzzles Joe and me as well. Someone holds the key to clearing John's name and making it right. Only then can Joe move to get John exonerated."

"Exonerated?" Marie asked with a puzzled stare.

"When evidence is brought forward that allows the Court to declare a person innocent of a previous conviction decision," I explained.

The hopeful twinkle in Marie's eyes erased the frustration of a moment ago. "Do you mean that John might be able to get his life back?"

"Yes, that'd be the case. But don't get your hopes too high, the Court doesn't enjoy being proved wrong. Let's not forget what's most important right now — John's coming home one way or another."

"I wish I could remember anything that might help," Marie said.

———

Marie's relaxed demeanor vanished once we stepped into the church's foyer. The buzz among groups of older women huddled nearby increased as we looked around.

With a quick glance toward the not-so-well-disguised stares, Judy Wright welcomed Marie with a warm embrace. She then clutched Marie's elbow, winked at Liddy and said, "Y'all excuse us a moment. We'll be right back." In most circles, smiles and cheerful chatter replaced the previous glares as Judy whisked Marie around the room.

Noticing how all eyes continued to focus on Marie, I leaned over to Liddy and whispered, "Judy sure knows how to nip gossip and warm hearts. Look how at ease Marie looks now."

Pete and Andy then appeared near the sanctuary entrance. I pointed toward Judy and Marie still engaged with another gaggle of women. They promptly approached Marie and Judy, offered their elbows to Marie and excused themselves as they escorted her into the sanctuary. We followed close behind while Judy merely smiled and watched.

Pete and Andy directed Marie to the far end of our usual row. Zeb offered her an awkward hug before she sat beside him. Sam, Susanna, and Jeannie stood, turned and greeted Marie from the next row. Larry and Martha slipped into their usual places between us and the center aisle. Marie's rosy cheeks and modest grin displayed how she felt about the fuss her young escorts made. Pete and Andy joined Jay and Jim in front of Marie.

Harold Archer made his best effort to whisper nonchalantly from the aisle over the piano music. "Psst! Psst! Misses Masterson, what a pleasant surprise. Did you get my letter?"

Marie nodded with a polite but guarded smile. Harold extended an obligatory greeting to the rest of us before he continued to his usual seat closer to the front.

Liddy nudged my side. "Look… Megan's here." We acknowledged Megan's waist high wave and quick grin as she and Phillip followed Harold to their seats.

Arnie winked with a smile in Marie's direction during his customary hearty welcome at the beginning of the service. His sermon on the "Prodigal Son's Return and the Older Son's Jealousy" struck a timely nerve, and I could not help but wonder how John's return would likely produce the parable's mixed emotions.

At the conclusion of his sermon, Arnie offered a challenge. "Consider your feelings and allow God to soften any hardness in your heart, so you may offer a warm welcome to any dear brother or sister who returns."

After the service, Marie's joy showed through streams of tears as we weaved in and out the crowd. Mary scooted from the piano and embraced Marie in the aisle. We worked our way into the foyer where Liddy gathered everyone.

"Okay, listen up," Liddy announced. "If you're free, we already took care of dinner. You're all invited to help decorate Marie's house for Christmas this afternoon."

Susanna looked at Liddy. "What time do you want us there?"

Liddy smiled and looked at her watch. "Let's say in about an hour?"

While Liddy spoke, Larry leaned towards me and whispered, "I'm sorry, but we've got other plans today. Will you stop by the office tomorrow? It sounds like your visit with John went rather well."

I nodded and whispered, "Don't worry about this afternoon. We'll have plenty of help. See you tomorrow."

Zeb pulled Jim and Jay next to him. "You can count on us. They've duly informed me. We're stopping by Bubba's." With that as their goodbye, the three left to get a head start.

Liddy said, "Judy and Arnie will be there as fast as they can get away."

Megan, Harold, and Phillip stood beside Harold's truck parked across the street. As soon as Liddy, Marie and I stepped onto the sidewalk, Megan ran over and thanked Liddy and me for sharing Thanksgiving with them. As she turned to walk away, she stopped and embraced Marie. Without a word exchanged, she raced back to an impatient Harold.

As soon as we returned to the house, I pulled Marie's tree off the back porch and placed it in the bed of her truck. Her eyes widened at the size and became even more tickled when she learned of the boys' generosity.

———

By the time we arrived at Marie's place, Pete's truck was parked beside Sam's silver Silverado. Susanna slid a peach cobbler into the oven as we entered by the kitchen door.

The loud thumps of the loose timbers of the makeshift bridge announced the arrival of Zeb along with Jay and Jim in a faded green Bronco. The boys yanked two large Bubba's BBQ coolers from the back of their vehicle. Before Zeb closed the tailgate, more thumps announced the arrival of Arnie and Judy in their Tahoe.

After we devoured two large aluminum trays of slow-roasted chicken and plenty of coleslaw and baked beans, the women helped Marie sort through old boxes of Christmas decorations. The boys brought the tree into the living room, and Sam and Arnie strung the lights. Marie asked Zeb and me to string strands of colored lights across the porch eaves and hang a wreath on both the front and kitchen doors.

After the women made short order of hanging ornaments on the tree, Judy found a large portrait of John and placed it next to Jessie's already on the mantle. Marie burst into a concert of "Oh my's!" and sniffles as the tree lights flickered off the framed photos.

Marie's cheeks glowed as she asked for help in the back bedrooms of the house. She felt John would feel awkward sleeping in Jessie's old room, so they prepared the spare guest room for him.

"John knows that room well enough anyway," she said. "He always slept there whenever he and Jessie studied films and prepared game plans late into the night."

With all tasks complete, the women gathered around the fireplace and talked about gift ideas and their upcoming shopping trip. The men landed in the comfort of Marie's seldom-used cane rockers on her front porch while the boys horsed around by the trucks. Our conversation soon ventured into the recollections of the "good ol' days." I sat back and listened to Sam and Zeb talking about John and Jessie's impact and influence on their boys. Even Arnie shared some insightful yet more objective observations.

At one point in his story-telling, Sam stood to watch his sons. "Theo, both my boys, just as Zeb will tell you about his sons, owe a lot to Jessie and John for the breaks they received to excel at Shiloh and go on to college. And that's no small feat in this neck of the woods." Sam looked over his shoulder at Zeb and said, "In your case, John and Jessie went above the call of duty to help your family after Miriam died."

Zeb leaned back in his rocking chair and glanced at Sam. With a soulful gaze, he turned and said, "Theo, I guess I oughta tell you my boys watched their mother lose her battle with cancer before they turned twelve."

Zeb glanced at Arnie with a sad grin. "Arnie here knows how I struggled after that. But I learned through those tough times that God brings good folks alongside to ease our pain. In addition to Arnie and Sam and their families, John and Jessie showed up whenever I needed extra help around the store."

Zeb's rocking pace increased. "I can't begin to tell you how many casseroles and cakes showed up thanks to Aunt Betty and Marie, and they
always seemed to know when I needed their warm hugs and smiles."

Sam leaned forward and slapped Zeb on the knee. "Friends care
for friends. We always have and always will."

Zeb reached for his handkerchief and blew his nose before he
continued. "Well, about John and Jessie, they never coddled my boys.
They made certain that Jay and Jim helped me at the house and the
business. Thanks to John and Jessie giving time off for the boys to help
me, I found time to get involved in the athletic booster club. On most
game nights, Sam and Susanna saved my seat in the bleachers while I
helped in the concession stand."

Sam laughed and bellowed, "Yeah, you should have heard us at
those games too! Ol' Zeb's hollering could be heard over the public address system." Arnie put his hands up when Sam asked for an unbiased
testimony to Zeb's raucous reputation.

Zeb stood beside the rocker and stared directly at me. "You can
quote this plainly if you want. If Jessie and John had not been there for
my boys, I'm dead certain they'd never have turned out as they did."
Zeb turned and stared at his boys. "They made sure neither Jay nor
Jim threw in the towel after their mom passed."

"What about Sanctuary?" I ventured to redirect the conversation.

Sam sat on the edge of his chair. "Theo, the boys loved their Sanctuary nights, but after we lost John and then Jessie, the meetings just
stopped."

"Do you think the guys might reconsider restarting Sanctuary? It'd
be a great tribute to Jessie."

Zeb and Sam looked at each other. Arnie nodded as if wanting to
hear more, so I continued. "Liddy and I will do everything we can to
help. What do y'all think?"

Zeb agreed but seemed to hold some reservation. "Sounds like a
fine idea. But, why not ask them?"

"I agree with Zeb," Sam said just before he let loose a blaring,
two-fingered whistle, and then yelled, "Y'all come over here a minute.

Mister P's got something to ask ya."

The four walked toward the porch, still poking fun at one another. Pete looked up and asked, "Yes sir, Mista P?"

I spent the next fifteen minutes explaining Liddy's and my offer to serve as benefactors but said we needed them to help get Sanctuary restarted.

Andy asked immediately, "Is Miss Marie okay with this?"

As soon as I said she gave her blessing, the boys all looked at each other and agreed to meet Tuesday evening to plan a kickoff event. The four scrambled inside the house to share the good news with Marie.

I said to Sam, "Before we join them, how about Jeannie? Do you think she'd like to help too?"

Sam laughed. "Sure. Jeannie adored John and Jessie as if they were uncles. I bet if you ask her about it, she'd be glad to help out too."

———

Just before we left late that afternoon, Liddy asked Marie, "How do you think John'll likely feel about us getting Sanctuary restarted?"

Marie grinned. "Won't know unless we ask him."

"Talking about John's return. Have you thought any more about anything that might be relevant to what happened to John?"

Marie hesitated. "Theo, I've thought long and hard about this. The only thing that comes to mind and offers some concern is how often Jessie told me about John losing his temper with Hank and Harold Archer, especially after all that school construction mess."

I looked intently into her eyes. "Did Jessie ever speak about someone John might've talked with or about; someone who might have caused unusual concerns between them?"

Marie scrunched her nose before her eyes popped wide. "Jessie did talk to me about a former female student that John stressed over because I think she approached him about a supposedly pregnant friend."

"Did Jessie say anything else?"

Marie paused and said, "Jessie told me that Hank Archer's name came up as the likely father, and John asked the girl to have her friend visit him if she needed any help. But that's all that Jessie said about it. Until you asked, I had forgotten about it."

"Do you remember when this happened?"

Marie paused to answer. "I believe not long after that ruckus between John and Hank happened at the school. I can't be sure."

"Interesting... thanks, Marie." I grew quiet in my distraction.

"I'm sorry I don't recall the girl's name. Besides, I don't think Jessie ever said and likely didn't know himself. John kept such matters pretty private." Marie revealed her disappointment and frustration.

I assured Marie that every little piece of information helped. Liddy and I hugged Marie and promised to stay in touch over the next few days.

CHAPTER TWENTY-SEVEN

LIDDY STIRRED BENEATH THE BLANKETS and mumbled, "I'll be up soon." Then she yanked the covers back over her head. This drab morning had brought winter's nip. The temptation to remain under our warm blankets crossed my mind, but the yearning to proofread my first of three articles on Jessie's story won out.

A few minutes later the warmth of a stoked fire and twinkle of the Christmas tree lights diverted my thoughts. I couldn't help but ponder the significance of this Christmas for Marie and John. Both faced the upcoming holidays with the loss of loved ones still fresh in their hearts. But thanks to God, they could find comfort sharing this Christmas together.

My first article dealt with Jessie's early years before he arrived in Shiloh, and the words had flowed as if Marie and Jessie dictated them. Aunt Betty's invitation to Marie to move to Shiloh served as the bridge to the next article. I added an ellipsis to the final word and set my pen down. That's when I realized Liddy with her ponytail tucked beneath the turned-up collar of her fleece robe stood mesmerized by the twinkling lights and flames in the fireplace.

Liddy curled up in her chair with her feet propped and tucked under her patchwork quilt. As we sipped our coffee, I shared my thoughts about our first Phillip's family Christmas in Shiloh.

Liddy appeared to listen but her focus turned to the Christmas tree, and she blurted, "Do you think there'll be enough room for all the gifts and toys under the tree?"

I laughed as I realized she hardly had heard a word I said. With a reassuring grin, I replied, "I'm sure we can make more room if needed."

Our conversation drifted to what took place yesterday at Marie's. I reiterated more of what Sam and Zeb said about Jessie and John. Liddy countered with similar tales from Judy, Susanna, Jeannie, and Marie.

When I jotted down a couple of notes, she interrupted and said, "Oh, I almost forgot, Marie wanted me to tell you what she remembered about Jessie and John."

"What'd she say?" I asked, still scribbling down what I wanted to remember for later.

"Marie told me about a particular night Jessie came home after one of those Booster meetings. He had arrived out of sorts and blew off steam about another fracas between John, Harold, and Hank. It evidently involved John's handling of money after home games. According to Marie, Jessie ranted about how they accused John of being too haphazard and lackadaisical, which riled Jessie. He knew firsthand John's headstrong attitude about such matters."

"I can imagine how that might have upset Jessie and stirred John up too."

"Yeah, Jessie told Marie that the Boosters decided that changes might be in the best interest of all concerned. Right after that, the school's bookkeeper met with John and set up a new audit procedure for all money collected, deposited and expended each week."

I gnawed on my pen. "You know, I'm sure Harold voiced his concerns in his usual charming, persuasive manner, while Hank might've seen this as an opportunity to embarrass and take a shot at John, parroting Harold's concerns."

Liddy sighed, "Maybe Zeb and Sam can shed more light on this."

I tucked my pen and pad aside. "Don't worry. I'll get to the bottom of this." I paused and scratched my chin. "But it still doesn't explain the missing money."

Liddy slid out of her chair, hugged me and planted a kiss on my forehead. "I'm so proud of you. I know you'll figure it out."

"Thanks, Sweetie. The fact remains, five thousand dollars wound up missing."

Liddy continued to rest her hands on my shoulders. "Now, follow my thinking. The evidence points to John, but..." She squeezed her eyes shut for a brief moment. "If John's guilty, why would he have left such an obvious money trail."

"I agree. The key's figuring out who John's protecting and why. But first things first. I need to get my first installment of Jessie's story to Larry this morning."

"Theo, would you mind if I tagged along?"

"Not at all. In fact, I'll treat you to breakfast while we're out."

———

Most of the early morning crowd had left by the time we parked in front of Bubba's. The mouth-watering aroma of hickory smoke already permeated the air outside as well as inside the restaurant. We felt remiss about not yet revisiting the first friendly faces we met in Shiloh as we entered and watched Cecil crack a couple of eggs and slap more bacon on the griddle.

"Good Morn'n Mista Theo and Missus Liddy," Cora said with a pleasant grin. "We've been talkin' bout y'all somethin' fierce these last couple of days. Your ears must'a been burnin'."

Cecil greeted us at the table. "Morn'n folks. We were pretty disappointed when Jay and Jim picked up y'all's order, especially after Bubba bragged about bumping into y'all at Zeb's store Saturday."

My smile twisted as I said, "Sorry we haven't gotten back sooner. We didn't forget about you, though. What's the breakfast special today?"

Cora tugged on Cecil's apron and gave him a cold stare. "Git yo'self back where you belong ol' man. Let me do my job. Now scat! Go on." Cora's scowl instantly transformed into a bubbling smile. "Lemme see. This morn' we've got homemade sausage, bacon, grits, the best buttermilk biscuits you'll ever put on your lips if I say so myself, and eggs as you like 'em, plus plenty of fresh coffee."

I ordered while Liddy stared at the menu. "I'm hungry Miss Cora.

I'll have the special with scrambled eggs."

"Want gravy with them biscuits?"

"No, ma'am. I'm watching my figure," I chuckled as I tapped my gut.

Liddy slapped my arm and said, "The special sounds scrumptious but is too much for me. I'd like... ah... two of Cecil's sausage biscuits and coffee."

Cora turned and yelled our order toward the kitchen. She disappeared briefly before reappearing with our coffee. Cora then grabbed a nearby chair and plopped down at the end of our table.

"Hope y'all don't mind, but it'll be a minute before that ol' coot has your orders ready. I hear y'all was at Master Harold's house for Thanksgivin'."

Liddy glanced at me with raised brows as I chuckled. "Yes, ma'am. We enjoyed meeting his daughter-in-law Megan too. But, why do I sense you knew that already."

Cora's smile blossomed. "Yes, sir. I gotta fess up. Maddie and I been friends a long time. We both attend Mount Zion on the edge of town. She told me all about your visit." Cora looked at Liddy, "Maddie sure likes you Missus Liddy and said Miss Megan talked about you long after you left. Maddie also said Mister Harold acted peculiarly pleasant the rest of the day, that is until them boys of his came home."

Liddy relaxed as she listened to Cora talk about the Archers. "Well, you can tell Maddie she's a mighty fine cook, and we think a lot of Miss Megan too. I think Megan enjoyed having some ol' fashioned girl talk. Know what I mean?"

"Yes ma'am, sure do. Maddie tells me how lonely and depressed Miss Megan gets in that big house. She's worried about how Hank treats Megan too, yellin' at her all the time."

Liddy's smile disappeared.

I swallowed more coffee, and asked, "So Cora, what's the latest scuttlebutt going around about Liddy and me?"

Cora's eyes opened wide. "Mista Theo, it's all good what I hear 'bout you two. They're saying you're a famous writer or sumthin' like that, and you're writin' about Coach Masterson, God rest his soul."

My smile tried to hide my discomfort. "I guess that's good."

Cora squealed, "Oh, Mista Theo, it's all good. Some folks even joke about how Mister Scribner can sure use your help over at that old newspaper anyway."

"CORA! Get over here and leave them nice folks be. Their plates are ready." Cecil snarled from across the counter.

———

At the newspaper office, Martha had her ear to the phone, Mary typed furiously on her keyboard, and Larry grumbled at someone on the phone in his office. Liddy remained with Martha and Mary and rambled on about Marie's newly decorated house, while I walked to Larry's office and rapped on the doorframe. Larry spun in his chair, tossed the papers he had been shuffling through back onto his desktop and motioned me to come in.

"I'll have to get back to you on that," he said before he hung up the phone.

"I'm sorry, Theo. Harold is a pain in my butt. He keeps making changes in this year's Christmas program insert. Doesn't seem to comprehend deadlines."

"Well, good morning Larry. Glad you're in such a good mood." I sat down with a sarcastic grin.

Larry stood behind his desk and mumbled. "Make yourself comfortable. I'll be right back."

A moment later, Mary poked her head in the doorway. "Good morning Theo. I'm getting some coffee for Liddy, do you want a cup? I just made a fresh pot."

"Thanks, Mary. That'd be nice."

Larry returned holding two cups of coffee. "Sorry. Here you go." He handed me a cup and sat back down. "It's been crazy this morning around here. I'm trying to finalize the four-page, full-color layout for Shiloh's Christmas celebration. Harold wants this year's insert to be more than just the usual advertisement. He thinks it should be a keep-sake program rather than just a schedule of events." He exhaled and forced a grin. "Alright, let's move on to our business."

He took a sip of his coffee as I handed him my handwritten draft. "Larry, I know you're busy, but I wanted to show you the first article about Jessie."

Larry stared at the paper-clipped pages. "Your penmanship is certainly legible."

I tried to determine the genuineness of his comments. "Sorry. Guess I'm still old school. My thoughts have always flowed better with a pen."

"No, no bother. Mary can type this up in no time."

Larry sat with one leg crossed over his other knee. He scanned the article and talked without losing focus. "This is good, very good, Theo. Now, tell me about your visit with John. I've been dying to hear how it went."

I hesitated until he stopped reading, and we made eye contact. "Glad you like it. I've already started on the second. As far as John's visit, we met for nearly ninety minutes. Joe had prepped him about my relationship with Marie, so after an awkward start, our conversation proved pretty productive."

"How soon will John be home?"

"Joe said, barring no surprises, next week. But it gets better."

Larry leaned forward. "Go on."

"John admitted he accepted the plea deal because he felt compelled to protect a promise he made to someone. He refuses to say who or why, though. Joe and I both agree the identity of this mystery person will be key to discovering what happened."

Larry scratched his cheek. "Tell me what we can do in the meantime."

I stood up and began to pace. After a few steps, I turned back around and said, "Larry, I've been giving this a lot of thought. Uncovering John's mystery person should be our priority. To do that, I think we've got to dig deeper into the days or weeks just before the money disappeared."

Larry joined my pacing. We chatted while we swapped ends of his office and came to the conclusion we needed to work two angles. First, we needed to find out who, besides John, handled the money after each game. Second, we needed to come up with ideas on who would likely be John's mystery person.

"Do you have any ideas where we can begin?" Larry asked.

"As far as who handled the money each week, I think I can get some names. There were some procedures implemented before the money disappeared that might shed some light. I'm going to start by talking to Zeb and see what he knows. On the second angle, Marie said that Jessie mentioned a former female student had approached John about a pregnant friend."

"Marie mention any names?"

"No. Jessie evidently wasn't privy, or maybe he maintained John's confidentiality when he confided in Marie."

Larry stood with his arms crossed and shrugged his shoulders. "I can't recall any rumor like that. Of course, in this town, such a secret would be impossible to keep for any length of time. From what you told me, at least three people know who the involved parties are – John, the inquiring former student, and obviously the pregnant young lady." Larry paused as he stared at the floor and then added careful consideration, "Young girls typically don't keep that sort of stuff to themselves. They have an innate need to confide."

"Sounds logical. Can you think of any former students from about that time who might be a good starting point?" I stared at Larry as I pondered my question.

Larry's eyes popped. "Hold a second." He stepped to the doorway and called out. "Mary!"

Mary appeared with a puzzled look.

Larry motioned for her to take a seat. Concern fell across Mary's face, and Larry's stoic stare certainly didn't help.

"Mary, we need your help." Larry hesitated before he continued. "There might've been a rumor floating around sometime after you graduated that you might have some knowledge about."

Mary's eyes darted between Larry and me. "Um, what kind of rumor?"

Larry looked in my direction, and Mary's eyes followed as I sat on the edge of Larry's mahogany desk. I cleared my throat and then calmly looked at Mary. "Mary, someone I trust told me that about four, maybe five years ago a former student at the high school might have become pregnant, and her friend evidently tried to get her some help. I'm sorry to ask such a question, but do you recall anything like that? It may be very relevant to what your father and I are working on."

Mary glanced at her dad before she cast her eyes upon the floor. "Uh... well... Something did happen that might be related. After Hank Archer got back from his time in the Army, he and his brother Hal had a huge falling out. Everyone talked about the night Hank and Hal fought in the center of town, much more than words got exchanged."

Larry interrupted, "What'd they fight about?"

Mary smiled at her dad. "Not what... who. Megan hung out with Hal back then, but after Hank got back to town, Megan stopped hanging with her usual friends, including Hal. A couple of months after their big fight, Hank and Megan eloped."

I cocked my head and asked Mary, "Megan Archer was Hal's girlfriend before she married Hank?"

Mary finally made eye contact. "Megan and Hal hung out as if they were going steady for about a year, but she dropped Hal and wound up as Hank's wife." Mary's head slowly swayed back and forth in disbelief as a look of disgust settled upon her face. "Daddy, I still can't understand it. Hank's at least eight years older than her, what did Megan possibly see in Hank?"

Larry interrupted. "I'm sorry Mary, I'm confused. Megan and Hank never had a baby. How's this story related to our question about a rumor of a pregnancy?"

Mary's eyes danced between Larry and me. "Dad, I know they never had a baby, but..." Mary's head sunk. "Maybe the rumors were true?"

I stepped from the edge of the desk and glanced at Larry briefly. I tried to stay calm as I looked back at Mary. "Mary, what rumors?"

Mary's voice cracked. "Some of the girls in town started a rumor right after Hank and Megan eloped. Until now, I considered it jealous gossip."

Larry reached over and put his hand on Mary's arm. "What'd they say?"

"Dad, you remember how Megan acted back then. She had quite a reputation because of her reckless behavior, and I think a lot of the girls and guys resented her popularity. Right after Megan and Hank got back and she wasn't showing any signs of being pregnant, rumors got started that Megan faked being pregnant just to get Hank to marry her. However, when Hank and Megan appeared happily married, the rumors died off."

Larry leaned back in his chair. "Mary, let's think this out a moment. Let's say she lied about the pregnancy like they said, or even lost the baby before or right after they got married? If she lied to Hank, I don't think he'd have married her as he did. And surely if she'd been pregnant and lost the baby, someone would've known. I'm confused either way."

"Daddy, it was only a rumor. Nothing more was said. That's why I didn't think about it until just now."

I squatted beside Mary and rested my hand on her arm. "Mary, Hank, and Hal seem to have healed their differences from what I can see. How well did you know Megan? She's only a little older than you, right?"

Mary tried to smile. "Yeah. As far as Hank and Hal, everyone knows their relationship hasn't been the same since Hank married Megan."

I peered at Larry before I said to Mary, "Thanks, Mary. You've been most helpful. If you think of anything else, would you tell your dad or me?"

Mary smiled politely and nodded before she looked at her father and left the office.

Larry looked intently at me after Mary left. "Theo, I think you're on the right track. I'd follow up on the story about Megan and Hank."

I confirmed with a slight grin and a nod. "I'm inclined to think she may be a possibility, but she certainly didn't have a baby, and all we have to go on appears to be a rumor."

"Well, see what you can find out anyway. Regarding the rest of Jessie's story, here's what I'm thinking. The City's Christmas program advertising begins a week from Wednesday." Larry stepped to his desk and pointed at his calendar. "Yes, the eleventh. Will you be able to get the other two articles finished in time? We'll print the first in the Wednesday edition, the second the following Saturday, and the final article on Wednesday the eighteenth, the first night of the city's Christmas program when Jessie's memorial and the new City Hall will be dedicated."

I chuckled as Larry finished his plan in a single breath. "That works. I promise I'll have at least the second article finished and on your desk by next Monday." I gave Larry a Boy Scout pledge and crossed my heart. "I might even have a bonus article about John Priestly if our investigation continues to progress."

"Theo, before you leave, I've got an envelope for you concerning the contract on the new City Hall. I managed to find how much the city in fact paid versus how much the original contract awarded. It appears there were some additions to that originally approved contract too."

Larry pulled a sealed manila envelope from one of the side drawers. He held it tightly as he said, "I had a hard time getting this from the city records. Be careful and don't lose this. Someone might've squealed to the mayor's office by now." He released the envelope into my grasp and led us back to where the women entertained themselves planning their upcoming shopping trip. I enjoyed seeing Mary light up when Liddy suggested Jeannie go too.

On the short drive home, Liddy asked about my meeting and what went on with Mary. I told her what Mary said. When we pulled in at the house, Liddy remained buckled in her passenger seat.

"Are you okay?" I asked.

Liddy turned toward me and said, "I may be wrong, but what Mary said about Megan and Hank is making me wonder about my conversation with Megan and what Cora said this morning. It's all making me believe you're on the right track."

CHAPTER TWENTY-EIGHT

LIDDY HAD BOLTED OUT THE DOOR early to attend a ladies breakfast social at church. I had capitalized on the solitude and completed my second article before I jaunted across town to Zeb's place. The colder air testified to December's arrival, as did the sight of the city workers mounting the last of the holiday decorations and strands of lights on the Town Square. Yellow caution tape likewise marked off the future location of the highly anticipated city's Christmas tree.

After the door announced my arrival, Zeb looked up from his stool behind the counter as I said, "Good morning. Hope I caught you at a good time."

Zeb let out an extended sigh of relief. "It's good you dropped by. I need a break from these darn receipts."

"I ordered a special Christmas gift for Liddy but don't want it mailed to the house… you know, just in case it arrives when I'm not around."

Zeb chuckled. "No problem, just have them mail it here in your name. How big is it?"

"Thanks, Zeb. It's not very big at all. It's a custom necklace a jeweler from Atlanta made for me."

"When will it be here?"

"Friday, while Liddy's off shopping."

"Don't you worry. I'll tell the boys, and we'll put it here under the counter when it arrives."

"If you've got a few minutes to talk, I'd also like to ask you about John Priestly and the Boosters. I'm particularly curious about the clashes between John and the Archers' over the handling of money procedures."

Zeb leaned on top of the forgotten receipts and stroked his whiskers. "I guess things did get pretty riled up, but John met with the school's bookkeeper. They devised a better paper trail to track gate receipts and monies from concessions and raffles. As a result, the Boosters, including Harold, seemed content afterward. In return for John maintaining the athletic department checkbook, he agreed to submit weekly accounting sheets to the bookkeeper. After reconciling bank statements, she'd submit a monthly report to John."

The account of the school's bookkeeper squared with what I'd heard, but I remained confused. "So the boosters were satisfied?"

Zeb grinned. "Pretty much. But Harold insisted the Boosters institute better safeguards. He felt the recent increases in money flowing into the program deserved additional oversight, and would better protect John and the program. However, other members — myself included — felt John had handled everything without issue up to then, and with the bookkeeper's approved recommendations in place, no further oversight made sense."

"Wait a minute… so the Boosters rejected Harold's proposals?"

"Kind'a… John's reputation put the motion to bed, but to appease Harold, John offered to provide a copy of the monthly financial reports to the Boosters."

"I don't see a problem then." I tried to hide my frustration and hoped Zeb would clarify what happened.

"Harold relented, agreeing to the compromise under one condition. He suggested a Booster member be assigned to assist John with the collection and counting of the money after each home game. He argued it would protect John because there'd always be at least two people to witness all money transactions. I was there that night when we all approved Harold's suggestion."

"So who did the Boosters appoint to help John?"

Zeb grinned. "Funny, the motion went out to the members, and Hank Archer volunteered. And, as a result, as odd as it might've seemed, Hank and John cooperated after each home game after that."

"Hank?"

"No one else wanted to risk their friendship with John."

"Interesting... Were there ever any discrepancies with the money or monthly reports before the discovery of the missing money?"

"Nary a one. Is this making any sense for you?"

"I guess... so no further tension existed between the Archers and John after that?"

A wide grin pierced Zeb's beard. "John tolerated Hank's presence and oddly seemed even to appreciate it. It's safe to say they didn't send Christmas cards to each other if that's what you mean, but by appearances, John and Hank got along."

"Not sure that's what I expected to hear, but thanks anyway." I glanced at my watch. "I gotta run. See you Friday."

I deliberated upon Zeb's recollection of the facts as I walked to City Hall. I couldn't completely grasp the apparently relaxed tension between John and the Archers, but learning John tolerated Hank intrigued me.

———

Christmas garland adorned the portico's granite columns of City Hall. Inside, a brightly lit Christmas tree decorated with ornaments made by local children sat over the city's seal in the middle of the foyer.

Megan's office desk surrounded her as she stared at a file with her phone propped against her shoulder. She raised one finger as I approached.

"Mister Phillips, it's a pleasure to see you again," Megan said as she hung up. "The mayor's out of the office. He had to make an unexpected trip to Atlanta, and I'm about to leave in a couple of minutes. Can I help you with anything before I run?" She fidgeted with some files on her desk.

"Well, I certainly don't want to hold you up. Will Harold be back in the morning?"

Megan locked her desk and gathered her purse and keys. "I'm not sure. Can I leave him a message?"

"Can you let him know I'd like to talk about restarting Sanctuary? And I've news about John Priestly."

Megan dropped her pen and with a frozen stare stuttered, "John Priestly? What kind of news?"

"I'm sure Harold's already heard, but Joe Arians expects a call about him from the Parole Board today or tomorrow."

"Mister Phillips, that's great news. I'll be sure Harold gets the messages. But, what's this about Sanctuary?"

"Liddy and I are looking into getting it started again as a tribute to Jessie Masterson."

A pleased look replaced Megan's gaping mouth. "I'm sure the mayor will be happy to talk to you about it. Who'll lead it?"

"Pete, Andy and Jeannie Simmons, along with Jay and Jim Adams, will likely spearhead the startup."

"Jeannie… We used to be such good friends." Megan looked at the clock on the office wall. "Oops, I've got a doctor's appointment, and Hank's meeting me there. Will you let me know how it goes with Coach Priestly?"

I nodded as she threw her large bag over her shoulder and raced down the hallway towards the exit.

———

When I arrived home, I called my jeweler friend in Atlanta, and he agreed to mail the package to Zeb's Feed and Hardware via second-day delivery service that afternoon. As I hung up the phone, I heard Liddy drive up.

The phone rang during dinner. A puzzled Liddy handed me the receiver. "It's Harold Archer."

Harold sounded distracted. "Sorry for interrupting your dinner, but Megan said you stopped by today. What's this about Sanctuary?"

"Thanks for calling Harold. When will you be back in your office?

I'd like to meet with you. We'd like to restart Sanctuary as a tribute to Jessie Masterson."

Harold paused before he responded. "Sounds good to me. How's Thursday right after lunch?"

"That'll be fine. Thanks."

Harold cleared his throat then asked, "Theo, what's this about John Priestly?"

"You may already know this, but Joe Arians said the Parole Board approved John for an early release, and he'll likely be home before Christmas."

Harold paused. "Um… that's certainly good news. Very good news indeed. Thank you. We'll talk more Thursday. Again, sorry to interrupt your dinner. Please pass my apologies to Miss Liddy."

Liddy stared at me as I hung up. "What'd Harold want?"

"He apologized for interrupting our dinner, but Megan had just told him about my visit. Sounds like he's open to Sanctuary's restart and we're meeting Thursday afternoon."

Liddy tilted her head with a pensive look. "That's good. What'd he say about John?"

"He thanked me for the information and said we'd talk Thursday about that too."

I put away the last of the clean dishes after dinner while Liddy slid a peach cobbler into the oven. While I dried my hands, the sound of a truck's engine drew me to the kitchen window. I recognized Hank Archer's black pickup and watched him approach the front door wearing a scowl. Before I could alert Liddy, Hank pounded on the door, making the glass rattle.

Liddy appeared in the hallway startled. I looked at Liddy before I opened the door. "It's Hank Archer. Would you go and check on your dessert?"

Liddy hesitated but stepped into the kitchen. I waited long enough for Liddy to at least pretend to be busy in the kitchen which instigated two more loud raps.

From the kitchen, Liddy whispered, "Should I call someone?"

"No, it'll be fine." I opened the door just as Hank raised his fist again. He stepped back as I swung the storm door open with a manufactured smile.

"Hank. What's up? Please, come in."

Hank crossed his arms and stood his ground. "Mister Phillips, what did Megan tell you today?" The smell of beer coupled with his apparent anger made me nervous.

"Hank, what's wrong? Please, come on inside." I stepped back, but he didn't budge. His wild eyes glared right through me.

"Mister Phillips, did Megan tell you anything about our private business?"

"Look, Hank, I came looking for your dad after lunch. Megan told me he was out of town."

"What else?"

"Megan said she'd give my message to your dad, and then mentioned she had to leave for a doctor's visit and then left. Why?"

"She didn't say anything else?" He flexed his crossed arms folded over his swollen chest.

"Did something happen? Is Megan okay?" I tried to remain cordial to counter his aggressive, gruff demeanor.

Hank snapped back, "Well…. then have you or your wife talked to my dad about Megan?"

My cordialness faded. "Hank, I'm really at a loss at what you want me to say to you. If you'd like to sit down, I'd be glad to calmly talk. We can continue this inside, or I can join you on the porch. I'm just not comfortable holding a conversation standing in my doorway."

Hank stepped further back onto the porch.

I turned my head toward the kitchen and shouted, "Hey Hun, I'll be on the porch." When I peeked towards the kitchen, I winked at Liddy's intense, concerned stare.

Our exterior Christmas lights provided ample lighting as I stepped away from the doorway and closed the storm door behind me. "Now Hank, what have I said or done to have ticked you off like this? I feel like you're accusing me of something."

Hank glared off into the darkness before he responded a little more composed. "Mister Phillips, look, you're new in town, but everyone knows you're snooping around and asking questions about my family."

"Well, my snooping as you call it involves my story about Jessie Masterson. Even your father knows about it. Why are you so upset about that?" I leaned against the pillar next to the steps, hoping my relaxed posture would help put Hank at ease.

"If you're only writing about Jessie Masterson, why are you asking about what happened to John Priestly?"

"Come on. You know how close they were. Learning about Coach Masterson naturally led me to what happened to Coach Priestly."

Hank gritted his teeth as the veins on his neck swelled, and his eyes glared through me. "Well, I think you're sticking your nose into places you've no business being." He uncrossed his arms and pointed at my chest. "I'm warning you. Stay away from me, and my wife!"

"Hank, I'm sorry if I've said or done anything to upset you. Have you spoken to your father?"

"This is between you and me. Stay out of our lives." Hank's effort to be more composed fell apart.

Just then, two trucks drove around the corner and pulled into our driveway. With one eye on the arrival of our guests, I began to reason with Hank. "I have a job to do, but I'll do my best to respect your concerns. But remember who survived the night Jessie died. As I understand it, he made it possible for you to be standing here tonight. So I guess you're a part of the story whether you like it or not."

Hank cocked his head and snarled, "Yeah, so what?"

"I'd prefer to hear your side of the story about that night along with anything you might be able to tell me about what happened to Coach Priestly."

"That's not likely to happen. Besides, why do you want to know what happened to John Priestly?"

Five shadows now observed Hank and me from the walkway below.

"Look, Hank. John'll be home in a few days, and I'm going to be interested in getting his story too."

Hank pushed his finger into my sternum. "This is all I'm going to say to you about Jessie or John..." He thumped his finger against my chest adding emphasis to each word. "I'm truly sorry about what happened to Jessie, but John got what he deserved. And you can quote me on that. Now back off! I'm warning you."

Pete stepped out from the shadows, unceremoniously interrupting Hank's exchange with me. "Mister P, is everything okay?" Pete asked as he glared at Hank. "Hank, who're you warning about what?"

Hank surveyed Pete and the four remaining shadows just out of the light. His finger fell to his side, but his distended veins on his neck swelled even more. "Pete, this has nothing to do with you or any of you guys!"

Pete stepped all the way onto the porch and positioned himself between Hank and me. Andy, Jay, and Jim remained at the foot of the steps with Jeannie two steps back. Andy caught my eye and winked with a confident look on his face.

Pete extended his finger just shy of Hank's chest. "How in the blue blazes do you know it don't involve us? If you think you can flex your muscles and intimidate one of my friends, you just made it my business." His stern warning and unflinching stare froze Hank. "I suggest you apologize to Mister P and then go home and mind your own business. Better yet, from the smell of your breath, maybe we should call Hal to drive you home."

Liddy stood by the storm door. Jeannie slipped past the boys and me and stood beside her. Hank surveyed Andy, Jim and Jay and then Liddy and Jeannie.

I stepped around Pete. "Look, Hank. I'm still not sure what brought you out here tonight, but let me be the first to apologize to you and Megan. I'm sorry if I said or did anything to upset either of you." I offered my hand, but Hank pushed it aside.

Hank peered at Liddy standing beside Jeannie. "Fine. Y'all just mind your own damn business." He turned and shoved his way through Andy, Jay, and Jim. All heads watched Hank jump into his truck and roar off.

"That was fun," I said as a smile returned to my face, and the others joined us on the porch.

Pete whispered as we walked into the house, "Mister P, you know we've got your back. Besides, it looked like you figured out that ol' Hank's more bark than bite anyway. But all the same, be careful. Hank's nothing but trouble." Pete's contagious laugh erased most of the tension still lingering from my confrontation with Hank.

Jeannie followed Liddy into the kitchen while the guys plopped onto seats in the living room. Andy added a log and stoked the fireplace and sat at the end of the hearth near the Christmas tree.

I eyed our four young friends, thankful for Jessie's and John's influences upon them. Jeannie broke our relieved silence. "Miss Liddy's peach cobbler with vanilla ice cream is ready. Come and get it."

I clapped my hands forestalling the mad dash to the kitchen. "First, let me thank y'all for not only being here tonight but also for showing up on time. Before we get our dessert, I've got some great news. I spoke to Mayor Archer tonight, and I meet with him Thursday to discuss Sanctuary."

We ate our cobbler and ice cream in the living room while the boys and Jeannie shared their favorite Sanctuary memories. The evening ended with their ideas to organize the first meeting. We tentatively set the third Wednesday in January as the launch date. Jeannie suggested we arrange for a photo with the Mayor to promote our plans in the *Sentinel*, and then ask the Mayor to mention Sanctuary during the dedication of Jessie's memorial.

The boys and Jeannie pulled away a little before nine thirty. Liddy put her arm around my waist as we watched them leave. "You know, I think we're undoubtedly dropping deep and lasting roots in our new community, even if there're still a couple of nasty weeds yet to contend with." She hugged me tighter and smiled. "I don't know what Hank's problem is, but you handled him pretty well for an old man. I think you impressed the boys too."

CHAPTER TWENTY-NINE

THE NEXT MORNING, I AGAIN read over the draft of my second article, Jessie's Glory Days. The article capitalized on my scribbled notes from those who knew Jessie best and offered insight into his teaching and coaching impact. Alex Thrope's memories reflected the most objective look at how Jessie's impact transcended wins, losses, and trophies.

I handed Liddy my handwritten final copy at breakfast while I perused the morning edition of the *Sentinel*. Several long minutes passed, Liddy laid my paper-clipped copy aside. "Here you go, Hun." She then left the table without comment nor hint of either her pleasure or displeasure.

I flipped through each page. Liddy continued to load dirty dishes into the dishwasher, her back to me. Confused, I inquired, "Sweetie, help me here. Um… You didn't make any notes or say anything."

"Hun, why do you think I didn't write or say anything?"

"You've always found something before." My angst grew in the seconds of silence that followed.

Liddy straightened her back and turned. With a tender-hearted look, she said, "Theo Phillips, I can honestly say not another comment is needed, other than this…" She brushed my hand aside, sat on my lap and put her head on my shoulder. "It's the best I've ever read from you. Everyone will be captured by your depiction of Jessie and John. At the same time, they'll be amazed at how well you got to know their impact upon Shiloh in the short time we've been here."

I looked into her soulful eyes and hugged her. We sat in silence before she lifted her head and asked, "Did you say if you didn't hear any more about John's parole you wanted to stop by Joe's office?"

"Why?"

"I'd like to tag along and make sure Nick and Joe won't mind losing Susanna and Jeannie this Friday."

"I almost forgot about your girls-only outing. Sure, we can go into town together."

———

Jeannie was not at her desk, but a shuffling sound of boxes came from beyond the open closet door. Jeannie backed out of the closet carrying a dusty storage box, lifted it onto the counter and wiped her hands on her dress jeans.

After inspecting her palms, Jeannie grabbed Liddy's hand and blushed. "I'm sorry. I wasn't expecting you." Jeannie dabbed her flushed cheeks with the sleeves of her blouse.

I chuckled and said, "Looks like you've been working hard."

Jeannie grabbed a tissue. "I've been busy all morning organizing and cleaning, and that darn old closet gets mighty stuffy in there. But, it's gotta get done, and Nick's certainly not goin' to do it." She elevated her voice as her protest for the lack of help.

I eyed the hall anticipating Nick's arrival. Liddy grinned and said equally loud, "We understand." Liddy hesitated and said even louder, "Besides, it's my fault we stopped by today."

Jeannie's reddened dimples accentuated her curious smile.

Liddy pulled a tissue from her purse and stepped in front of Jeannie with a mother's grin. "You've got a small dirt smudge on your cheek." Liddy lightly wiped her cheek, took a step back and surveyed Jeannie's face with a triumphant grin.

"Thank you, Miss Liddy."

Liddy said, "Before it slips my mind, with all that went on last night, I meant to ask if you and your mom might like to go shopping this Friday? Mary and her mom are going, along with Judy Wright and Miss Marie."

Jeannie's curious smile broadened. "Of course. I'd love it. That is if I can get off work."

"I thought I recognized your voice, Miss Liddy. What are you conspiring with my assistant?" Nick asked, laughing as he stepped from his office.

Liddy bit her lower lip and greeted Nick with a determined glare in her eyes. "I've got a bone to pick with you, Nick Arians."

Puzzled, he put his hands up in front of him, as if uncertain whether to protect himself or surrender. "Liddy, what'd I do?"

Jeannie began to step towards Liddy, but I rested my arm on her shoulder and whispered, "Shh. She won't bite him."

"You're overworking this poor girl. Why she's ruining her nice outfit and sweating like a farm hand." Liddy stopped abruptly put one hand on her hip and wagged her forefinger at Nick.

Nick looked beyond Liddy at Jeannie and me standing out of the line of fire. Then he looked back at Liddy. "Uh... Uh...."

"Oh, quit your stuttering. Jeannie's been so helpful to us since we first arrived in town. We wanted to do something nice to show our appreciation. And now we see how you're making her bust a sweat today. It seems to me that this poor girl has earned a day off. How about this Friday as a matter of fact?"

I smiled at Nick and shrugged my shoulders. Jeannie stood speechless, puzzled by Liddy's brazen tirade.

"Miss Liddy, since you put it that way, I guess we could work something out," he relented caught between a grin and a grimace.

Liddy's snarl became a snicker and then a loud laugh. "Oh Nick, I was just messin' with you. I just thought Jeannie would enjoy going on a ladies day out a few of us have planned."

Nick's brows arched as he glanced at Jeannie, who shied away from returning direct eye contact with him, but her flush cheeks and clinched lower lip spoke volumes. "Jeannie, if *we* finish decorating the office before we close tomorrow, I think I can handle the office Friday by myself."

Jeannie let out a huge sigh, and her breathing returned to normal.

"Thanks, Nick. I'm nearly done organizing the closet. *We'll* be finished decorating long before *we* go home tomorrow."

Nick bellowed, "Ho! Ho! Ho! That settles that." He hugged Liddy and winked at Jeannie before he asked me to step into his office.

In his office, Nick asked, "Did you hear anything about John?"

"No, not yet. But, Joe thought we'd hear today."

Nick rubbed his cheek. "Joe hasn't said anything to me either."

"I'm sure we'll hear by this afternoon." Nick conceded with a slight nod, and then I added, "By the way, hope you don't mind, but I'd like to mention you in the last of the articles I'm writing about Jessie."

Nick grinned. "If it'd help, that's fine with me."

"Well, you helped inspire me to write the articles in the first place. It'd only be fitting to give credit where it's due."

Nick smiled. "If you say so. Thanks. Will I see you and Liddy to-night?"

"Yea, we'll be there. And thanks for being a good sport with Liddy's little charade."

"Don't worry about it. Besides, Jeannie knows she can take a day off anytime she needs it," Nick admitted with a chuckle.

Before we walked up the stairs leading up to Joe's office, Liddy pulled me aside. "Hun, while you and Nick were in his office, Jeannie and I talked about Hank's visit last night."

"What did Jeannie have to say?"

"She said she felt awful that Hank threatened you, but she's more concerned about how he may be treating Megan."

"I understand. What else did Jeannie say?"

"Jeannie met Megan during Jeannie's freshman year. Even though Megan was a senior, they became close friends, and their friendship continued after Megan graduated, at least until Megan married Hank." Liddy then added, "I believe Jeannie wanted to say more, but you and Nick came out of his office before I could ask."

"Maybe she'll let you know if there's more on Friday."

———

Susanna's frazzled look greeted us as she fumbled through a stack of files, glanced at the glowing light on her phone, and grabbed papers from her printer. Her busyness instigated her abbreviated greeting. "Thought you might've been here earlier. Joe's been on and off his phone all morning. Whatever's happening must be good news, though. He's been whistling between calls and requests for files on John."

Liddy peered at my smiling face and said to Susanna, "Glad to hear he's in a good mood then."

Susanna looked up from her desk. "What do you mean?"

Liddy shared how Nick let Jeannie take Friday off and suggested that Susanna should get off too. I heard enough to know I needed to find a safe seat on the sofa and put my nose in a dated *Sports Illustrated*. Another incoming call interrupted Liddy and Susanna chatting about the shopping trip.

Susanna put her hand over the mouthpiece and looked in my direction. "It's the DA's office calling for the third time about John." She returned to her caller. "Yes, do you want to hold a moment? Mr. Arians's still on the phone." Susanna intently listened before she interrupted the caller. "Mr. Arians just hung up. I'm sure he wants to speak with you." She put the phone on hold and apologized to us as she disappeared beyond Joe's office door.

The blinking hold light went dark a moment later. Susanna reappeared wearing a big grin. She carefully closed the door behind her and provided a non-verbal okay with her forefinger and thumb.

Back at her desk, she whispered, "Theo, this is the call Joe's been waiting for. It should confirm if John's motion for release has been fast-tracked for approval." Susanna pointed to the door. "In another moment or two, you'll know how the call went when Joe comes out of his office."

I gave a thumbs-up and pointed upward to share my belief that

God was in control. I set the magazine on the sofa, leaned forward, and offered a brief silent prayer for God's will to be done.

Susanna whispered to Liddy loud enough for me to hear, "Joe's been keeping me busy these last few days. I'm overdue for some time off to get some Christmas shopping done. Friday sounds like a great idea. Besides, it'll be fun spending time with Marie." Susanna slouched in her chair and stared at the desk littered with files and papers. A dejected and forlorn look came over her. "I just don't know if I can take a day off on such short notice. There's so much going on right now."

Joe's office door swung open. He stepped out with his chest puffed out and a congratulatory look on his face. "It's done except for some last-minute signatures. John will be out in a week."

Joe and I celebrated with a fist bump.

"William Paraman from the DA's office said his boss and Cal Barnard at the State Parole Board office received several well-timed calls from Atlanta encouraging them to cooperate and do what it took to facilitate the parole process so John would be home before Christmas. Whoever was behind those calls should get a huge thank you." Joe took a big breath and slowly exhaled.

Liddy said, "Joe, that's terrific news. When are you going to let Marie know?"

"Just as soon as the signed order from the Parole office gets faxed over. No need to rile her emotions up until then. Besides, the order will tell me exactly when John will be released."

"Do you think it'll be here today or tomorrow?" I asked.

Joe confidently said, "The Parole Board meets this afternoon. I hope before tomorrow morning. Why do you ask?"

Liddy smiled. "What if I told you Marie and some of the women are meeting Friday for a ladies outing? That would be great news for Marie to celebrate while we're together, wouldn't it?"

Joe grinned at Liddy and Susanna. "Susanna, I bet you'd like to celebrate with Marie on Friday too, wouldn't you?"

Susanna offered a hopeful grin.

"She deserves to celebrate the news with you too Susanna. You've earned it."

Liddy's sheepish look triggered Susanna's full-fledged smile.

Joe added, "We should be able to get whatever needs to be done by tomorrow night. I'll handle the office Friday. Go ahead and get your shopping list made up."

"You sure?"

"Absolutely. Besides, if it gets too crazy, I'll ask Theo to give me a hand." Joe winked at me before letting out a boisterous laugh.

Susanna hugged Joe. "This is for all the long hours helping John." Then she kissed his forehead, leaving a noticeable red lipstick mark.

Joe blushed. "Okay, okay, but please remember to carry your cell phone. I might need to find something while you're having fun on Friday."

Liddy then asked, "Joe do you think Missy will want to go with us?"

"I'm sure she'd love to, but I'll have to see if mom will watch the twins. Why don't you call Missy later, and see what she says."

I grabbed my handkerchief from my back pocket and handed it to Joe. "You probably want to get rid of Susanna's lipstick on your forehead before you have to explain it to Missy."

CHAPTER THIRTY

"LIDDY, WHEN YOU'RE DONE ON the phone, please let me know. I've got to make a quick call."

"Almost done, just finished confirming with Missy Arians about tomorrow, and I need to make a quick call to Judy. I'll only be a minute more."

My thoughts shifted to my appointment with Harold after lunch.

Liddy's voice rang out. "Theo, I'm done and headed to the church to help Judy for a bit. Do you need the car?"

"No. Have fun and say hello, for me."

Harold's voice surprised me when he answered. He confirmed our appointment and said he looked forward to seeing me right after lunch.

Though nearly noon, my anxiousness about John's pending release demanded a quick stop at Joe's office before I went to City Hall. Lunch could wait.

I heard Susanna and Joe in an inaudible exchange in the back office just before she appeared clutching a handful of papers. "Theo, Good morning. I was just about to call you. Joe's got John's papers on his desk. I'll let Joe tell you the news."

Susanna's rushed, business-like demeanor gave me the sense that the news was not as we expected yesterday. I wondered out loud, "Did the Parole Board finalize John's parole decision?"

Susanna walked by me to her desk and said, "Yes, but let Joe explain it to you." She saw Joe's line free up, looked towards Joe's open office door and shouted, "Joe, I just talked with Theo Phillips for you."

Joe's voice echoed back, "What'd he say?"

"Why not ask him yourself? He's out here."

Joe appeared from his office with rolled up shirtsleeves and loosened tie. "Theo, I'm glad you're here. Come on back."

Joe reached for a file on his desk, pulled out a faxed letter from the Georgia State Board of Probation and Parole, and handed it to me. He pointed to two highlighted parts. John received approval for his early work release motion, and his release date from Clearwater State Prison was December thirteenth, next Friday.

"I've already made some calls this morning to confirm next Friday." Joe stared at my raised brows and smugly confessed, "The extra couple of days comes without too much surprise. Everything in Georgia takes longer because of the bureaucratic red tape in Atlanta, but it's done. I'm going to invite Marie to come with me to pick up John."

"That's good news. I'm sure John won't mind a couple more days to get home. Congratulations." I smacked Joe's shoulder.

"I'm pleased, but I'll feel a whole lot better once John's beyond barbed wire and back in Shiloh." Joe walked me to his office door. "What do you have planned today?"

"I'm heading over to Harold's office to solicit support for Sanctuary getting started again. I'm sure he'll ask about the latest on John's parole if he doesn't already know."

"Sounds like fun. Be sure to give my regards to our dear mayor," Joe said with a tinge of sarcasm. "Oh yeah, did Liddy tell you? Missy's goin' with the ladies tomorrow."

"I heard. Your mother agreed to watch the twins?"

His distorted grin spoke first. "Not exactly. Momma suggested I take the day off. Momma insisted Missy ain't goin' without her. Missy said I deserve some time off anyway."

"I agree. You've earned a day off. Enjoy time with the twins."

———

The sound of city employees scurrying about echoed from the granite hallways and grand marble staircase as I walked past the Christmas tree in the foyer toward the mayor's office. Megan hung her coat and stashed her purse behind her desk as I approached when I noticed her puffy eyes and flushed cheeks as her forced smile greeted me.

She sniffled and said, "Mister Phillips, I forgot about your appointment. Harold just called and said he's on his way." She pulled a tissue from the box on the corner of her desk and turned away to blow her nose.

"That's fine. I'm early anyway. Do you mind if I sit here?" I pointed to the chair next to her desk.

"Not at all, please do," she replied. She stared at her empty desk, and tears flowed from the corner of her eyes. "I'm sorry. I just need a minute." She grabbed a handful of tissues and walked down the hall.

Megan's cell phone began buzzing right after she left and continued until she reappeared and frantically fumbled through her purse. "I need to take this," she said. She swiveled in her chair until her back faced me. I tried not to listen, but her louder than intended frustrated whispers made it hard to ignore.

"Look, Hank, I can't talk now! I'm back at the office, and Harold will be here any second." She ran her fingers through her blond hair. "Please! Let's talk about this tonight. I'll call when I leave." Another brief pause, and though I could not make out Hank's words, his growing anger came through loud and clear. Megan broke her whisper. "No. I promise, as soon as I leave, I'll call you!" Her finger clung to the face of her smartphone as she turned her chair back around.

"Everything okay?"

Megan sighed. "Not really. We got some bad news this morning." Her focus retreated to her bare desk.

Lost for words, I leaned closer and whispered, "I'm sorry."

She did not look up but tilted her head slightly to make a little eye contact. "Do you remember when you and Liddy visited the house, and I told you how Hank and I planned to start a family?"

"Of course."

Sniffles followed by a long sigh created a tear-filled pause. "Theo, my doctor told me I can't have children."

I sat back in my chair and searched for words. "I assume Hank knows?"

She answered through her sobbing. "Yes, but he doesn't know why."

"What about Harold, does he know?"

Her teary eyes connected with mine, and I saw fear in her face. "Oh no, not yet! But, I'm afraid Hank won't keep it a secret for long."

I wished Liddy was here as I grabbed another tissue and handed it to her. I asked, "Have you talked with anyone else, like your mother or father?"

"Theo, you're too kind. Thank you. I'm not sure how to tell my folks."

"Look, I admit I'm not very good at this kind of thing. I raised two boys." I tried to hold onto a grin as best as I could.

Megan generated a polite grin as she surveyed the office and wiped her eyes again. "I'm sorry. I just don't know who to talk to."

"Liddy's just across the street. Do you want me to reach her?"

"Oh no. Please, not right now."

"Well, when you feel ready, you can certainly talk with Liddy. In the meantime, why not call Pastor Wright? I know he's a good listener and can offer you and Hank solid advice."

"That actually sounds like a good idea. I'll give him a call in a little bit."

"Good. Pastor Wright can help you get through this, and he'll keep it between just you and him."

Megan's swollen eyes and reddened cheeks finally appeared tear free. She even provided a tight smile and nod. The sound of heavy footsteps and a door opening and closing announced Harold's return through his private office door. The intercom on Megan's desk buzzed a moment later.

Megan grabbed the receiver, listened and said, "Yes, sir. Yes, sir. No, sir. Oh, Theo Phillips is out here waiting for you... Okay." She looked up and whispered, "The Mayor will see you now." As I stood, she clutched my forearm. "Thanks, Mister Phillips."

I leaned closer and whispered, "Everything will be fine. You'll see.

God works everything out for the greater good of all who love him."

"Thanks. I want to believe that, but I'm not sure God's listening to me right now."

I pointed to the phone. "Call Pastor Wright. I'm sure he'll put in a good word for you."

As I entered his grandiose office, he pointed to two leather armchairs separated by an antique table. "Theo, sorry. Lunch got interrupted with some personal matters."

"Don't fret about that. Megan kept me company. I know you're busy, but I'd like to talk briefly with you about an idea Liddy and I want to explore, but we need your help."

"Is this about Sanctuary? Harold pushed his chair back and stepped around his desk. "I thought about it after we spoke a little on the phone. If you want a place to meet, I should be able to get the general purpose room in the basement approved for your meetings. Heck, it'll be like the old days again. Besides, the room's only being used as a break room for the janitors since we moved in a couple of months ago."

"That'd be perfect, Harold. It'll be a great tribute to Jessie Masterson's legacy to have Sanctuary up and running again. What do you think?"

Harold rocked his feet with his thumbs tucked into his vest pockets. "Yes, it's a splendid idea. Would you like me to say something about it during the Jessie Masterson memorial dedication?"

"You read my mind. Also, would you care if Mary Scribner took a publicity photo for the paper with you and Sanctuary's leaders? Of course, I'm sure Larry will also mention your generous support in his article."

Harold paused in thought. "Of course. Have Mary call Megan. Now tell me about John Priestly? What's the latest?"

"I just left Joe Arians' office. It's official. He'll be home next Friday. From what I understand, the DA's office and State Parole Board received a few well-placed calls that spurred the decision along. You wouldn't know anything about that would you?"

A smug look appeared on Harold's jovial face. "That's good to hear. By the way, where's John going to live? You and Liddy own his old house."

"Marie Masterson wants him to stay at her farmhouse."

"That's mighty generous of her."

I rose and shook Harold's hand. "Thanks for the help Harold. I know you're busy. Hey, one more quick question. When's the city's Christmas tree arriving?"

"Next Friday. It's coming from upstate. Hal told me it's the biggest we've ever had. He said he needed to arrange for a special crane to offload it when it gets here."

"Can't wait to see it. Thanks again, Harold." I turned and walked by Megan's desk as I left.

Megan's blue eyes hesitated to make direct contact, but she did provide a composed smile. "Mister Phillips, thanks. I called the pastor. We're meeting this afternoon."

"That's good to hear. Everything'll work out just fine. I'm sure."

———

I found Liddy busy in her back room painting poster boards for the church's children's department. Wearing one of my old flannel shirts over her blouse and jeans, she looked up from her easel. "How'd your meeting with Harold go?"

"Oh, it went fine. Harold agreed to have his picture taken for the paper's story and to mention the restart of Sanctuary during Jessie's memorial dedication."

"Did he fuss about it at all?"

"Not at all. Harold loved the idea and the publicity even more. He also said getting the room beneath City Hall should be no problem."

Liddy giggled. "That doesn't surprise me."

"I also told him the latest news on John."

"Oh? What'd you find out? Did you talk to Joe this morning?"

"Sure did. John'll be home next Friday."

"How did Harold respond to the news?"

"Curious enough, he appeared a little smug about it. More importantly, you need to know about Megan."

"What about Megan?"

"She got some bad news. The doctor informed her that she can't have children."

Liddy laid her paintbrush aside and stepped around her easel. A frown fell on her face. "How did you find that out?"

"When I got to City Hall, Harold wasn't back yet, but Megan was at her desk crying. She told me the news when I tried to console her."

Liddy walked up, put her arms around my waist and looked up at me.

"I wished you were there. I overheard her brief cell phone exchange with Hank, who from the sound of it, responded poorly to the news. When I asked if she talked to her parents, she said she wasn't sure how to tell them. She appeared scared about the thought of telling Harold but felt certain Hank would probably break the news by tonight."

"So what's she going to do? It sounds as though she needs someone to talk to?"

"She agreed to call Arnie and is meeting him this afternoon."

Liddy hesitated and then said, "Arnie's a good person for her right now, but I'm worried about her and Hank. I gathered she was banking on things improving between them after they had a child together."

I squeezed Liddy's shoulders and looked into her sad eyes. "You don't know how badly I wish you'd of been there with me. I felt uncomfortable and unsure responding to all the tears Megan shed."

Liddy sighed. "Theo, sounds like you did just fine."

———

Liddy left right after sunrise to meet Marie for breakfast before catching up with the others at the church. With so many going, Arnie had suggested Judy take the church's van.

While I sipped on my morning coffee and enjoyed the paper, the phone rang. Zeb let me know that my special package arrived.

Nick Arians stood outside his office locking the door when I walked up and looked through his front office window. "Nick, it looks like y'all did an admirable job decorating your office." A small artificial Christmas tree sat on the counter, and silver garland hung throughout the front office. A twinkling wreath decorated the back wall. I laughed at the painted cardboard fireplace display affixed to the wall across from Jeannie's desk. A sign above it read, "There's no place like home for Christmas."

I looked at Nick and pointed to the sign. "Nice touch. Where are you heading anyway?"

"Larry's. He's printing some posters for me. Are you headed over there?"

"I'm on my way to see Zeb. Have fun checking on Larry with both Martha and Mary away."

———

I found Jay busy at the front counter. He pointed toward the warehouse. When I stepped through the sliding door, Zeb stood on the loading ramp engaged with a customer. He waved and indicated he'd be five minutes. I waved back and leaned against a pallet.

Jim dismounted the fork truck and walked up the aisle with papers in his hand. He removed his leather work gloves, and we shook hands. "Looks mighty busy today?"

"Yeah, everyone knows we always shut down between Christmas and New Year's, so these last two weeks before Christmas are always pretty crazy around here."

"Bet you guys are looking forward to having off that whole week."

"Yes, sir. We sure are."

"I don't blame you. Hey, I'm just here to pick up a package your dad has for me. And by the way, I spoke with the mayor, and he's going to let Sanctuary use a meeting room at City Hall. He also said he'd arrange with Mary to have a photo taken with you guys to publicize the group's kickoff."

"That's awesome."

"Tell Jay and the others, will you?"

Jim smiled. "Yes, sir. Thanks, Mister P. Looks like Pop's free now." He quickly headed toward the front of the store.

"Sorry, Theo. We're just so busy this time of year," Zeb said brushing himself off as dust floated off his flannel shirt.

"No problem. I'm glad business is good. Jim told me that you close the entire Christmas week."

"Yep, but we'll do a whole month's business these next two weeks." He led me back into the store. "If you don't mind me asking, what's in the package? It ain't real big."

"Like I said the other day, it's a custom-made necklace for Liddy. My sons helped me design it."

Zeb bent down behind the front counter and handed me a padded envelope.

I peeled the flap and removed a velvet jewelry box. "Do you want to see it?"

"Sure. I bet it's pretty."

I carefully removed the gold chain necklace with the custom-made cross pendant and draped it across the palm of my hand. Jay and Jim joined Zeb at the counter. Eight pairs of eyes admired the birthstones and diamonds that sparkled in the sunlight.

"Wow. Mister P, that's really pretty. Miss Liddy's going to like that for sure."

Jay reached out to touch the necklace, but Zeb swatted his hand away. "Son, that's too pretty for your grimy fingers to be touching."

"Sorry Pop."

Zeb slipped his hands into the top of his bib overalls and smiled. "Your wife sure is a lucky lady."

I returned the necklace to the box and slid it back into the padded envelope. "Thanks, Zeb. I appreciate your help with this. I'm going to wrap it before Liddy gets home tonight. It'll drive her crazy knowing she has two weeks before she can open it."

———

Liddy arrived home well after sunset. I raced to put the final touches on the dining room table. The aroma of marinara sauce with sausages filled the house.

Liddy looked exhausted as she pushed her way through the kitchen door carrying two large shopping bags. "Mmmm. Smells good. How soon before we eat?" Her eyes scanned the cluttered counter tops and dirty pots in the sink as she took her coat off. "Sure looks like you worked hard to surprise me with dinner. Thanks"

"It was fun. Now go wash up. Dinner's ready." I then placed her wrapped gift in her seat with a note attached that read, "Do not open until before Christmas Eve. Merry Christmas. T"

CHAPTER THIRTY-ONE

LIDDY HANDED ME A CUP of coffee with the morning paper and nestled into her chair and sipped her coffee. I opened to Larry's editorial article that suggested Harold Archer was about to throw his hat in the ring for the open state senate seat.

Before I could mention it to Liddy, she broke her contemplative silence. "Theo, I feel just awful. I just can't stop wondering how Hank reacted to Megan's news. Heavens, it wouldn't surprise me none if he rolled around the corner again and blamed us."

I lowered the paper. "What do you mean blame us?"

Her soulful eyes met mine. "I just mean… well, you know, how irrational Hank can be. When Hank stormed over here the other night, it was fairly obvious to me that he wasn't interested in protecting her."

"Wow, come to think about it, you're right. I didn't buy Hank's heated plea had much to do with their privacy. His anger had another purpose."

"From what you told me about Megan's call with Hank, he likely could've flown off the handle last night," Liddy said, definitely unsettled. "She had every reason to dread Hank's reaction. I wonder if he's even stopped to consider how Megan's struggling with the news?"

"The thought definitely crossed my mind. Should we check in on her today?"

Liddy fiddled with her coffee cup. "My instincts tell me Megan's not much more than a trophy wife to Hank. Even Cora affirmed what Maddie told me about how lonely Megan is in that big old house and how often Hank berates her. I'm just not sure what we should do yet."

"Hmm…me neither, but I'm concerned enough to wonder why she married him in the first place."

"Why'd you say that?"

"I wonder if the rumor Mary shared might be closer to the truth than we realize."

"Do you mean Megan's phantom pregnancy story?" Liddy raised her eyebrows as she pondered the thought.

"I'm not sure, but I surmise Hank's trying to live up to his father's expectations." I pointed to Larry's article in the morning newspaper. "Larry confirmed what Harold told me in confidence about his political aspirations. Maybe Hank's too concerned about winning back his father's approval and not letting him down again." I stopped and scratched my chin. "Harold's previous plans to run for the Senate three years ago derailed after all the cumulative bad publicity over the school contract scandal, John's arrest and Jessie's death surfaced. Maybe Hank's trying too hard to regain Harold's confidence so he can take over the family's business again. He might even see himself as the next mayor when Harold wins the Senate seat and heads to Atlanta."

Liddy muttered. "Like father, like son?"

I chuckled. "Only in Hank's eyes. Harold's shoes are too big for Hank. Besides, he's already stumbled once in those shoes."

Liddy sighed. "Enough about Hank. Let's focus on Megan."

"Well, I hope her visit with Arnie helped."

Liddy stared back out the window. "I just can't grasp how hard this news must be for her. I just feel horrible. She'll never have a child of her own." She dabbed her cheek with her robe sleeve.

I leaned out of my chair, wiped her tear-stained cheeks with my fingertips and placed my arm around her. "Do you know who drives a Red Jeep?"

"Why?" Liddy curiously asked.

"One just pulled up out front, and the driver's talking on his phone."

Liddy pulled back from my embrace and turned toward the window. "I don't know. I haven't seen it before."

Phillip Archer stepped out of the Jeep when I arrived onto the porch. He adjusted his shirt and hair as he walked toward me.

"Good morning Phillip." I braced the storm door open and invited him inside.

"Thank you, sir." Phillip stomped his pointed leather boots on the welcome mat and removed his sunglasses.

Liddy greeted him in the living room. "Please excuse my robe. I wasn't expecting company."

"Sorry, ma'am. I probably should've called first." Phillip dangled his glasses in his hands and avoided eye contact.

Liddy directed him to the sofa. "Would you like a cup of coffee or some juice?"

"No thank you. I'm fine." Phillip cleared his throat and inspected his glasses. "Mister Phillips, Hank came home last night all fired up and started a huge fight with Megan in their room. He then stormed downstairs and dad confronted him. Hank raved on and on about you meddling in the family's business and his personal life."

I stared at Phillip before I responded, but could not get his eyes to meet mine. "How did your dad respond?"

Phillip's head popped up. "Mister Phillips, my dad defended you. He said you've been respectful and straightforward. He told Hank any questions you've asked have dealt with your interest in Coach Masterson."

"Well, I'm glad to hear your dad said that."

"When dad asked Hank why he was so upset, Hank dropped some bad news about what the doctor told Megan."

"Megan told me about it yesterday. We feel sad for Megan and Hank. How'd your dad handle the news?"

"At first, he just sat without saying anything. He looked numb. He tried to talk to Hank, but I think dad struggled with his own emotions. He asked about Megan and scolded Hank for treating her like he did. Hank claimed he got mad at Megan because she shared the news outside of the family."

Liddy left her chair and sat beside Phillip. "That's understandable.

But why would Hank be so angry at Megan and not recognize about how badly she feels?"

"Miss Liddy, my dad asked Hank the same thing, but Hank told dad to butt out of his and Megan's personal affairs. The more dad tried to calm him down, the more infuriated Hank became. Hank got so steamed up I thought he'd take a swing at dad."

I leaned forward in my chair. "Oh no! He didn't, did he?"

"Thankfully, Hal arrived home. He took Hank for a walk while I talked with dad. That's when dad suggested I stop by this morning to see if you were okay and apologize for Hank's visit the other night."

"Tell your dad we're fine. More importantly, how's Megan?"

Phillip's eyes darted between Liddy and me. "We don't know. She stormed out of the house lugging her suitcase before we could talk to her. We think she went to her parent's house."

Liddy looked intently at Phillip. "Anything else happened that caused Megan to leave?"

"After Hal returned with Hank, Hank went back upstairs. This time we heard Megan's voice as much as Hank's. That's when Megan stormed downstairs and drove off. At breakfast this morning, Hank told dad and me that he blamed you two for Megan walking out."

Liddy peeked out of the corner of her eye. I sank back into my chair trying to make sense of Hank's accusation. "Phillip, did he say why he thought we were at fault?"

"No. Hank was just blowing steam like usual. Dad told me on the phone as I drove up that he warned Hank to leave Megan alone. She needs time to sort this out, and he said to tell you that he warned Hank to stay clear of both of you as well. Dad wanted me to make sure you understood how sorry he feels for Hank's behavior."

Liddy wrapped her arm around Phillip's shoulder and said, "It'll be okay." Phillip continued to stare at the floor but appeared comforted by Liddy's attention.

I scooted to the edge of my chair. "Liddy's right, everything will work out. Tell your dad how appreciative we are that he sent you to talk with us."

Phillip raised his head and let out a long sigh. "Mister Phillips, please don't let this stop you from doing what you're doing." A small smile appeared on Phillip's reddened face. "And I want you to know that dad told me about y'all's desire to restart Sanctuary. Will you let me know how I can help?"

"I'll be sure to tell the others about your interest."

Phillip stood and extended his hand. "Thanks, Mister and Missus Phillips. I'm glad my dad suggested I stop by this morning."

I pushed his hand aside and hugged him. "Look, tell your dad we'll catch you both at church tomorrow. In the meantime, we'll be praying for Megan and Hank."

Liddy stared into his eyes. "If you talk to Megan, please let her know we're praying for her and are here if she needs someone to talk to."

"Yes ma'am, I sure will. Thanks. I gotta' run."

When the taillights of Phillip's Wrangler disappeared, Liddy wrapped her arm around me and said, "The more we learn about the folks in this town, the more we discover how little we in truth know."

Liddy occupied herself throughout the afternoon creating last-minute gifts while I took advantage of the uninterrupted time to attack my final article on Jessie Masterson. I inspected my notes and realized the two persons who last saw Jessie alive were Hal and Hank. Without their firsthand accounts, Jessie's story remained unfinished. I grimaced at the thought of approaching Hank, and up to now, Hal seemed unapproachable too. I became sidetracked with the notion that I still needed to find the right opportunity to interview Megan. More than ever, I wanted to delve into the possibility that she might be John Priestly's mystery person. However, I wasn't sure when I could speak with Megan.

The ring of the phone provided a temporary distraction. Liddy shouted from the back of the house. "Honey, it's for you. It's Harold Archer."

"Theo, sorry to disturb you. I wanted to call personally. Phillip just told me about his visit this morning."

"No problem Harold. Liddy and I appreciated him stopping by."

"He's a good kid, but I feel terrible how my oldest has been acting lately. It appears I haven't been much help to him or Megan. It's times like these I wish their mother hadn't of left."

"Look, Harold, what Hank and Megan are dealing with would unsettle anyone."

"I agree, but I expect more out of Hank. I think what's happened has created a serious problem between him and Megan."

"Have you heard from Megan?"

"No. I tried to call her but just get her voicemail. Even her mother says she doesn't want to talk to anyone right now."

"Well, at least we know she's safe with her parents. Give it some time."

"You're right, Theo. Maybe I'll have some news by tomorrow."

I hung up the phone as Liddy appeared. "Hun, everything okay?"

The evidence of her artistic handiwork decorated the flannel shirt she wore and brought a warm smile to my face. I licked my fingertip and wiped an evergreen paint splotch from the tip of her nose. I inspected the rest of her face while I answered her inquiry. "Everything's fine. Harold felt he needed to personally apologize."

Liddy wrinkled her nose. "I feel bad for Harold."

"I told Harold to not worry about us. He then said Megan's not taking phone calls, but at least we know she's at her parents."

Liddy blew some stray hairs from her face. "Well, is there anything we can do?"

"Not sure. Maybe Arnie can offer some advice. He'll at least want to know how the situation escalated last night if Megan hasn't already called him again."

I reached Arnie at the hospital coffee shop between visits. He listened while I updated him and told him about Phillip's visit and the call from Harold.

"Theo, thanks for calling. I'm sorry to hear things have gotten worse. I'll try to reach her, but if she doesn't want to talk, all I can do is leave a message."

"Thanks, Arnie. Let us know if we can help. See you tomorrow. Oh yeah, you might also want to check on Harold. He sounds out of sorts over this whole mess."

"Will do. Hey, gotta run."

———

Sunday morning at the church, after we removed our jackets, two huddles formed among our growing clique of friends. The women cackled about their outing, while the men bemoaned the sudden weather change.

When Harold and Phillip appeared, I slid out into the aisle to greet them, and we stepped back into the foyer. "Good morning, Harold. Glad you and Phillip could make it."

Harold shook my hand. "Thanks, Theo. Megan hasn't returned my calls, and Hank isn't talking either." Phillip kept focused on his dad, but his young eyes showed the strain of the last couple of days.

"Did Arnie reach you?"

Harold's voice and demeanor showed signs of growing fatigue and stress. "Yes, late last night. I appreciated talking with him. He offered the same advice you did and wanted to reach Megan and Hank. I told him Hank's not in a real receptive mood right now."

"Well, Liddy and I'll keep Megan and Hank in our prayers and thoughts. We just have to believe God knows the 'what and why' of such matters long before we ever do."

"I know you're right, thanks." He sighed, making his dejection even more pronounced.

"Harold, why don't you come say hello to everyone before the service begins."

We weaved our way to where Liddy remained engaged with our friends. As soon as Phillip and Harold arrived, conversations ceased, and wide-eyed stares greeted us.

Liddy gave Phillip a motherly embrace while Zeb extended his hand to Harold. "Harold, why don't you join us this morning? You look worn out. Is everything alright?"

"Thanks, Zeb. I've had a couple of rough days," Harold confessed with a doleful tone. "It seems Hank and Megan are experiencing marital problems after she got some terrible news from the doctor."

"Is Megan okay? Can we do anything for ya'?"

Harold tried his best to answer Zeb with an appreciative nod. "Just keep them in your prayers, I guess. And it wouldn't hurt to add a prayer for me. I just don't know what to do to make this right."

Zeb pulled Harold close for a bear hug. Harold's discomfort showed, his arms hung loosely by his side. Zeb said to Harold, "God wrote the book on fatherhood, and he takes extra special care of us, single dads." Zeb stepped back and winked, which drew a small wrinkled grin to Harold's face.

"Thanks, Zeb. Never thought about God in that light, but it does make me feel a little better."

I observed Liddy next to Phillip during the hymns, and tried to understand how hard growing up must have been without the comfort and consolation of a mother. I considered how different Hank, Hal, and Phillip were from each other and how each represented a different aspect of Harold's personality.

After I felt Liddy's nudge, she whispered, "Are you okay?" I smiled and placed my hand on hers. At that moment, I realized the reason I struggled understanding how Harold truly felt was sitting right next to me. I wondered when Harold last received an elbow nudge to get his attention.

The sanctuary emptied quickly after the service. I told Larry I'd stop by in the morning and suggested that Mary ought to schedule a photo shoot with Harold regarding the announcement about Sanctuary in the paper.

Harold said goodbye to Zeb before he and Phillip joined Liddy and me as we stopped to see Arnie and Judy at the door. Harold and Arnie shared a whispered exchange and shook hands. Arnie likewise smiled at Phillip and thanked him for making sure he and his dad went to church.

After Harold and Phillip left, Arnie whispered, "I want you to know, I spoke with Megan. I can tell you this much... she's wrestling with some mighty tough decisions, but I think she'll make the right choices."

I pulled back to observe Arnie's eyes. "I sure hope so. What's your prognosis with Hank and Megan?"

"God's going to be busy with them over the next few days."

CHAPTER THIRTY-TWO

I SCURRIED TO THE KITCHEN, grabbed the receiver in the middle of the second ring, and answered just above a whisper.

"Mister Phillips?" A barely-audible whimper asked.

"Yes, who's this?"

"Mister Phillips, sorry to call so early. This is Megan, Megan Archer."

"Are you okay, Megan?"

"Would you mind if I stopped by this morning? It's important I see you and Miss Liddy."

"Of course. What time?"

"Would you mind if I stopped a little before eight?"

"Sure. That'll be fine." I glanced at the clock and then down the dark hallway to our closed bedroom door.

"Thank you so much. I'm sorry I disturbed you so early. I promised Harold I'd be at work this morning, but I need to stop by your house first."

"No apologies necessary. We'll see you in an hour."

My thoughts churned about the nature of Megan's urgent visit. I walked down the hall and opened the bedroom door. Liddy, barely awake, clutching her pillow asked, "Who called?"

"Megan."

Liddy's sleepy eyes sprung open, and she propped herself up on her elbows. "Megan called? Why? Is everything all right?" Liddy's instincts woke her fully. "What time is it?" She squinted at the clock.

"She wanted to know if she could stop by this morning. She said it was important."

"What'd you tell her?" Liddy asked in a dry, raspy voice.

"Of course I said yes. However, she apologized but said she'd be here a little before eight."

Liddy rose to the edge of the bed and stared at the clock. "She's going to be here within the hour?"

"Yes. Coffee, juice and a buttered bagel will be ready in five minutes."

A couple of minutes before eight, Megan's crimson Mustang pulled into the driveway. Megan arrived at the door wearing a sequined black leather jacket over a white blouse and gray dress pants. Her black high heels clicked as she walked across the porch's wood floor.

"Megan, please come on in," Liddy said opening the door.

I offered to take her jacket. "Hello, Mister Phillips. I'm good, thanks. I don't want to stay too long."

Liddy invited Megan to sit in her chair. "I feel just awful for you. I can't even begin to imagine all you've dealt with the last few days."

Megan sat upright on the edge of the cushion and smoothed the wrinkles in her slacks. "Thanks so much for seeing me so early. I wasn't even sure I'd be welcome after I heard how Hank's been behaving." She continued to avoid eye contact but put extra emphasis on each word. "But, I felt I needed to apologize."

Liddy stood beside Megan with a vulnerable look and rested her hand on Megan's shoulder. "Apologize? Why should you apologize?" Liddy then sat down on the arm of my recliner.

Relieved that Liddy engaged Megan, I stood and gestured for her to take my seat. "Would you young ladies like some coffee or tea?"

"Thanks, Mister Phillips…" Megan nodded with a forced grin. "If it wouldn't be much trouble, hot tea with just a little sugar would suit me fine."

"I can handle that. What about you Liddy?"

Liddy focused her eyes on Megan. "Yes, please. You know how I like mine."

While I waited for the water to boil, I admired how Liddy gave Megan the attention she needed. They held hands and spoke softly back and forth. I couldn't make out the words, but Megan no longer looked uncomfortable and stiff.

"Here you go, ladies. Two hot cups of tea." I went back into the kitchen to get my coffee before I took a seat on the sofa. Megan enjoyed the full comfort of Liddy's chair while she savored her tea.

Megan's attention drifted from Liddy to me. "I want to thank both of you…" She hesitated long enough to see my smile. "I'm not sure where to begin." She sighed as she hesitated. "Harold told me about Phillip's visit, so I assume Phillip told you what happened between Hank and me?"

Liddy's affable grin and nod encouraged Megan to continue.

"First, I feel terrible that you were victims of Hank's unpredictable temper. I heard Pete and the others showed up before Hank did any real harm. I feel I'm to blame for his threatening tirade. And now that I finally walked out on him, I'm more afraid. Just having my car parked in your driveway makes me nervous."

Liddy snickered, leaned over and patted Megan's knee. "Oh, don't you fret none. You're safe here. Theo and the boys sent a strong message to Hank the other night."

Megan exchanged her first genuine smile with my awkward grin, then turned back toward Liddy. "I've little doubt that's true. Miss Liddy, more importantly, the reason I came here is that your husband helped me when I dumped my terrible news on him. I sure wish my father had been as helpful and compassionate." Her grin faded and eyes dropped as she talked about her father.

"Look, I trust your father will come around in time. But, to be honest, Liddy and I've been worried sick about you, and here you're worried about us," I said a bit lighthearted before I turned serious. "Phillip told us how ugly it's been for you at the house."

"Hank didn't get physical, but he sure said a lot of dreadful things that hurt far worse than if he had beaten me." Tears streamed down her cheeks. "Y'all have been so kind, much more so than my mother and father."

Liddy pulled out a box of tissues. "Listen to me. Parents often struggle to respond well when their children are hurting. Especially the grownup ones. Trust me, I speak from experience."

Megan looked into Liddy's eyes, and a tear-filled grin surfaced. "Miss Liddy, now I know why everyone likes you and Theo so much."

I swallowed the knot in my throat. "Megan, we've come to a point in our lives where we see how God showed us through our mistakes and we've learned that compassion and mercy build much better bridges than when we point out the faults and failures in others."

Megan dipped her head. "Oh, it's so hard to be that way when others are focused on my mistakes, but I do want to do the right thing." Her voice quivered.

Liddy took Megan's hand and spoke softly. "Megan, what do *you* want to do? Do you want to work it out with Hank?"

Megan grabbed a tissue and blew her nose. She then turned to both of us with an extended pensive stare, and after what seemed like a minute, Megan stammered, "I…I'm not sure, but I…I told Harold that I'd like to come back to work this morning." A twinkle in her eyes and a slight grin appeared. "He's probably panicking without me to keep him straight." She dabbed a stray tear as her red-faced smile grew.

I chuckled. "Harold told me just yesterday how much he missed you." Though not Harold's exact words, I had little doubt that he relied upon Megan both at the office and at home.

Megan's lightheartedness escalated into healthier giggles. "I can only imagine what my desk looks like, and it's only been a day." Megan looked out the window in the direction of City Hall. "I'm not sure how to tell Harold what I need to tell him… it'll break his heart." A long sigh followed.

"Megan, Harold knows about your diagnosis, and I know that he still cares about you. I sure don't know everything, but I do know Harold's not pleased with Hank at this moment."

Megan suddenly turned away from the window before she burst out in frustration. "No, you don't know. Harold doesn't know. Nobody knows. Hank and I got married for all the wrong reasons, and because of that, I'll never have children… And in Hank's eyes, it's my fault. Whatever glimmer of hope I clung to for our marriage has been ripped away." Her swollen red eyes defiantly refused to shed another tear.

I sank into the sofa. Liddy appeared equally stunned. Megan's trite, emotionless admission interrupted the momentary silence. "Hank and I have finally received the consequences of *our* mistake!"

Liddy broke Megan's blank gaze. "What mistake? I'm not sure I understand what you're trying to say."

"I don't know what you and Theo know, but four years ago Hal and I had been dating for several months. We enjoyed hanging out with each other, but we were just friends, though I knew he wanted more…" Megan monitored us as she spoke and paused mid-sentence.

Liddy attempted to finish her statement. "So, you and Hank connected in a way you didn't feel with Hal?"

"Yes, ma'am. I felt bad about it too, but at first, I wasn't certain about my feelings for Hank either. One thing led to another between us while I continued to hang out with Hal, but Hank and I met more and more, as often as we could…" Her lips quivered, and she struggled to stifle her tears.

I felt uncomfortable as I tried to imagine how my two sons would have reacted. "So, how did you break it off with Hal?"

Megan no longer made eye contact and preferred the view through the window. "This is so hard. I haven't even told my parents. Lord, especially my parents! You haven't been here long enough to know how small this town really can be. But I've got to tell someone. Only Coach Priestly knows the truth about Hank and me. I couldn't even tell Pastor Wright everything when we talked."

"Liddy and I'll do our best to help you if we can." Mary's rumor story came to mind.

Sniffles and tears drowned Megan's words. "Please bear with me. I've carried the shame with me for the last four years. In the beginning, I prayed daily, but all those unanswered prayers just numbed my pain after I resorted to unanswered pleas with Hank to make it right."

Liddy got up, sat on the arm of Megan's chair and hugged Megan like a caring mother. "There's nothing that you and Hank have done that God doesn't know about and already offers his forgiveness. We're here to help, not judge, you and Hank."

Megan tilted her head and examined Liddy's gentle face. "But did God forgive me for taking the life of our unborn child? I allowed Hank to talk me into it. He promised he'd marry me but said we couldn't afford to have the baby. He swore we'd start a family the right way at the right time. Please don't hate me." She buried her head into Liddy's shoulder and sobbed.

I sat dumbfounded. Part of me wished I had not gotten between Pete and Hank the other night, but then began to feel sorry for Hank as well. Why did he encroach upon Megan and Hal's relationship and break his brother's trust? Why did he coerce Megan into an abortion and paint it over with a doomed marriage? I wondered if his own mother's faults and failures shaped Hank's view of how he treated women. My heart ached as I silently watched Liddy comfort Megan.

Megan nestled closer to Liddy and whispered through their shared tears. "I'm so sorry."

Liddy tried to comfort Megan but her empathetic tears began to flow too. "Don't mind my tears. I feel your broken heart and want to help you. Please, keep talking about it if you'd like."

Megan focused on my empty recliner. "Hank and I slipped out of town late one night. No one knew, not even Hal. Oh, poor Hal… but Hank promised he'd straighten it out after we got back. We drove to a clinic Hank contacted in Ocean City, Maryland. A few days later, a local justice of the peace married us. As far as anyone knew, we returned from a happy honeymoon. Sure, we heard some gossip among my so-called former friends, but it faded quickly."

Liddy asked, "What about your parents? How did you tell them?"

Liddy stroked Megan's hair as she continued her blank stare. "My parents hardly tolerated Hal, but Hank has never received their approval. I called from Maryland to tell them that we had eloped and would be home in a few more days. You can guess how well that went over. My father cried when I told him. I can't begin to imagine how he would've reacted if he knew what happened."

Feeling useless, I walked into the kitchen to ponder the significance of Megan's confession and how no one could ever know from us what happened.

Liddy's motherly voice and touch comforted Megan. "What're you going to do now? How can we help you?"

Megan returned to her upright posture on the edge of the chair. She searched for where I went and found me standing in the kitchen doorway. She looked back to Liddy. "I can't explain it, but I feel a lot better finally telling someone about my horrible secret."

Megan shifted her hips and shoulders to look directly at me. "Theo, when I shared the news I got from the doctor with you, I couldn't tell you then how upset and devastated I felt. What a horrible price I've paid for that terrible decision. But because of this, I now realize what I have been afraid to admit. Hank had convinced me that becoming an Archer was worth what we went through, but inside my heart, I knew what we did was wrong in God's eyes. Initially, Hank spoiled me with lots of nice things. Harold welcomed me into the family with open arms and immediately made me his administrative assistant. When I look back, though, none of it truly gave me peace about myself. When Hank said the things he did the other night, I realized this was my answer from God."

My eyes captured hers. "How so?"

"When I first discovered I was pregnant, I reached out to Coach Priestly. He told me not to give up on God. He said God knew what happened, and Coach offered to help me talk with Hank about doing the right thing. But when I told Hank, he promised he'd handle it and make it right. He then told me not to say anything more to anyone else, especially Coach Priestly. I felt scared and trapped. Regretfully, I listened to Hank, not Coach."

"Did you ever talk to Coach Priestly after you got back?" Liddy asked.

Megan sighed. "Yeah, I went to see him right after we got home. He told me how sad he felt for Hank and me once he realized what had happened. He told me the choice we made was wrong, but God's love and compassion come with unconditional forgiveness. Coach said that God's plan would likely have consequences, but it'll be for my good if I would just love God enough to tell him how sorry I am."

I returned to the living room. "That's true Megan. Coach Priestly's a wise and godly man."

Megan looked up. "I tried praying for forgiveness, but I've never really felt forgiven. I turned away from God until the news the other day reminded me of Coach Priestly's words." Megan reached out and held my hand. "Thanks to you, I heard the same message of God's compassion and mercy from Pastor Wright. It's hard to swallow that I'll never have a baby, but I desire God's forgiveness more. I've got a lot to work out with a lot of people, but this morning is a good place to start."

Liddy and Megan stood and embraced each other. "I can only imagine how hard it was for you to come here this morning, but it's the beginning of God's healing process. You can count on us to help you any way we can."

My arms wrapped around both of them. "Don't allow this terrible secret to imprison you any longer. Remember what Jesus told the wayward woman after her self-righteous accusers wanted her stoned? All her accusers recognized their sinfulness and walked away. Jesus then shared with the woman, 'Go and sin no more.' Megan, I don't know how this will work out for you and Hank, but you've got a choice to make with God's help. Begin by discovering the forgiveness of those who genuinely love you. Allow those who choose to judge you and withhold forgiveness to walk away."

Megan's twinkling blue eyes and rosy dimples revealed that she understood as she said, "Thank you, both of you."

Liddy inspected her tear free cheeks. "There are plenty of good people in this town who'll support you in whatever decision you make. If you need me, I'll be glad to help you begin the journey to forgiveness with your parents."

"Thank you, Miss Liddy. I'd like that." Megan glanced at her watch. "Oh my, I need to get to the office. I'm not sure what all I should tell Harold just yet, but I'll begin by asking his forgiveness."

Liddy hugged Megan again before she prepared to leave. "You have our phone number, and our home will always be open to you."

"Oh Megan, after Coach Priestly gets home, I'm pretty sure he'll be glad to hear from you too."

"Thanks, Theo, I'd like that."

———

"How do you think Megan made out with Harold?" Liddy asked while preparing dinner.

"The same thought crossed my mind earlier when I drove by City Hall. I've got an idea, though. I need Phillip's cell phone number anyway, and I'm not going to risk calling his house number."

The phone at the Mayor's office rang several times before Megan's frazzled voice spoke over the answer machine's message. "Please hold a moment." She sounded flustered once the recording abruptly ended. "I'm sorry. Mayor's office. Can I help you?"

"Megan, hey, this is Theo. Is everything alright?"

"Yes, everything's fine. Harold and I just wrapped up a meeting to catch up on some city business. I couldn't answer the phone fast enough."

"Sorry to interrupt. It sounds as though everything's good then, with Harold I mean. The reason I called is to get Phillip's cell number. I need to reach him about my last article on Jessie. I only have the house number and thought... You know what I mean?"

Megan gave me Phillip's cell number, thanked me and said she'd contact us again in a day or two.

Liddy's impatience blurted, "Well? What'd she say?"

"Megan's fine. She said she'd stop by or call in a day or so."

Liddy's maternal instincts took over. "Theo, if we don't hear anything from her by Wednesday, I'll find a reason to stop by her office."

I chuckled, which earned me a swift love tap on my arm. "Hush. We told her we'd help her. I don't suspect she's told Harold everything yet. You take care of your article, and I'll take care of helping Megan."

CHAPTER THIRTY-THREE

THE USUAL LUNCH CROWD HAD dispersed except for two couples extending their lunch breaks. Alex met me as soon as I entered and pointed towards the booth in the back. "Mister Phillips, good afternoon. By the way, who'll be joining you today? Missus Phillips, Nick or Joe?"

"Phillip Archer, the mayor's son."

Alex stopped wiping the table. "Phillip. I know him. Please go sit down. I'll direct him to you."

Although Phillip assured me that neither Hank nor Hal ever ate lunch there, the lone rear booth offered a little more peace of mind.

As I turned towards the booth, Bernie Thrope in her throaty broken English greeted me. "Welcome, Mistor Phillips. Are you having lunch with us today?"

"Yes, Bernie, I am. How are you today?"

"Good, very good. Thank you, so very much. You just missed that sorry husband of mine. He's headed to Mistor Zeb's store, again." She spoke with a wily snark, but her wink indicated she knew about Silas' secret checker games with Bubba.

"But Bernie, I came to say hello to you," I said with a playful grin.

As I slid into the booth, I heard Alex greet Phillip at the door. Moments later, the two appeared, and I gestured for Phillip to sit across from me. "Thanks, Alex. I'm glad to hear you know each other."

Phillip laughed. "Yeah, Alex and I share a lot of good Sanctuary memories."

Alex snapped back. "But since you started working across the street, I don't see you much anymore. You don't eat lunch?"

Phillip tucked his head. "Guilty. No excuse. But I'm here today…"

Alex grinned and said he'd give us a minute before he took our orders. I positioned myself to keep an eye on the front of the restaurant. With a slight tilt of my head, I could easily see anyone enter the front door. For both of our sakes, I made sure we could talk without interruption or be overheard.

"Mister P, I have to admit, I've just never been comfortable ordering from their Greek menu. I guess the food's pretty good, though. What'd you suggest?"

"Let me see," I said staring up at the menu over the counter. "I know. Souvlaki is nothing more than a Greek shish kabob. Do you prefer chicken, beef or lamb?"

"I've never eaten lamb."

"Alex's mama makes the tastiest lamb Souvlaki. You should try it." Phillip offered a trusting nod and shrug of his shoulders.

Alex took our order, then walked toward his mom with two raised fingers. "Two lamb platters." He returned a few seconds later with two large glasses of iced tea.

Phillip and I chatted about his school days until Alex returned and placed our lunches in front of us and refilled our tea glasses. Phillip only had an hour for lunch, so I directed our conversation to the reason I invited him. After I swallowed my first bite, I asked, "Phillip, how's everything at your house? Liddy and I sure feel bad about what happened between Megan and Hank."

Phillip set his pita aside and held up a finger while he swallowed. "It's as good as can be expected." A big gulp of tea followed. "But dad's been oddly quiet. Certainly not his usual, fun self."

"How so?"

"Well, he sits in front of the television oblivious to what's on, and then he disappears for hours behind the closed doors of his study. To make matters worse, Hank and Hal aren't talking to one another, much less dad or me for that matter. Maddie's the only person I can share a civil conversation with, but even she struggles to talk with my dad or brothers. She usually ends up throwing her hands in the air, retreating into the kitchen, shaking her head, grumbling to herself."

I nodded and swallowed another bite with my eyes focused on Phillip's long face. "What do you think about Megan and Hank?"

Phillip raised an eyebrow. His sad blue eyes searched mine. "If Megan's smart, she'll end it and never come back." His decisive, sternness matched his emphatic stare.

"What makes you say that?"

"Between you and me," Phillip looked over his shoulder before he continued. "Hank's never treated Megan right. The latest news only made matters worse. He made it abundantly clear to the whole family that he had the right to be angry with Megan."

"You mean he's blaming Megan for the bad news they got from the doctor?"

"Yeah, and he called her all kinds of awful names before she finally stormed out in tears. I may be young and naive, but even I know that Hank doesn't love Megan. I don't believe he ever has." Phillip swayed his head back and forth and stared at the table. "It's a crying shame to watch Hank strut around the house as if he's relieved that she left, and then a minute later, rant and rave because she left him. Just last night, he flung his dinner plate across the dining room when dad told him she came back to work yesterday."

"I'm sorry to hear that. No doubt Hank's got a real anger problem. I'm sure it's been tough for Megan to put up a sweet front when he's so mean to her."

Phillip swallowed a swig of his tea. "Megan's been like a big sister to me. I remember before she married Hank or even dated Hal, she and her friends would stop by some of the Sanctuary meetings. We used to joke that she had a crush on Coach Masterson, but I soon realized most of the girls acted the same way around him."

"What was Hal and Megan's relationship like?"

Phillip paused. "Well, mostly just convenient friends, I guess. More platonic than one of those mushy gushy relationships. You know what I mean?"

"So Hal and Megan didn't share a romantic relationship?"

"No, it never appeared that way. I think Hal relished the attention Megan offered him, that is until Hank came back home from Afghanistan. After Hank came home, well, let's just say he came back different and Hal and Hank's relationship changed."

"What do you mean different?"

"Mister P, no one's told me much, and Hank surely won't talk about it. I know he spent three months in some fancy army hospital in Maryland." Phillip paused. "Dad said, we shouldn't say anything about what happened to Hank to anyone."

"I understand. You don't have to say anything you're not comfortable sharing, Phillip."

"I know I can trust you Mister P. No one needs to know about this, but it's important to explain what happened. I didn't understand what PTSD meant when I first heard the term. In the beginning, Hank came home moodier, more unpredictable, and he preferred being left alone. However, dad always wanted him to run the family's business. His duties as mayor took so much of his time, and it only got worse when he prepared to make a run for the State Senate. Hal stepped aside from the family business after Hank returned, and dad appointed Hal as the Director of the City Utilities."

"So Hal wanted to run the family's business?"

"I'm not sure. Hal seemed happy enough with his city position, and when dad asked him to assist Hank during the final phase of the school contract, I don't think that sat well with Hal. The extra time to help Hank also cut into his time with Megan."

"So let me ask you this. Did Hank know of Hal's relationship with Megan?"

"Gee, I don't know. Probably."

I leaned back and checked the front door. "Do you think Hank's interest in Megan came by accident or…"

Phillip's blunt response anticipated my question. "You mean was Hank jealous enough to break them up and marry Megan?" Apparently, Phillip didn't know the real reason Hank and Megan eloped.

I sipped more tea and stretched my shoulders to gather my thoughts.

"Yeah, you're right. That's too far-fetched. So why do you think Hank and Megan ran off and got married?"

Phillip sank into the back corner of the booth and stretched his long legs into the aisle. Only the noise from Alex cleaning tables interrupted Phillip's pause. "Do you think Megan wanted to marry Hank so badly she concocted a story about being pregnant?"

"Why would you ask that?" My abrupt response caught Phillip's attention.

"Well, I heard Hank yell at Megan the other night. He blamed her for them getting married in the first place. I also remembered the stupid rumors right after they first married."

I straightened my back and stared at Phillip. "If only a stupid rumor, why would Hank blame Megan for them getting married? Anyway, I thought Hank instigated their marriage?"

"Hal confided that Hank admitted that they secretly left to get married because Megan had been pregnant, but she lost the baby before they returned home. Hank told Hal that he loved Megan and they'd start a family the right way, at the right time."

My mind wrestled with this version of the story. How would Phillip react if he knew the truth? I then asked, "Did Hal tell you when Hank told him about this?"

"Sometime after Coach Masterson died. Hal said Hank wanted him to forgive him for what happened and to set things straight between them."

"Interesting…" I thought for a moment. "Not to change the subject, but since you mentioned the fire… I'm curious about what happened that night."

"What can I tell you that you don't already know?"

I looked intently at Phillip and leaned forward. "I want your version. What you saw and heard. I only have what the news articles said. Why were Hal and Hank there that night? You just told me that they didn't see eye-to-eye before the fire."

"That's right. Hal dropped me off for the meeting and told me he had some work to do in his office, which back then was on the second floor. He told me he'd meet me after the meeting."

"When did Hank arrive at the Courthouse?"

"I don't know. I've wondered about that myself."

"Okay. Let's just leave it that Hank and Hal wound up meeting upstairs for whatever reason. What happened when you first realized the building was on fire?"

Phillip's eyes closed as if rewinding the events in his mind. "Lemme see... Coach Masterson hung out with the high school students in the main room. He had asked me to keep an eye on the middle school students, so I took them outside to play games near the side entrance to the basement. I remember the kids yelling 'Fire!' and pointing up as smoke and flames shattered windows above our heads. Then things got hectic. The kids panicked and yelled for Coach Masterson. We evacuated the basement and corralled everyone underneath an old oak tree that used to be on the corner where Jessie's statue is now."

"What happened next?"

"I helped Coach account for all the students and then watched the flames blow out more of the front and side windows on the second floor. Dark gray smoke then poured out of the first-floor windows moments after that. The rooftop lit up with flames rising above the bell tower. That's when I remembered Hal told me he'd be in his office."

"Did you tell Jessie?"

"No. I started running toward the building, but Coach chased me down. I yelled that Hal might still be in his office upstairs. I panicked when I saw Hal's empty truck parked beside the building. Coach told me to stay put and watch the kids. He raced to the front door and found it unlocked. Smoke billowed out of the open door as Coach entered."

I pictured the scene Phillip described by remembering the photos I had seen of the old antebellum wood and brick courthouse fire. "Then what happened?"

Phillip's blank stare held firm. "Sirens and flashing lights filled the air as emergency vehicles arrived within minutes. The flames grew and swallowed the smoke that tried to escape every window on the second floor. Hank screamed from a second-floor front window just before Coach Masterson pulled him back. Coach yelled from the same window that Hal was with them, and they were trying to get out."

"When did you realize they were in trouble?"

"Coach looked calm when he yelled, but I ran to the fire chief as soon as he arrived and told him about Hank, Hal and Coach Masterson. Two firemen charged the front entrance, but flames overhead showered broken glass upon them and heavier black smoke gushed out the cracked front doors. The firemen leaped back and ran around to the side of the building. Before the first water hose could begin dousing the fire, the front doors flung open. Hank and Hal landed face down on the portico steps and scrambled on all fours down the front steps and onto the grass. Both of them looked back as if they expected Coach Masterson to be right behind them, but only a huge gush of smoke and ash followed as the main floor ceiling collapsed. Flames immediately engulfed the whole building. The fire department could only manage to contain the fire after that."

My heart pounded as I considered how vividly Phillip recalled the horrible details of that tragic night.

"Mister P, I haven't told this story to anyone since that night." Tears attempted to extinguish the flames in his mind's eye. "I ran to my brothers. They were laying on the courthouse lawn gagging from the smoke. Hal looked up at me and said that Coach Masterson cleared the way when the stairwell became blocked with burning timbers and debris. He said Jessie told them to run, and he'd be right behind them, but he never came out."

"Oh my God! That must have devastated Hank and Hal."

Then I heard Alex's voice at the end of the table. "I'm sorry, I heard Phillip talk about the fire. What he said is true. His brothers screamed, 'Jessie! Jessie! Jessie!' as they stared back into the flames." Alex began to tear up as he looked at Phillip who stared back at Alex in tears.

I glanced at both of them and asked Alex, "You were there that night?"

"Yes, sir. Every day I see his shiny statue, I remember how brave Coach was that night." Alex slid into the booth beside Phillip and put his arm around Phillip's shoulders.

The retelling of the horrible night came, as I had hoped, through the eyes of Phillip and surprisingly corroborated to by Alex. Phillip took another gulp of his drink. We sat in silence for several minutes.

"Phillip, Alex, I'm sorry. I can only guess how hard it is to recollect that night. It's not a memory anyone your age should keep bottled up."

Phillip shook his head and muttered, "Coach, forgive me."

I stared at Phillip. "Why'd you say that? It wasn't your fault."

Alex leaned closer to Phillip. "Phillip, there was nothing any of us could've done. God sent Coach in there to save your brothers."

Phillip sat upright and glared. "Neither of you understand. It should've been me who ran back into the building, not him. They were my brothers." Tears flowed as he pounded his chest.

I glanced at Alex and realized he appeared as confused as I felt. "Listen carefully to me, son. There are no easy answers to why this happened, but as Alex said, God has reasons for choosing Jessie and not you. I believe Jessie knew what he risked. If you had run in there, all three of you could have died."

Phillip ran his hands through his hair. "I know you're right, but it hurts whenever I think about it. Coach Masterson sacrificed himself, so my brothers could live."

"That's how you should honor Coach Masterson."

A few minutes later, Alex held the door open as Phillip and I walked onto the sidewalk, and the three of us looked at Jessie's bronze statue across the street. Phillip shook my hand. "Mister P, thanks for moving to Shiloh. I hope what I told you today helped so that you can finish writing Jessie's story."

"Thanks, it most definitely helped. However, I gotta tell you, I know the officials declared the fire an accident, but unless Hal or Hank tells their side of it, when this story hits the paper it'll likely raise more questions about their presence that night."

"I know. I'll give them a heads up that we spoke and that your story is going to press in a few days with or without their side being told."

I patted Phillip on the shoulder. "Thanks. You can also tell them that if either wants to share their version of the story, all they need to do is come see me by this weekend."

———

That evening, I sat in my recliner by the window as Liddy talked about how she and Judy helped Marie put the final touches on John's room. Liddy mentioned that Marie apologized to Judy for not being at church Sunday. She was still not ready after all this time to come back regularly. While I shared about my lunch with Phillip and Alex, I positioned myself to keep one eye on vehicles as they drove by our house.

Liddy fell off to sleep right away that night, but scenes of the fire played out in my head as did the haunting echoes of Hank and Hal yelling Jessie's name, as I wondered why were they were there together that night?

CHAPTER THIRTY-FOUR

AFTER TOSSING AND TURNING FOR half the night, the conclusion of Jessie's story weighed on my mind. The key to unlocking Jessie's and John's stories remained beyond my grasp. On my yellow legal pad, I wrote the one question that I believed held the secret. "WHY WERE HANK AND HAL IN THE COURTHOUSE THE NIGHT OF THE FIRE?" I traced each capital letter, again and again, hoping the answer might appear out of them. Behind the now bold question mark, I drew an exclamation point to emphasize that the answer, not the question, would deliver closure to Jessie's story and bring me closer to the truth behind what happened to John.

Beneath the question, I scrawled "HANK" on the left, and "HAL" on the right. Then I circled both names and linked them with a bold line. While my pencil lead retraced the link between the names, I wondered whether Phillip relayed my message to his brothers. If so, whether either would step forward to share his version of the story. I grimaced at the prospect of Hank's response but remained undecided about Hal's.

Above "HANK" and "HAL," I wrote "MEGAN." Her testimony served as the apex of the triangle connecting the three. I promised myself, no matter what the truth revealed, this story needed no more victims. Megan deserved no further scandal.

The first hints of daylight arrived as I sipped my coffee in the kitchen and Timmy launched Wednesday's edition of the *Sentinel* onto the foot of the porch steps. A minute later I sat in the kitchen, unfolded it and discovered a photo of Jessie Masterson's memorial on the front page. The caption read, "Jessie Masterson Memorial dedication scheduled for the opening ceremonies of Christmas in Shiloh." Beneath Larry's article about this year's celebration, readers saw that the first of a three-part tribute to Jessie Masterson written by Theo Phillips waited for them on page three.

My heart sped up as I flipped to the article. Jessie's school photo filled much of the page, and the headline read, "Jessie's Road to Shiloh." I skimmed the article, neatly filling the left three columns, and smiled in appreciation of Mary's meticulous transcription of my manuscript. On the right side of the page, a picture of Harold Archer with an article by Larry confirmed Harold's decision about the vacant State Senate seat. Larry quoted Harold as stating, "a final decision will come out after the first of the year."

I refilled my coffee mug and prepared a tray with coffee, juice and today's paper for Liddy. Her sleepy smile greeted me as I entered the bedroom. "Good morning, hun. What time is it?" she asked with a stifled yawn.

"It's time for you to get up. You told me that you wanted to go back to Marie's today."

"Yeah." Liddy stared at the clock and moaned.

"Here, I brought you some coffee and juice."

She grabbed the paper and looked up with a curious stare. "Is it?"

"Page three. Would you like some toast or a bagel?"

She lowered the paper with a coy look. "No, but how about a little oatmeal with butter and honey, if you don't mind?"

By the time I returned, the paper lay folded on the bed next to the tray, and the shower revealed Liddy's whereabouts. "I put your oatmeal on the tray and refilled your coffee."

"Thank you, dear. I'll be out shortly. Oh, I think a whole host of folks in town will be wondering about you after today."

Minutes later, Liddy grabbed the car keys. "Gotta run, hun. Judy's expecting me." She leaned over and kissed me. "I'm proud of you. We'll talk later, but if Judy and I don't hurry over to Marie's, she's going to bust fretting about John's arrival Friday."

——

I entered the Sentinel's front door after a thought-filled stroll through town. Determined to use this visit to perk myself up, I hid my uneasiness with a forced grin. "Good morning Martha. Good morning Mary."

Mary's over-sized computer screen hid her face, but she briefly peeked above it with a welcoming smile. In obvious work mode, Martha returned an equally strained grin and pointed right away to Larry's office.

I stopped by Mary's layout desk and saw her intense focus rested on various photos for the Christmas program insert planned for Saturday's edition. "Looks good, Mary."

Mary huffed before she looked over her shoulder and said, "I wish dad and the mayor would stop making changes. I'm running out of time. I already can't finish this until the mayor's grand Christmas tree arrives Friday. I just don't understand why the mayor waited until now to have it delivered. But, he's adamant about having a picture of his grand tree in this year's program. Doesn't anyone understand deadlines?"

"I'm sure you'll get it done in time. Oh, by the way, I thoroughly enjoyed how the first article turned out in today's edition. Your suggestion to use Jessie's school photo was spot-on."

Her grimace morphed into a grin. "Thanks, Theo. At least one person appreciates my hard work around here."

Martha rolled her eyes as I winked at her, headed to Larry's office.

Larry stood behind his desk, staring out the window at the idle printing presses. The smell of printing ink and solvents from the early morning run of the paper still filled the air.

With hands on hips and still facing the window, Larry said, "Come on in Theo. Do you have something for us today?"

"Just a compliment," I said stepping into his office. "Liddy and I are both pleased with how Jessie's first article looked in this morning's paper."

Larry turned with a tight-lipped grin. "Mary deserves most of the thanks."

"Already let her know too."

"No doubt y'all will also like Saturday's edition. The second article will be opposite the City's Christmas Program center pullout. But — "

"Before you ask, the final article is at home waiting for its conclusion."

Larry leaned on the edge of his desk. "And when do you suppose it will get one?"

"Can't say, but unless I hear from Hank or Hal by this weekend, there's certainly going to be a stir around town when everyone reads the current ending."

"What do you mean?"

"Unless I receive Hank's or Hal's versions, I plan to end the final article questioning their reason for being in the courthouse that night and why they didn't get out when the fire broke out."

"Do you think one of them will fess up?"

"Let's just say I laid my cards on the table. It's now up to them to call or fold by this weekend." I smugly pulled my arms tight across my chest.

Larry scratched his head. "I hope you know what you're doing. Hank and Hal have been evasive on that question up to now. Why do you think they'd come forward now?"

"Three reasons. First, I've made it clear that I'm at a dead end, and they're the only ones who can provide an accurate conclusion to the story. Second, they now know how I'll end the article if they don't come forward. Finally, both have good reason to believe I know more than either is comfortable with me knowing."

"Sounds like a big gamble to me. You sure you know what you're doing? Hank threatened you once already."

"Larry, my daddy taught me never to gamble. Until they find out for themselves what I know for certain, I don't think there's any real danger." I hardened my look to assure Larry of my resolve on the matter, though inside I struggled with my uneasiness.

Larry raised a brow. "Okay. I guess you know what you're doing. We'll wait 'til Monday afternoon for the final article." He stepped away from his desk and glanced toward the print room again. "John Priestly will be back in town Friday. Have you thought about what you want to write about his return?"

"I'm working on an angle, but I need to get Jessie's story done before I can tackle John's next week."

"I trust you, Theo. Before you race off, stop by Mary's desk. Remind her to schedule Harold and whoever else you think needs to be in the picture for our Sanctuary article. She's already grumbling about having to be at the Town Square Friday afternoon to get photos of Harold's almighty Christmas tree. Maybe you can suggest she kill two birds with one stone, figuratively speaking of course."

Mary nodded and provided a sarcasm-laced chuckle before she relented. "Oh, what's one more last-minute photo layout for Saturday's special edition anyway." She then playfully growled and glanced at her father's office.

———

Liddy pulled into the driveway just before dusk. I greeted her by the kitchen door stoop. One of her arms threaded through three evergreen wreaths, her other hand clutched two bags of wrapping paper and ribbons.

"Where'd you stop? Thought you were visiting Marie before making a quick stop to City Hall?"

Liddy offered a sly grin as I held the door for her. "Well, women talk best when shopping."

"By the looks of things, y'all did a lot of talking."

"Marie came back into town with us. After we dropped Judy off at the church, we swung by Zeb's. She needed a few last minute items, and of course, you know me, I couldn't just watch her shop." She then grabbed one of the naked wreaths and pulled out a piece of the broad red ribbon. "What do you think? Thought we'd put one over the mantle and hang the other two on the front and side doors."

I enjoyed the twinkle in Liddy's eyes. "Sounds good, Missus Claus."

While she added ribbon to another wreath, Liddy squinted at me and raised an eyebrow. "Is everything alright? You look out of sorts about something. Your meeting with Larry went okay?"

"Oh, fine. Larry gave the credit for today's article to Mary. Guess I'm just a little on edge about the ending of Jessie's story. I hope my gambit with Hal and Hank doesn't backfire."

Liddy put down her wreath and ribbon and sat across from me. "Why do you think it'd backfire?"

"Oh, I'm just a little worried how Hank and Hal will react to Phillip telling them what I said about my article's ending."

"Well, let me tell you about a call Megan got when we stopped by her office." Liddy hesitated. "Hal called and asked to meet her, and by the puzzled look on her face, Marie and I both agreed something's up."

"Maybe Phillip spoke to Hal. Did Megan say anything else?"

"No. I didn't want to ask either, but when I hugged Megan, she whispered that it's not a good time to talk, but she's okay."

"Was Harold there?"

"He stepped out of his office briefly and greeted Marie. I told him we just stopped to see Megan and appeared to be his usual jovial self. He told Marie how pleased he felt that John would live out on the farm with her. Then he disappeared back into his office."

"Do you think Harold knows the whole truth about Megan?"

"No, I don't. Megan grimaced when Harold first stepped out of his office. She caught my eye and shook her head slightly as if to tell me not to say anything. Megan appeared uneasy throughout our visit, but I wasn't sure if it was because of Hal's phone call or what."

After a quiet dinner, Liddy grabbed my arm and pointed to the wreath we hung over the fireplace. "That adds a nice touch to our living room for Christmas. I can't wait for the family to get here in one more week."

———

Church began with the noticeable absence of all the Archers. When

Arnie ended the service early and ducked out the back, Liddy and I gave each other puzzled looks. Judy smiled and greeted everyone alone by her post at the door, and I overheard her tell others as they left that "Arnie had to take care of something important."

When Liddy and I approached Judy on our way out, she pulled me close and whispered, "Arnie wanted me to tell you he'll call first thing in the morning."

Before I stepped back, I whispered. "Arnie didn't say anything more?"

"There are some things even the preacher's wife isn't privy to know. I'm just the messenger."

I shrugged my shoulders and said, "We'll know soon enough I reckon," as I grabbed Liddy's hand and we exited.

CHAPTER THIRTY-FIVE

RIGHT AFTER BREAKFAST, I GRABBED my cell phone, slipped it into my coat pocket and winked at Liddy. "If you hear from Arnie, call me." I blew her a kiss and pulled the door shut behind me.

Arnie's empty parking spot revealed what the church office staff confirmed. No one knew his whereabouts since he ran out the door last night.

At Joe's office, Susanna looked frazzled as she hung up and sighed. She jockeyed papers into an envelope before she finally looked up. "Good morning, Theo. And no, Joe's not here. He's visiting with Marie this morning about their trip to pick up John tomorrow."

"That's all I wanted to know. Liddy's headed out to Marie's shortly. I'll let you get back to whatever you were doing."

"Theo, hold up. Do you know why Arnie disappeared so quickly last night?"

"Afraid not."

Susanna nibbled gently on her pencil. "Hope everything's all right."

"Me too. If you hear anything, I'll be home."

As soon as I hit the sidewalk, I dialed the house. "Hey hun, any news from Arnie?"

"Not a word. I'm sure he'll call soon, though."

"No one at the church has heard from him either. But, I just talked to Susanna. Joe stopped by Marie's this morning to talk about tomorrow's trip to fetch John."

"That's great. Are you on your way home now? I'm about to leave."

"Yes, but you don't have to wait for me. I love you, and I'll see you later this evening."

After I tucked my phone into my coat pocket, Arnie's red Tahoe rolled up to the curb. "Good morning. Want a ride? I was just headed to your house."

"Arnie, is everything alright? Judy gave me your message, but when I didn't hear from you first thing this morning, I got concerned and visited your office."

"Sorry about that. I'll explain after we get to your house, but I've been with Harold and Phillip." Arnie's tired eyes and wrinkled forehead provided evidence of a sleepless night.

A Shiloh City pickup was out front alongside the curb. A slouched figure leaned against my porch railing. As we approached, Hal's long, scruffy face hid beneath his baseball cap. His scraggly, uncombed dark hair coupled with bags under his droopy eyes aged him ten years.

Hal yanked off his cap. "Mister Phillips, sorry to stop by like this, but we need to talk."

Arnie rested his hand on Hal's shoulder. "Hal, you okay? You look like you've been through a rough night or two."

Hal mustered a semblance of a grin. "Yes, sir. Guess it's been more like a tough week."

I unlocked the front door. "Liddy's not here. Come on in and take a load off."

Hal asked to use the bathroom. After I hung our coats over a kitchen chair, Arnie gave me a puzzled look and whispered, "Should I excuse myself?"

"Lord no."

"Good. I'd like to hear what Hal has to say."

Hal returned with his hair combed, looking more refreshed as he tucked his shirt. He sat on the far edge of the sofa, fidgeting with his ball cap. His initial interest appeared to focus more on one of my sports magazines on the coffee table than Arnie or me.

"By the way Hal, you must've just missed Miss Liddy."

"Yes, sir. She drove past me as I turned the corner. I stopped anyway because I hoped you were still home. Sure glad you pulled up when you did. It was hard enough coming here in the first place. I sure didn't want to leave without talking with you." Hal forced himself to make eye contact. "Phillip told me about y'all's lunch meeting and that I should trust you." Hal's eyes drifted to Arnie and his reassuring grin.

"Hal, would you rather speak with Theo alone?" Arnie asked.

"No, sir. Please stay. I'm glad you're here. What I have to say I should've shared with you long ago." They engaged one another with tired eyes.

"Well, you can trust Theo. We both want to help you and hear what you have to say."

Hal's head fell as he cleared his throat. "Um, this is hard…" Hal refocused his attention on his hat before he lifted his eyes and continued. "Mister Phillips, do you want to know what happened the night Jessie died?"

My eyes widened. "Well, I reckon you know I do. Jessie's story deserves a proper ending. Only you and Hank can provide it."

Hal and Arnie glanced at one another before Hal's attention returned to the coffee table. "Hank's not likely to step forward, but I can't cover for him anymore. Since Phillip told me what you said, I've not slept a wink thinking about what I should do." Hal's jaw tightened, and his eyes shut.

"Why not just start from the beginning?" Arnie suggested in his calm pastoral voice.

Hal nodded and opened his bloodshot eyes. "Fair enough. It's time I got this monkey off my back. The truth is, I've never forgiven Hank for what he did to me and how he's treated Megan and everyone else in my family."

I raised my brows and interrupted. "But you and Hank seem to get along when I've seen you together. When Phillip indicated a rift existed between you, I thought he meant in the past."

Hal huffed. "Hardly. I've tried to move on, but Hank's got this knack for scraping the scabs off old wounds. What Hank said and the way he treated Megan last week was just… well, dead wrong. After Megan stormed out of the house, I tried to calm him down, but his propensity for spinning lies finally backfired. Phillip and dad filled me in on how Hank cussed out Megan, blaming her for the terrible news she got from the doctor. I decided then and there I was through with Hank."

Arnie asked, "So, am I to understand that these old wounds between Hank and you go back before Hank married Megan?"

Hal snapped at Arnie. "Yes!" His fiery eyes quickly retreated to the safety of the coffee table. "You think you know what happened between Megan, me and Hank? Not even Phillip knows the half of it."

"What's the truth then?" I asked.

"After Megan and Hank moved into the house, for the sake of the family I tried to forgive both of them for hurting me. I honestly tried to move on, but Hank's shenanigans right from the start kept getting in the way."

Arnie said, "I can only imagine how mad and disappointed you must've felt."

"As for Megan and me, she... uh, well... I pretty much realized early on that she wasn't ready to commit to a deeper relationship, but what they did broke my heart all the same. I felt betrayed, but I also knew what Hank's temper could be like and didn't want her to get hurt."

I asked, "Did you fear for Megan from the start of their marriage?"

"Theo, the Pastor knows some of this, but Hank returned all messed up from the war. The Army hospital helped Hank adjust, and as long as he stayed away from alcohol, he appeared okay. After dad placed Hank back over the family's business, he seemed to settle down and only experienced occasional temper flare-ups whenever stress got the best of him, but, for the most part, he controlled his outbursts pretty well and settled back down quick enough."

Arnie asked, "I remember well those first early weeks of adjustment."

Hal smirked. "Yeah, but he became a master at masking his ongoing struggles dealing with his PTSD. Even dad became too busy to notice, but I witnessed how he wrestled with his demons. So, was I concerned for Megan? You bet ya! But early on, I was too focused on how hurt I felt after their so-called honeymoon and we co-existed under the same roof. I tried to forgive them, and gradually I put my hurt feelings aside for Megan's sake."

"What about Hank?" I said to Hal as I noticed Arnie's intent stare.

Hal struggled for words. "Megan and I moved on, but I still placed the brunt of the blame on Hank and kept my distance until the night of the fire."

"What happened that night?" The time for truth finally arrived, I scooted onto the edge of my chair.

"I dropped Phillip off for his Sanctuary meeting and decided to hang out in my office. Not long after, Hank walked into my office."

"What did Hank want?" I asked.

"He wanted to apologize for going behind my back with Megan. He claimed he just didn't know how to tell me. He made it sound as though they fell in love after Megan hinted she wanted more than friendship, and that's when their discreet meetings became more frequent. I tried to listen calmly, but snapped and flew off the handle at him." Hal looked up and glanced at both Arnie and me with a brief grin. "Funny now that I think about it. Hank was the calm one that night. I was the one who lost his cool." Hal appeared to rewind that evening in his mind as his hands massaged his temples.

I looked at Arnie. "Under the same circumstances, forgive me Arnie, but I'd likely have lost my temper too." I looked back to Hal as he looked up. "What happened next?"

Hal's voice got louder and tenser. "Words weren't enough. The lid blew off my bottled up hurt. I remember tossing my cigarette as I walked around the desk and yanked the chair out from under Hank. He fell back onto the floor while I stood over him and shouted, 'How's it feel to have your seat jerked out from under you?' Hank jumped up swinging. For the first time since middle school, I took on my older brother. I was actually deathly afraid of what he could do to me as we exchanged blows. He kept hollering at the top of his lungs that he didn't want to fight, but I wouldn't stop. I couldn't stop. We tumbled into the hallway. Hank got up first, stepped back with both hands raised and yelled, 'You don't know the truth! Let me tell you why we had to elope.'"

Arnie interrupted Hal. "What did Hank say?"

"Pastor, Hank told me they became scared because Megan got pregnant, and had promised Megan that he'd take care of it and agreed to marry her."

Arnie stood and looked at Hal. "Megan, pregnant?" Arnie's shock revealed that Megan had not told him everything.

Hal stared at Arnie and then turned his focus in my general direction. "Hold on Pastor. Hank then told me she miscarried while they were on their honeymoon. That's why they stayed away longer than planned."

"So let me get this straight. Hank concocted the story that they impetuously eloped because they wanted to be married before anyone knew about the pregnancy?" The pieces of the stories I had heard from Megan and what little I heard from Phillip ran through my mind.

"Well, that's what Hank told me. But hearing he got Megan pregnant and lied about it only infuriated me all the more. Hank then stepped back and said, 'That's what I came to tell you.' When he turned to leave, I followed him down the stairs to the main lobby. I shoved Hank when my words failed to stop him, and we fought again until we smelled the smoke."

I leaned forward. "You were downstairs when you first realized there was a fire?"

"Yeah, outside of dad's office. We raced upstairs and saw flames crawling up the back wall of my office. I then remembered the two five-gallon plastic pails of flammable solvent on the floor beside my desk and yelled for Hank to run, but we didn't get two steps before the pails exploded. The force blew Hank out the doorway, clear across the hallway. I wasn't as lucky. I slammed headlong into the wall beside the doorway and fell to my knees, dazed and disoriented." Hal rubbed the back of his head as if remembering the blow.

Arnie said, "That must have been frightening for you."

"I never felt that scared before or since. If my desk hadn't deflected the blast, I might not be standing here today. The explosion shot the flames into the ceiling, and the old timbers became kindling. The fire grew out of control fast. Hank ran to the window at the end of the hall but came right back and dragged me out of the growing inferno. The flames consumed my office, and the adjoining rooms burst into flames. I began to choke and gag. That's when I remember hearing Jessie's voice. Hank panicked, shoved Jessie aside and ran to the window again. Flames blocked our exit, so Jessie pulled Hank away from the window and said he'd find another way out. Hank helped me up after Jessie told us to stay put and he disappeared into the growing smoke that filled the hallway." Hal scrunched his baseball cap into a ball, and his glassy eyes stared past us.

Arnie asked, "Hal, you okay?"

"Thanks, Pastor. I've never told anyone this story, but I gotta finish it now."

I tried to make eye contact with Hal. "Take your time Hal."

Hal stood and paced the living room. "While we waited for Jessie, the overhead sprinklers finally popped open. The water pressure sputtered and had little effect dousing the fire, but the sprinklers bought us a little time. Jessie returned through the smoke and yelled that we had to leave now. We stood at the top of the stairwell and saw the fire had spread into the sub-floor timbers. Heavy black smoke filled the foyer below, while flames broke out all around. Jessie followed Hank and me down the steps. I leaned on Hank until we were almost to the bottom of the stairs, and that's when the ceiling above us collapsed. Hank took a direct hit and slammed into the wall. Jessie grabbed me and helped Hank back onto his feet. Jessie then yelled at us to run. I felt his hand shove me towards the front doors just before a blast of hot air blew the doors open. I landed on the front portico steps and heard a loud crash behind us, so I grabbed Hank, and we scrambled onto the lawn. When we looked back for Jessie, he wasn't there." Hal focused on the glare of the noon sun shining off the peak of the bronze dome atop City Hall.

"You two were saved by the hands of God," Arnie muttered.

"If God saved us, why not Jessie too?" Tears formed in Hal's eyes.

Arnie paused before he stuttered. "I don't know. I wish he had, but I know God sent Jessie to save you. Jessie knew the risk when he entered the building that night. He trusted God and knew he had to shove you to safety. He probably wasn't even thinking about himself."

Tears flowed on Hal's face while I struggled to contain my own. "Look…" I said to Hal. "The fire was an accident, and Jessie gave his life for your lives. You can't change those facts. However, you can honor his sacrifice by making your life worth the price he paid. I believe that's what God's trying to get you to understand."

"But… it was my cigarette that started the fire." Hal sobbed.

Arnie said, "Look at me. I knew Jessie well enough to know he understood what he was doing. He exchanged, redeemed if you will, his life for yours. Whatever the actual cause, the fire was an accident. It wasn't your fault Jessie died. You need to forgive yourself, Hal."

Hal openly sobbed. "We got scared after the fire. We were concerned about anyone knowing why we were there that night and that my carelessness caused the fire. The thought of a cigarette to this day makes me sick to my stomach."

"Don't you feel better telling the truth?" I asked.

Hal barked back. "No! What I told you about Hank and Megan was more of Hank's lies!"

"What do you mean?" Arnie pleaded.

Distraught, Hal tugged on the sides of his jeans as he paced back and forth. "Hank slipped up the other night and told me how Megan's abortion, not a miscarriage, caused her not to be able to have children. His lies finally caught up with him."

"Are you sure?" said Arnie, undoubtedly shocked by the revelation.

Hal's red eyes cut through me. "That idiot brother of mine cursed Megan because she couldn't have kids. When I asked what he meant, he yelled at me like I was stupid. 'Because she had that botched abortion!' He tried to backtrack when he realized he had slipped up and apologized over and over for lying to me."

I collapsed back into my chair. Arnie followed suit in Liddy's chair. I looked directly at Hal. "How does Coach Priestly fit into this?"

Hal froze, and then sarcasm spewed. "My dear brother tried to blame Coach Priestly for Megan's botched abortion." Hal huffed. "When I asked Hank what he meant by that, he shouted, 'You know too much already. Butt out!' That's when I walked away from Hank."

Arnie stood and rested his arm on Hal's shoulder. "The truth always frees us to do the right thing." I watched as Arnie comforted Hal's broken spirit. Hal asked for forgiveness, and Arnie assured him that God forgave him. Arnie then prayed for Hal and asked God to give him the courage to confess to Megan and Marie about what he knew. Hal reluctantly agreed but feared they might not want to talk to him.

I stood and said, "Hal, Megan deserves to move on in her life. She needs to know who she can trust and with whom she can share the truth that haunts her too. Hank's hurt both of you, but I believe you can be the friend she needs now. I also believe Marie'll forgive you."

Hal expressed his uncertainty about his family's future. "I hope we can move forward from this even if Hank never really does."

Before today, Hal seemed more of an enigma to me than either Hank or Phillip. He walked in the shadows of his older brother and their father, but now I saw a young man ready to make his own decisions.

Arnie smiled as Hal drove off. "Theo, my friend, I believe we just experienced a divine appointment."

I turned toward Arnie. "For sure. I'm just glad God invited you to the appointment too."

"How so?"

"Arnie, I wanted to talk to you about Megan's visit Monday but wasn't sure how to broach the subject with you. I didn't know what you knew or didn't know. Hal pretty much erased that concern."

Arnie hesitated before he confessed, "Megan never told me everything. Guess she was too embarrassed and ashamed. I suggested she find someone she felt comfortable with and talk to them."

My knees went limp, and I leaned against the door as Arnie's response sunk in. "So you never knew what happened between Hank, Hal, and Megan?"

"Nope. All I just heard was news to me. Though Harold and Phillip did fill in a few details when we talked last night, but it appears they said nothing you obviously don't already know."

I stood motionless assessing my thoughts. "Well, I'm still at a loss. Megan and Hal both carry deep wounds thanks to Hank, but what about Harold? How's he going to wrap his head around this when Hal tells him?"

"Theo, let me ask you something." Arnie's subtle pastoral voice returned. "Why do you believe you and Liddy came to Shiloh when you did? Why have Megan and Hal come to you like they have when they haven't known you long?"

"I'm not sure."

"Has it dawned on you that God might've directed you and Liddy here? Consider your uncanny connection to Marie and Jessie. Think about the uniqueness of this house. Is that any more amazing than how so many people in this town have been drawn to both of you so quickly? Do you still think it was chance or coincidence? Or maybe providence?"

"But... I..."

"Theo, there are no buts where God's concerned. God brought you here. Just keep doing whatever you're doing, and let God do the rest."

I chuckled at the premise, though I still felt utterly confused. "But what'll be the town's response once Megan's story gets out? Do you think Megan will be okay?"

Arnie considered his response. "Let those without sin cast the first stone. God's forgiveness and grace haven't run dry. Megan's still wrestling with the consequences of her choices, but I don't believe this town will shun her. Sooner or later we all seek forgiveness from God for something. When we do, God reminds us all that his forgiveness is conditional on how we forgive others."

"I know you're right about God. I just hope you're right about this town too."

"I am. Trust me. Now, my friend, I gotta run."

———

Shortly after Liddy arrived home and told me about her afternoon with Marie, I delved into what happened with Hal. She propped herself up in her chair, attentive to every detail as I retold Hal's story as best as I could recount the details.

"So Hank continued to lie even to Hal about Megan's pregnancy?" Liddy squeezed her cheeks between her hands as if to grasp Hal's hurt. "Now what?"

"We helped Hal realize the fire was an accident and, to honor Jessie, he should meet with Marie and Megan separately, ask for their forgiveness, and share what he knows."

"What about Harold and Hank?"

"We'll just have to wait and see what happens."

"By the way, how did Arnie react to learning about Megan's pregnancy and abortion?"

"Arnie's a great friend and pastor. He cares about people's hearts first and foremost."

Liddy kissed me and grabbed my hands. "I sure hope so. When John's back in town tomorrow, we'll most certainly get a taste of this town's open-mindedness."

CHAPTER THIRTY-SIX

THE CONTINUAL SOUND OF RAIN pronounced a soggy and dreary day lay ahead. Though this particular Friday the 13th arrived inauspiciously, I trusted God's providential hand rather than juvenile fears of black cats and misfortune. By the end of this fateful day, John Priestly would be home out on Marie's farm.

While watching the raindrops hit the window, Liddy's apparition appeared on the glass. "What ya' thinking so deeply about?" Liddy whispered as she snuggled into my lap.

"Just realizing how God shapes our lives through dreary, bleak days like these." I pulled her tight. "Have I told you lately how much I love you?"

"You know I never tire of you telling me. I love you too."

Though Timmy took the utmost care to protect this morning's paper, Liddy gingerly peeled away the soaked pages and found a brief article about today's arrival of the city's Christmas tree. Also, to our relief, Larry had avoided any mention of John Priestly's parole or return to Shiloh.

The waterlogged news landed in the kitchen trash as Liddy said, "Do you know that Judy told me that Megan reminded her of Harold's ex-wife."

"Did you ask Judy why she mentioned that?"

Liddy tapped her lips with her fingertip. "No, but she also noted that Dixie, Harold's wife, left out of the blue one day, leaving Harold with a toddler and two rowdy teenage boys to raise on his own."

"Did Judy know what happened to Dixie or where she is?"

"The last she and Arnie heard, Dixie remarried and settled near New Orleans. But to their knowledge, Dixie's never been back even to visit her sons."

"It's hard to comprehend of any mother walking away from her children, no matter what happened in her marriage."

"Just think how that likely affected Hank and Hal. And, Phillip, poor Phillip. Maddie's likely the only mother-figure he's ever known."

I sipped my coffee and tried to dwell on more pleasant thoughts. "Hun, on a cheerier note, how about you and I think about caring for our own family. They'll be here in a few days. Is there anything we need to do?"

"Oh my goodness, we've gotta go grocery shopping."

"All right, I think I'll go with you. Go get ready, and I'll clean up in here."

Just as we turned onto Main Street, a city worker held a stop sign while a flatbed trailer backed along the curb next to the taped-off site where this year's city Christmas tree would stand. The crane on the adjacent corner waited with its boom raised and a sling dangling.

Liddy squealed when she realized the trailer's cargo. "It's the tree! It's larger than I envisioned." The eighteen-wheeler finally found its designated place and a city worker waved us around the parked rig.

As we drove slowly past, the truck driver removed the yellow straps that anchored Harold's prize tree along its journey. "They sure picked a great day to erect that tree."

Liddy craned her neck to watch as men wearing yellow rain gear directed the crane's boom into position. "The temperature's dropping. I can see the workers' breath in the rain."

I found an empty parking spot out front of Shiloh's IGA, and we dashed into the store. Even though I never enjoyed shopping, I loved watching Liddy work her way through the aisles with repeated glances at her detailed and extra long shopping list. She had anticipated everyone's favorites and made sure there'd be enough leftovers until well after Christmas.

After the groceries found their proper place in the kitchen, I embraced the challenge of sorting through the bags of candies and trinkets purchased to fill our grandchildren's Christmas stockings. I sat on the floor in front of the fireplace, wrote each child's name on a separate brown paper bag, and made certain that each received equal amounts of goodies. Liddy joked from the safety of the kitchen that I looked like a jolly old elf as I stashed the packed bags in the closet. I laughed because I knew we both looked forward to Christmas Eve when we both became Santa's elves and would deposit the contents of the bags into the now empty stockings decorating the mantle.

For the rest of the afternoon, Liddy busied herself in the guest bedrooms between her baking priorities. In short order, the tantalizing aroma of Liddy's Christmas cookies, fresh out of the oven, filled the house. I grabbed a few samples, stretched out on our sofa and soon dozed off watching an old John Wayne western.

Liddy stirred me from my nap. "Hun, it's Harold on the phone, and he sounds upset."

I grabbed the phone. "Hello, Harold. What's up?"

Harold sounded out of breath and alarmed. "It's Hank!"

"What about Hank?" My mind raced over the possibilities of what Hank could have done.

"Sorry to have to call you, but… well, Hank got into a heated argument with Hal and Phillip this afternoon and stormed off in his truck."

"What'd they fight about?" Liddy leaned close trying to hear Harold's answer.

Harold took a deep breath and then said, "Hank found out Megan, Hal and Phillip had been to see you. I can't remember everything that was said, but Hank began hollering and ranting and called Hal a backstabber. Hank started to blast into Phillip, but Hal jumped between them. I thought for sure it would escalate beyond words, so I got involved. That's when Hank threw his arms in the air and stormed out filling the air with irrational, curse-laced threats directed at all of us, including you."

"Are you okay?"

Harold moaned. "I'm feeling pretty confused about everything.

Outside of my elevated blood pressure, I reckon we're all okay."

"Well, maybe Hank just needs some time and space to cool off. I'm sure he'll be back soon enough. When he does, I suggest you pull him aside and talk to him one-on-one. He'll listen to you."

"Maybe, but can you and I meet to talk? You appear to have a better handle on what's going on than I do. Hal and Phillip both suggested it."

I covered the phone and looked into Liddy's bewildered eyes. She put her hand on my cheek and said, "Do what you have to do. I'll be fine."

"Where and when do you want to meet?"

"How about I swing by your house in, say, thirty minutes? We can take a drive and talk."

"Okay, I'll watch for you."

Forty-five minutes later, Harold's diesel truck rumbled out front. His haggard, disheveled appearance testified to the sea of misery and pain he had been trying to navigate.

"Thanks, Theo." Harold put the truck in gear as I snapped my seatbelt. "Sorry to drag you out like this tonight, but I need some reliable answers to what's happening to my family."

I gripped his forearm. "Hey, listen to me… Father-to-father, I understand. Why don't we find somewhere to sit and talk?" Harold stared quietly out the windshield until he pulled into his usual parking space across the street from the church near Jessie's illuminated bronze statue.

The moist, cold air greeted us when we climbed out of Harold's truck. The rain-soaked streets downtown appeared empty as we began to walk. I refrained from talking and instead listened to our footsteps. With my hands tucked into my jacket pockets, the damp night air felt chilly but tolerable. Harold walked with his head down as if deliberately choosing each step, and I adjusted my stride to match his.

After several minutes of awkward silence, Harold stopped and said, "If this mess at my house can't get straightened out soon, I'm afraid another catastrophe won't be far behind."

"How so?"

Harold peered at me, openly examining my sincerity. "Theo, I feel for the first time in a very long time, I've lost control. Raising those boys hasn't been easy, and they've certainly been a handful over the years, but they're grown men now." He slowly shook his head.

We stopped beneath a lamp post at the corner near the city's grand Christmas tree, decorated with ornaments and lights, though not yet illuminated. "Harold, why do you think they've been hiding all this from you?"

"I wish I knew. Hank stormed out after Hal challenged him to tell me what's going on with Megan. When I asked Hal what he meant, he said it wasn't his place to say." Harold paused and stared more intently. "What's Hank and Hal not telling me? As one father to another, I need to know if you know anything."

I wondered if I should hold back what Harold deserved to know and paused to consider what I could tell him without breaking any confidences. "Harold, did Hank tell you why he visited me and why he blames me for what's eating at him?"

"No, and none of this makes any sense either."

"Would you consider the possibility that Hank's afraid?"

"Afraid?"

I pointed to the nearby bench. "This might take a few minutes."

Harold sat while I remained standing.

"I'm pretty sure that Hank's afraid of what I discovered after I started to look into what happened the night the courthouse burned down." I gazed at the old courthouse's replacement.

"What does the fire have to do with why Hank would be afraid? I'm sorry about what happened to Jessie, but my sons were spared. I'm confused."

"Did you know Hal visited me two days ago?"

"Not until I heard it mentioned during the argument between Hal and Hank."

"Well, I suspect you'll have a one-on-one with Hal in the next day or so, but I'll tell you this much. Hal was afraid too, but unlike Hank, he wanted to clarify what happened that night."

"What does your story about the fire have to do with this?"

"Harold, think back to the time before the night of the fire. How would you describe their relationship?"

Harold paused and stared at the entrance to City Hall. "Well, I guess they had their differences. For certain, whatever went on between them got worse after Hank married Megan."

"Haven't you ever wondered what prompted Hank to visit Hal in the courthouse that night?"

Harold nodded with a slight shrug.

"Hal, Hank or Megan will have to tell you everything, but I guess it's okay to share that the rift between Hank and Hal came to a head in Hal's office that night. Hal also blames himself for the fire because of a carelessly tossed aside cigarette during their exchange of words. He's also carried the burden that Hank and he fought that night and were too caught up their scuffle to recognize a fire broke out until it was too late."

"Do you know what caused their fight?"

"I'd rather they tell you, but it involved Megan."

Harold's confusion added to his weariness. He turned his head toward Jessie's statue. "But, because of what they did-"

I raised my hand. "Before you say another word, the fire was an accident. I reminded Hal of the same conclusion. And Jessie knew the risk when he entered the building to save your sons."

"But why hasn't Hank or Hal at least talked to me about what happened?"

"Harold, they each had their reasons for being afraid."

Harold's whole face, even his voice, wilted. "The other night when Hank lost his temper with Megan after she told him what the doctor said, he blamed her for her condition. What did Hank mean by that?"

"Please Harold, talk to Hal and Megan before you talk to Hank."

Harold stood and paced, all the while running his hands through his hair. "Theo, please what did Megan tell you?"

"Trust me, Hal will tell what you need to hear, but you have to talk with him."

Harold's arms dropped to his sides, his labored breathing made visible by the night air. "Why would Hank lie? Why?"

"Do you want my honest opinion?"

Harold nodded.

"Because he didn't want to disappoint you. Running your family's business provided a huge opportunity for Hank after he returned from Afghanistan, but I think he tried too hard to please you."

Harold turned to face me. "Hank thought he'd disappoint me?"

"Sometimes respect and fear are strange bed-fellows inside a son's heart. Hank wanted to manage Archer Construction as good as you, and he wanted his marriage to produce grandchildren for you too."

"But I never expected him to be me. I never wanted him to be anything but who he was." Harold stood motionless.

I put my arm on his shoulder and guided us slowly toward Jessie's image. "Look, I'm afraid I can't say anything more until you talk with Hal and hopefully Hank, but you deserve to hear the truth even if it's difficult to swallow."

Harold glanced at me and sighed. "Okay. Whatever Hal tells me, though, I feel somehow responsible." He stopped opposite Jessie and looked up at his face. "What about Jessie? What about poor Megan?" He turned to City Hall and pointed. "What about all the people affected by what happened?"

I looked at his tired, dejected face and squeezed his shoulders. "We can't change the past, and only God knows what the future holds. We can only take one step at a time in the present."

"What's my next step?"

"I suggest you start with your family. Sit down with Hal and Phillip. Sort this out with them, so all of you are on the same page. Listen to Megan with a father's compassionate heart, and then sit down with Hank. Get him to fess up, and help him remove the fears burdening his shoulders. And, maybe talking to Arnie at some point might be a good idea too."

"What about Marie Masterson?" Harold asked as we started walking toward his truck.

"I believe she understands and blames no one. Jessie's decision that night had nothing to do with why the fire started or who needed help. He put himself at risk just because lives were in danger."

We shook hands before I got out of the truck. Harold drove off at least knowing what he should do to get the answers he deserved.

Liddy greeted me at the door. "Everything okay?"

I sighed. "I hope so."

She hugged me and grinned. "Well, I've got some hot chocolate and cookies for you. And, if it'll make you feel any better, Joe called. John's at Marie's."

CHAPTER THIRTY-SEVEN

A BREAK IN THE DREARY weather arrived after two dismal days. The sun parted the remaining gray clouds, but a wintry chill whistled through the trees. At church, few dared to linger outside and the foyer and sanctuary aisles brimmed with incessant gossip and chatter. John Priestly's name floated alongside opinions about rumors of unrest in the Archer family.

Liddy and I huddled near the front entrance, removed from the grip of icy blasts of air whenever the doors opened and closed. We watched as still, mostly strangers milled about, and smiled in the direction of unfamiliar glances. We inched our way toward the familiar smiles of our friends and found Megan beside Jeannie, chatting with her brothers, and Jay and Jim.

Liddy gravitated toward Martha and Susanna who were talking about Marie and John. Zeb, Sam, and Larry pulled me into their discussion directed at the gossip floating among the church members. I half-heartedly listened as I made brief eye contact with Megan. Seeing her reconnect with old friends warmed my heart.

My attention returned to the potshots emanating from Zeb, Sam, and Larry. I finally interjected. "For what it's worth, I have to agree on this much with you... there's certainly a whole lot more than the usual harmless chit chat in the air this morning."

Zeb straightened and stared over my shoulder, which caused me to gawk at Marie weaving her way toward us. Phillip and Hal accompanied her, nudging those unwilling to pause briefly from their conversations to allow them to pass.

Hal arrived clean-shaven, his long, brown hair trimmed and neat. He followed Marie while Phillip navigated their way. Before I could signal Liddy, she darted between Zeb and me. I wondered if Hal knew Megan stood just a few steps ahead beside Jeannie.

Zeb greeted Phillip first. "Good morning, young man. Who've you brought with you this mornin'?" Zeb then reached out his hand to Hal while Liddy embraced Marie. Hal cautiously surveyed each face in our group.

Before Hal left Marie's side, I discreetly asked, "Is your dad coming?"

"No, sir. He stayed home in case Hank comes back."

Liddy asked Marie, "Where's John? How's he doing?"

Marie said, "John's not quite ready to venture into town, but he encouraged me to come to church this morning. I found my two hand-some escorts milling around outside."

Jay shook hands with Hal. "Hey, Hal. It's been a long time."

Hal replied. "Yeah, it certainly has," but Megan's quiet voice di-verted Hal's attention. She walked up, wrapped one hand around Hal's arm, the other around Jay's, and guided both to join the other young adults who now included Phillip, as well.

From his chair on the platform, Arnie looked over the more than usual pre-service crowd. His smile widened when he recognized Marie, Megan and Hal standing together. As we took our seats, Hal appeared at ease sitting between Jeannie and Megan. Marie, directly behind them, leaned forward and whispered to each of them while her hands rested on Hal's shoulders.

As the music began for the first hymn, Joe ribbed Nick. Both smiled at Marie before they started singing from their usual places in the choir.

Arnie opened the service offering a reminder about Wednesday evening. "The lighting of this year's Christmas tree on Town Square will follow the dedication of our new City Hall and Jessie Masterson's Memorial Statue. There will be no evening service so that we all might attend this auspicious event, which begins at seven-thirty."

During Arnie's closing prayer after his message on God's Timeli-ness, Marie stood with her head raised skyward engaged in a private conversation with God. I squeezed Liddy's hand and thanked God for answers received and answers yet to come to all our prayers.

Mary scooted from her piano and warmly greeted Megan right after the service ended. Zeb and Sam invited everyone to Bubba's for dinner.

Hal escorted Jeannie and Megan into the aisle and then tugged my arm. "Thank you. I heard Arnie's message in a whole new light this morning."

"Liddy and I are especially pleased you and Phillip came today. Marie obviously enjoyed your decision too. I hope that opens the door for you to talk with her soon."

Hal smiled and nodded.

———

Our vehicles commandeered the empty parking spots in front of Bubba's. Barb Patterson's jovial voice greeted us while Cora and Cecil frantically shuffled tables and chairs to accommodate our large group in the back of the restaurant.

Hal and Phillip settled in well among the others and sat next to Megan and Jeannie. Arnie and Judy arrived last and took the two remaining seats across from Hal and Phillip. I enjoyed seeing Arnie and Hal engaged in friendly conversation throughout dinner.

After dinner, Liddy pulled Marie aside in the parking lot. "Please let John know we understand why he stayed home, and we look forward to seeing him as soon as he's up to it."

Marie assured Liddy that John wanted to meet her as soon as he got settled, and got used to life outside of prison. As the parking lot emptied, we watched as Megan and Jeannie, both captured in laughter, climbed into Megan's Mustang.

After a brisk walk home, Liddy and I spent the afternoon talking on the phone with both our sons and their families. We laughed as we listened to stories of recent happenings in their lives. Each grandchild, in turn, sounded excited about their visit to Shiloh.

———

More rain arrived during the night and exacerbated an already restless sleep. I ventured into the kitchen for some coffee only to be followed a few minutes later by Liddy. She let out a pretentious yawn just as she stepped behind me. I gazed out the window into the darkness. She wrapped her arms around my waist and said softly, "The rain woke me too."

While waiting for Monday's edition to arrive, I took Saturday's paper tucked away on top of the fridge, clipped the second installment of Jessie's story out, and placed it inside my attaché, alongside my handwritten draft of the revised final article.

My morning entailed a visit to deliver Larry the conclusion to Jessie's story and a stop at City Hall to check on Harold. I asked Liddy to join me so she could chat with Megan while I checked on Harold.

Liddy beamed. "Sounds like a good idea. I also need your opinion. Do you think there'd be any harm in baking something special to bring over to Marie's tomorrow?"

I scratched my early morning stubbles as I sensed her growing curiosity about John. "Maybe you outta call her later this afternoon and see what time would be best for them."

———

Just after nine, the Expedition splashed through the large puddle at the end of our driveway. Even with a reprieve in the weather, the rain-soaked streets and gray skies dominated the balance of the day.

We entered the Sentinel's office and were amused to find Jeannie leaning on the counter engrossed in conversation with Mary. Martha looked up from her desk and told us that Nick sent Jeannie to see if Mary could help with a layout design for an advertisement for the paper's special edition on Wednesday.

Liddy and I watched a few moments before I blurted, "Good morning ladies."

Jeannie jerked her head around, and Mary's head popped up. Both smiled as Mary said, "Oh! Good morning." Both then returned their focus to the urgent work at hand.

Martha turned her attention back to her desk but lifted a finger while she calculated the cost for Nick's advertisement. Jeannie turned from her elbow propped position. "How are you two doing this morning? Haven't seen you two since, let me see, yesterday."

Liddy walked over to talk with Jeannie and Mary while I looked for Larry. I first stopped to grab some coffee, but the pot felt lukewarm. As I turned around empty-handed, Jeannie walked up.

"Theo, I just wanted to tell you how much I appreciate how you and Miss Liddy have made yourselves available to Megan."

"Megan's gone through a lot the last few days. Liddy's been a real godsend to Megan." I looked up and saw Liddy engrossed with Mary and Martha.

"It's just that, well, Megan's troubles go much further back." Her head dropped, and she fiddled with her hands as they dangled in front of her.

"I think I understand." I sensed she knew far more than I previously realized.

There was a quiver in Jeannie's faint voice as she looked up. "It's just that Megan and I have known one another a long time, and I'm well aware of what happened between Hank and her… I know why they got married."

"I knew you and Megan were in school about the same time but didn't she graduate with Pete?"

"Yes, sir. She and Pete were seniors when she took me under her wings after I tried out for cheerleading my freshman year, and we continued to be good friends after that."

"That's great, but you said you know what happened when Megan and…" My mind froze a brief moment as I recalled what John said about a friend of Megan's approaching him. "Ah, I mean, Megan and Hank got married."

"Yesterday is the first we've talked in a very long time. That's how come I learned about her visit with you and Miss Liddy." Her down-cast eyes looked helpless.

"How's she doing? She seemed pretty relaxed with y'all yesterday."

"Considering all she's been through the last few days, she's doing pretty well, I guess. But she's deathly afraid of Hank."

"I don't blame her. Hank's been missing the last couple of days, and not even his family knows what he's apt to do at this point."

A sense of urgency came over Jeannie as she asked, "Would you mind if we got together later today, with Miss Liddy of course?" Her eyes accented her hopeful plea. "Last night, Megan urged me to talk with you. I'm scared because Megan made me promise to tell you what I know. You know, just in case."

"She must be terrified."

"Yes, sir."

"Don't worry. We'll stop by your office right after we leave City Hall later this morning. Is that okay? I'll let Liddy know what you told me and we'll work out something about getting together then."

After a half-hearted grin and nod, she turned and disappeared into the ladies room. By the time Jeannie rejoined Liddy and Mary, I had made a fresh pot of coffee and poured myself a cup. When Liddy smiled in my direction, I raised five fingers and pointed to my watch.

Larry stood in his office doorway with an inquisitive smirk and arms folded on his chest. I grabbed my attaché and coffee.

"So, what secrets did Jeannie share with you?" Larry queried as I walked past him.

I offered only a tight-lipped grin before reaching into my leather attaché. "Here's the final article on Jessie Masterson with a proper ending as promised."

Larry took the paper-clipped pages, walked behind his desk and skimmed them for a couple of minutes. He looked up with eyebrows arched. "You're happy with this ending?"

"Yep. The story's about Jessie, his heroic yet tragic life story. It's best to have an ending that doesn't detract from that." I leaned back in my chair and clasped my hands behind my head with a satisfied grin.

Larry closed the folder, then rocked back in his chair. "I agree." His furrowed brows disappeared.

"Thanks, Larry. I wrestled with this but felt I've hidden nothing that'd make a difference. In the end, it was a tragedy destined to happen."

Larry moved to the chair next to mine. "What would you like to do about John's return? Part of me wants to get something into the paper now." He inspected his feet as he leaned forward in his chair and waited for my reply.

I pulled my hands down from around my head and sat upright. "Well, I'm not one hundred percent certain quite yet. I believe John's story is still being written. If we rush an article for the sake of printing about his parole, speculation and rumors may stir up more harm than good. Waiting another day or two should prove beneficial. Is that okay?"

Larry raised his head and inspected my face. "Do you know something you're not telling me?"

I firmly planted both feet and leaned toward Larry and connected with his inquisitive glare. "I promise we'll have a story worthy of the wait. I can feel it."

"You just want me to trust your gut again?" Larry's voice cracked as he countered back.

I nodded. "You trusted my gut when we first discussed Jessie's story, right?"

"All right. I'll focus on getting the conclusion to Jessie's story printed. I plan to have it across from the special holiday insert in Wednesday's edition." Larry stood up. "Let me do my job now. You take care of John's story. Maybe we can print something before Christmas."

CHAPTER THIRTY-EIGHT

WE PARKED ACROSS THE STREET from the Arians Building and walked into City Hall. Megan greeted us as we approached her desk. "Good morning." Her pleasant demeanor brought some relief after hearing Jeannie's concerns. "I imagine you'd like to see the mayor."

Before I managed a response, Liddy whispered to Megan. "Theo volunteered to distract your boss while you and I had a little chat if that's okay with you." Liddy straightened her back up with her hands clasped in front of her.

Megan looked at me with a puzzled grin, and I chuckled under my breath. "Don't take Liddy too seriously. I really would like to speak with Harold for a moment." I looked at Liddy smiling. "I hoped you'd keep this instigator preoccupied while I meet with him."

Megan exhaled in relief as she raised her eyes to Liddy. "You two are too funny for words." She grabbed the phone. "Mayor, I have Mister Phillips here if you have a couple of minutes."

Harold's footsteps provided his answer just before he appeared in his doorway, glanced at his watch, then produced one of his patented smiles. "I see you brought your lovely wife with you this time. Come on back. I can certainly squeeze in a few minutes for you Theo."

I hoped Harold's tongue-in-cheek attitude indicated a degree of progress on the home front, but his baggy eyes said otherwise.

We chatted briefly about what he missed at church, and afterward at Bubba's. Harold leaned back and said, "Sorry I stayed home. Would've enjoyed seeing Hal mingle with your growing circle of friends. Sounds like y'all had a good time." He patted his stomach.

"It's a shame I missed out, but under the current circumstances —"

"Don't worry about it. Hal told us."

"Hal's a good son. You know, he talked Phillip into going to church. We talked at great length last evening about Arnie's message and the great time he and Phillip had afterward. He mentioned that Megan came to church too." Harold's eyebrow raised.

"Both Megan and Jeannie seemed to enjoy Hal's company."

"Theo, Hal mentioned they ran into Marie Masterson at church."

"Yeah, Marie appeared to welcome their attention when they escorted her into the sanctuary."

"Glad my boys took good care of her. Hal also mentioned how much he likes you and Liddy," Harold said with an inquiring look.

"Liddy and I like him too." Harold's curiosity made it clear that Hal had not mentioned anything about his most recent visit with us.

"You know, I'm proud of Hal. Probably don't tell him as I should. He's done an admirable job heading the city's utilities department, and he's never complained when I've asked him to manage some special projects either. I suggested last night that he should hang out more with his old friends."

"You'd be proud of him. He evidently followed your advice from what I could see yesterday. I'm confident you and he'll talk more in the days ahead."

Harold paused before answering, "I hope so. He needs to climb out of his shell and speak up more. Oh yeah, Phillip mentioned your final article would be in Wednesday's edition of the paper. I've enjoyed the first two installments so far. You certainly uncovered a lot about Jessie. Everyone I've talked to seems anxious to read the conclusion."

"You'll be glad to know that Larry got it this morning. I believe you'll be happy."

Harold's eyes widened. "If you don't mind… What did you mention about the night of the fire?"

I recognized the sudden absence of his jovial spirit in his inquiry. I leaned forward on the edge of my chair. "Jessie's story was always the intended focus of the article. The only reference to your two sons will be at the end of the article. I quoted you as expressing your heartfelt gratitude for what Jessie did saving them that night."

Harold sighed. "I only hope Wednesday night's ceremony will do justice to Jessie's memory. Oh, I also plan to announce the restart of Sanctuary during the tribute ceremony."

"Harold, that's great, but how are you doing? You still don't look your usual self, more than just tired."

Harold gripped his knees as his head drooped. "Theo, I don't know what to do about Hank. For one of the few times in my life, I don't have any answers. I don't understand what's happening to my own family. I feel I've lost control."

"Have you heard from him?"

Harold wiped his face with his hand as he grumbled. "Nothing and no one knows where he's run off to. He's not been to work and doesn't answer his phone."

As a father, I tried to empathize with his pain and grief. "Has he disappeared like this before? Where do you think he's gone off to?"

Harold eyed the family portrait on his desk. "I suspect he'll show up soon enough. He's always had a short fuse, but it seems more often than not to ignite a powder keg within him that harms the lives of others lately. He just needs time to regain his senses. No doubt, what's happened between him and Megan has given him a lot to brood about."

I nodded but struggled to maintain my assuring grin. "Maybe you're right. He's holed up somewhere stewing over what's happened these last few days."

"I don't know Theo. Hal's usually managed to help Hank through some of these rough patches. Not this time. I suspect he's hanging out at our old hunting cabin deep in the woods on the back of our property. You know, I oughta have Hal and Phillip run out there and check it out this evening." Harold got up and paced with his thumbs tucked into his vest pockets. "Yep, he's probably at the cabin with a case of beer and a bucket of fried chicken right now."

I put my arm around his shoulders. "I'm sure you're right. Would you rather that we drive there right now?"

"You'd do that?"

"Sure. If the shoe were on the other foot, I'd want to know as soon as I could."

Harold paused. "Thanks, Theo, but I reckon it'd be best if Hal and Phillip went. No telling what's on Hank's mind right now. Besides, hasn't it crossed your mind that you're not exactly his favorite either?"

"You're probably right about that. Will you at least call me if you hear anything?"

Harold patted my back. "Sure. I do appreciate your offer, though."

"If I can help, please let me know. I feel partly at fault for this mess."

Harold gripped my hand. Both of his hands felt cold and clammy. "It's not your fault. What's happened has been brewing for quite some time. I should've stepped in sooner. I've been too busy taking care of my career and this town better than my own family. I'll call you. I promise."

Harold apologized and asked if I'd see myself out. After I closed the door behind me, I leaned towards Megan and whispered, "Did she behave herself?"

Megan whispered loud enough for Liddy to hear. "Of course. She's awesome." She then asked as I took Liddy's hand, "Is Harold okay? I'm worried."

Before I responded, Harold opened his door and leaned against the frame with his hands in his pockets. His forced smile and half-hearted wave answered Megan's question.

"Hold all my calls for the next hour," he said and then closed the door behind him.

Megan walked with us into the foyer. "See what I mean?"

I said, "He needs lots of rest, but I'm afraid there'll be more trouble brewing soon enough."

Before we walked across Main Street to visit Jeannie, we briefly stopped to watch workers in a lift bucket stringing more lights onto the grandiose Christmas tree in front of City Hall.

Liddy leaned close and whispered, "Megan verified what Jeannie told you this morning. She also feels awful how she's neglected Jeannie since she married Hank, especially since Jeannie's kept her secret all this time."

I absorbed what Liddy said. "All of this is nothing but a tangled mess," I finally responded, squeezing her hand. "When it comes un-raveled, it could get real nasty, real fast. Harold's heard nothing from Hank, and I'm sure it's eating at him more than he's letting on."

———

Jeannie told us Nick would be out of the office all day and asked if she could stop by the house after she locked up. Liddy told Jeannie about her talk with Megan and invited her for dinner.

A little before six, a truck drove up out front and drew Liddy's at-tention. "Come here, Theo. It's Jeannie. Check out who brought her." She waved for me to hurry.

I got up from resting my eyes on the sofa and joined Liddy at the front window. Hal walked a step behind Jeannie with his hands in his pockets. Jeannie stepped onto the porch, but Hal waited at the foot of the porch steps.

Liddy whispered. "Find out if Hal will join us for dinner too."

I held the storm door open. "Is everything okay Jeannie?" She looked at me and then at Liddy who wiggled around me to greet them.

"Hey, Miss Liddy. Hal gave me a lift, but he can't stay."

Liddy looked at Hal. "Hal, you're more than welcome to stay for dinner."

"No thank you, ma'am. I just came to drop Jeannie off."

Jeannie grabbed Liddy's hand and glanced at me. "Hal's gotta pick up Phillip. They're heading out to find Hank."

"Did you hear from him?" I blurted hoping that any news would be good news.

Hal looking displeased said, "Megan got a threatening phone call from him this afternoon. Evidentially, he's fallen completely off the wagon this time. Dad called me just a short while ago when I was talk-ing with Jeannie."

"Is Megan okay?" Liddy asked as she peered at Hal.

"Miss Liddy, dad told me to tell you she's fine." He glanced at me. "Would you mind taking Jeannie home?"

"Of course not. Tell your dad, thanks. Don't worry about Jeannie. We'll take good care of her."

Hal's slow gait indicated someone, not in a hurry for what awaited him. His eyes remained glued to the windshield as he slowly pulled away.

Jeannie stayed put until Hal's truck taillights disappeared. Liddy took her by the hand. "Come on inside. He'll be just fine." Jeannie's wrinkled grin and glassy eyes expressed her anxiety.

I used my free arm to shoo them off the porch and into the house as I peered up and down the street one more time. Not really expecting to see anything, my gut wrenched over what may happen in the hours ahead. The twinkle of the lights both inside and out provided some comfort as the sun gave way to a chilly evening.

Jeannie apologized after only a couple of bites of her dinner. "Miss Liddy, this is great, thank you, but I'm afraid I'm just not too hungry with all that's going on."

"Don't you worry. If you get hungry later, let me know. Just eat what you can."

In between forced chit-chat, the three of us finally cleared the table and settled into the living room. Jeannie relaxed as she gazed at the Christmas tree lights. Our conversation began to flow more comfort-ably than during dinner. We talked about Jeannie's mom and dad, and soon Jeannie found comfort picking on Pete and Andy. She mentioned how Nick admitted feeling anxious about John's return and how peo-ple would treat him, but that triggered Jeannie's uneasiness again. She retreated to a glassy stare at the colored Christmas lights.

"Mister P, I've got to get some things off my chest," Jeannie said as she began to fidget.

Liddy reached over from the opposite end of the sofa and held her hand. After a moment of silent eye contact, Liddy said, "Hun, whatever you need to say, we're here to listen."

Jeannie squeezed Liddy's hand and peered at me. "Mister P, I'm sorry about this morning. I've been trying to get up the nerve to speak with you for a couple of days. Megan and I talked this weekend, and she apologized to me for distancing herself from me. But all that's happened in the last few days reminded her of the dark secret we've shared all this time. She told me about her visit with you and said there's no reason to keep the secret anymore."

Jeannie's eyes became teary. "Megan confessed how she's paid the price for her secret and didn't want me to be burdened by it any longer."

"What secret, Jeannie?" I urged as she focused on the outside lights glistening on the window.

Tears flowed freely as her chin and lips quivered. "Oh, Megan was right. You two are the only ones in town I feel remotely comfortable talking to about this."

Liddy inched closer and placed her arm around her shoulders. Jeannie smiled at Liddy through tears and continued her confession.

"I couldn't possibly tell momma or daddy about this... Before Megan and I grew apart, they accepted Megan as kind of a big sister for me. Heck, I used to tag along with Hal and Megan all around town until the night Megan told me about her relationship with Hank. Then I found myself between her and Hal. She asked me on more than one occasion to give Hal some excuse because she wanted to meet Hank. She swore me to secrecy because her mom and dad were already uneasy about she and Hal hanging out so much, but her dad despised Hank even more. Our secret grew a few weeks later when she came to me in tears and admitted she might be pregnant."

Liddy asked, "What'd you do?"

"I promised not to say anything but felt I needed to talk to someone. I didn't know what to do or what I could say to help her. Out of fear, I went to the one person I knew Megan and me could trust."

"Coach Priestly?" I uttered matter-of-factly.

Jeannie broke her teary stare and bobbed her head as she wiped her cheeks. "Coach Priestly's been like an uncle to me for as long as I can remember. I knew Megan looked up to him. I trusted he'd give her sound advice without judging her. I knew Megan already felt scared sharing with me about her situation, so I approached Coach for her and tried not to mention Megan's name. However, there wasn't much in Shiloh he didn't know about. He spouted Megan's name to me and said he'd already heard the rumors of Megan running around with Hank behind Hal's back and he knew how close we were."

Liddy asked, "How'd Coach Priestly react?"

"He wasn't upset or angry. In fact, he stayed much calmer than I anticipated. I think he knew how uncomfortable I felt being in the middle. He sat me down and explained that while neither Hank nor Megan wanted something like this to happen, God's grace would provide a way through this for them. That's when I mentioned that Megan was considering an abortion, but that I thought it was more as a result of Hank pushing her into it."

"Did Megan ever visit with Coach?" I asked.

"He asked me to tell Megan that he wanted to talk with her before she made any decisions. But as far as I know, she was too embarrassed and frightened. Megan told me Hank assured her that he'd take care of everything. Not long after that Megan freaked out when she started to show, if you know what I mean, and they disappeared without telling anyone, not even me." Jeannie's head swayed back and forth.

Liddy calmly asked, "Do you think she panicked and felt Hank offered the only solution to her problem?"

After a few moments, Jeannie raised her eyes. "After Megan and Hank returned to town, she visited me in tears. When I asked what happened, she begged me that if anyone asks about the pregnancy to say she miscarried. I tried to sort out in my mind that they returned married and lost the baby, but that's when Megan told me the truth about the abortion and made me swear not to tell a soul."

I looked at Jeannie and tried to comprehend the confusion and pain she must have felt. "Jeannie, you were still a teenager at that time?"

Liddy said, "That would be a lot for any young woman, at any age, to handle. Does Hank have any notion that you know anything?"

"No ma'am, not as far as I know. Megan kept the secret too. Only Coach Priestly knows."

"What do you think Megan meant when she said Hank would take care of everything?" I sensed Hank's guilt fueled his behavior toward Megan during their marriage, especially when she told him what the doctor told her recently.

"According to Megan, Hank arranged a private clinic in Maryland to handle the abortion because she was so far along. Megan told me how she tried to back out, but Hank got upset because he had already arranged everything. He even threatened not to marry her. Megan said she felt trapped and tried to believe Hank when he promised they'd raise a proper family later."

I asked, "Did Coach Priestly ever find out?"

"Yeah. Megan confessed to him after they got back. She felt so guilty and depressed. She believed God would certainly punish her."

"You've every right to cry," Liddy said, as Jeannie sobbed on her shoulder. "You've been carrying this secret for far too long. Megan did the same thing you're doing, not but a couple of days ago."

Jeannie inquired sobbing, "What'll happen to Megan now? Was the doctor's news God's punishment?"

Liddy stroked Jeannie's hair. "What's happened to Megan was just an unfortunate consequence of the procedure she had. God loves her no less or no more than he loves you or me. God has a plan and purpose for Megan in the days ahead. You best leave that to Megan and God."

I sat in my chair, lost in the lights flickering outside. I sifted through all I had heard over the past few days. Megan, Hal and now Jeannie revealed their terrible secrets. Hank hung out somewhere distraught, agitated all the more by his drinking. I considered how Susanna and Sam would need God's understanding to help Jeannie in the coming days. She had covered up a secret that in the eyes of many in the church meant aiding and abetting a murder. I wondered how Pete and Andy would react. Would they change how they felt about Megan now? Even more troubling, how might they respond to Hank after they realize what in truth happened. How about Harold when he learns about this? He seemed utterly clueless, but I still wondered if he spoke to me in complete honesty yet.

Liddy suggested Jeannie take a few days before she told her parents the whole story. "If it'll help, tell Pete and Andy first. They may be a big help when you talk with your parents." Jeannie's swollen red eyes undermined her efforts to smile.

Based on what I knew of Susanna and Sam, I felt their response after the initial shock would be nothing but understanding, and assured Jeannie as much when we drove her home.

———

Our alarm clock read 12:41 when the phone stirred us from our sleep. I cleared my throat while fumbling for the phone. "Hello..." I muttered.

Liddy stirred and whispered. "Is that one of the boys?"

I shook my head as Arnie spoke with grave urgency. "Theo, sorry to call so late, but I thought you'd want to hear right away."

My groggy mind struggled to make sense of the call. "Arnie, is that you? What's going on? It's almost one in the morning."

"Theo, sorry to wake you, but I'm at the hospital. Harold's being admitted."

CHAPTER THIRTY-NINE

ONLY A HANDFUL OF VEHICLES littered the parking lot when we arrived at the Shiloh Medical Center and pulled beside Arnie's Tahoe. We spotted Arnie on his phone near the coffee vending machine in the waiting room.

I asked as he put his phone away. "How's Harold?"

He took a deep breath. "Glad you're here. Phillip brought Harold in about an hour ago and called me right away. He said they found Harold passed out on the floor of his study."

Liddy's grip on my arm tightened as her eyes scanned the waiting room. "Where's Phillip now?"

"Probably with Harold."

I asked, "Have the doctors said anything?"

"The nurse told me the doctor arranged for Harold's admittance. They want to run some routine tests in the morning. Otherwise, the doctor believes Harold will be okay."

Liddy's grip eased as she sighed, "Thank the Lord."

"Do they know why he collapsed?" I asked as Liddy's hand fell into mine.

"Doctor said, probably a toxic combination of stress and poor diet, on top of a lack of sleep. The tests will confirm his initial diagnosis in the morning. Thankfully, it appears his heart's fine, and they ruled out a stroke."

"Where's Hal? Is he here as well?" I asked.

"Phillip told me they had a nasty run-in with Hank tonight. Hal decided to stay behind at the house in case Hank showed up," Arnie said shaking his head back and forth.

A nurse appeared next to Arnie. "Excuse me, Pastor Wright. You can go back now."

Arnie did not ask permission but prompted us down the hall to a curtained area where Phillip stood at the foot of the examination table looking between his father and the flashing and beeping monitors tethered to his father's body. The nurse attending Harold double-checked his readings and surveyed the IV before she excused herself.

Groggy and embarrassed, Harold struggled to lift a weak smile when he saw Liddy and me next to Phillip. In a dry, raspy whisper Harold said, "I'm sorry to drag you two out of bed at such a dreadful time of night."

Liddy spoke with a rosy smile while she gently stroked Harold's fingers. "Hey, we're retired, we can sleep in tomorrow. How are you feeling?"

Arnie smiled. "Hey, thanks a lot, old man."

Harold eyed Arnie. "Of course I expected you to be here, and be careful who you call old man." He strained as a cough broke his smile.

The nurse reappeared. "Sorry folks, but you'll have to say goodbye. We're moving the mayor to a private room upstairs."

Phillip stepped beside the bed and lightly squeezed his dad's hand. We dismissed ourselves with a promise that we'd visit him after he got some sleep. The nurse yanked the curtain closed behind us.

In a quiet corner of the waiting room, Phillip sat between Arnie and Liddy. I pulled a chair around to face them. Phillip inspected the torn pocket on his heavy flannel shirt until his bruised and swollen knuckles took priority. As a father of two boys, I had no trouble recognizing a young man after a scrap. Liddy turned to Phillip and inspected each of his knuckles. Satisfied there appeared to be no serious injury, she patted his hands and relaxed back in her seat.

Arnie looked at Phillip and pointed to his hands. "What happened?"

"We found Hank where dad thought he'd be." Phillip directed his words to Arnie. "You remember the cabin when dad took us all bird hunting together?"

Arnie smiled and nodded.

"Well, sure enough, Hank's truck was out front when we drove up, and a kerosene lantern on the table glowed inside. Hal yelled for Hank to come out, but Hank told us to go away." Phillip turned to Liddy and apologized. "Hank's actual words were a bit more colorful than that, but you get the idea."

"Thank you for being so considerate Phillip. Please continue." Liddy's motherly tone seemed to relax Phillip and encourage him to continue.

"Thank you, ma'am. Well, Hal grabbed my arm and said it sounded like an invitation." Phillip paused and glanced at each of us. "The smell of cheap moonshine and greasy fried chicken met us at the door. Hank remained rocked back in his chair with his boots propped atop the table, but as soon as we entered, Hank pointed at Hal and began cussing up a storm. I won't repeat what he said. Hal just waited for Hank's barrage to end and then shared a few of his own choice words. That stirred Hank, and he jumped to his feet. I stepped between them, so Hank turned on me. In so many words, Hank told me to butt out before I got hurt. I got caught up in the heat of the exchange and let him know in pretty plain terms that I was tired of being treated as his half-pint little brother, and it was him who needed to back off and quit acting like a drunken fool."

Arnie smirked when he glanced at me and saw my grin. We both turned back to see a modest smirk and nod from Phillip before he looked at me and continued. "Hank spouted on and on about the trouble you've stirred up snooping around and sticking your nose into our family's affairs." Phillip put his hand up with a slight grimace on his face. "Mind you those are Hank's words, Mister Phillips."

"I understand." I motioned for him to continue.

"Thank you. Well, Hank's face and neck turned three different shades of purple. He brushed me aside and stared down Hal. Again, what he exactly said I'd rather not repeat, but the gist of what he said was none of this would have happened if Hal had manned up and took care of Megan when he'd had the chance. Hal pointed to himself and made it clear he wouldn't allow Hank to dump the blame on him this time. Hank walked up to Hal and poked him in his chest as he spoke real slow and clear. 'Yeah Hal, it's your fault. If you had satisfied Megan, she'd never have snuck around your back with me.' Hank then stepped back with crossed arms over his chest just staring at Hal. Before Hank saw it coming, Hal landed a right jab and caught Hank flat-footed. Hank fell head over heels into the back corner of the room." Phillip smiled with satisfaction.

Liddy winced and grabbed one of Phillip's hands. "Why are your knuckles like this and your shirt torn?"

Phillip answered looking pretty pleased with himself. "Miss Liddy, Hank was so drunk that Hal's punch hardly fazed him. He got right back on his feet, wiped the blood off his lip and said, 'This has been coming for a long time.' Hal prepared himself as Hank stomped across the floor. Hank then said as he pushed up his sleeves, 'We never finished our fight little brother, and no fire's gonna stop us tonight.' Hank drove his shoulder into Hal's chest and rammed him into the door. They stumbled over one another onto the floor. Hank straddled Hal and delivered one punch after another. I couldn't let it continue, so I dove into Hank, and he fell off of Hal. I landed on top of Hank and became so scared I wailed blindly at Hank's face until Hal dragged me off of Hank. That's when Hank grabbed hold of my shirt and tore my pocket." Phillip looked down and seemed to admire the evidence of the fight, while we sat silently and stared at him.

Arnie put his hand on Phillip's shoulder with an expression on his face that offered no criticism, only acceptance. After a moment of eye-to-eye contact, Arnie asked, "What happened to Hank after Hal pulled you off?"

Phillip rubbed his sore knuckles as he continued. "Hank got to his feet a bit dazed and glared at Hal, wiped the blood flowing from his lips and nose, and swore he'd settle with both of us. He said we didn't have any idea what he had done to protect the family and then ranted that without him, Archer Construction would not be the business it is today. He stared at Hal and boasted how his fancy city position was his doing. He looked at me and pointed to my Wrangler parked outside and said the business bought it as a gift for his baby brother."

"I'm sorry you had to go through that —" I began to say.

"Wait, there's more. Hank then grabbed the lantern, flung it into the back corner of the cabin and yelled, 'You can now blame me for this fire. Hey, baby brother, why don't you give Coach Priestly a call, maybe he'll show up to save you guys this time. I hear the jail bird's found his way out of prison after I got him arrested!' The fire spread swiftly, but Hank blocked the doorway and glared at the flames until he shoved Hal out of his way and slipped out the door. Hal and I grabbed blankets from the bunks and tried to put out the fire, but the cabin's dried out timbers fueled the spreading blaze. Within ten minutes, the roof collapsed. We just sat in my Jeep and watched."

I tapped Phillip's shoulder. "What do you think Hank meant about getting Coach Priestly arrested?"

Phillip gave a puzzled shrug. "But, Hal sure fumed on the drive home. He didn't say a word the whole way. When we pulled up at the house, he jumped out before I came to a stop and raced inside. That's when we found dad on the floor of his study."

On the way to our vehicles, Arnie said to me, "If we can, we probably should talk to Hal in the morning before we see Harold. Call me as soon as you get out of bed." Arnie peered back over his shoulder as he walked beside Phillip toward Phillip's Jeep. "Talk to you in the morning so we can get a game plan together. Now the two of you go get some rest."

———

I crawled out of bed just before seven and right away noticed the blinking red light on our answering machine. "It's Larry. Call me first thing. Harold's been taken to the hospital." I erased the message and felt satisfaction knowing that this time I scooped even Larry.

I sat at the kitchen table and contemplated all Phillip conveyed at the hospital. Little doubt remained of the priority over getting Hal's version of the ruckus last night. Arnie and I also needed to decide what Harold should hear concerning the altercation between his sons and the news about his cabin. I reminded myself that Liddy and I already had plans to visit Marie and John later that afternoon too. I became even more anxious when I also realized our two sons would be here with their families in just twenty-four hours. I looked up and selfishly prayed the Archer drama would miraculously subside before my family arrived.

Liddy remained fast asleep, and an hour later I left a note on her nightstand saying I'd be back by lunch. I asked her to call Marie about our afternoon visit and said I had my phone and would call with any news about Harold. I drove to the newspaper office and while I waited for someone to arrive, scribbled some notes for Larry to use in an article about the fire at the cabin and about Harold being in the hospital. I decided to keep the news about what happened with Harold's sons to myself for the time being.

Martha unlocked the front door of the office and waved until she caught my attention. Inside, Martha maneuvered around bundles of undelivered papers, pulled a proof copy of the holiday insert with its festive front page framed in green and red and handed it to me. "Thought you'd like to have this."

Larry yelled from the break room. "Good morning! What do you think of the holiday insert?"

"Looks fine, Larry." I carefully folded the proof copy to show Liddy later.

Larry leaned against the corner of his desk with arms crossed. "Okay, so I got a call from the hospital about Harold being admitted after midnight last night."

Although curious about his source, I remembered how my father had his contacts at hospitals and police stations who fed him news about arrests and admittances during the wee hours of the night. "Yeah, Arnie called, and Liddy and I went straight over. They're running tests this morning, but doctors say it's probably due to excess fatigue and stress, nothing too serious."

Larry hesitated with an intrigued raised brow. "Since you were there already, what can I print? Do you have any notes?"

I pulled out my hastily scribbled notes. Larry's head popped up with a dumbfounded look after he looked over my notes. "What's this about Harold's cabin?"

"Evidently, Hank had holed up in their old hunting cabin the last couple of days and torched the place last night."

"Does Harold know about this?"

"I don't think so. Arnie and I are going to stop by and check in on him this morning. Do you want to come along?"

"Would love to, but I've too much to do. Mary's headed to Marie's about lunchtime to interview John and get some pictures. Are you and Liddy still going over there?"

"I think so. We'll likely head over there after lunch. Please remind Mary that I'm working on a follow-up story with Coach Priestly. Maybe we can use some of her pictures for my story as well. Do me a favor. For the time being, when you print something on the cabin, leave the cause unknown."

Larry nodded with a twisted curious smile.

———

By the time I walked into Arnie's office, he had Harold's room number but looked irritated because he could not reach Hal. When we arrived at the hospital, the nurse informed us that they had finished the cardio tests and blood work and that the doctor should stop by Harold's room in a few minutes with preliminary results.

Harold sat propped up on the bed staring at the local station's morning talk show with the volume muted. Tired and haggard, he mustered a semblance of a grin when we knocked.

"If it's not the Preacher and Theo. Somehow I remember seeing you two not long ago, but where's Liddy?"

"Still sleeping. How're you feeling?"

Harold pressed the buttons on his bed's controller to raise himself into almost a sitting position. "Still a little tired. I don't know how they expect anyone to get any rest around here. They woke me before dawn, rolled me down the hall and then probed and poked me for the better part of an hour. Otherwise, I reckon I'm not too worse for wear." His humor remained intact, but his energy still seemed lacking.

Arnie slid a chair toward the bed and sat down. "You had us a little scared last night. I'm glad Phillip and Hal found you when they did."

"Me too. They're good boys. But what's this about them fighting?"

We shared as much as we dared concerning what Phillip told us and gave him the sad news about his hunting cabin.

He managed a glib wisecrack. "Heck, I ain't worried about that rickety old shack. It should've burnt down years ago." Harold's smirk faded as he stared at the ceiling. "Anyone get hurt? How's Hank and Hal?"

Arnie tapped Harold's foot. "Hey, Harold. You okay?"

Harold broke his fixed gaze with a barely recognizable grin. He raised his hand with an okay signal but said nothing. Though not the closest of friends, Arnie knew Harold well enough to push a bit to get him to open up.

"Harold, Theo and I didn't traipse over here this morning with only a couple hours of sleep just to paint you a rainbow and sugar coat things for you."

Arnie's candidness hit its intended mark. Harold stirred in his bed and sighed before slowly muttering, "Hank stopped by earlier."

Arnie appeared a little uncomfortable with Harold's distraught and bewildered expression. "Hank was here?"

"I was in the middle of eating a little breakfast when this apparition appeared at my door. His three-day beard, dirty jeans, and ragged shirt made him almost unrecognizable. Heck, even the nurse apologized for Hank's intrusion. She asked if I needed security, but I shooed her away. Hank's nose and eyes showed he took more punches than he likely delivered, but when I asked him about it, he dismissed it and claimed Hal and Phillip ganged up on him."

Arnie asked, "Was he sober? Phillip indicated that Hank was pretty lit up last night."

"No doubt he grappled with a hangover, but he seemed clearheaded enough this morning." Harold's description of his son told the story of a young man with the same macho gritty spirit that landed his father in the hospital.

Harold turned somber and asked me to close the door. I got up and told the nurse we wanted some privacy for a few minutes. Harold's jaw clenched as his facial features hardened.

"Arnie, no doubt about it, Hank messed up real good this time. He confessed that he lied to me about him and Megan." Harold's eyes became glassy, and his voice trembled. "He admitted Megan had been pregnant and that he had arranged an... an abortion" Harold's fists tightened, and tears flowed from the corners of his eyes. "What were they thinking? Why didn't they come to me?"

Arnie glanced at me before we both focused again upon Harold who wiped the corners of his eyes with the back of his hands and kept his focus glued upon the distant gray clouds blanketing the mid-morning sky.

"Hank told me when Megan shared the news she received from the doctor that she could no longer have kids, he felt God punished them for what they'd done." Harold's chin quivered, and he struggled to continue.

Arnie rested his hand on Harold's white-knuckled fist, and asked, "You don't believe God's responsible for what happened to them, do you?"

Arnie bowed his head and winced. "No, and I believe you don't either. You and I need to hold onto our faith that God will use what's happened between Hank and Megan for his good purposes."

Harold sniffed. "But, Hank told me Megan refuses to forgive him for coercing her into the abortion."

I said, "Both seem determined to blunt their pain by blaming one another for the choices they made. I agree with Arnie. God'll work his good purposes through everything that's happening even though for now, it's causing a lot of pain for so many people."

Harold turned and tried to focus his glazed-over eyes upon Arnie and me. "What I don't understand is where Hank got the money for Megan's procedure and their expenses during the so-called honeymoon. Back then, he spent nearly every dollar he earned, and Megan sure didn't have much money."

I asked, "Did you ask Hank?"

"Yeah, but he grumbled that he did what he had to do, and I should leave it at that." Harold shook his head in disbelief. "When I pushed him on what he meant, Hank said the money didn't matter anymore. He and Megan were done."

Arnie asked, "Did Hank say anything more?"

"He plans to leave town and only stopped by to tell me he was sorry for letting me down and making a mess of things." Harold glared at Arnie with fear in his eyes. "Arnie, do you believe I'm responsible for what happened? Did I expect too much from him?"

Arnie hesitated before he answered. "Hank probably tried too hard to live up to what he thought he needed to be. He's had a rough five years, but it's not your fault. You've done everything you could to give him a chance to succeed. Give him some time."

Harold's dark, sad eyes looked at me. "Theo, one more thing worries me. Hank said he wanted to find Megan before he left town and emphasized doing so before she has the opportunity to talk with John. I'm troubled about what might be going through his head right now."

Just then, the nurse knocked on the door and poked her head into the room. "I'm sorry to interrupt you gentlemen, but the doctor wants to see if the mayor would like to go home this afternoon. He also wants to share the good news about your tests when you're ready."

Harold forced a grin. "Give us five minutes."

Arnie assured Harold we would keep our eyes open for Hank and watch out for Megan. After Harold called Phillip to pick him up, he dismissed us with a strained but genuine smile.

As we turned to leave, Harold said, "Can't wait to get out of here. There's still a lot to be done before tomorrow night. Hey, Theo, I assume your family will be there?"

I grinned and nodded before I pulled the door shut.

CHAPTER FORTY

AFTER LUNCH, LIDDY AND I ARRIVED at Marie's farmhouse. We recognized Pete's rust bucket beside one of Marie's dated farm tractors in front of the barn. Pete stepped from the front of the tractor, grabbed a filthy rag hung across his truck's tailgate and wiped his greasy hands. He waved and pointed towards the house. "Y'all head on in. Marie and Coach are expecting you." As he reached for a wrench and returned to his work, Liddy and I giggled as Pete whistled his rendition of *I Saw Mommy Kissing Santa Claus*.

Marie, wearing her usual blue jeans and denim top with rolled-up sleeves, greeted us with her pulled-back hair complimenting her youthful spirit.

The smell of a pecan wood fire mingled with the tantalizing aroma from the kitchen oven as we followed Marie into the great room. John Priestly stood beside the easy chair next to the fireplace. He looked relaxed in his faded jeans and white crew t-shirt beneath a gold-embroidered green Shiloh Saints sweater vest. His groomed hair and clean-shaven face matched the framed photo of him and Jessie on the mantle.

John offered a friendly grin and his hand. "You must be Liddy. I'm honored to meet you finally. Marie's talked nonstop about you." Liddy blushed as he shook her hand.

For the first hour, we shared our impression of Shiloh so far. Liddy tried her best to paint a picture of the changes we made to his family's old home. At first, we felt awkward talking about the house John knew so intimately, but his relaxed manner and conversation set to rest all our apprehension.

I mentioned Harold's brief scare at the hospital, which led John to inquire about Megan and Hank. After I conveyed only the basics about their recent split-up, Liddy directed her attention to John. "Did Marie tell you the news that likely precipitated their breakup?"

John sighed, showing obvious concern. "Yeah, in fact, we spoke quite a bit about Megan last night and about how Hank reacted to the news." He lowered his head and asked, "How's she doing?"

"Much better. She's back at work and for the time being staying with her parents." Liddy's calm demeanor seemed to reassure John.

He looked up at her and asked with a bit less emotion in his voice, "Is she still at City Hall?"

Liddy nodded. "Harold's been very good to her."

"Good," John said, relaxed even more. "But I can see the awkward pressure Harold must feel, caught in the middle between Megan and Hank."

"Before we hang a medal on Harold, the next couple of days could prove rough on him, Megan and Hank."

Marie got up and looked at Liddy. "Maybe we should move on to a more pleasant conversation. Liddy, would you give me a hand in the kitchen?" They left, and moments later sounds of the oven opening and closing and coffee being poured mixed with their chatter.

I leaned closer to John and said privately, "I'd like to talk more about Megan and Hank with you later." John's detached stare made me wonder if I had stepped on his toes somehow. John slumped against the back of his chair and sat in silence until the ladies returned.

As Liddy handed John his cup, she also extended an invitation for him to visit his old home. "John, I want your approval. We've tried to capture the charm of the old home. Besides, I'd love for you to meet our two sons and their families while they are visiting."

John smiled and peered at Marie's grinning face. "That sounds fine with me. Marie, whatever you work out between the two of you is good." John set down his coffee cup, stood and looked at me. "While the ladies talk, would you join me for a walk? I need to stretch my legs."

Marie asked us to cut a piece of cake and give it to Pete. A few minutes later, we left Pete sitting on his tailgate munching a hunk of Marie's spice cake. John and I walked along a path that led from the barn and along the fenced pasture.

John spoke first, staring at the well-worn path beneath his feet. "Sorry, I'm not too talkative. I'm still getting adjusted to life outside of prison. It's, well, it's different."

We continued down the path as he shared a little about his prison experience. We shared some laughs over a couple of his funnier stories about some of the prisoners and guards, but mostly he described some situations and people he wanted to forget. He grew detached and distant again, so I stopped walking.

"John, I don't get it. You knew you were innocent. Why'd you take the plea deal?"

John stood still a moment before he turned toward me. "Theo, integrity is more sacred to me than innocence. What good is innocence if we betray a trust to prove it?" He kicked a rock loose and off the path.

"Well, John Priestly, I've got to admit that you are a uniquely rare young man. Be honest, though, do you have any lingering regrets?"

John stared at the threatening clouds in the distance and then lowered his head with an odd smile. "No, not really. I believe God's the only judge that matters in the end, and I find all the comfort I need in that."

I remained speechless, admiring this unusual man. After a few moments, I decided to confide in him. "John, what if I told you Megan and Jeannie told me everything about why Hank and Megan got married."

John's brows arched, and he crossed his arms. After inspecting the early winter colors in the fields for a long moment, he finally spoke. "When did they talk to you?"

"Right after I visited you with Joe. I told you I suspected a connection existed between Jessie's death and what happened to you, but I couldn't figure it out exactly. Megan's doctor visit opened the floodgates. Right after Megan walked out on Hank when he went postal over the news from the doctor, all the pieces of the puzzle began to fall into place."

John's stoic stare gave way to a long sullen face. He shuffled the sole of his right foot back and forth as he absorbed the gravity of my revelation. "So Jeannie confided in you about this?"

I continued to look at John, but his focus remained in the distance. "Hal Archer as well. In fact, Harold just this morning learned about their abortion and how Hank and Megan have lied to cover it up."

John remained motionless except for the slow shuffle of his foot. The silence we shared encroached upon eternity before John asked, "Theo, is Megan still in town?"

"Yeah. Like I told you, she's back at work, at least for the time being." My hands sank deep into in my pockets. While he seemed held captive by his thoughts, I decided to try to push him to talk more.

"John, what I'm about to ask you is off the record and between you and me. First, I know Jeannie Simmons came to you about Megan's pregnancy. However, I'm still not clear how that connects with what happened to you unless Hank's linked to the missing money. Was he?"

John turned his head and inspected me, finally making eye contact. "Joe told me how you've delved into what happened to Jessie and now me, and said I should trust you."

I met his stare. "Well, do you? Have I earned your trust?"

"If I didn't trust you, we wouldn't be out here."

I allowed a cautious grin to appear, resulting in a widening smile from John. He slapped the back of my shoulder, and we continued along the path again.

As we walked, John conveyed what he knew about what happened to the money. He shared that he suspected Hank all along but knew proving it risked revealing Megan's secret because it provided a motive. He knew Megan didn't have much money, and he suspected Hank's frivolous spending prevented him from having the kind of funds needed to pay for their so-called honeymoon and the medical expenses on such short notice.

John went into detail about why he felt Hank was behind the missing money. "Not even Jessie had access to the cash deposits after games like Hank. Thanks to Harold's incessant harping at the Booster meetings, I agreed to Hank helping with the collecting and counting of the cash after each home game. We even developed a system whereby signed-off receipts were required as the money passed along until it arrived in the office. Hank always sat across the desk from me anytime we counted the money and cross-checked it against the receipts. He made out the bank deposit slip while I wrote the deposit amount in the athletic department's checkbook. We made certain the amounts matched before we put the money and a deposit slip into the sealed night deposit envelope. Hank deposited it on his way home a couple of times, but normally I made the drop."

I tried to picture John's fail-safe system. When he paused, I asked, "How much money was in a typical deposit?"

"Depended. Home basketball or baseball games ranged from $1,000 to $5,000 or so, but home football games could be as much as $20,000-$30,000. Shiloh might be a small school, but our championship seasons drew bigger and bigger crowds, especially during the playoffs."

"But $5,000 came up missing."

John nodded his head. "Yeah, and with our system in place, as well as the school's internal audit system, any discrepancy would sooner or later get discovered. That's why when the $5,000 discrepancy showed up, the audit revealed there should've been $35,000 in cash alone deposited that night. My athletic department checkbook ledger confirmed the proper amount, but the bank statement received by the school bookkeeper recorded only $30,000 in cash had been deposited. After the bookkeeper audited the account, the bank re-verified their safety checks, which included auditing their video surveillance. I was called into the office and presented with the deposit slip the bank received in that deposit bag, and it reflected a cash deposit of $30,000. I had no explanation since I made the deposit myself that night. When the school officials questioned Hank, he testified that he couldn't explain the difference. He also explained the double-check process we used. He said the amount was correct when we sealed the night drop envelope, and he saw me place it in the top drawer of my desk as usual before he left that night."

"How long after the deposit did the discrepancy come to light?"

"I guess at least three weeks went by, but that wasn't unusual for the audit process to verify the books. It was long enough that Mister and Missus Hank Archer returned from their honeymoon and stirred up a lot of fuss and rumors around town."

"Why didn't the bank sound the alarm sooner?"

"However it happened, the amount the bank credited the account matched the amount on the deposit slip that got deposited. Nobody at the bank had reason to question the deposit."

"Did you ever figure out what could've possibly happened?"

"No. Right after the discrepancy came to my attention, I double-checked my records but found nothing."

I recalled what Harold said earlier that morning about money and Hank. I grabbed John's arm. "Do you think Hank figured out a way to take the money?"

"I'm sure that's possible, but we've no evidence. If I give this to Joe, I risk Megan's abortion becoming public."

"Look, John, do you believe Megan would want you to keep her abortion secret if it prevented you from proving your innocence?"

"Theo, I've served the time already. Why should I stir this up now and add to Megan's problems?"

"First of all, I think I know what she'd say. Second, Hank's about to leave town. I think he fears all his lies are coming unglued. Most importantly, it's the right thing to do. Don't you want to teach and coach again?"

John picked up a chunk of gravel and heaved it into the tall grass getting Marie's old mule to stir. "Let me think about it. I just want to get all this behind me. What makes you think I could ever get my old positions back at the school anyway?"

"Just like Joe told you, I've been busy since I arrived," I said with a sly look. "There're an awful lot of people in this town who'd do about anything for you. This town needs Coach John Priestly as much as John Priestly needs this as his home again."

"Give me another day or two. Okay?"

We found our way back to the house and saw Pete exit the kitchen door with another huge hunk of Marie's cake. He wiped the crumbs from the corners of his mouth and smiled as he walked past us.

Liddy met us at the door. "What have the two of you been up to? You've been gone over an hour. Thought we'd have to send Pete after you."

"Just enjoying the fresh air and talking more about the changes in town."

———

When we got home that afternoon, we discovered a message from Harold on our answering machine. "Hope you had a pleasant visit with Marie. I'm home and doing fine, thanks to the outstanding care of Shiloh's medical staff. I know your family's arriving tomorrow, so I've taken the liberty to reserve extra seating for all y'all in the bleachers next to the stage. Please try to be there a bit early. If you've got any questions, call my office."

CHAPTER FORTY-ONE

WINTER'S CHILL STUCK AROUND WEDNESDAY morning, but clear skies heralded a gorgeous South Georgia afternoon for the arrival of our family. Liddy woke first and began cooking breakfast well before I got out of bed. Coffee and the morning paper welcomed me at the kitchen table. Liddy had opened to the centerfold where the Christmas Program schedule of events and related articles filled the right side. A picture of Jessie's bronze statue accompanied the concluding article about him on the opposite page.

Shortly before eleven, a honk announced the arrival of Tommy and his family. Before he could get out from behind the wheel, the rear passenger door on their blue van sprung open. Teddy and Sissy bolted toward the house as Stacey frantically unbuckled a screaming Buzz, abandoned and imprisoned in his car seat's grip.

Tommy greeted me with a smile and a hug on the porch amidst the activity of the grandkids at our feet. "You made excellent time," I said.

"We got on the road early, and the kids slept most of the way." He looked at his watch. "Just over five hours from Chattanooga to Shiloh, and we only stopped twice. We managed to squeak through Atlanta before morning rush hour traffic."

Not able to wait any longer, Sissy and Teddy wedged between Tommy and me. "Poppy, Poppy." I leaned down and gave both a big hug and kiss.

Inside, Buzz had wasted no time and waved his arms. "Poppy, come here." He grabbed my hand and dragged me toward the Christmas tree and pointed to all the presents. "Which one's mine?"

I lifted Buzz into my arms. "I'll show you later, but I believe there's more than one down there for you." Another honk and I pointed out the window. "Looks like your uncle and aunt just pulled up."

Buzz squirmed out of my arms, scooted out the door and met Conrad and Bubba in the front yard.

I greeted Bubba with a squeeze before he jumped into the hammock alongside Teddy and Sissy. They giggled as Conrad arrived a step ahead of Buzz and raised his arms. "Poppy!"

Buzz pulled on Conrad's pants leg. "Come on! You gotta see the Kwist-mas tree. Come on Poppy." I followed them back inside to monitor their combined exuberance.

While I occupied the two youngest, Liddy gave a tour of the house to the rest of the family. Afterward, the older kids explored outside and inspected the Santa and Nativity decorations in the front yard while Buzz, Conrad and I swayed in the hammock. I kept their attention talking about what they'd see later that night. "Shiloh's Christmas tree is as big and tall as that tree in my front yard, and there'll be decorations and lights on it and people from all over town that we'll get to see tonight."

After lunch, while the kids played, Tommy and Junior joined me on the porch, and the Phillips' women enjoyed time chatting in the kitchen. My conversation with Tommy and Junior took our usual drift to football, and we discussed watching a couple of the bowl games while they were here.

"Talking about football, I've got some new young friends for you to meet. They were quite the talk around town a few years ago when Shiloh High School won back-to-back state championships. I'm sure y'all will be able to share a few war stories."

Junior said, "Tell me more about this Coach Priestly you told me about on the phone."

Tommy said, "Mom told me about Marie Masterson and John Priestly. How's it going with John's situation?"

"It's still working itself out. And, Junior, I think you'll especially like John. He's about your age."

We focused on John's days as the head coach and athletic director before we talked about Zeb Adams and his store and each of our new friends in Shiloh.

———

With five kids to corral, Liddy gathered them right after dinner and had everyone bundled and ready to head for downtown before seven. The entire family enjoyed the cool but pleasant evening walk. Liddy occupied the kids by commenting on the decorations and light displays of every house we passed. When we arrived on Main Street, the kids' eyes lit up as they saw how Town Square glowed with its own unique Christmas displays. However, when the two spotlights in front of City Hall turned on, and their huge beams crisscrossed the dark sky, even Liddy and I looked at each other.

I leaned toward Liddy as we headed to the bleachers across the street. "I'm sure glad we walked. It looks like there isn't any parking available."

The kids "oohed and aahed" as Shiloh's two dated, red fire trucks and an Adams County Sheriff car crept past with lights flashing and sirens screaming. Barricades redirected traffic from the center of town.

Phillip greeted us and escorted the entire family to the bleachers near the stage, a flatbed trailer disguised in Christmas decorations. Liddy and I introduced our family to Arnie and Judy already talking on the front row with Larry, Martha, Zeb, Sam, and Susanna. Mary Scribner moved about snapping photos for the newspaper. Hal Archer huddled with the Simmons and Adams brothers at the end of the trailer near the foot of the stairs.

Liddy poked my side and pointed to Jeannie speaking with Megan and Harold near the main entrance of City Hall. Megan clutched a clipboard and inspected the green and red ceremonial ribbons draped across the columns of the portico.

We settled into our seats near the top of the bleachers where Buzz and Conrad sat mesmerized by all the lights and commotion in the laps and firm grips of their dads. Liddy tugged on my jacket and then waved to four silhouettes in the second story windows of the Arians Building.

At seven-thirty, the Christmas music playing over the public address system faded. Harold, who looked much better than yesterday morning, stepped up onto the stage. His seasoned smile beamed as he tapped the microphone.

"Ladies and gentlemen, citizens of Shiloh, young and old, welcome to the opening ceremonies of this year's edition of Christmas in Shiloh." Cheers, applause, and whistles filled the air until Harold raised his hand. "At this time, I'd like to invite Doctor John Mason from the First Methodist Church to officially open our program tonight with the invocation."

After Reverend Mason prayed, Harold returned to the microphone. "The first order of business tonight is the dedication of two recent additions to our town. To assist me, I'd like to ask my son, Mister Hal Archer, Director of Shiloh's Utilities Department, to join me on stage."

Hal walked onto the stage with an awkward grin that bordered on a grimace. Phillip's whistle cut through the ruckus of the crowd as Hal approached the microphone.

Hal pulled index cards from his coat pocket and shared his carefully scripted introduction. More applause erupted when he pointed to all the lights on Town Square while he scanned the faces watching him.

"Doesn't Shiloh look great with all the lights?" He turned and looked back to his father. "By the way, Mayor, who do I send the power bill to for all the electricity we're using?" Harold laughed with the crowd and slapped his knee.

Hal waited for the crowd to quiet down while he nonchalantly wiped the corners of his eyes. "I'm honored and humbled by this opportunity to stand before all of you tonight, my friends, and especially my dad, the Mayor of Shiloh. Three years ago, almost to the day, my brothers and I could've died in the fire that razed our beautiful landmark that symbolized Shiloh's deep historical roots here in Adams

County. On what was otherwise a typical middle-of-the-week, dull evening in downtown Shiloh…" Snickers mimicked Hal's wry grin as he spoke to a crowd that understood the nature of Shiloh.

"Sanctuary's assembly of young students gathered in the basement of that old landmark, enjoying their usual fun, food, and fellowship with each other. Each week they met with Sanctuary's leader and sponsor, a beloved teacher, coach, and friend to many of us here tonight. His name was Jessie Masterson. My younger brother, Phillip, helped Coach Masterson as they supervised over fifty middle school and high school students in attendance that particular night."

Hal paused to compose himself. "After I dropped Phillip off, my brother Hank joined me in my office upstairs. A fire then broke out that shattered the peace and tranquility of our town. My brother and I attempted to put out the fire, but the fire raced out of control. We became trapped until Coach Masterson appeared through the smoke and flames and guided us down the burning stairs before he shoved us to safety just before the ceiling collapsed behind us, taking him from us forever." Hal took several deep breaths, grabbed his handkerchief and stepped away from the podium.

The crowd remained silent with every eye glued to Hal until he returned to the podium. "Coach Masterson didn't grow up here, but while he graced Shiloh, he made it a better place to live. He modeled what is good and right about Shiloh. He'll always be remembered as an exemplary champion on and off the field. I believe God looked down on his life and smiled, and when death came for Coach Masterson, God welcomed Jessie home and said, 'Well done my good and faithful servant.' Tonight, I'm honored to represent our town as we dedicate this statue of Coach Jessie Masterson as our way to say we will never forget his life and sacrifice. I know my family never will." Hal turned toward the bronze statue as two spotlights lit up Jessie's face.

Everyone rose to their feet and applauded. During the ovation, Joe Arians escorted a tearful Marie Masterson through the crowd. Hal escorted Marie to the podium. "Shiloh, please welcome Jessie's mother, Missus Marie Masterson!" Hal stepped back and offered his own applause before they shared a tearful embrace. Harold left his chair and hugged her as Hal tendered a tear-filled smile to his father and turned to escort Marie off the stage.

Harold grabbed the microphone. "Hold up Marie." Harold held a commemorative plaque with a replica of the statue engraved on it. Harold read the inscription. "Shiloh will never forget." Marie sobbed as she hugged Harold again and clutched the plaque against her chest in one hand while clinging to Hal's arm with the other as they exited the stage.

Harold turned and announced, "Can I have Pete, Andy and Jeannie Simmons, Jay and Jim Adams, and Phillip Archer on stage? While these young people are working their way onto the stage, there are two other people that I'd like to recognize. They're our newest residents in Shiloh, but they arrived ready and willing to invest themselves in our community. From the first night they arrived, Mister Theo Phillips dedicated himself to research and wrote about the young man we are honoring tonight."

"Many of you have undoubtedly enjoyed learning more about Jessie Masterson thanks to the Sentinel publishing Mister Phillips' heart-rending articles this past week." Harold returned his attention to Liddy and me. "Mister Phillips, would you and your lovely wife Liddy please stand?" I held Liddy's hand as we stood and looked out upon the faces of the crowd and saw their acceptance of us as a part of Shiloh.

As a polite round of applause subsided, Harold continued. "At this time, thanks in part to Theo and Liddy, I'm proud to announce that Sanctuary will once again impact the youth of Shiloh. The City Council unanimously offered the use of City Hall to accommodate their weekly meetings beginning next month." Harold raised his arm toward the group assembled on stage. "This fine group benefited from Sanctuary in the past and agreed to spearhead the program." Each of them waved and departed the stage.

As the crowd settled down, Harold took the opportunity to change the focus to City Hall. "The future for Shiloh is bright. The charm of our town has changed, but the future of Shiloh will forge a new heritage. The courthouse could never be reconstructed with its old antebellum charm." On cue, the massive spotlights lowered from criss-crossing the sky and focused on the portico entrance with the brilliant green and red ribbon draped between its columns.

The lights illuminated Marie standing beside Megan and Joe. With some assistance from Megan, Marie cut the ribbon with a pair of scissors. "Thank you, Miss Marie," Harold said. "But there's another reason we chose you for this honor." Her wide-eyed stare fell upon Joe and Megan as they escorted her to a green cloth draped across a portion of the wall next to the main entrance. After Megan whispered in her ear, Marie pulled the corner of the fabric to reveal a newly mounted bronze plaque anchored to the brick exterior.

Harold announced to the crowd, "What most of you can't see is that Marie Masterson not only dedicated the building by cutting the ribbon she also just revealed a newly installed plaque, visible to all who visit City Hall from this day forward. The plaque identifies that our new beautiful City Hall will henceforth be officially known as the Jessie Masterson Administration Building."

Amidst the outburst of applause and whistles, Buzz and Conrad started wiggling, ready to get up. Harold turned everyone's attention to the Christmas tree on the far corner of Town Square. The spotlights swung their bright beams from the front of the Jessie Masterson Administration Building to high above the unlit tree. Buzz and Conrad froze.

"As the Mayor of Shiloh, I officially command that the lights of the city's Christmas tree be turned on and remain on for the next two weeks." The tree's lights sprang to life, and the kids gasped with amazement. Christmas carols played again as Harold invited everyone to come back Saturday night at eight o'clock for more special events to celebrate Christmas in Shiloh.

As the crowds dispersed, Kari and Stacey gathered the kids on the sidewalk next to the bleachers. Marie hugged each of our grandkids and then turned to Liddy and me. "John and I'd like to visit tomorrow if that'll be okay with you?"

Liddy smiled. "Of course. Did you know about the naming of the new building?"

Marie shook her head.

We looked up at the second-floor window of Joe's office and saw Nick and John watching Marie and Joe walking across the street. A moment later the lights turned off.

Liddy and I gathered our family and said goodnight to everyone before we walked across the street. Liddy squeezed my hand to direct my attention toward the front of Nick Arians' office. Jeannie and Megan stood talking with John and Marie. Liddy waved as I hollered, "Goodnight!" They waved back and then returned to their conversation while we wrangled the family down the sidewalk towards the house.

CHAPTER FORTY-TWO

ONLY AN OCCASIONAL SIP OF COFFEE and flip of a page broke the silence as I scribbled down my thanks to God for the joy of family in my journal. As dawn broke, noises from opposing directions prompted me to cap my pen and put my journal aside. The sound of the morning paper's arrival drew me toward the front door, but a muffled whimper from the foot of the stairs gained my attention. There sat Buzz hugging UGGA, his well-traveled stuffed bulldog.

"Buzz, you want to join Poppy for some juice?" I whispered.

His tears dried by the time he sipped his juice. The sounds of shuffling feet and giggles caught my ears just before Tommy said in a strained whisper, "SHH! Y'all be quiet."

Liddy followed the grandkids into the kitchen. "Would you like a hand, Poppy?"

"Grammy, why don't you and Tommy pour some juice and see what they want for breakfast."

An increasingly louder chant rose from the table. "Pan-a-cakes. We want Poppy to make pan-a-cakes!"

Within minutes, "pan-a-cakes" arrived onto their plates, and Liddy smothered each stack with syrup. After all were served and a platter of seconds sat on the table, I retrieved the neglected morning paper.

Amid a chorus of moans and whines as their mothers wiped the syrup from their faces, the phone rang. "Theo, it's Joe," Liddy said with an inquisitive look. I shrugged and lifted the phone to my ear.

"Theo, I'm sorry to call this morning, especially with your family in town, but I need you to stop by my office."

"Is something wrong?"

"I can't tell you over the phone. Trust me. Ten o'clock."

I stared at Liddy as she helped Kari and Stacey. "Um, I guess ten o'clock will be okay."

———

Susanna held a thick file of papers and an out-of-character sneer. "Joe's expecting you. Go on in." Her look and tone indicated that my tardiness held up whatever waited beyond the closed door.

Joe leaned back in his chair behind his cluttered desk. At the same conference table where Liddy and I signed the papers for our house, Jeannie sat beside Megan, and John slouched with feet fully extended and crossed in an armchair pulled out from the head of the table. Their conversations ceased, and they all focused on my bewildered look.

Joe walked to the door and stuck his head out. "Susanna, please hold all calls unless it's Jared from the DA's office." He closed the door and walked to the edge of his desk with a business-like, unemotional demeanor. "Thanks for coming, Theo. We all agreed last night that you needed to be in on this."

My curiousness darted from John to Megan to Jeannie. "What's going on? What happened?"

John mustered a silly smirk beneath his bloodshot eyes. Megan and Jeannie looked at me with equally weary but benign expressions. John jostled himself upright and planted both feet firmly on the floor. "Mister Phillips, I promised you I'd give our conversation more thought." John glanced at Joe. "After the crowd dispersed last night, Megan and Jeannie joined Marie, Joe and me in Nick's office." John then stared at Megan. "Megan's ready to move forward with her life without any more secrets or lies." Megan's reserved smile affirmed John's statement.

Joe began to pace. "Theo, Megan's agreed to confront Hank and help us get to the truth behind the money John purportedly stole." Megan gnawed on her upper lip and squeezed Jeannie's hand as Joe continued. "The obstacle we need to overcome, which John and Megan understand, is how we can provide testimony of Hank's strong motive and argue that in addition to John that night, Hank also had ample opportunity to orchestrate the money discrepancy. But, to overturn John's conviction, we need irrefutable evidence or Hank's confession."

"So what can we do?" I blurted.

"Good question Theo. After we broke up last night, John and I went back to my office and scoured over the case files again. We focused on the deposit slip the bank turned over as evidence from the night deposit pouch they received." Joe handed a photocopy to me along with comparable slips from previous deposits. "What do you see?"

"Other than the amounts, they appear identical, except for the last one," I answered with a puzzled look.

Joe placed copies of the checkbook register on the table, pointed and repeated his question.

I slid the register closer and inspected them. "Nothing unusual or different that I can see. The entries are consistent."

John then slid the deposit slips beside the checkbook ledger copies. "Now, are they identical?" Joe asked.

"No. The writing is different." I looked up, more puzzled.

Joe leaned on my shoulder. "How so?"

"The deposit slips aren't written by the same person as the checkbook ledger. But, John already told me Hank filled out the deposit slips while he filled out the duplicate amount in the check register."

John smiled. "Exactly. Why we didn't recognize this from the beginning is beyond me. The actual deposit slip that accompanied the cash and checks deposited that night is similar but not the same as previous slips. The investigators originally claimed the difference was due to a hasty, poor attempt to duplicate Hank's writing, but I contend Hank had to scribble in a hurry another deposit slip for expediency sake and possibly to disguise that he, in fact, actually made out the replacement deposit slip."

Joe leaned over my shoulder and pointed to the differences. "The State pointed out early on that the differences in the writing of the numbers gave them enough reason to believe that John made the switch in deposit slips after he removed the money. Their argument was confirmed when the only fingerprints other than the bank employees were John's, not Hank's on the outside of the deposit pouch."

"I'm still confused. The fingerprint evidence clears Hank."

"Just as I discussed with you," John said. "Thanks to Harold, only two sets of eyes were present when the money and original deposit slip were sealed inside the bank's tamper-proof, quick-seal deposit envelope. Hank's and mine."

"Was there any possible way he pulled the money out and altered the deposit slip without you knowing before the pouch was sealed?" I asked.

John relented. "No. We sat across from each other until I tucked the sealed deposit pouch into my top desk drawer where it remained until I left to make the deposit each evening."

I looked over my shoulder at Joe and then back to John. "Was the pouch in fact tamper-proof once sealed?"

Joe held up a similar pouch. "Absolutely. Once the adhesive strip seals the flap, you have to rip or cut it open. The bank inspected each pouch before they opened and processed the deposits inside."

"It sounds like Hank's original testimony is pretty air-tight," I said and sank into my chair even more confused.

"Sounds that way," Joe added with a lawyer's unemotional statement of the facts. "And the bank's security video along with the fingerprint evidence certainly appears to leave John as the only likely suspect, but each of us knows John didn't make the switch. It must've occurred after the deposit was sealed but before John delivered it to the bank. Unfortunately, we've no evidence Hank made such a switch even though we can now provide a likely motive and show Hank at least had a brief window of opportunity. That's why Jeannie and Megan are key."

I said, "Do you believe Megan can get Hank to incriminate himself?" Putting Megan in Hank's path on purpose struck me as risky on several fronts. Plus, Hank had already told his brothers and father enough to implicate himself.

"Mister Phillips," Megan said before Joe answered, "We're meeting right after work."

Megan's revelation increased the mixed feelings stirring in my gut. "Megan, you sure you want to go through with this?"

Megan glanced at Jeannie and then managed a gritty stare. "Jeannie will be with me." When I looked at Jeannie, I caught a glimpse of her brothers' tenacity and confidence.

Joe leaned back on the edge of his desk. "We know Hank's a loose cannon, and I'm as concerned as any of us, but in his current state of mind he's more likely to drop his guard if Megan and Jeannie are the ones badgering him."

I stood up. "I'm not sure about this! Hank's too unpredictable. How can we protect Megan and Jeannie?"

Joe raised his hand and motioned for me to sit down. "They'll be wired, and the meeting will take place in that corner of the employee parking lot behind City Hall... I mean, the Jessie Masterson Administration Building." Joe smiled as he pointed out the window to the visible end of the rear parking lot. "If we hear or see anything, we can respond immediately."

Jeannie stirred in her seat. "Look, Mister P, we're counting on Hank being, well, Hank. But don't worry. He will NOT lay a hand on Megan! You have my word." Jeannie accented her pretty facial features with a rigid flex of her jaw.

Joe slapped my shoulder. "Look, Theo, nobody outside of this office knows what we know." He winked at Jeannie. "Not even Susanna knows all the details of our plan."

"What can I do?" I relented.

John tapped my arm. "Go home. Enjoy your family. Marie and I'll stop by right after lunch for a visit. You and Liddy keep Marie preoccupied after I excuse myself and shoot back here this afternoon."

I looked at each of the others and reluctantly said, "I just hope Hank's temper works in our favor, not against us, and nobody gets hurt."

Marie and John arrived shortly after one. My sons and I rose from our seats on the porch to greet them as Liddy appeared at the front door and said, "John, I'm so pleased you finally have the chance to see your old home."

John laughed as he observed our grandkids swinging in the hammock. "Well, it's been a long time since I can remember five youngsters enjoying this old porch." He inspected the exterior of the house. "Miss Liddy, from the outside it looks as nice as I've ever seen it. I always told mom this house only needed a little lipstick and rouge. But she was unable, and I was too busy."

I laughed. "Let Liddy show you the rest of the house before she busts." Marie grabbed one of John's arms, Liddy grabbed the other, and they disappeared.

Minutes later, John returned to the porch with a pleased grin. "Theo, thank you. You and Liddy are godsends. Mom would be proud, and that attic renovation was long overdue. Sam and his boys did a first-class job up there."

John took a seat on the porch and swapped stories with my sons. Teddy and Bubba disappeared into the backyard, while Sissy slipped into the house and left Buzz and Conrad asleep on the hammock.

A little before four, John excused himself, promising to return before dark. I walked beside him to Marie's truck. I closed the driver's door behind him and looked intently into his eyes as he cranked the ignition. "Godspeed, and may he keep the girls safe."

John dropped the truck into gear and yelled as he pulled away, "Thanks, Theo. Take care of Marie. I'll be back as soon as I can."

Teddy and Bubba turned on the Christmas tree lights as darkness descended. I walked outside with Buzz and Conrad, and they inspected the lights decorating the outside of the house, the illuminated Santa directing his reindeer, and the Nativity on the front lawn. The four-year-olds giggled and ran around each ornament while I kept an anxious eye out for John.

Liddy kept Marie distracted as they helped Kari and Stacey prepare and serve dinner. Marie engaged in conversations at the table, but she eyed John's empty chair more than once.

Stacey began dishing out dessert when the sound of Marie's truck turned our heads toward the window.

John walked straight into the room with a painted smile and sat down. "Sorry, I'm late. Did you save me any dinner? It sure smells good." Liddy brought out the set-aside plate from the kitchen, and John said, "Sorry I took longer than I expected. Mmm, looks good Liddy. Thanks."

A few minutes later, after a couple of bites of his dessert, John glanced at me and nodded. He leaned back in his chair, rubbed his belly and pushed aside the remaining pie. "Thank you, ladies. That was excellent." Then he looked at me. "I think I need to stretch my legs a second."

I peered at Liddy and Marie and laid my napkin on the table. "I know what you mean John. I'm right behind you."

Marie looked at Liddy and the others and said, "While they're on the porch, let me tell you a couple of stories about John since y'all have shared your stories already."

John laughed. "Marie, don't embarrass me too much."

John walked to the far corner of the porch and peered at the stars while I sat in one of the rockers. He chuckled under his breath, "Harold sure got a big tree this year." He stared at the golden glow emanating from the center of town. "I guess you're kinda curious how it went?"

"Of course. How's Megan and Jeannie?"

"They're fine. I left Joe and Susanna finishing up their deposition. Susanna sure took her pent-up anxiety out on her keyboard and the printer while I was there. I'm not sure she was overly thrilled with Joe and me over the whole scheme."

"When did you tell her what was going on?"

"We didn't. Jeannie said something to her just before she left to meet Megan in the parking lot. Susanna paced behind Joe and me as we watched the meeting unfold from the office window."

"What happened when Hank arrived?"

"He rolled up behind Megan's Mustang right on time, and the

three stood in front of Megan's car. Hank appeared annoyed that Jeannie showed up, but Megan did a great job convincing Hank that she wouldn't be there without her. Megan then told Hank about her intention to file for a divorce and asked him not to contest it. She ranted on about her deep remorse for believing his lies and putting up with his deceit from the beginning of their relationship. She told him that only God knows how many times he lied to her and the rest of his family over the last four years."

"How did Hank handle that?"

"Hank tried to justify some of the lies and argued with her to reconsider. That's when Megan stopped him cold and told him that she figured out how he paid for her abortion and their make-me-feel-good honeymoon following their hasty justice-of-the-peace wedding. Hank emphatically claimed it was his money, but Megan laughed and said, 'There you go again. More lies.' Hank got madder and yelled, 'Look, I got the money without asking my dad for a single dime. I scraped together what we needed because you didn't have the time to wait any longer.'"

John stood at this point as his retelling became even more animated. "The whole time, Hank's arms flailed about as he snarled and strutted in front of Megan and Jeannie. He called Megan a 'lying bitch,' but that only infuriated Jeannie enough for her to step between Hank and Megan. 'You're wrong Hank. You're the liar! I know it. Coach Priestly knows it, and now your entire family now knows it too.' Jeannie dodged Hank when he tried to shove her aside, and she pushed him backward and snarled, 'Go ahead Hank, put your hands on Megan or me. I promise you'll never get out of Shiloh.' I almost gave in to the urge to run downstairs when Hank clenched his fists and let out another barrage of expletives. What we heard froze Susanna in her tracks with scarlet cheeks and a wild-eyed stare."

"I can only imagine what Susanna feared at that moment."

"Fortunately, Susanna listened long enough to hear Jeannie stand her ground. 'Why don't you act like a real man Hank! Admit you're behind the missing money and, like always, cast the blame on someone else, namely, Coach Priestly.' Hank stood with his mouth wide open before he shouted, 'Hell, Coach owed me anyway, but good luck proving that I took the money. And Megan, if this goes any further, I promise, you'll never get that divorce!' He then jumped into his truck and peeled out from the parking lot."

"So Jeannie meant it when she promised to protect Megan."

"Joe got it all on tape, and he's preparing a motion to the court with a copy to the District Attorney's office." John looked into the night and mumbled, "I hope it's enough."

I placed my hand on John's shoulder. "Sounds like there's enough reasonable doubt to reopen the investigation at the very least."

John sighed. "I learned in prison to expect disappointment with our justice system. If you don't mind, I'll hold off any optimism until we see what tomorrow brings. But thanks for everything you've done and for believing in me."

"You're most welcome. But remember, it was Jessie who made it possible."

CHAPTER FORTY-THREE

BEFORE THE REST OF THE FAMILY woke, Liddy and I got out of bed early and shared a quiet cup of coffee. Liddy blew across the top of her coffee cup and said, "Thanks for confiding in me last night about what took place. There's such a stark contrast between Hank and John. Hank focuses on himself at the expense of others, whereas John protects others at his own expense. Sounds to me as though John acted with the same unselfish passion as did Jessie."

"I'd hate to be in Harold's shoes," I said. "I can only imagine what's going through his mind this morning."

Liddy squeezed my hand. "Don't forget about Hal and Phillip. As far as we've seen, they've braved the storm for the better."

"I agree," I mumbled, deep in thought. "And what about Megan? God appears to be orchestrating a transformation in her life."

The sound of the front door opening drew our attention. Tommy raised his forefinger to his lips and then pointed to Sissy fast asleep beneath Liddy's patchwork quilt on the sofa.

Tommy brought the paper to the kitchen and sat down next to Liddy. "Sissy woke me about four this morning. I didn't want to disturb Stacey or the boys, so I brought her downstairs. Guess we both fell back to sleep."

Liddy asked, "Did we wake you?"

Tommy's grin softened his confession. "I stirred a bit when you first made coffee. I half-listened but didn't want to disturb you either." He looked back toward the sofa at Sissy with her auburn curls covering her face. I stared at Tommy, and a knot swelled in my throat. I struggled to stifle my empathetic concerns for Harold and his family.

The aroma of biscuits in the oven and sausage sizzling filled the air and enticed the rest of the family downstairs after Sissy awoke and assisted Liddy in the kitchen. The two youngest climbed into my lap, and we laughed together at the comic strips in the paper until the phone rang. Liddy answered but immediately turned and held the phone out to me. "Joe."

"I hate to do this again to you, but can you break away later this morning?"

"Is it Hank?"

"Harold called me after speaking with Arnie early this morning and said he wanted to bring Hank by the office at eleven. He requested you, Arnie and John be there as well."

"What's going on?" I asked. Liddy looked over her shoulder at me as she scooped the last of the scrambled eggs from the skillet onto a serving dish.

Joe said, "Hank came home last night to pack some clothes, and told Harold that Megan was spreading lies and he just needed to leave town. Harold convinced him that they needed to get to the bottom of this mess before he left. Hank's agreed to clear up her lies to appease Harold. So, can you be here?"

"Of course I'll be there." I wondered what Hank might have said that stirred Harold to agree to the meeting in Joe's office.

I hung up the phone, and Liddy asked, "What's going on?"

"Harold requested I attend a meeting he arranged with Hank."

———

My anxious strides brought me quickly to Main Street. I glanced in the window of Arians Realty and Property Management. Nick occupied Jeannie's desk with the phone to his ear. When I entered his office he clutched the phone to his chest and lifted a curious grin. "Rumor has it that it's going to be a busy day upstairs."

"I guess so, although I'm still puzzled by what's supposed to be happening." My eyes darted around the office. "Where's Jeannie?"

Nick brought the phone back to his ear. "I'm truly sorry. I'll be just another moment." This time he placed the caller on hold and set the handset down on the desk. He sighed as he turned in the chair to face me. "Jeannie's with Megan until this hoopla with Hank gets resolved. Until it does, I'm worried about both of them after what Jeannie and Joe told me took place yesterday." Nick clenched his jaw and reached for the phone once again.

I back-stepped toward the door. "I'll check back with you later. I hope for Jeannie and Megan's sake all this will be over in the next day or so."

Nick forced a grin as the phone landed back against his ear.

———

Joe leaned against the corner of Susanna's desk, engrossed on the phone. He sounded agitated and cringed in response to what he heard. At an appropriate pause, he looked up and pointed to John quietly reading a copy of today's newspaper.

I left Joe to his intense exchange. "Good morning John. What do you think about the article on restarting Sanctuary?"

John folded the paper and pointed to the picture of Harold with the leadership team above Mary's article. "She's becoming quite a journalist. Bet Larry's proud of his little girl."

"I just hope Larry can find a way to keep her here in Shiloh. Otherwise, I'm afraid Mary's aspirations will lead her to bigger horizons."

John laid the paper in his lap. "Mary always struck me as being ambitious and smarter than most. In fact, I figured when she went off to school Shiloh would lose its hold on her."

"That'll be Shiloh's loss for certain if that happens. By the way, where's Arnie?"

On cue, Arnie stepped through the door and complied with Joe's finger pointed toward us. Joe's train of thought never diverted from whoever bartered back and forth with him on the phone. The conversation sounded heavy in legalese.

Joe audibly exhaled as he dropped the phone onto its cradle. He stared at his watch before he turned, slapped the desk as he stood facing the three of us with a slight smirk on his face. "Glad y'all made it."

Arnie spoke my thoughts. "Is everything okay?"

"All's good. Harold should be here momentarily, hopefully with Hank," Joe said. "Here's what I should tell you since Harold's the one who requested the three of you be here too. The DA conditionally agreed to support our motion to Judge Fitzgerald requesting that he overturn John's conviction."

John scooted upright in his chair as Arnie said, "That's good news right? You don't seem as excited as you should."

Joe looked at John until they locked eyes. "The District Attorney's support hinges upon Hank confessing. Otherwise, we have no compelling evidence to cause them or the Judge to consider the motion."

John stood with his hands on his hips, his casual smile gone. "And how do you propose we do that?"

Joe put his hand on John's shoulder. "We haven't crossed the goal line, but we know what we need to do to score. To begin with, I'm going to confront Hank with his own words from yesterday's meeting with Megan and Jeannie. I'll ask him to clarify what he meant by his comments and what he meant about John owing him anyway. I'm hoping he'll either clarify his meaning enough to reinforce his motive or make a careless comment about the money's disappearance between the time John and he sealed the bank deposit envelope and when John dropped it off at the bank that night."

"Do you think John being present might pose a problem?" I asked as I glanced at John.

Joe's slight smirk reappeared. "I'm counting on John's presence as a deterrent to any further attempts by Hank to put his own farcical spins on what's he's heard, or we present today. I'm going to advise him that he can't be charged with embezzlement, since John already served time for that, so he might as well try telling the truth."

Arnie interjected. "Are we going to lie?"

Joe turned to Arnie. "If he confesses as I believe his ego will stir him to do, by the letter of the law, we won't be lying to Hank."

"What about Harold?" I asked.

Joe stepped beside my chair and placed a hand on my shoulder as he glanced at Arnie and then me. "That's where you and Arnie come in. You'll remain out here with Harold while John, Hank and I go into my office. Harold will likely be on edge, but he's got his reasons for getting Hank to come here."

Arnie scratched his cheek. "Don't you think Hank'll suspect something's up and refuse to talk or request a lawyer?"

"As far as Hank knows, I just want him to clarify what he'll hear on the tape of his meeting with the girls yesterday. Hopefully, he'll be more intimidated by John's presence in the meeting than what I'll be trying to pull out of him. Let's be clear about our purpose this morning. Harold instigated the meeting, and we're not here to bring charges against anyone. We just want John's conviction overturned by the Judge with the support of the DA's office. As far as any charges against Hank, I'll leave that decision up to the DA or the sheriff. We're here to help John." Joe glanced at John and Arnie. "Everyone onboard?"

Arnie and I nodded as John stepped to the window. "Harold's on the steps outside of City Hall, and Hank's with him."

Joe looked at Arnie and me. "I have one more favor to ask. Susanna's with Megan and Jeannie. After I take Hank and John back into my office, will one of you answer the phone if it rings?"

Arnie grinned. "Do you want all your calls held boss?"

Joe laughed. "Absolutely."

Hank stepped into the office showered and shaved, his jet-black hair slicked back and wore a clean pair of jeans and a sweater. His silver-tipped, custom leather boots clicked as he entered Joe's office with Harold leading the way.

Hank scanned the room and paused when he noticed Arnie, John and me in the waiting area. Harold leaned towards Hank and said, "It's all right son. I asked them to be here. We want this whole mess cleared up properly before you leave town."

Hank peered over his shoulder at his dad and then glared at Joe. "What do y'all need from me? Let's get this over with so I can get out of here."

Joe directed Hank and John back to his private office and closed the door behind them.

Harold took a seat on the sofa across from Arnie and me. He tried to engage in conversation, but the muffled sounds emanating from Joe's office proved too much of a distraction. None of us could make out any words, but we had little difficulty discerning the voices. I stared at Harold and sensed he likely knew what Hank might be facing, but I felt the damning fact that Hank was responsible for John's incarceration haunted him more.

Harold broke eye contact and let his head sink toward his chest. "Guys, thanks for being here. I'm not sure what y'all are thinking right now, but I want you to know... I've little doubt Hank messed up and allowed an innocent man to go to prison. Bringing him here wasn't easy, but it's high time he accounts for his actions." Harold peered at Arnie. "I'm praying for leniency and mercy after I convinced Hank that running would only make matters worse. When he asked if we should have our lawyer come, I told him a real man stands behind the truth, not a lawyer."

Arnie reached over and put his arm around Harold's broad shoulders. "Harold, you and I go back a lot of years. In fact, I've known your boys for most of their lives. I know this isn't easy, but it's the right thing to do."

Harold closed his eyes, and his chin quivered. He mumbled to himself before he cleared his throat. "It's my fault." Harold looked up. "I expected too much from him before he was ready. I thought all along I was helping him, but coddling him was a mistake. I've tried to make sure he and his brothers had every opportunity after their mother abandoned us." He pulled a handkerchief from his back pocket and blew his nose. "I regret how I snapped to judgment against John and blindly trusted Hank's testimony."

Arnie patted Harold's shoulder. "There were plenty of mistakes made by a host of presumptive, well-intended people. It's time we place this into God's merciful hands. He'll reveal to you what you need to do to right the wrongs."

"GO TO HELL, BOTH OF YOU!" Hank's outburst reverberated through the walls. Harold, Arnie and I immediately stood up and stared at Joe's office door expecting them to come running out. Hank's raised voice continued. "WHAT MORE DO YOU WANT ME TO SAY? DO YOU WANT ME TO TELL YOU COACH SERVED THREE YEARS OF HIS LIFE FOR SOMETHING HE DIDN'T DO? DO YOU WANT ME TO TELL YOU I STOLE THE MONEY?" The conversation from the other side of the walls then returned to muffled exchanges.

Several long, anxious minutes passed before the door opened and Joe stepped out followed by John with his arm around Hank's shoulder. Hank sobbed and looked defeated.

Joe made a brief call from Susanna's desk and asked Harold and Hank to go with him back into his office. John dropped his arm from Hank's shoulder. "Hank, I promise you're doing the right thing. God'll bless you for telling the truth."

Hank and Harold disappeared into the office. John poured himself a cup of water, gulped it down and tossed the crushed cup into the trash. "I feel for Hank. Joe prodded and pushed Hank until, well, I reckon you heard Hank. That's when Joe reminded Hank that his dad was right outside. He told him that everyone knew the truth, even his dad, and it was now up to him to finally do the right thing." John's ambivalent stare indicated mixed feelings over Hank's confession.

Two Adams County sheriff deputies entered the office. The sergeant held a clipboard and looked at the papers attached. "Where can I find Joseph Arians and Harold Archer, Junior?"

John walked over and shook hands with the sergeant. "Good morning, Mitch. It's been a while. I see they've made you a sergeant now."

The sergeant's harsh business-like demeanor relaxed. "Coach Priestly. Yes. sir. I heard you got out on parole."

"Thankfully that's true. Hank Archer's in Joe's office with Hank's father. They should be out any moment. Have a seat. I don't think there's a back door." John offered them coffee as the deputies removed their hats and sat down on either side of Arnie and me. John and Mitch held a half-hearted conversation about the changes in the Shiloh football program.

Joe exited first and stepped aside beyond the doorway as Harold stepped out and eyed the two deputies. Harold knew them both and raised his hand as a request for them to wait another moment. Hank followed in the shadow of his father. Sorrow filled Hank's downcast face. "I'm sorry, Dad." Harold put his arm around him. Mitch stood and looked at Harold as if waiting for permission.

Harold looked into Hank's sad eyes. "These deputies will take you to Alexandria. Don't say or do anything until you hear from our attorney or me. Do you understand?" Harold stepped back, and the deputies escorted Hank downstairs to their patrol car. Harold followed and walked swiftly to City Hall after they drove away.

Joe said to John, "The Judge can't act on the motion until Monday or Tuesday at the earliest, but I'm confident the DA and Judge Fitzgerald will approve our motion to overturn your conviction. You'll be a free man. Your record expunged."

John cracked a cautious smile and hugged Joe.

Joe broke the somber mood and chuckled. "Let's celebrate. I'm buying lunch next door."

"Thanks, Joe, I'll take a rain check. I promised my family I'd come straight home. But first, I have a question."

Joe put his hand on my shoulder. "What's that?"

"How did Hank pull it off?"

"Turns out it was my carelessness that made it possible," John sighed before Joe could answer. "I always slid the deposit pouch into my desk drawer before I checked in with Jessie to make sure all the players left the locker room and we locked all the doors. Hank realized it gave him the perfect window of opportunity. He even smirked as he told us how easy it was for him. Hank left that night as usual but slipped back in through the gym. He knew I kept the extra bank deposit envelopes in the bottom drawer of my file cabinet and ripped out the entire last page of deposit slips from the back of the checkbook. Hank used my scissors to open the original envelope, placed all but the money he wanted to keep back into the new envelope, and exchanged the new seal strip. He stuffed the old strip and envelope into his jacket pocket. He intentionally disguised his normal writing and hastily scribbled the adjusted totals. Hank wiped the envelope clean and slipped it into the drawer. He proudly admitted that it took all of two minutes. The money and remnants of the original deposit envelope and deposit slip went back out the gym door with him. I never had a clue about the switch when I grabbed the bank's envelope from my desk, turned out the lights and made the drop at the bank on the way home."

"I wouldn't be too hard on yourself, John. Besides, doesn't it feel a little better knowing how he did it?" I looked at John. "At least I can begin to construct a happy ending to the article I'm writing about you."

CHAPTER FORTY-FOUR

A MYRIAD OF EMOTIONS CHURNED within me after I left Joe's office. The distraction my family provided helped, but the end of John's story remained unclear.

"Hank confessed, and he's in the custody of the Adams County Sheriff's department."

Larry's initial silence during my phone call told me he was oblivious to what had taken place. I promised to hand him my piece on John's return to Shiloh by Monday. I explained there would be a follow-up story after Judge Fitzgerald ruled on Joe's motion to overturn John's conviction and Hank's arraignment took place.

Larry returned to his colorful self as we ended our conversation. "Enjoy your family. God knows you deserve it. But, please get us something to print by Monday morning. I want it in the Christmas Eve edition."

———

I invited my two sons and the three oldest grandkids to join me on a special errand. When I pulled into a parking spot in front of Adams Feed and General Hardware, five sets of anxious eyes surveyed the store's dated exterior and well-traveled, scarred steps leading into the store.

Junior turned toward me. "Do you want us to stay here while you run in?"

I opened my door and barked, "Everyone out! I've got some friends for you to meet."

Zeb and his twin sons leaned against the counter cracking peanuts and sipping soda when we entered. They promptly brushed their hands off and greeted us. I introduced Junior and Tommy while the kids eyed the entrance to the Old General Store. Junior hollered, "Y'all just stay right here where we can see you."

Zeb smiled at Jim and Jay who immediately stepped toward the kids. "We'll watch 'em. I think they'll enjoy what's in here." Junior and Tommy glanced at each other before Junior waved and said, "All right, but y'all behave and listen to Jay and Jim."

Five minutes later, the kids scrambled back, yelling over one another with a bottle of soda in one hand and a small bag of peanuts hoisted in the other. "Please, please! They said we could have these. Is it okay?" Sissy said pointing at Jay and Jim.

Zeb laughed as I glanced at Tommy and Junior. "I don't think that'll spoil their dinner." Both nodded and they each cracked open a peanut, mumbling an obligatory "Thanks."

Zeb chuckled. "You're most welcome. But I don't know your names yet."

Sissy nervously looked up at her dad and then at Zeb's bearded smile. "I'm Sissy. I'm eight." She pointed at Tommy. "That's my daddy." Sissy's innocent curiosity then fell upon Zeb's mostly white beard and long hair. She inched closer and whispered, "Are you Santa?"

Zeb laughed and got down on one knee. "No, not today anyway." After he gave her a sly wink, he added, "My name's Zeb Adams, but you can call me Uncle Zeb." Sissy giggled as she resisted her urge to touch his bearded smile.

Teddy stepped beside his sister. "I'm Teddy. Sissy's my sister." Teddy's adolescent hand disappeared into Zeb's gentle grip.

Bubba set his bag and bottle on the floor, wiped his hands on the sides of his jeans, and extended his hand. "Bubba's my name." He pointed to Junior. "That's my dad." Bubba then pointed to the merchandise on display. "Do you own all of this?"

Zeb stroked his beard. "I reckon I do, at least until somebody buys something. Then they can say they own a little piece of my store."

Bubba scratched his head. "Daddy, can we buy something?"

I looked as Jim and Jay. "Would you fellas mind helping them pick out a special Shiloh Christmas present from me?"

Jim and Jay motioned for the kids to follow them. They disappeared into the General Store, but this time their dads followed to monitor their choices. Zeb grabbed hold of my extended hand and yanked himself off the floor while I shared the news about John and Hank.

"How's Harold?" Zeb asked.

"As good as one could expect. He confessed to Arnie and me about his regrets and fears, but that he knew Hank couldn't run from his mistakes. Too many lives already had been hurt."

Zeb sighed. "Well, I feel awful for Harold. He did the right thing, though, and we gotta believe Hank'll be a heap better off because he fessed up rather than run." Zeb paused and ran his hand through his beard. "I wonder what'll happen to Coach Priestly? Do you think he'll stay in Shiloh?"

"Is there any chance he'll be able to get his old job back?" I asked. "If I remember right, the school's looking for a new coach again."

Zeb's face lit up. "I reckon I can find out if I still have any sway left on our school board. It's worth making a couple of calls."

Giggles and footsteps arrived ahead of Jim and Jay as the kids raced around the corner. "Poppy, Poppy, check out what we found." The three dragged me into the General Store. Zeb followed with a curious stare. They pointed to the painted miniature house in the center of the Christmas village display.

"The three of you want to buy the house? Why?"

Sissy giggled. "Because it looks just like your new house, Poppy." Teddy's and Bubba's heads bobbed in agreement. Tommy and Junior handed me two miniature carolers and the lighted Christmas tree from the display.

I became speechless and stared at the figurines before I asked, "What're you going to do with these and the house?"

Bubba laughed. "Oh, Poppy! What are YOU goin' to do with them? They're for you and Grammy." He pointed to the carolers in my hand. "This one is you, and this one is Grammy. It's our special Christmas present to both of you."

Junior stopped chuckling long enough to confess. "Pop, it was all their idea."

Zeb scratched the bottom of his chin. "Um, what do you think boys? Isn't that fifty percent off sale effective today?"

Jim declared, "Absolutely!"

Junior said with a broad grin, "It's settled, and I want no arguments. Tommy and I'll pay for this too."

As we were leaving, Teddy tugged on my jacket. "Poppy, does this mean we own a piece of Uncle Zeb's store now?"

I ruffled his brown hair with my fingers. "If Uncle Zeb said so, I reckon it's so."

———

Liddy helped the grandkids to display the miniature house, carolers and the lighted Christmas tree on the mantle. My sons and I sat on the front porch when Pete's rickety truck clamored around the corner, followed closely by Megan's Mustang. Andy and John climbed out of Pete's rusty back end. Jeannie and Megan joined them as they walked together to the porch.

"News about Coach Priestly raced through the streets faster than saucy gossip through the aisles at church," Andy announced. "We just had to stop over. Hope you don't mind."

Megan and Jeannie went inside with Liddy and the rest of the family. Tommy, Junior, and the older grandsons remained on the porch with me and listened to John tell stories about Coach Masterson for the next hour. By the time we finally joined the ladies inside, Buzz and Conrad were sound asleep, nestled between Megan and Jeannie on the sofa. Sissy, struggled to keep her eyes open and leaned against Megan. Bubba and Teddy plopped down at Liddy's feet with equally droopy eyes.

When our surprise guests prepared to leave, Andy stared across the room at Megan. She nodded with a coy look. Andy cleared his throat as Pete whistled to get our attention. "Megan asked me to tell you she's decided to go back to school. Coach made some calls, and she has an interview lined up for an open cheerleader intern coach position at GCU, and already applied for admission this coming semester."

Liddy slid out from between our two groggy grandsons and embraced Megan. "Congratulations. I guess that means you'll be leaving Shiloh then? But you'll stop back and visit?"

John put his hand on her shoulder. "I'll make sure of it."

I looked at Megan. "Have you told Harold yet?"

"No, not yet. I'll wait a couple more days with all that's happening, but I don't suspect he'll be too surprised or upset."

Pete looked at the grandkids still fast asleep and sighed. "Well, I guess it's time we hit the road and let these people get these sleepy heads to bed."

Liddy and I stood on the porch and waved as they walked to their vehicles. Liddy gave me a curious smile as Jeannie jumped into Pete's truck with John stretched out in the truck bed, while Andy drove off with Megan.

Just before dinner Saturday evening, Liddy pulled me aside in the kitchen. "Who do you think will serve as the Master of Ceremonies tonight?" I shrugged with an uncertain stare.

While the kids dug into their apple cobbler, I cleared my throat and looked at Liddy. "Grammy, I hear Santa's making a special visit to Shiloh tonight. Folks tell me he stops by every year just before Christmas."

Buzz and Conrad's heads popped up. Whipped cream decorated their smiles as they broke out singing. "San-ta Claus is com-ing to town." Sissy, Bubba and Teddy laughed and shouted, "Oh boy, Santa!"

We arrived on Main Street with the kids bundled and eager to see Santa. Tommy and Junior lugged folding chairs, while our wives carried extra blankets. I managed to corral the two eager toddlers until we found room in front of The Butcher Shoppe.

Bernie, Silas, and Alex sat at one of the tables outside their restaurant. Bernie came over and smiled. "Mistor Theo, Missus Liddy. We've gotta lots of fresh hot chocolate inside. Please let me offer some to your beautiful family." I smiled and nudged Bubba and Teddy to follow me.

A few minutes later, we returned with plenty of hot chocolate for everyone. Liddy had laid blankets on the curb for the kids to sit on. The grown-ups sat in the folding chairs behind them as Christmas music filled the air while we waited for the official start of the second evening of festivities.

Across the street, Megan nudged Hal until he nervously adjusted his tie and stepped onto the platform. The fading music drew a round of cheers from the excited crowd. The crisp breeze danced through Hal's hair.

"Ladies and Gentlemen, friends, on behalf of your city officials, thank you for sharing another evening with us as we all celebrate another Christmas in Shiloh. This annual tradition has been a part of the community for as long as I can remember. Tonight, I'm honored to stand in for my father, the Honorable Harold Archer, your Mayor. He'll be here shortly, but in the meantime, he asked me to make sure the program started on time. Please sit back and enjoy this evening's musical program."

Choir members stepped to their rehearsed places in front of the stage. Miss Phoebe Thatcher, the high school's music teacher, stepped in front of the tightly assembled choir, and with raised hands and a nod, their voices rang out as they sang familiar Christmas carols.

During *O Little Town of Bethlehem*, Harold's rotund body and rapid gait bolted up the walkway from the newly dedicated Jessie Masterson Administration Building. When the song ended, Hal and Harold appeared together on stage.

Harold beamed as he took the podium. "Ladies and Gentlemen, fellow citizens of Shiloh, dear friends, and family, before we continue with this evening's outstanding festive musical program, please allow me five minutes of your attention. I just left a couple of very important meetings that impact all of us. First, I want to thank all of you for the last twenty-five years, but I'm formally announcing tonight that as of the end of my current term as your mayor, I am stepping away from public office."

A sudden gasp swept through the crowd, but a crescendoing buzz ensued. Silas leaned from his chair. "Mistor Theo, did you know about this?"

Though I shook my head, I understood Harold's possible motivation for his decision.

"Folks, I know this may come as a surprise to many of you, but I'm also well aware there may be some in attendance who may want to express their pleasure at the news. Truthfully, I'll gladly join in their celebration." Pockets of laughter and jeers broke the tension in the air. A brief round of applause followed, which Harold joined as promised.

"Seriously, serving this fine city has been my life and the life of my family. My father stood on this same stage as your mayor before me, celebrating with many of you, but like with him, there comes a time for new blood to step up. The truth is, it's my time to step aside and enjoy my family and friends as just another fellow citizen of this wonderful, historic community." Applause broke out again until Harold put both his hands high into the air.

Harold cleared his throat, wiped his tears, and glanced back where Hal sat behind him. "But I'll not leave without offering a special Christmas gift for this town that I love so much. My attorney has begun making arrangements for the City of Shiloh to receive twenty acres of my family's land. This particular parcel sits along Shiloh Creek on the edge of town. However, it's a conditional gift. The town must allow me to construct a new park facility on the grounds, which will include a badly needed multi-purpose community building." A round of applause laced with whistles and youngsters hollering emanated from the crowd.

"Also, as my personal and ongoing commitment to the future growth and well-being of Shiloh, I'll coordinate with the local Habitat for Humanity office and sponsor the construction of two homes each year for as long as I can do so."

Hal and Harold waved goodbye and stepped off the stage as the choir began to sing Christmas songs again. All the youngsters in attendance stirred when the choir started to sing *I Saw Mommy Kissing Santa Claus.* Those who had attended the annual event before knew this served as Santa's cue and they began to work their way up and down the curb. As the song neared its end, an all-too-familiar figure dressed in a bright red suit with shiny black boots and matching wide black belt appeared on stage dragging an oversized green sack.

Larry and Martha found their way to where we were. Larry stood over my shoulder and bragged how this was Zeb's annual gig to portray Santa. Liddy smirked as she tugged on Larry's jacket and pointed to Zeb standing at the far end of the stage zipping up his leather jacket.

This year's Santa Claus "Ho-Ho-Hoed" and called all the children to come towards the stage. Jay, Jim, Andy, and Jeannie served as Santa's helpers and distributed candies from Santa's stuffed green sack to every child while Santa paced. "Ho-Ho-Ho! Merry Christmas!"

Liddy leaned her smiling face against my shoulder. "Is that who I think it is?"

"Who do you think it is?" I replied before I saw and laughed at the red curls peeking out from under the white beard and wig. A new Santa tradition had been passed on to the next generation.

Santa grabbed the microphone. "Ho-Ho-Ho! Here's how I'll remember how to find my way back to Shiloh with my reindeer and sleigh on Christmas Eve." He pointed upward as the first firework lit the sky. After the last burst and the "oohs" and "aahs" faded, Harold stepped to the podium, thanked everyone for coming and wished all a very Merry Christmas. Phillip and Hal joined him at the foot of the steps where Megan greeted him with a warm hug before she exited alongside Andy towards City Hall.

CHAPTER FORTY-FIVE

THE SUNDAY SERVICE BEFORE CHRISTMAS, Harold did not sit in his traditional aisle seat up front, but with Zeb among our circle of friends. Hal and Phillip managed to squeeze into the pew in front of their dad. Our entire family overflowed into the last row just behind our friends. Missy and Momma Arians shuffled in beside Zeb and Harold.

Liddy asked as Mary began to play. "Do you think Marie and John are here?" She scanned the sanctuary, brimming to capacity.

Right after Arnie took his customary seat behind the pulpit, Mary cued the organist, and they played "March of the Tin Soldiers." The choir wearing coordinating red blazers and dresses marched into the sanctuary down the center aisle. Heads turned as Marie filed in among the ladies in the choir. A buzz spread throughout the pews as Nick and Joe stood on either side of John Priestly, almost unrecognizable in his red blazer, but his deep-set dimples stood out among the smiling faces around him.

Larry looked over his shoulder and whispered to us, "It's been four years since John and Marie sang in the choir."

Our entire family enjoyed the festive music and familiar carols. Arnie shared his holiday message with all the children nestled around him on the platform steps. He narrated the story of a humble baby born in a small, country town much like Shiloh, who grew up to win the favor and blessing of his heavenly Father and gathered a ragtag collection of young people to become his disciples. Arnie stressed how this unlikely band of misfits overcame adversity and persecution to launch what we know as the church, which now proclaims the good news of God's love and mercy to all people.

"Enthusiastic, dedicated followers such as Peter, John, James, and Andrew passed on Jesus' legacy to the next generation. Who, in turn, passed it on and so on. We sit here today bearing the same responsibility to pass on Jesus' legacy and message to the next generation of disciples right here in Shiloh." Arnie pointed to each of the smiling young faces staring back at him from the platform steps.

After Arnie's prayer, the organist played Handel's "Messiah." The choir rose and added the beauty and splendor of the magical lyrics, celebrating the birth and eternal message of Christmas. Right after Arnie dismissed the children, the aisles swelled as pews emptied. Waiting for the crowd to clear, I overheard Zeb ask Harold, "What exactly are your plans? You retiring?"

"After I left Hank yesterday, I knew what I needed to do. Until Phillip proves he's ready, I'm taking control of the family business. I already ordered an audit of the company's books. I suspect retiring will just have to wait a bit longer."

"I'm sorry for interrupting, but what about Hal?" I asked.

A wide grin grew on Harold's face. "Hal's proven over the last few days that he doesn't need my help for what's in store for him." Harold stared at Hal and Phillip talking with their renewed friends. Harold dropped his thumbs into in his vest pockets. "I'll personally oversee the completion of that new community center before I step down as mayor. I can visualize it as the centerpiece of the new Priestly Recreational Park, surrounded by a properly equipped children's playground, large pavilion with plenty of picnic tables, all overlooking Shiloh Creek."

John, Marie, Joe, and Nick joined us still wearing their holiday attire. John recoiled when Harold extended his hand to him until he measured Harold's smile. "Will you ever forgive me?"

"Forgive you for what?"

Harold laughed and slapped John's shoulder. "Thanks, John. By the way, the city's new Priestly Recreation Park will need a facilities and grounds director. Think you might know of anyone interested?"

John locked eyes with Harold. "I'll have to get back to you on that, but it does sound like a wonderful opportunity for the right person."

Hal barked as the aisle cleared, "Dad! Come on. We promised Maddie that we'd pick her and Cora up at Saint James. Besides, everyone's already headed to Bubba's." Phillip grabbed Harold's elbow and dragged him away.

Liddy yelled above the commotion. "Save us some seats!"

———

Barb Patterson left a memorable impression when she greeted our family at Bubba's. Liddy and I looked at one another and laughed when we realized Barb directed us to the same table in front of the front window where we first ate dinner in Shiloh. Barb shoved another table up to ours to make room for the rest of our family. At the table behind us, Harold, Hal, and Phillip laughed at Maddie's playful exchange with her longtime friend, Cora, who fussed over them while she waited on their table. Barb and Cora frantically hustled between the tables while Cecil and Bubba prepared our orders in the kitchen.

When we first arrived in Shiloh, we knew no one, but now Liddy and I sat surrounded by new friends as well as our own family. Marie and John stirred boisterous laughter as they shared memories with Pete, Andy, Jay, Jim, Jeannie, and Megan. Judy and Arnie arrived last and sat with Nick, Joe and their family.

When everyone prepared to leave, I turned to Tommy and Junior. "Would you mind if mom and I walked home? The fresh air will do us good." After they drove off, we realized it was a little chillier than our first evening walk in Shiloh.

As we walked past the Sentinel's office, Liddy asked, "Are you going to keep writing for Larry?"

I stared at our images in the plate glass windows. "Well, my dad once told me a writer's never done as long as there are stories to write. So, I guess I'll keep dabbling at this, at least until Larry shows me the door."

Liddy squeezed my arm. "I thought that's what'd you say." Then she began to giggle uncontrollably.

"What's so funny?"

Liddy struggled to talk through her watering eyes and giggles. "You gotta admit that you've become a much better writer since those first articles you wrote for *The Red and Black* forty years ago." We both laughed as we continued arm in arm, remembering our days in Athens.

On Town Square, Liddy looked up and grabbed my elbow. "Thinking back over all the years we've been together, what inspired our journey sure hasn't changed that much. We might've gotten sidetracked, but here we are again dreaming, not dreading what tomorrow will bring our way."

———

Two days later, two special closed hearings convened in the Adams County Courthouse. The State Circuit Court Judge, the Honorable Gerald Fitzgerald, presided over both hearings. During the first, he acted on Joe's motion to overturn the verdict and conviction against John. Harold insisted he should be allowed to speak on John's behalf, and the Judge smiled when he obliged Harold's request. After Harold said his peace, the Judge looked over to William Paraman, Assistant District Attorney, who smiled at Joe and John and confirmed that the State had no objection to the motion. With the loud clap of Judge Fitzgerald's gavel, John became a free man with a spotless record.

Zeb, Sam, and Larry sat beside Marie and me throughout both hearings. Between sessions, I took one more look at a copy of the *Sentinel*'s Christmas Eve edition folded to my article about John's tragic arrest and wrongful conviction. I tucked it back into my attaché and pulled out the digital camera Mary loaned me. Taking pictures at the courthouse that day was my gift to her, so that she could stay in Shiloh.

As soon as Judge Fitzgerald disappeared from the courtroom, John greeted Marie with a hug and a wrinkle-free smile. "Now I know what it feels like to be truly redeemed." John's brown eyes glistened as his grin appeared.

Zeb gripped John's shoulder. "Well, how about feeling restored too?" John turned to Joe who stood beside him with an equally puzzled look.

"What Zeb's so eloquently eluding to…" Harold interjected before Zeb responded. "The City of Shiloh and the Shiloh School Board have an immediate need for a social studies teacher and an athletic director at the high school. The positions are yours if want them."

John examined their faces. "Are y'all serious?"

"It's yours if you want it," Zeb affirmed.

Marie clung to John's arm and smiled. "Jessie would be very pleased, and so would I, if you said yes."

John slowly bobbed his head as tears formed.

"We'll take that as a yes." Zeb jested.

At the top of the hour, a sheriff's deputy escorted Hank into the courtroom. Hank had exchanged his fancy clothes and boots for an orange jumpsuit with shackled wrists and ankles. He sat beside Harold's family attorney, Gus Appleton, at the defendant's table. Harold moved to a bench directly behind them. The sheriff's deputy stood off to one side and eyed John with a tight grin.

Sam tapped my shoulder. "That deputy played at Shiloh with Pete and Andy."

When Judge Fitzgerald re-appeared, far more subdued than before, he immediately called the two attorneys to his bench. They exchanged inaudible responses and nodded or swayed their head each time the judge spoke. After they returned to their seats, the Judge gave a summary of the charges and nature of the hearing. Hank remained motionless and without expression while his attorney scribbled notes on a legal pad.

Paraman stood and announced to the Judge that a plea bargain had been accepted by the defendant and his counsel. "Your Honor, the State agrees to withdraw the perjury charge and only asks the Court to consider the minimum sentence for the felony theft charge."

Judge Fitzgerald flipped through the papers in front of him and then looked over the top of his reading glasses at Hank and Gus Appleton. The young assistant district attorney looked over to Joe Arians and winked. The Judge continued, "Mister Appleton, I expect your client is agreeable to this agreement?"

Appleton looked at Hank. "Yes, sir. He is."

The Judge motioned to Hank. "Mister Archer, would you stand." Hank rose, but held a firm blank stare. "Before I accept this agreement, Mister Archer, do you understand that you are waiving your right to a trial by jury by accepting this agreement?"

Hank nodded and muttered. "Yes, sir."

The Judge nodded. "According to this agreement, the State of Georgia, subject to my approval, has agreed that you only serve the minimum mandatory twelve-month sentence and it is to be served out here in the Adams County jail facility with credit for time served since your arrest. It further stipulates you pay $5,000.00 in restitution to the Shiloh High School Athletic Department and serve 1,000 hours of community service under the supervision of the Georgia Department of Corrections in the city of Shiloh. Mister Archer, you also will be required to complete court-approved anger management and psychological counseling. And lest I forget, you'll pay all court costs and fines." The Judge looked at Appleton and Hank. "Before I make my final ruling, I have been asked to hear from Mister John Priestly."

John rose to his feet, stepped through the bar's doors and stood beside Hank and his attorney. "Mister Priestly, I'd like to put it on record that you requested that the Court accept this most favorable plea agreement. May I ask why?"

"Your honor, as you know, this hearing seeks to properly convict the person who committed the crimes I'd been wrongfully charged with and convicted. However, I can't get back the three years I served in the state's prison system. Your honor, I'd like the time I served to have meant something. Mister Archer surrendered himself and willingly confessed when he could've easily fled justice. I'm begging the Court to credit my served time as time already served for Mister Archer and accept this favorable plea agreement in that light."

Judge Fitzgerald scrutinized Hank as John returned to his seat. He reviewed the case documents again and then peered at Paraman before he raised an eyebrow at Hank's nervous stare. "Mister Archer, did any-one promise you anything in return for accepting this agreement?"

"No sir."

"Are you fully aware of the content of this agreement?"

"Yes, sir."

"Do you have anything more to say?"

"No sir."

"In that case," Judge Fitzgerald tapped his gavel, "So be it. Mr. Appleton, please assist your client in signing the plea agreement and then present it to me for my signature." The formalities of paper-work took place, and the deputy escorted Hank as he glanced briefly at his father's sad face before he and the deputy disappeared behind the same door he entered only thirty minutes before.

Outside the courtroom, Paraman raced up to John walking with the rest of us as we congratulated him. "Mister Priestly, the judge asked to meet with you before y'all left. Please wait just one moment."

Judge Fitzgerald emerged a moment later from his office down the hall. No longer wearing his black robe, he approached donning a gold golf shirt beneath a brown leather aviator's jacket, which he zipped up as he approached.

Judge Fitzgerald extended his hand and a smile to John. "Mister Priestly, I wanted to shake your hand. What you demonstrated in my courtroom was most admirable. If we had more people like you, we'd need less old judges like me. May God richly bless you for being so gracious and magnanimous. I'm sorry I can't stay and talk more, but I have to run. My grandkids are arriving shortly. I promised my wife I'd not dilly-dally. Merry Christmas to you all!" He waved as he quickly stepped out the door to the nearly empty parking lot.

Harold looked at John. "I know you heard this from me before, but thank you again for Hank's sake. I pray by this time next year Hank'll have put the past behind him and be able to thank you himself."

John smiled at Harold. "Don't we have a Christmas Eve celebra-tion and service to attend?"

EPILOGUE

SHILOH'S CHRISTMAS EVE MUSICAL PROGRAM went off without a glitch. The mayor's absence caused a little buzz among the crowd, but Hal admirably stood in his father's stead as the emcee. The *Sentinel's* articles about Hank and John would not circulate about town until after Christmas. While the orchestrated singing of carols stirred the crowd to sing along, the city's Christmas tree overlooked the life-size Nativity creche animated by eager costumed characters reenacting the real reason for Christmas. A laughable moment occurred when the swaddled infant tucked in the manger apparently had had enough and went off script crying out loud during the finale as everyone sang "Silent Night." Hal dismissed the crowd by reading a letter from Santa addressed to the children, which promised that Santa and his trusty reindeer were on his way to Shiloh.

Liddy and I herded our family back home. Without much reluctance, all our grandkids scurried upstairs and soon fell fast asleep. Junior, Tommy, Stacey and Kari sat with Liddy and me around the dining room table nibbling on cookies and reminisced while presents magically appeared under the Christmas tree and once empty stockings overflowed beneath the mantle.

Shortly after midnight Liddy and I climbed into bed sharing giggles of anticipation, but our giddiness shifted to the somber reality that not every home in Shiloh eagerly anticipated Christmas morning. Liddy's eyes watered as she rolled over and her voice cracked. "Poor Harold, I hope he's okay. What kind of Christmas morning will he and his sons share? Hank will awake in a jail cell, and Megan will arise as a guest in her parent's home."

Liddy rolled onto her back and squeezed her eyes tightly shut. "I just wish we could do something. I'm worried about Harold."

———

Sanctuary held its first official meeting in January. Liddy and I dropped by from time to time and made sure plenty of snacks and refreshments satisfied the growing number of students. John Priestly remained in the shadows, but he hosted regular meetings with the leaders out on the farm and steered new prospective students at the school to Sanctuary's meetings.

John remained out on the farm with Marie but invested in a rustic log cabin erected beside the pecan orchard on the property.

———

Zeb Adams and his two sons, Jay and Jim, announced the reopening of the old lumber mill. After Zeb's wife passed away, he had closed the mill down because it became too much to manage. Zeb sensed that Jim and Jay needed a more significant challenge than helping around the store, and he negotiated with Harold Archer to harvest the timber on his property and placed Jay and Jim over restarting the mill. The dilapidating eyesore on the edge of town got spruced up and added new job opportunities for Shiloh again.

———

Harold stepped down as mayor shortly after the first of the year. With the support of Zeb, Arnie and Larry, Hal accepted with some trepidation the city council's offer that he serve as Shiloh's Mayor Pro Tem. Three months later, a citywide referendum dropped the Pro Tem from Hal's title. Phillip struggled as the new manager of Archer Construction but coped with Harold's behind the scenes assistance. Harold, however, spent most of his days in his sanctum, the study in his home. Maddie shuffled around the house nursemaiding over Harold but shared her concerns about him to her friend Cora.

———

Thanks to Liddy's insistence, I accepted an offer from Cornerstone Publishing, my former company, to publish *Jessie's Story*, if I expanded the articles I wrote for the paper into a full-length manuscript. Larry insisted that I continued to write special interest articles for the *Sentinel* but made sure I had plenty of time to meet Cornerstone's deadlines. Larry encouraged me to take advantage of Mary to transcribe my handwritten drafts.

ACKNOWLEDGEMENTS

THE FOUR-YEAR JOURNEY VENTURED to bring this story to life demands many thanks, beginning with a myriad of friends and family who offered encouragement along the way and are just too many to name. I am genuinely grateful to each and every one.

However, I am compelled to share a few special thanks:

Noah, Brannon, Natalie, Eli, and Dillon, my five very special grandchildren served as the inspiration behind tackling the daunting task of writing a novel. Their unique personalities appear in each of Theo and Liddy's grandchildren. When they have grandchildren, I pray they might share with their grandchildren the books that their Poppy wrote as a legacy of love for them.

Connie, my wife and best friend for over forty-four years, thank you. She endured reading each of the many drafts and shared numerous long walks together hatching the plot twists in the story. Her patience and love encouraged me never to lose sight of the dream. She too nudged me into early retirement so I could tackle the challenge of expanding my writing.

Early on I recognized how formidable the task of writing the nascent story stirring in my head would be and I sought a willing writing partner. That's when God directed me to a talented young lady, Kari Scare, my writing coach and editor. I shall remain forever indebted to her patience, persistence, and at many times, perseverance. Without her tutelage, my stories about lil' ol' Shiloh with its colorful setting and memorable characters may never have been more than an idea bouncing around in my head. I am pleased to have witnessed how her coaching and editing aspirations have blossomed since we partnered up four years ago.

Special thanks to Hancock County and Sparta, Georgia. They lost their beloved courthouse in 2014 to an accidental fire, and the images and accounts of their loss aided in depicting Shiloh's antebellum courthouse and tragic fire scenes in the story. In 2016, the reconstruction of "Her Majesty" - Hancock County's beloved courthouse - was completed and rededicated as a testimony to the spirit and legacy of Sparta. (Photo of Hancock County courthouse courtesy of Brian Brown, vanishingnorthgeorgia.com)

Likewise, thank you Coweta County, GA, my home for the past seven years. The historic Court Square in Newnan provided the quaint shops, offices, landmark cinema theatre, Carnegie Library, and obligatory downtown churches that ended up in Shiloh.

Finally, but not the least, I thank God for planting the seed that sprouted into this story, and...

Testament - An Unexpected Return, 2018
Purgatory - A Progeny's Quest, 2019

ABOUT THE AUTHOR

T. M. BROWN IS A SOUTHERN BOY at heart, although he's lived and traveled in many states far removed from his beloved boyhood roots in Georgia and Florida. He returned to his Southern roots several years ago while his two sons were still in school and regularly traveled throughout the South before returning to college shortly after his youngest son graduated. In the last fifteen years he has preached, taught and coached in Alabama, Georgia and Florida until his wife and he moved outside of Atlanta and retired to write, travel, and spoil grandchildren.

www.TMBrownauthor.com
info@tmbrownauthor.com